THE WITCH
and the
Priest of Lies

by

John Baldwin Large

DORRANCE
PUBLISHING CO
EST. 1920
PITTSBURGH, PENNSYLVANIA 15238

The contents of this work, including, but not limited to, the accuracy of events, people, and places depicted; opinions expressed; permission to use previously published materials included; and any advice given or actions advocated are solely the responsibility of the author, who assumes all liability for said work and indemnifies the publisher against any claims stemming from publication of the work.

All Rights Reserved
Copyright © 2022 by John Baldwin Large

No part of this book may be reproduced or transmitted, downloaded, distributed, reverse engineered, or stored in or introduced into any information storage and retrieval system, in any form or by any means, including photocopying and recording, whether electronic or mechanical, now known or hereinafter invented without permission in writing from the publisher.

Dorrance Publishing Co
585 Alpha Drive
Suite 103
Pittsburgh, PA 15238
Visit our website at *www.dorrancebookstore.com*

ISBN: 978-1-6386-7317-0
eISBN: 978-1-6386-7665-2

With a lot of help from Humphries.
To Mom, I will never forget…
I love you.
John

This book is a work of fiction. Any references to historical events, real people, or real places are used fictitiously. Other names, characters, places and events are products of the author's imagination, and any resemblance to actual events or places or persons, living or dead, is entirely coincidental. Thank you and enjoy the novel!

The artwork on the cover of this book is by Alesia Ventura-Large. For more of her artwork go to; www.artistrybyalesia.com.

ACKNOWLEDGMENTS

I first want to thank my beautiful wife, Alesia, for her endless and unwavering support through this endeavor. She is also known as Alesia Ventura-Large, an artist of extraordinary talent. Alesia is the artist who created the awesome cover for this book. You can find more of her artwork at www.artistrybyalesia.com. I love you, baby. Thank you.

I also wish to thank my cousin, Emily "Lili" Carey, for her encouragement, tireless proofreading, and helping me to correct the one zillion-million-billion mistakes I made in the early drafts. Thank you, Lili, for all of that and your pure heart and magnificent brain. I love you.

Thanks to another cousin, Fran MacMaster. You encouraged me from the beginning, too. Your suggestions and observations helped immensely. You are truly a love, and you have a lion's heart to go with it! Thank you, Fran. I love you.

I also must thank my cousin Meade Carey for her reading, and positive support throughout as well. I love you, Meade.

Thanks also go out to Suzie Buck. Suzie read and critiqued the work faithfully right up to publishing time. I am so grateful. Thank you, Suzie, and Phineus the ferret, too! I love you.

I also want to thank Kris for everything he did. Thanks, man. I love you.

Thank you, Humphries. I never would have made it without you, little dingo dog. I love you and miss you.

Thanks go to Mr. Karl Jeffrey Etshied, for everything. Godspeed, and I love you, man.

I wish to thank my brother, Henry Large, and my sister, Stormy Large. I am so proud of you both for the incredible humans you both grew up to be. Thank you for the support and the belief. I love you, Henry. I love you, Storm.

Finally, there are the two people most responsible for this book and the following books: my mom, Suzi Large, and my aunt and godmother,

Emily "Bitsy" Carey. In my darkest hours, and my darkest thoughts, you both somehow managed to shine a light for me to follow out of that darkness. You never gave up on me and believed in me, no matter what. This book, and the subsequent books that complete the trilogy, are written for you. They were written because of you. You are both gone now, for many years. Yet I know that you are both still here, angels in life, and angels in the hereafter. Thank you, Aunt Bitsy, for everything. I love you. Thanks, Mom, for everything. I love you. I hope you like the book!

Love, John 4/30/21

"…but there is a terrible cogency in the self-evident;
ultimately it breaks down all defenses…"
—Albert Camus, *The Plague*

"The devil…the prowde spirite…cannot endure to be mocked."
—Thomas More

PART ONE
The Rat in the Hat

"To pay attention, this is our endless and proper work."
— Mary Oliver

CHAPTER 1
Day Dream Believer

Julie opened her eyes. The black night shimmered. She was certain that she had heard somebody say something. The voice was familiar to her. She couldn't be sure from which direction it came. And then she heard it again. It was softer, this time, more distant than before. It seemed to echo all around her in a strange, ethereal way.

"Pray for me."

"Hello? Is anyone there?" Julie said. She listened. There was no response. She was alone in the darkness. The air felt cool on her face and skin. She could smell the moisture of dew and the fresh pine of the forest. She could hear the soft singing of crickets and the gentle breeze blowing through the trees of the Great Woods. Julie looked up into the night sky. She could not see any stars, or the moon, or even clouds above. There was only the night and the darkness. Hot fear flared in her belly.

A voice whispered into her ear. "Once upon a time, a devil fell, then sang a rhyme."

Julie whirled around but there was no one there. She had felt the warmth of someone's breath on the back of her neck. It smelled sweet. The sounds of the forest ceased. There was now only silence and darkness. All Julie could hear was the sound of her own breath. She held her breath for a moment and listened intently to the night. The entirety of the Great Woods seemed to join with her in this silence, listening, observing, waiting. What was that? she wondered. She waited. The faint sound of drums beating in the far-off distance could be heard. It was as if the sounds were being carried through the woods and the wilderness on a silent wind.

"But now we live and how they cry that only Christ was blessed to die."

It seemed as if many different voices had chanted this together in unison. They could only be heard faintly along with the sound of the drums. The sounds rose on the wind, then fell, muted by the thickness of the forest. Julie turned to face the music. The light, cool breeze blew into her face.

"The rest are doomed to earthly Hell; the devil laughed and further fell."

A tiny light appeared to her, flickering in the darkness and the distance. All of the sounds, the voices and the drums, seemed to be coming from where that light had appeared. Julie began to make her way carefully toward that distant light. She felt so light. Her footsteps seemed to fall silently. It seemed to her that she was flying, or floating. At the thought of herself, the shifted focus on her movement, her progress seemed to slow down. It was as if she was in a slow motion. Julie tried to concentrate, but the harder she tried to move, the slower her progress seemed to be. She felt as if she had stopped moving completely. It all felt to her as if time itself had ceased. It was as if there was a heavy weight in the pit of her stomach.

"Down cast he falls from black night's sky, his smile widens, a grin quite wry." The voices chanted distantly, but the words seemed to appear in her mind as they were sung. It stopped her from thinking momentarily and her mind cleared.

She did not know why she did this, but Julie let go. She stopped fighting the slow motion. She refocused her eyes and her mind on the distant, flickering light in the wilderness. The weight in her stomach dissipated. The weightlessness and light feeling of movement returned in force. She began to move again. As she slowly drew closer, she could see many more lights in the distance flicker to life as they appeared around the original light. Julie could now make out a multitude of candles and torches amidst the trees and foliage of the dark woods. They formed a large ring of small, individual flames, licking the darkness. The center of this ring was as black as pitch. It looked like a large doorway framed by an ancient glow.

A lone, small flame appeared in the very center of the ring. It danced in Julie's wide, green eyes as it suddenly burst outward in all directions until it had taken an enormous size. She realized it was a large bonfire that lit the whole of the doorway. The light of the bonfire illuminated the darkness in the center of the ring to reveal figures in long, dark red robes and hoods. They appeared to Julie like droplets of blood silhouetted against the darkness of the Great Woods, only to return to obscurity when blending with the high yellow and orange flames of the bonfire. These figures sang and danced around the fire to the beat of the drums, which were being played somewhere along the perimeter of an enormous clearing in these woods.

"Bring anger and ego, gray selfish confusion; blind the weak, meek, damned fools of delusion."

The voices and drums grew louder as Julie crept closer. She was careful not to leave the safety of the darkness. The drums reverberated in her chest. The smell of the forest and of autumn now mixed with the cold, acrid odor of the bonfire's smoke in Julie's nostrils. No heat or warmth seemed to emanate from the bonfire. The dancers swayed and moved rhythmically, hypnotically, and gracefully around the great flame. The cold firelight cast their shadows ghoulishly against the forest canopy surrounding the clearing. The figures all joined hands.

"Bring hate upon man."

Somewhere, a church bell rang. And slowly the dance picked up pace.

"It's the turn of the worm and the rise of the shrew and the slaughter of lambs that we give to you."

Julie saw something moving on the opposite side of the clearing. She could not see clearly because of the light and glare from the fire, the haze from the smoke and the dozens of revelers spinning and twirling around the bonfire and the surrounding darkness. Julie left the safety of the dark forest and crept to the edge of the clearing.

A tall, thin man dressed in a long, black, hooded robe stood near the bonfire's rage. He held his long arms and large hands up over his head. Long, boney fingers clutched a large book in his right hand. His left hand clutched a large, ornate knife that seemed to wrap itself down and around his arm. Three of the hooded revelers stopped dancing and broke off of the main group and joined the tall man near the bonfire. He led them across the clearing to a point on the opposite side. The three revelers sank down onto their knees around this man. Julie bit her lip as she silently crept along the edge of the clearing toward the tall man.

"Nearby the witches, who gave pause to listen, sensed the thundering silence on the moonlight's glisten," the voices chanted.

The tall man stood before a large tree. The revelers rose back up onto their feet and began to do something at the foot of this tree. The tall man held the book up over his head. He spoke in a language that Julie did not recognize. Something was moving up above the tall man. Then Julie saw; someone was tied up onto that tree.

As the tall man began to speak, all the revelers removed their hoods, revealing strange theatrical masks, painted white, red, and black. The masks bore the gamut of emotion—joy, fear, rage, sorrow, agony, ecstasy, and madness. The masked revelers continued to dance and sing.

The three revelers who accompanied the tall man removed their masks. They were young girls, Julie thought. Maybe in their mid-teens? One of the girls held up a large silver cup above her head while the other two danced around the tree. The young girl turned to face the leader.

Kneeling down onto the forest floor, she handed the chalice up to the tall man. He took the chalice and held it up to his face. It looked to Julie as if he were drinking from the silver chalice. He handed the chalice back to the young girl. Each young girl would take a turn holding the chalice up and then handing it to the tall man so that he could drink. Then the young girls carried the chalice over so that the rest of the group could drink from it. One by one, each of the revelers were handed the silver chalice. Each would stop dancing, raise their mask, and sip from this cup. They would then lower their mask and resume the feverish dancing. Julie tried to focus her eyes on the person tied up on the tree, but she was not able to see who it was. What she did see was the crimson of blood flowing downward from the figure up on the tree.

Julie's green eyes sparkled. Anger burned in her belly. She rose up out of the underbrush along the edge of the clearing and marched straight into the center of the chaos. She had only just stepped over the threshold of the clearing when everything seemed to change. The entire scene seemed to slow down into a gruesome, macabre slow-motion. The dancers still danced, the flames still licked, snapped, and crackled. But the pace was nightmarish.

Julie heard a strange cry from down on the clearing floor. She looked down and gasped. A small, mostly white rat stood on her hind legs, regarding Julie. It clutched a large, black mushroom cap that it seemed to be nibbling on. The rat stood in the center of what looked to Julie like a maze that had somehow been formed from the underbrush of the forest floor. This maze began to spiral outward. The spiral spread itself endlessly around the rat and throughout the entire clearing right before Julie's eyes.

"Start round again slowly round dizzying dance, with the elixir of tongues and the tonic of chance."

She looked back up. The pace of the dance had returned to its original, normal speed.

The tall man was chanting and the blood was flowing. When Julie looked back down at the forest floor, the rat and the strange spiral in the underbrush had vanished.

She resumed her way across the clearing toward the tall man. It surprised her that none of the revelers seemed to notice her, or care. They were all deeply engrossed as they smiled through their masks, beaming and glowing in an ecstatic trance. They sang and chanted the same strange language along with the tall man. The ritual had reached a fever's pitch.

Julie finally got close enough to the tree and the tall man to see that it was a young woman, or girl, who had been tied up to that tree several feet above the forest floor. Her arms had been tied straight up, over her head. Her wrists and ankles had large spikes driven through them, holding her fast up onto the tree. Blood flowed thickly down her arms, her head and face, her torso, and her legs into the silver cup held aloft by the three girls as they stood together and chanted the dark language. Dark crimson ran delicate rivers down the pale, white skin of these young girls' arms.

Dark rivulets fell slowly and thickly, dotting their smiling faces. Julie stopped and stared wide eyed. She felt dizzy and nauseas. Everything was moving in a sickly strange slow-motion despite the now frantic pace of the dancers.

The sound of the drums pounded in her head. Julie closed her eyes and wished that they would stop pounding. To her surprise and amazement, the drums suddenly stopped. The revelers all stopped dancing and chanting. Julie opened her eyes. They all turned their masked faces and stared silently at Julie. The tall man had stopped speaking. He turned and looked at Julie.

Slowly, he reached up with one hand and carefully removed his hood. He was not wearing a mask.

He was wearing the enormous skull of a deer, or a goat. Antlers seemed to be growing out of his head right before her eyes. He then pulled this skull up and off of his head. Julie could see him clearly in the light of the full moon and the bonfire.

He had a mane of wild, white hair. The flames from the bonfire seemed to dance in his hair and all around his head, creating an aura of fiery yellow and orange. His high cheek bones, a long, gaunt and chiseled face, old, pale skin, and a wide, yellow-toothed grin were all dominated by his piercing blue eyes. Julie looked at the knife he held. The razor thin blade morphed into a serpentine handle that wrapped itself up the tall man's long, thin arm. He was grinning at Julie. He began to laugh. His laughter echoed all around her and seemed to reverberate all around the great clearing.

The drums resumed beating and the revelers cheered and resumed their dancing.

Julie tore her eyes away from this man and looked up through the haze of smoke into the face of the young girl who was up on the tree. Though her eyes still could not fully focus on the girl, Julie knew who it was now. The girl looked down at Julie. Her brown eyes wept tears that mingled with the blood that covered her face and neck. Julie could only shake her head in disbelief.

Then something stirred overhead. The tall man, the drummers, and the revelers all paused their ritual. They seemed, to Julie, to be confused. The revelers all looked at the tall man. He was silently looking up at the canopy of this large clearing. They all then turned their attention to the canopy. Julie turned to see. Silence thundered. Time stopped. The whole of the clearing was now bathed in the raw and naked light of the full moon. In that moment Julie felt all of existence and creation outside of herself cease to be. Her awareness heightened.

Time passed. Creation held its breath. Somewhere above the clearing there was the sound of wings flapping overhead. Church bells rang in the distance. They seemed to signal that a safe haven is here. But they were far too far away and out of reach. As suddenly as they started, the church bells stopped. There was silence for exactly one heartbeat. Then all of the dancers started screaming. They were looking upward. Julie looked up, too. Something large descended down into the clearing with a crash and the deep cracking sound of large tree limbs splintering and snapping. It all landed right on top of the bonfire. A wall of wind and flame burst in every direction, knocking every mortal there off of their feet. Julie was lifted up and violently thrown to the edge of the clearing onto her back.

She heard men and women screaming. She tried to look but her head was too heavy to lift. A deafening, primal growl, low and guttural, roared from somewhere inside the pitch-black darkness of the clearing. Julie rolled over and struggled to get up onto her knees and pick up her head. Peering through a haze of smoke and ash, she could only hear the sounds of people dying.

There were screams, some piercing and others that were muted by gurgling, tearing and crunching sounds. Whatever it was that was thrashing around in the clearing caused the forest floor beneath her to shake and shudder. She could feel it, but she still could not see. The bonfire had been completely extinguished by what appeared to be a giant, black shroud. The pitch darkness had returned to envelope everything.

"Julie," a voice called. Despite the din all around her, Julie heard it quite clearly. It was deep and resonant. She covered her ears with her hands. "Julie." The voice tugged at her. Her entire body vibrated and shivered.

"Help me!" Julie looked up when she heard this. It was the voice of the young girl up on the tree. Julie painfully got up onto her feet and staggered back into the clearing. "Help me, please!"

Julie could see just enough by the light of the full moon to make her way through the sheer chaos and horror to try and find the young girl. It was as if hell was on earth. There were bodies and body parts strewn everywhere upon the forest floor. Julie tripped and fell over someone. His young, bloodied face was turned lifelessly up at the night sky. His eyes were missing. Julie thought she was going to be sick. She cried out and covered her mouth, struggling to get back onto her feet, looking wide-eyed and warily toward the growling sounds.

It sounded like a huge wolf. Julie could see just well enough to make out what she thought must be its eyes. They glowed like cinder from the shadows of the clearing's edge. She could hear it thrashing in the leaves, branches, and underbrush among the desperate and terrible cries of the revelers as it continued to feast. Finally, Julie found the tree and looked up at the young girl.

"Help me!" The voice came from right behind Julie. She whirled around and cried out involuntarily. Standing just a few feet away was a tall, thin, shadow of a man. His face was dark and featureless, except for his eyes. They were a pale, light blue. Then they changed right before Julie's eyes into a dark crimson red, then deep purple, then black. Though she could not be sure, Julie sensed that this man was smiling. She felt ice cold. There was the odor of feces and rotting flesh. All of the Great Woods fell silent.

"Who are you?" she said.

"Do you not know me?" the voice whispered low and clear.

Julie heard music. She looked around. She looked back up only to find that the shadow was gone. She heard the music again. Julie recognized it now. Whenever her cell phone received a text message, it played "Superstition" by Stevie Wonder.

Julie opened her eyes. She sat up and realized that she was in her bed. It had been a dream. She was soaked in sweat. "Very superstitious…"

She looked at her cell on the side table. It was indicating a received text message. She peeled off the covers and swung her legs over the side of the bed. A low-pitched groan came from her large malamute, Rasputin, who had been asleep next to her in the bed. Julie smiled and reached over and scratched behind his ears. He stretched and yawned. She opened her texts to read the message. Chills ran down Julie's spine and the sweat froze on her body as she read it: "pray for me." †

CHAPTER 2
Bonfire of Insanity

Pale blue and white lights illuminated the dark wood's edge, pulsating in a silent rhythm and giving a heart-beat to the night. A patrolman stood in the center of Deerfoot Road signaling with a flashlight. Julie Bernard slowed her Jeep Cherokee and pulled the vehicle around a gentle bend toward where he was standing. The lights from all of the patrol cars made her blink her sleepy eyes.

Julie was out of bed, dressed, out the door and in her car in less than five minutes after receiving that text. It was from a student named Megan Streeter. Megan was not answering her cell. Julie planned to drive to her office where she worked at the local high school in order to look up Megan's home address in the hope that she could find Megan. When a patrol car silently sped by her driveway with its lights flashing, Julie started her Jeep, put it into drive and followed the patrol car. She didn't know why she did this; she simply did it. It led her here to Deerfoot Road.

Julie parked on the shoulder and climbed out of her Jeep. The young patrolman approached her.

"Can I help you, ma'am?"

"I'm not sure. What happened here, officer?"

"We're not sure. We received an emergency phone call at the station just about five minutes ago. But everything seems to be quiet here, ma'am." Julie hated to be called *ma'am*.

As the young patrolman was speaking, Julie watched as several other patrolmen searched along the edge of the woods along a steep embankment. Their flashlights were trained on the trees and underbrush. They spoke in hushed voices.

"Would you mind waiting here, ma'am?" the young patrolman said. Julie smiled and shook her head. Her long, dirty blonde hair tousled in the wind.

A tall man emerged from the shadows of the wood's edge. She watched as he seemed to glide up the steep embankment and stride toward where the young patrolman was standing. The other police officers followed him and they gathered in the middle of the road. The young patrolman spoke with the tall man.

Julie shivered. It was much colder out than she expected when she hurriedly left the house ten minutes ago. She had thrown on her old jeans and a green sweater, which she laid out the night before. She planned to spend this Sunday cleaning the yard and raking leaves. Rasputin loved to go charging into leaf piles. Julie wrapped her arms around her chest for warmth. The tall man walked over to her.

"Hi, I'm Inspector Dahms. Can I help you, ma'am?"

"Hi inspector, I'm Julie Bernard. I'm a psychologist at the high school. A few minutes ago, I received a text from one of our students. She was in my office with a problem three days ago. I think she's in trouble."

"Why do you think she's in trouble, ma'am?" Julie showed the inspector the text message on her cell phone.

"Right." The inspector nodded his head. He towered over Julie, despite her being five feet and nine inches tall. His face was still just a shadow. The streetlights here on Deerfoot Road somehow seemed dimmed by the black night. "And you believe she may be here, somewhere?"

"No, actually. I saw a patrol car speed past and thought it may be for Megan. So, I followed, I guess." Julie shrugged. The inspector was nodding his head. Julie looked up into his face. "What happened here, Inspector?"

"Megan, that's her name?" The inspector asked.

Julie hesitated before replying. "Yes, sir, Megan Streeter."

"What was the nature of the problem that brought her to your office?"

"Oh, well, you know I can't tell you that, I'm sorry. That's a confidentiality issue."

"Right. Of course. Well, Miss Bernard, if we hear anything at all concerning Megan Streeter, we will contact you immediately. You have a good night." The inspector turned back toward the woods where his patrolmen were waiting. Julie began to follow him. He stopped and turned back around to face her.

"Miss Bernard?"

"Yes, Inspector Dahms?"

"May I ask where you're going?"

"You certainly may." As she said this, Julie walked around the inspector and across the road. The patrolmen all watched as she carefully made her way down the embankment and to the edge of the woods. The inspector had followed.

"Well?" he asked.

"Well, what?"

"Where are you going, Miss Bernard?"

"I'm going to look for Megan," Julie said.

"Miss Bernard, we're responding to a call that a noisy party was heard to be ongoing at a large clearing in these woods. It's where the local schools hold their pep-rallies and bonfires." A chill went up Julie's spine when the inspector had said *bonfires*. "Now, would a troubled child text you from a pep rally, Miss Bernard?" Julie stared up at the inspector, his face still just a shadow. But his voice, low and clear, had kindness in it. Julie swallowed.

"I don't think we'll find a pep rally there, Inspector," she said.

"What do you think we'll find?"

"I don't know." Julie shook her head. "But I have to find Megan."

"Have you checked her home or called her parents?"

"I don't have to. I know she isn't there."

"How do you know?"

"Shall we go?" Julie smiled as she said this. Her eyes searched for his in the darkness. The inspector nodded.

"I must ask you, Miss Bernard, to please stay back behind us a little in case of any danger."

"That's reasonable. I will do as you ask, Inspector."

"Thank you, ma'am." The inspector turned toward the tree line. "Tubbs, you and Jonesy will be ten yards or so to the left of the path. Marconi and Evers will take the right side. Franklin, you come with me on the path. Lydon, stay back here just in case. Miss Bernard," he handed Julie a large flash light, "stay on the path, maybe ten feet behind us, right?"

"Yes, sir." Julie took the flashlight. It was quite heavy.

"Eyes open, flash lights on, silently, please. Let's go."

The search party began to make their way into the woods. The lights from the patrol cars flashed intermittently amidst the trees and branches and faded fast in the thick wood. An avid hiker and runner, Julie was familiar with the path that she was on. Many of the folks in the town used it. It led to several different clearings, fishing ponds and reservoirs, and a myriad of other paths that wound through the woods, fields and farmlands of Littleborough. The walk was over a mile.

Julie's heart pounded in her chest. The darkness of the forest seemed to swallow the light from the flashlights whole. She smelled the pungent forest, the pine and the dew. She felt the cool autumn air. It was all too familiar. A shiver went straight down her spine. Julie shook her head slightly and refocused her mind on Megan. The soft, crunching sound of the patrolmen as they stepped through the thick underbrush on either side of her as they made their way through the woods was of some comfort.

A soft voice in front of Julie broke the silence. One of the patrolmen was checking the radio signal back to Officer Lydon on Deerfoot Road. Julie tried to look around with her flashlight. But she found herself mostly using it on the ground right in front of her as she tried to make her way along the path. She periodically looked up to make sure that she could still see the inspector and Officer Franklin up ahead. A voice came out of the darkness from Julie's right. It was one of the patrolmen.

"Wait, what's that sound?" Everyone listened.

"I hear drums," someone said. Julie's heart jumped. She could faintly hear the drumming, primal beats that sounded Native American, or African, in origin. Julie felt her entire body fill with dread. Despite the cool air, her hands and feet felt clammy. For one brief moment, Julie wondered if this, too, was only a dream.

"There's a light up ahead." This voice came from in front of Julie. It wasn't the inspector. It must be Officer Franklin, she reasoned. She looked up ahead of them on the path into the darkness of the forest. Her belly burned with fear as she made out a faint, orange glow. It seemed to appear and then disappear alternately amidst the trees of these thick woods. It could only be a bonfire, she thought.

"I think it's a bonfire," Officer Franklin said. Julie rolled her eyes in the dark.

They pressed forward silently. It seemed an eternity to Julie. They were well along the path now. The flashing lights from the emergency vehicles behind them were now completely out of sight. But the dancing flames of the bonfire didn't seem to get any closer. The drums were getting louder, though. Voices could now be heard. There was singing and chanting. Julie was thinking about Megan. Could this really be happening?

As they all inched closer to the clearing, they could see movement inside it. Blurry red figures seemed to be floating in a counter-clockwise motion around the bonfire. The smell of smoke wafted through the trees and mingled with the deep smell of pine and dew. The search party had almost reached the mouth, or entrance, to the clearing. That was when the drums and voices stopped. There was a pause. Somewhere off in the distance a church bell rang.

"Inspector, I think this is going to be bad," Julie said.

"What, Miss Bernard?"

"She said she thinks this is going to be—" A scream pierced the dark woods and the night.

"Let's go!" Inspector Dahms burst into a full run. But Julie had started running the moment she had heard the scream. Ungodly shrieks and screams came from inside the clearing. She ran past Officer Franklin and followed the inspector's dark shadow toward the chaos. Her mind raced her body as she ran. Julie was aware of the other patrolmen on either side of the pathway as they crashed through the woods and underbrush toward the screaming. The search party had reached the very outer edge of the clearing.

Julie could see the tall, thin frame of the inspector silhouetted by the flames of an impossibly large bonfire as he entered the mouth of the clearing. Crimson-robe-clad revelers scattered in every direction, screaming. Something enormous seemed to manifest among the treetops directly above the clearing. The large, dark shape descended rapidly. There was the deep crack of huge tree limbs snapping and breaking. The huge, black shroud landed right on top of the bonfire.

A deafening roar, a scream of anguish, and a wall of wind and flame burst outward in all directions, singeing the forest canopy at the very edges of the clearing. It knocked Julie off of her feet and onto the cold forest floor. Something howled in agony. Julie heard screaming and growling, crunching and tearing, crying, gurgling, death, and more church bells ringing. She knew what was happening now. There was no doubt. A deafening howl shook the ground. She couldn't look. Then Julie began to feel electricity all over her entire body. At first, it tingled, almost tickling her hands and her feet and her face and head. But it then increased in its intensity. It evolved into an overwhelming vibration. Though she could not hear it, Julie could feel a low, powerful vibration emanate throughout the entire Great Woods as well as throughout her entire body. It pinned Julie down flat on her back. She lay perfectly still on the cool forest floor until finally, after an eternity, the vibration and the cacophony subsided. The forest was now still and silent.

A moment passed. Julie began to get up onto her feet. At first, she wasn't sure in which direction the clearing was. The bonfire had been extinguished and the forest night was pitch dark now. A horrible, acrid smell of smoke permeated the night. She knew Megan would be in there, somewhere. Julie hoped with all her might that she would not be up on some tree. She could hear the sound of the radio dispatch asking what all that noise was. Julie wasn't sure if she was hurt. She could hear the police officers nearby as they were getting back up onto their feet.

"What the hell was that?" a voice from Julie's left said.

"Something hit the fire," the inspector said.

"Put the whole damn thing out!"

15

"What could do that?"

"I don't know."

Julie turned toward the voices and took a cautious step. She bent down and felt around the ground for her flashlight. She did not find it. Julie took another step forward, and then another. She kicked something hard. She squatted down and began to feel around the ground with both hands. She found her flashlight, or a flashlight. It was still on.

Julie looked at her feet to see if she was still on the path. She was not. She then looked up and saw that another flashlight was on up ahead of her. It shined into her face briefly.

"Miss Bernard, glad you're okay." Julie recognized Inspector Dahms' voice. "Quite a bang that was, hmmm?" he said. "Check in, please. You okay, Benjamin?"

"Got knocked on my ass, but I'm fine, sir," Officer Franklin said. His high, boyish voice came from well behind them on the path.

"Same here. Evers and I are both fine. What was that?" Officer Marconi said.

"I'm not sure. The bonfire looked like it burned out of control. Now it's gone and I don't hear anything. Tubbs, Jones, you okay?"

"Yeah, we're fine. What was growling and howling?" Officer Tubbs said.

"It sounded like a wolf," Officer Franklin said.

"Yes, it did," the inspector said. "Lights on, forward, easy. Remember, this may be a crime scene." They entered the clearing.

"God, what's that smell?" Everyone started gagging.

"That's the smell of burnt flesh and burnt hair," Inspector Dahms said.

Julie removed a handkerchief from her pocket and held it over her face. Her eyes stung and watered from the soot and smell.

Seven lonely beams of light from the flashlights arced up and down, left and right and along the smoldering forest floor. It was dead quiet. A soft, warm and very light rain started to land gently on the leaves and canopy of the forest and everyone below.

"Why is it raining warm water on a cold, clear night?"

"That's an excellent question, Franklin," Inspector Dahms said.

Julie looked up at the night sky. It was as beautiful a night sky as she could ever remember. It was crystal clear and the stars and the full moon shone brightly. A warm drop of rain touched down gently on her face. It landed at the corner of her mouth. Julie gagged, then spat. She retched violently and began vomiting.

"Oh my God, this is blood! It's raining blood!" Officer Marconi said. Blood was dripping down from the leaves and limbs of the trees above the clearing.

"Yes, it is. I'm afraid you're right. Stay cool, Marconi. Everybody, easy now." But despite the inspector's words, Officer Marconi was vomiting and repeating the Lord's Prayer alternately. He was joined by Officers Evers and Jones. Officer Tubbs added his two cents with several carefully chosen expletives. Then Officer Franklin joined in the chorus of vomiting.

Julie staggered back onto her feet, still retching and crying softly. She knew exactly what she was looking for. She knew exactly where to look. She went to her right, stumbling over bodies, over downed tree limbs and human limbs and through the blood rain until she reached the foot of a large tree that had been surrounded by countless candles that had all been blown out. Julie shined the flashlight up and into the face of Megan Streeter. Megan was dead. She had been crucified on that tree.

"Oh, my God..." †

CHAPTER 3

Julie stared up into Megan's contorted face while tears rolled down her own. She could feel the blood rushing from her head and face. She became dizzy and felt faint. She staggered over to the edge of the clearing, just beyond Megan's tree and all the candles, knelt down, and vomited again. She remained there on her hands and knees on the cool forest floor for several minutes, vomiting, retching, and sobbing alternately. Finally her body had nothing left to vomit and the retching stopped. Her stomach ached. Sit-ups are going to hurt today, Julie thought.

Her breath came back to her slowly. The fresh night air with the pungent smell of dew and the forest were, to Julie, heaven sent. She got up slowly and stiffly. The dizzy and light-headed feeling was still there. Julie closed her eyes and breathed in deeply and slowly, as she always did before going for a run. She held each breath for a second or two, then breathed out slowly. Julie opened her eyes in the darkness of the wilderness. She brushed herself off and took another handkerchief from her pocket and cleaned herself up as best she could. She then walked back into the stench and horror of the clearing where Megan was.

Julie aimed her flashlight upward and looked up at the young girl. Megan's face was covered in blood and soot. Tear streaks ran down both of her child-like cheeks and had washed some of the soot away. Julie turned away. She could hear Inspector Dahms and several of his officers carefully examining the scene. The powerful beams from their flashlights darted and waved along the ground and the forest canopy above.

"You've gotta be fucking kidding me..." Officer Tubbs said.

"These people have been crucified!" Officer Marconi began gagging again after he said this.

"Not all of them. Some of them have been ripped apart," Officer Franklin said.

"This isn't real."

"Easy, everybody, take it easy. We've got to keep our heads." Inspector Dahms was standing next to Julie. "Is this Megan Streeter, Miss Bernard?" Julie nodded her head. She could not speak at that moment.

"I'm sorry, ma'am. I'm truly sorry." Julie nodded. Inspector Dahms wrote in his pad. He then sent a text to the chief.

"Lord, God, this can't be happening," Officer Marconi said.

"Why would anybody do any of this?"

"I think a wild animal did most of this."

"What the fuck are you talking about, Franklin? Wild animals don't crucify people, you wing nut!"

"I know that, Tubbs. I'm talking about all the bodies down on the ground here."

"Oh." Officer Tubbs shined his flashlight along the forest floor. "Jesus, it's more like body parts than bodies."

"I know."

"This can't be real."

"Jesus Christ." Officer Tubbs had his light on the severed head of a young man. His eyes were missing.

"Did this really happen?"

"This guy over here was crucified upside down, Inspector," Officer Franklin said.

Somewhere in the deep recesses of Julie's mind she thought, Oh, no.

"What the fuck?" Officer Tubbs said.

"Okay, this is a crime scene," Inspector Dahms said. "Anyone who wants out, to leave this place, can. I would understand. But we're going to need to preserve this scene until daybreak so I can get a good look at this. Has anyone found any survivors?" No one answered. "I want you all to stay calm and stay focused. We need to search for survivors until we're sure. Let's be alert. Those wolves could come back."

The thought of possible survivors helped the patrolmen begin to focus. They trained their flashlights on the forest floor and began searching for anyone who might still be alive. The inspector began to look over the victims who were up on the trees. There were four people who had been crucified. Two men and two girls were the victims. One of the men had been crucified upside down. The blood-rain had let up, and was now only dripping intermittently from the leaves and branches.

"This is old Jed Prescott," Inspector Dahms said. Officer Franklin looked up.

"Yes, it is." He swallowed hard, fighting back the nausea. The inspector then walked carefully over to the third cross and shone his flashlight up into the victims' face.

"Another young girl, I'm afraid," he said. Julie walked over and looked.

"That's Caroline Hart. She's also a student at the high school." Tears filled Julie's eyes. Her eyes burned from the grief. She realized she had a dull headache.

"I am sorry, Miss Bernard." The inspector wrote the name on his little pad. He then texted the chief: *old jed prescott and caroline hart, too.*

"Does anyone recognize the man upside-down on the tree?" Inspector Dahms asked. No one did. "Okay. We have no survivors in this clearing, and four victims of crucifixion, hmmm."

The inspector walked into the center of the clearing, where the bonfire had once raged. He then looked around, surveying the crime scene. "Franklin, would you say that these victims are all placed at a cardinal point?" Officer Franklin walked over to where Inspector Dahms was standing and looked.

"Yes, I would. We entered from the west. The upside-down guy is directly north. The other three all correspond as well." Inspector Dahms' cell signaled a text with a soft vibration. It was from the chief: *thank you keep me posted-going to prescotts place - be in touch.*

The remaining patrolmen had extended their search for survivors beyond the edge of the clearing. They began to trickle back to the clearing, one by one.

"We didn't find anyone?"

"No, sir," Officer Evers said.

"No," Officer Tubbs said. Officer Jones shook his head.

"Not a soul," Officer Marconi said. He was still crying.

"Is this real?"

"This is real, Evers," Officer Tubbs said.

"I'm afraid it is," the inspector said. Julie had walked back over to where Megan was. She was looking up at her, weeping softly, when she realized Inspector Dahms was speaking to her. "...to leave ma'am."

"I'm so sorry, what...what were you saying, Inspector?" Julie was embarrassed, but Inspector Dahms simply smiled warmly.

"I was saying that I need you to leave this place, ma'am." But Julie was already shaking her head. Inspector Dahms continued anyway. "Well, the fact is, Miss Bernard, this is an official crime scene now. I'm going to have one of my men escort you back to Deerfoot Road." The inspector turned to one of the uniformed officers, "Officer Evers here will get you back to the road, ma'am." The tall, pale patrolman stepped forward out of the darkness, but Julie hesitated.

"Inspector," she stared up into his face, "you can't tell me to leave now." Officer Evers stopped in his tracks, looking from Julie to the inspector and then back again. She continued, "Do you even know what it is you're looking at?"

"What are we looking at, Miss Bernard?"

"These people were sacrificed. Megan and Caroline were…sacrificed!"

"What do you mean by 'sacrificed'?"

"How much do you know about the occult, Inspector?"

"Very little, ma'am." The inspector's tone was low and even. It was the first time Julie had been able to really see him. His suit and his coat were black. He wore a fedora, also black, that seemed to Julie to suit him to a tee. He had hard, ice-cold gray eyes that squinted in perpetual thought, thought Julie. He was older, has to be in his forties, she guessed. He had a long, thin nose and a graying mustache. His high cheekbones and weathered complexion suited the intelligence in his eyes.

"Can you read any meaning at all from the crime scene?"

"No, ma'am."

"Two of our children are dead, and who knows how many more are in here somewhere? If you don't read this correctly it could happen again!"

"Miss Bernard, can I take it that you are knowledgeable about the occult?"

"In addition to psychology, I received a doctorate in mythology and the occult, yes."

"I see. What do you mean by 'read' the scene, ma'am?"

"This was some kind of ritual, Inspector. The crucifixions lead me to believe this was done by some sort of devil worship cult, something like that."

"That makes sense. Well," the inspector looked at his men and then back at Julie, "since you're an expert on this, I can let you stay if you want. We would appreciate your help. But you must do all you can to not interfere with any evidence or this crime scene itself. Sound okay?"

Julie nodded. "Yes, sir."

"Are you sure you want to do this?"

"Yes, I'll be fine," Julie lied. She clenched her jaw and steeled herself. "I need to examine the victims' necks, throats, and faces as closely as possible."

"You wouldn't want to start somewhere else?" Officer Franklin said. He was serious.

"No." Inspector Dahms nodded. "We will start where Miss Bernard suggests we start."

"Let's go," she said.

"Let's go." †

CHAPTER 3.14
A Lamb unto Unholy Waters

"Oh, dear," sighed Father James Knight. He knew this was going to be a dirty job. He never imagined this. He peered in through the doorway but could make out very little. The lights in the hallway did not penetrate the darkness of the closet at all. "Cobwebs thicker than my skull, and dust bunnies the size of my leg," he said aloud to Ezekiel, his small and very old German shepherd. The dog was stretched out on a thick rug at the other end of the hall. He wagged his tail, thumping the floor with it three times before yawning and going back to sleep.

Father Knight heard the unmistakable *scrabble, scrabble* of mice or rats scurrying from the invading light. It was a closet built in underneath the main stairwell of the church known as St. Mark's in Littleborough. Today was his first day at the new assignment. Oh, the glamour! Oh, the glory! He laughed at himself as he took the broom and duster out to pick up what he was sure would turn out to be oodles of mouse poop.

Everything had happened so fast. It all seemed like a blur to Father Knight. He was thirty years old, fresh out of seminary. He had only just been assigned to a parish called St. Anne's, in a small town neighboring Littleborough. He was to assist and learn from Father John Freeman. Despite what the church authorities considered rather risqué teaching methods along with a certain degree of risqué living, Father Freeman seemed perfect for the task. He was an old friend of Father Knight's family.

It was his second day at St. Anne's. Father Knight was working in the garden when Father Freeman had come for him. His face was dark and ashen in stark contrast to his normally red-cheeked look.

23

"James…" Father Freeman paused for breath. Father Knight thought, *was he running?*

"Yes, John?"

"Bishop Richter is here. He's in the study. He wants to speak with you."

"Of course." Father Knight rose up onto his feet and brushed himself off. He smiled as his St. Christopher's medal fell out of his collar, dangling from the silver chain around his neck. He kissed it and tucked it gently back into his shirt as he followed Father Freeman through the rear entrance of St. Anne's. Despite running several miles daily, he had to hustle to catch up with Father Freeman, who could move well for a man of his age and size. Only about five feet and ten inches tall, Father Freeman was a bull of a man. He had broad shoulders and big, thick arms and a barrel chest. Even his face and balding head were large.

"John," Father Knight said to his old friend just outside the study door, "are you okay?"

Father Freeman smiled. His wide blue eyes peered from behind a slightly crooked nose, the result of a successful amateur boxing career. He patted Father Knight's shoulder.

"Yes," he whispered. He then opened the study door and both men entered.

"Father Knight, James…" Bishop Richter smiled as he got up out of his seat and shook hands with Father Knight. He then waddled his short, stout body back behind the desk and sat down heavily, smiling at Father Freeman. "Ah, these old bones of mine, John, I don't know how much longer they're going to be able to haul my considerable bulk around like this; I really don't."

Father Freeman laughed. He walked over to a small cabinet almost hidden between two bookshelves and under a pile of papers. The room could have been a library. Bookshelves lined the entire study. They were filled, end to end and top to bottom, with books and periodicals. Prayer books, songbooks, and holy scriptures such as the Bible, the Bhagavad Gita, the Dead Sea Scrolls, teachings of the Buddha, the Jewish mystics, Gnosticism, Alan Watts, Zoroastrianism, the Egyptian Book of the Dead, the Koran, Zen teachings and many other disciplines of every edition and language filled the lower shelves. The upper shelves had textbooks, history books, books about religion, mythology, archaeology, anthropology, psychology, sociology, and philosophy of every kind. There were books on ancient languages, ancient history, recent history, physics, quantum mechanics, astrophysics, geology, and, of course, hidden in the back were Father Freeman's *Playboy* and *Penthouse* magazines. There were so many books and shelves that it left room for only a small calendar of cute kittens on the wall behind the desk.

Father Freeman had taken a bottle of scotch out of the cabinet along with two glasses.

"Let's start this off right, hey Pat?" In private these priests were never formal with one another in terms of names or titles, no matter what their "rank." "How about a nice glass of super holy water?"

"Amen!" smiled Bishop Richter, "none for James?" Father Knight smiled and shook his head politely.

"No, James doesn't touch the stuff, which is excellent because it leaves so much more for me." All three men laughed. Father Knight sensed a tension in the way the two older men laughed. He remembered how ashen Father Freeman had looked only a few minutes ago. Whatever it was that the bishop had told Father Freeman must have been awful for him to look like that, because nothing ever fazed Father John Freeman.

"Sit down, please, gentlemen." The Bishop lit a cigarette. "Sorry about the smoke, James."

"Oh, no…don't ah…no problem…there." Father Freeman smiled to himself as he accepted a cigarette from the Bishop. He and Father Knight were seated in front of the desk at which the bishop now sat as he smoked, drank, and regarded them through spectacles perched on the end of his nose.

The bishop had to slightly tilt his round, balding head back in order that his beady, intelligent blue eyes could focus on the two priests. His lips were full and in a perpetual pout when he wasn't smiling or laughing. His complexion was ruddy from years of drinking and smoking. There was also an undeniable hint of mischief in his face.

"I need to speak with you both. The hard part of this I have already told to John." He paused, and then he and Father Freeman exchanged sad glances. He took a deep breath. "Father Torrez, our pastor at St. Mark's in Littleborough, passed away last night. Did you know him, James?"

"No, I didn't," Father Knight replied softly. "But it's clear to me that you and John knew him well enough." The two older men nodded. It seemed for a moment neither could speak. "I am very sorry for the loss of your friend and our church's loss of a shepherd. What can I do?"

"You're very kind, James. I've heard that from every teacher, student, counselor, and priest that has ever known you." The bishop leaned his fat, frumpy frame back in the chair and stretched out his legs under the desk. He then lit another cigarette with the one he had just finished. "But God help me for what I'm about to do." Bishop Richter looked hard at Father Knight. "I'm asking you to replace Father Torrez at St. Mark's." His look intensified as he leaned over the desk. "I want you to ease those people's pain and shock. I want you to help them…to protect them…damn!" He slammed the wooden desk with a pudgy fist. "I'm sorry…I'm…sorry."

"Easy, Pat, easy." Father Freeman had risen from his chair and leaned over the desk, putting a hand on the shoulder of his friend. "Hey, how about a refill?" The bishop nodded while Father Freeman poured a bit more scotch into their glasses. The bishop took his glass and raised it.

"To Father Miguel Torrez, may his beautiful soul rest in peace."

"Amen," Father Knight said.

"Amen," Father Freeman echoed. The room fell silent. The bishop sipped his drink. He was staring out the window of the study. Father Knight could tell that Bishop Richter was not looking at any one thing in particular. His thoughts and reminiscences were light years away. He looked over at Father Freeman, who had also momentarily turned his thoughts inward. Though awkward, periods of uncomfortable silence like this one did not faze Father Knight. He was aware of their benefits and believed in the power of silence. The moment passed.

"That's good scotch, John," the bishop said. He then looked at Father Knight, smiling sadly.

"When shall I begin my new duties, Bishop?"

"Whoa! Whoa, there Pocahontas! Not so fast, James. I'm not assigning you to this; I'm asking you to do this." Both Father Knight and Father Freeman looked quizzically at the Bishop, who went on. "Despite my rank and authority, despite your vows of obedience and service to God and all His flock, no one has the power or authority to assign this to any man, woman, or child." The bishop finished his drink. "And frankly, gentlemen, I've got a lot of damn balls even asking this of James." Pocahontas? Father Knight thought as he smiled to himself.

"I don't understand, Pat." Father Freeman had risen from his seat to refill their empty glasses. "This is a terrific chance for James, albeit a bitter sweet one due to Miguel's passing. I can tell you with one hundred percent certainty that James is ready for his own ministry. He's better prepared than you or I when we were at that age."

"That is certainly true. However, there is much more to this than I have told you so far. I hate to sound like a bad movie, but what I'm about to tell you both is being done so in complete confidence. This edict comes from the Teacher. Anyway, before you accept this new position, James, there are some...details we all have to go over first." Father Freeman and Father Knight leaned forward to listen.

"Father Torrez died of what the coroner is calling a massive heart attack. Because Miguel was so young, they have to do an autopsy, I guess, so we may learn more." Bishop Richter shrugged as he spoke. It seemed to Father Knight that the bishop did not like the idea of an autopsy being performed on his friend.

"How old was Father Torrez?"

"He was forty."

"Did he leave a family?"

"No," Bishop Richter said, "no wife, or children."

"There is his sister…Anna?" Father Freeman said, looking at the bishop for confirmation.

"Yes, I think that's right. She's a volunteer with some charitable agency; they send her all over the world—you know, flood relief, famines, refugee camps and that sort of thing. It worried Miguel no end, I can tell you that." The bishop lit another cigarette.

"Anyway, the death of Father Torrez is suspicious. And, for reasons that will soon become clear to you both, the police and our church are keeping the rest of the details quiet for right now."

"Pat, what are the rest of the details?" Father Freeman asked.

"They are sick. They are…sick!" Bishop Richter sprang to his feet and began to pace back and forth. For such a rotund and robust man, he was deceptively quick in his movements. Father Knight vaguely remembered being told that the bishop was an all-American wide receiver on a great college football team back in the sixties. The bishop sat as suddenly as he had gotten up. He closed his eyes and breathed out slowly, puffing his pudgy cheeks out as he did so.

"From what I gather from the initial investigation, which was conducted by an Inspector Dahms, something woke up Miguel around midnight last night." The bishop spoke barely above a whisper. "Whatever it was he heard was coming from the church itself. The police think that Miguel went straight along the walkway that leads right from the little rectory to the rear entrance. He entered the back door and walked into the kitchen and prep area. Whatever he was hearing drew him straight into the chapel.

"I guess someone had lit a bunch of candles on the altar and on all the pews… everywhere. The altar and the carpeting all around it were soaked in blood. Miguel must have seen something or someone at the main entrance, or out in the atrium. The Inspector was able to track Miguel's steps right through the blood that was all around the altar, right down the center aisle toward the entrance door." The bishop stopped short, and swallowed hard. Despite his round face and perpetual squinting of his eyes, he could not mask the pain and sorrow….and rage. "It is there that the police found him, in his pajamas…and his slippers…" Father Knight poured the bishop more scotch, filling the glass almost to the very top. Bishop Richter accepted it gratefully.

"Thanks, kid. The police found what they think caused Miguel's heart attack, if that's what it really was. In the holy water we keep right by the entrance…they found a heart, a human heart!" The bishop shouted this. Father Knight and Father Freeman simply froze in their chairs; James could feel the hairs on the back of his neck standing up as chills worked their way down his spine. A tremendous weight of dread formed in the pit of his stomach. "From the size of the heart, the inspector thinks it was taken from a newborn baby."

This last sentence seemed to sap the bishop of his strength. He glanced briefly at his old friend, Father Freeman. He then stared straight ahead, past his two ministers and out the window. And there the three holy men sat in total shock and silence. The still and somber mood in the room contrasted with the bright, sunny day outside. †

CHAPTER 4
A Mourning Star

As he cleaned out the closet in his new parish, Father Knight thought about the meeting yesterday with Bishop Richter and Father Freeman over and over. He never imagined that his first assignment would be in such a difficult circumstance. He was confident that he would be able to heal the congregation over time. But this business with candles and blood on the altar and a heart left in the holy water, what could that mean? And what was the significance of the heart having belonged to a newborn baby? As sick as it is, removing anybody's heart is an equally depraved act, thought Father Knight.

But it was the look that the bishop and Father Freeman exchanged at the mention of the infant that had caught Father Knight's attention. There was rage and sorrow in their faces, but also recognition. It was almost as if they had been expecting it. But what could that mean? Father Knight wondered. What was the significance? He certainly didn't get any answers from Father Freeman.

When the shock of the entire, sordid story about Miguel's death began to wear off of Father Knight, the question of honesty occurred to him. He had just left the meeting with the bishop and went back to the Vestry to pack his and Ezekiel's things. He stopped and looked at the little old German Shepherd.

"I don't know, Zeke," he said. The dog stared into Father Knight's eyes. Then he blinked his eyes once. Father Knight could swear the little old dog had understood him. They went out the door together and climbed into Father Freeman's old Chevy pick-up truck. It was a short drive to St. Mark's Church of America in Littleborough. Father Knight had to ask.

"Father Freeman?"

"Yes, James?"

"I'm not sure about lying to our congregation about what has happened last night. It just doesn't seem right to me."

"Well, I can understand that, James. We fully intend to tell everybody everything just as soon as we know what exactly has happened. Because the truth is, we don't know. I think the Holy Mother and the Judges feel it's best to protect our people from the unknown. You know, to prevent rumors and gossip and the whole thing snowballing out of control. Once we have all the information, we'll share it with everybody."

"But we've already lied, John. How are they all going to feel when they realize that we lied to them?"

"Oh, I think most will understand. Right now, we need to worry about one thing and one thing only: healing this group of people and easing their shock and sadness." Father Knight looked at Father Freeman.

"That's certainly true enough," he had said.

Father Knight found himself simply standing outside the closet, clutching the broom with white knuckles as he thought about this conversation. He still had that heavy feeling in the pit of his stomach. He looked at his watch. He would have to finish cleaning the closet later. It was time to prepare for a special memorial service for Father Torrez. Father Knight washed up and dressed.

Bishop Richter had felt that it would be better for all involved if a special Saturday service was held in order that the congregation could meet Father Knight before the regular Sunday services. Father Freeman, who had been a long-time minister at St. Mark's before moving one town over to St. Anne's, would help with the introductions. There would then be a cookout on the grounds, and croquet and badminton for the children.

The memorial service for Father Torrez was held in the church. Bishop Richter and Father Freeman both read lessons from the Bible and the congregation had joined them in prayers and a hymn. Then the bishop introduced Father Knight to the entire congregation as their new priest. Father Knight spoke briefly.

"Hello, all of you." His soft, brown eyes looked straight into the eyes of his new parish. "I first must express my deepest sympathy to you all for this shocking loss, the sorrow, and pain. I cannot and will not ever be able to replace Father Torrez. As I look out into all of your faces, I can see the true depth of grief, and pain, and sorrow. It tells me that he must have been wonderful. Together, we must embrace this pain. We all must be courageous enough, and strong enough to acknowledge this terrible loss. We must do this together, as one. We must peer unabashedly into the face of our own grief. For the true measure of this pain that we all feel is also the truest measure of what Father Miguel Torrez meant to us all. Here on this earth, this Creation, we have lost a loved one.

"But we have not lost that love. Love is eternal. It is through love that his memory can be honored and cherished by every one of us. It is with love that we can all act as individuals and as a community to honor our lost loved ones. And so, we all shall.

"As I say, I cannot, nor ever will be able to fill his shoes. I can, and shall, however, do all I can to carry on his good works. Our doors shall remain open to you at all times. I hope you will feel free to come see me anytime if you feel the need to talk, or cry, or to just hang out. I will see you all tomorrow at Sunday service. May God bless Father Torrez, and may God bless each and every one of you."

"Thanks, Father Knight," Bishop Richter said.

"Murder!" A single voice rang out from the midst of the congregation. "Murder!"

Everyone in the church turned to see who had spoken up. It was Madeline Anastazio. She was looking at Father Knight. "It was murder, young man!" Madeline stood up out of her pew, which was about halfway back in the right row. Father Freeman had quickly gotten to his feet and was walking hurriedly down the center aisle toward her.

"Madeline, what are you talking about, honey?" he said. Several parishioners, including Michelle Floria and Julie Bernard, had risen and were gently trying to calm her.

"It's true! Evil is here! He is here, with us, among us! Father Torrez was murdered, and you have brought an innocent lamb to slaughter!"

"Sssshhh." Julie put her hand gently on Madeline's shoulder.

"Sssshhh, it'll be okay, honey," Michelle said in a soft, throaty voice. She and Julie had been crying. Most of the congregation had cried during Father Knight's talk. Madeline, who appeared to Father Knight to be in her sixties, was dressed in all black. Her pale, gaunt face was streaked with mascara from crying. She looked exhausted. The sheer desperation in her voice was matched by the look in her blue eyes. Father Knight started for her, but the bishop stopped him.

"It's okay, my boy. John will take care of it. Father Torrez's death has shocked her terribly."

"Can't any of you feel it? Can't any of you see it? I can! It was murder! I hear you! I can hear you! I can hear you laughing at us!" Madeline looked around at everyone with wild-eyed fear as she exclaimed this. Father Freeman reached where Madeline stood.

"Ssshhh, Madeline. Take it easy, take it easy. You're frightening everyone."

"But he was murdered, Father, taken away by someone he trusted, I just know it!"

"Ssshhh, Miguel died from a heart attack, honey. Now come on, come with me. We'll get a little fresh air and some food and you'll feel better." Father Freeman gently took Madeline by the arm and the two had started for the door, but Madeline then stopped and looked back at Father Knight.

"He's here, Father. Evil is here. Evil is here for you." Her eyes filled with tears. "Be careful."

"All right, Madeline, come on." Father Freeman began to gently steer Madeline for the door.

"Please, be careful, Father Knight! He's here for you! Evil is here for you, dear!"

"Don't worry, he'll be very careful. Now, come on, dear."

"But, he's here, Father, I just..."

"I know. I know..." The two exited the church, closing the large, oak door behind them.

"Okay, don't worry, folks. We'll get Madeline calmed down and she'll be fine," the bishop said, then added to the congregation, "hey, let's eat!"

Bishop Richter stayed by Father Knight in the enormous parlor as he met, one by one, his new flock. Father Freeman manned the grill, cooking burgers, hot dogs, and chicken.

"Bishop Richter, so good to see you again!" A smartly dressed woman in her thirties approached Bishop Richter and Father Knight. She smiled a gleaming, white-toothed smile that did not seem, to Father Knight, to be very genuine. Her cheeks dimpled slightly through her heavily applied make-up as she leaned forward slightly to greet the bishop without actually touching him.

"Hello Daphne, how are you?"

"I'm well, dear." She turned toward Father Knight. "And so, this is the prodigal?"

"Daphne Phoeble, this is Father James Knight."

"So good to meet you, Father. I am the principle Selectperson here in Littleborough. We're so excited to have you back in our little community!"

"Well, thank you, Miss Phoeble."

"Not at all, not at all!" She turned back to the Bishop; her expression was dead serious. "Have you heard anything from Inspector Dahms or the chief? Have they found anything?" He shook his head.

"Not that I'm aware of, no. But it is awfully early in the investigation. I'm sure they will find out who did this."

"They had better find out, and quick. We're not going to be able to keep this quiet for very long. People are already talking. And now that fucking drunk, Madeline, is making noise." The bishop nodded his head.

"I am not happy that this happened on my watch; that much I can tell you. The next election is only days away." She paused and looked around. "When we all met late last night, I made it clear to the chief that this needs to be resolved, like, now. I'm not going to be the one blamed for keeping the town in the dark while some devil worship cult is running around doing…doing that."

"Take it easy, dear. You and the rest of the board insisted on all of us remaining mum until an arrest is made. That does make the job more difficult for the chief and the inspector."

"I'm just thinking about our town, Bishop, the panic it could cause. I think everybody's going to be pissed when they find out what happened after the fact."

"Maybe we should tell everybody, then?"

"Absolutely not. I can't believe this…I'm not going down for this."

"Well, it certainly wasn't your fault, Daphne. I'm sure the police will get to the bottom of it before too long."

"Quickly enough to save my re-election?" She turned and quickly walked away, her high heels clicking on the linoleum floor. Father Knight looked at the Bishop. The bishop smiled and shrugged his shoulders.

"Why, hello Mrs. McGillicuddy, I'm so glad you could come." Bishop Richter took the hand of a very plump, very redheaded woman in her mid-forties. She was accompanied by a gaggle of women who all seemed to Father Knight to look and sound the same.

"Oh, my God, Bishop!" she replied in a loud New York accent,. "I wouldn't have missed it for the world." She took the Bishop's hand and tut-tutted. "Poor Father Torrez. His passing was so sudden! Strange, he never married." She said this to the women standing next to her, who both nodded. Father Knight looked at the Bishop, who was suppressing a smile. She seemed to Father Knight to be totally insincere.

"There, there, now." Bishop Richter patted her pudgy hand, which had been expensively manicured and bore several enormous rings on it. "May I introduce you to Father James Knight? Father Knight, this is Paula McGillicuddy, Tessa Nusbaum, and Frieda Whiteapple, all great supporters of our little parish here."

"Ladies, it is a great pleasure to meet you. Please accept my deepest sympathy for the loss of Father Torrez to you and this parish." They all shook hands. Mrs. McGillicuddy's grip was firm.

"Thank you, dear." She smiled a perfect-toothed smile. "You said the nicest things during the service, honey. I was so impressed!" The other ladies clucked their approval.

"Yes ma'am, thank you."

"Oh! I think that's wonderful! So polite and young and handsome!"

"Well, he's young, anyway." Bishop Richter said. Father Knight burst out laughing.

"Oh! Bishop Richter is very naughty, isn't he? You pay no attention to him at all, Father Knight! Ooooh!" she squealed. "Crullers!" A tray of donuts, muffins, and the aforementioned crullers was set out as a dessert spread next to a tray of fruits and hot pots of coffee and tea.

"Oh please," Bishop Richter said, "help yourselves."

"It was very nice meeting you, Father Knight."

"Yes ma'am, it was nice meeting you all, too." The ladies then swarmed the dessert tray.

"I hope none of them sprains her esophagus," the bishop said in a low tone. Father Knight covered his mouth as he chuckled softly.

"Hello Father Knight, my name is Barbara Wordsworth." A tall woman in an expensive suit and glasses stared into his eyes and shook his hand firmly.

"How do you do?"

"Doing great, padre, doing great. I'm a Selectperson here in Littleborough." Father Knight was guessing she was in her mid-thirties. Tall and thin, her hair was cut into a perfect bob and frosted. She reached a long arm towards an older man in his fifties. "Father, this is Selectperson Dick Pale." The man stepped forward and shook Father Knight's hand.

"Nice to meet you, Father. I thought what you said was terrific. You could be my speech writer!" He smiled and winked.

"Thank you, sir. It's nice to meet you, too."

"And this is Selectperson Candy Dahlbright."

"Hi Father Knight, I'm Candy Dahlbright." A lovely young woman in her mid-twenties, she was blonde and blue eyed. Her figure was petite. "I loved what you said at the service, thank you."

"Well, thank you, too. It's nice to meet you."

A short, stout man stood behind Selectperson Candy Dahlbright. He reached out and shook Father Knight's hand.

"Selectperson Bert Snodgrass, Father. It's nice to meet you. I knew your father, good man."

"It's nice to meet you, too, thank you."

"And this is Selectperson Tim White."

"Hello, Mr. White." A tall, elderly gentleman shook hands with Father Knight while speaking without making a sound.

"That's good, Tim." Selectperson Barbara Wordsworth gently moved him along. She looked back at Father Knight. "Please feel free to contact me if there's anything you need."

"Oh, well, thank you very much…Selectperson Wordsworth." This delighted the Selectperson into a perfect-toothed smile as she and her fellow Selectpersons then greeted the Bishop.

Bishop Richter introduced Father Knight to Julie Bernard, a psychologist at the high school. Father Knight observed what a breathtakingly beautiful woman she was. Her smooth, peaches and cream complexion dimpled when she smiled. Julie's lips were full and curved upward in a slightly wry smile. Her face was made even more sensual by a small, curved nose set between the intelligence and curiosity in her wide green eyes.

"Hi Father. I loved what you said at the memorial."

"Thank you. I was touched by how kind you were to poor Madeline at the end of the service."

"Oh, thank you, Father, that poor dear."

"Please call me James, Miss Bernard."

"Okay, James. Call me Julie."

"Okay, Julie it is." Neither of them could stop smiling. "Maybe we could have coffee, or something, at Dick's tomorrow?"

"I would like that, James. How about in the morning?" Still smiling, he nodded. Their eyes locked for a moment. Neither one of them wanted to let go of the other's hand. There was something in that moment, a warmth and an authenticity. The world seemed to stand still. But there was a long line of folks behind Julie all waiting to meet Father Knight.

"You old dog, nicely played," the bishop said. He grinned at Father Knight, who grinned back. As the line continued to stream past him, Father Knight would occasionally look up to see Julie. As she chatted with other parishioners, she would playfully glance over at Father Knight. They smiled each time their eyes met. From the first person in line to the last, Father Knight tried to connect with everyone he met that day.

"Bishop!" The bishop and Father Knight, who were now alone in the reception hall, turned around to find a tall, impossibly thin man striding toward them. "How wonderful to see you again!" He was dressed in an all-white suit and white tie with a white top hat and white shoes. Father Knight couldn't recall seeing this person during the service, the cookout, or any of the other activities that followed.

"Oh, I am sorry," the man seemed only interested in the bishop as he faced only him and really took no notice of Father Knight at all, "but don't you recognize me, Pat?" The man smiled a white-toothed smile that seemed to Father Knight to be devoid of warmth or humor.

"No, I don't recognize you, sir. Forgive me and my truly poor memory, and you are…?" There was an awkward pause as the tall man's smile vanished, then returned in a more menacing form.

"Oh, that is disappointing, Bishop. And here I was expecting so much more! You see, where I come from you have a very naughty reputation! Believe you me, everybody down that way is really looking forward to meeting you, Pat."

"Well, it's always nice to meet new folks." As the bishop spoke, he had turned toward the dessert tray. "Cruller?" the bishop offered a large, jelly cruller to the tall man.

"So, you still say you don't recognize me, Bishop?" The man no longer smiled.

"Oh, well, now don't feel so bad. Some folks just aren't that memorable." The bishop was smiling now. He put the cruller inside the top breast pocket of the tall man's white jacket, smearing jelly all over the lapel as he did so. "There, that's in case you get hungry later." Father Knight's jaw dropped. For his part, the tall man did not seem to take notice of it, at all.

"It truly is a shame about Miguel, Pat." The tall man spoke in a lower and more menacing tone. He bared his white teeth as he spoke. There was a pure malice in his voice. The tall man seemed to be circling the bishop as he spoke. He had bent down so that his face was mere inches away from the Bishop's. Father Knight could see that Bishop Richter's face had turned serious at the mention of Father Torrez. "Just heart wrenching, don't you think? Gosh! It just breaks my heart in two… I mean, something like that just isn't good for the old ticker, you know?"

The tall man straightened himself up suddenly, still staring down at Bishop Richter. He covered his own chest with one of his long, bony hands, patting his chest lightly, and rhythmically. "Pitter-patter…pitter-patter…pitter-patter…thump thump, thump thump, thump-oops!" He shook his head at the Bishop, "No more Miguel…boo hoo, oh, boo hoo hoo! Oh, boo hoo hoo hoo! See you sooooon. See you sooooon. See you soooooon." The tall man left while he seemingly sang this, his long strides took him out of sight almost instantly. But the bishop and Father Knight could still hear the singsong in their heads. Then, it seemed as if it was coming from right behind them.

"See you sooooon. See you sooooon." They both turned around to find a little girl in a pink and light blue dress with a pink bow in her blonde hair. She was standing in the archway that led out to the main hall singing the same strange tune and staring at Father Knight. She can't be more than five years old, maybe six, he thought.

"Are you all right, honey?" asked Father Knight. She stopped singing, but did not answer. Bishop Richter stooped his wide frame over to get down to her level.

"Everything okay?" They waited for the little girl to respond. Her wide blue eyes stared at Father Knight.

"I can't find my heart," she said. The two men froze, and Father Knight was sure his heart had skipped a beat, maybe even two.

"Your...heart?" Father Knight could only whisper.

"I can't find it any place. I've been looking and looking!"

"What do you mean, dear?" The bishop tried his best smile. "Your heart is right here, in your chest." The bishop was pointing to his own chest. "Don't be afraid, child. It's right there, I promise."

"He's right sweetheart, you have nothing to worry about." Father Knight had squatted down and taken the child's hand. It was cold to the touch. Father Knight found himself resisting the powerful temptation to try to see if the little girl's heart was, in fact, beating in her little body. He stood back up, still smiling. "What's your name? Can you tell me your name?"

"Sandra!" A voice boomed down the hall that made the bishop and Father Knight almost jump out of their skins. The little girl never even flinched. Her eyes simply continued to stare at Father Knight. The two men turned to see whose voice that was.

Another tall, thin man stood in the doorway. He wore blue overalls with a red-checkered flannel shirt underneath. His sleeves were rolled up, revealing a dark tan from hours of labor in the sun. He looked to Father Knight to be thirty years of age. Striking blue eyes peered intelligently from his dark, tanned face beneath the lid of a Red Sox baseball cap.

"Sandra, c'mere little bug. What're you playing at now?" Father Knight recognized a deep southern accent.

"Nothing, Daddy!"

"Oh, I do declare that'll be the day." Sandra giggled and her dad smiled. The man then looked at Bishop Richter and Father Knight. "Father Knight?"

"Yes, I am Father Knight." The man smiled warmly as they shook hands.

"I'm Jeb, the caretaker here at St. Mark's. Please excuse Sandra. She's my little girl and sometimes she gets to pretending." Then Jeb and the bishop shook hands, they apparently knew one another. "Hi, Bishop."

"Hi, Jeb, I'm very sorry about Father Torrez. I know that you were very fond of him. We all were."

"Thank you, sir. Father Torrez was a fine man, and a fine shepherd."

"You did a bang-up job cleaning up the altar and church for the service, Jeb. That must have been awful. Thank you for doing that." Father Knight found himself staring at Jeb's wide, staring blue eyes.

"Yes, sir, it was terrible, so much blood. It had to be done, though. The good Lord's work must be done no matter how terrible it may be."

"Yes, that's certainly true. I didn't know you had a little girl, very lovely." Jeb regarded his daughter as the child played leapfrog with a large stuffed animal down the hallway and out the door. The three men smiled.

"Why, thank you, sir. Yes, she very truly is the apple of my Eden, Fathers. I'd better keep up with her," Jeb said. "It is good to see you again, Bishop. And it is nice to meet you, Father Knight. Bless you for the very kind words you had for our beloved shepherd." The men all shook hands.

"It's good to meet you, too, Jeb." Jeb nodded and exited, closing the door gently on his way out.

"Well!" the bishop exclaimed. "Don't you just love a cookout? Jesus Christ!" Father Knight, who usually cringed when the bishop or Father Freeman cursed, burst out laughing. †

CHAPTER 5
The After-School Special

Thyra Lane was an eighteen-year-old cheerleader at the local high school. She was so beautiful. Long, brown hair with just a tinge of auburn splashed onto her shoulders like sunshine on a meadow. Her blue eyes were wide and innocent. Yet, when she was at ease or misbehaving, those eyes were positively bewitching. A brilliant student, she had been accepted to the pre-med program at the University of Massachusetts.

But today Thyra was down—upside down. When she awoke from the drug-induced sleep two hours after she had been tricked, she found herself bound and gagged, hanging upside down in total darkness. Her tears and mascara stained her temples and forehead. Her head truly ached. Fortunately, because of the drug, Thyra could feel nothing else. Her body felt numb. Her ankles had been tied tightly together and the rope ran from her ankles up and over a hook. Thyra's hands were bound behind her back. She did not even know that she was naked.

But the worst part for Thyra, by far, was that it was in the room with her, watching. It. Although Thyra could not see through the darkness that was her prison, she could sense it, and surely smell it. The stench was overwhelming. It was shit, or sewage of some kind, she thought. Through the haze of the powerful narcotic, she tried to think, to remember. How did this happen? Thyra vaguely remembered drinking something… Oh, that smell! She could feel herself begin to fade again, but this was a different kind of blackness. She couldn't breathe. Thyra felt that if she let herself go into this blackness, she would never see light again. As Thyra began to panic in the dark, she heard something move toward her.

She froze and went as silent as she could, listening intently. Her eyes opened as wide as possible to see what was coming. Time passed. The darkness and unknown were unbearable for Thyra. *Oh my God*, was all she could think over and over again. Because of the gag, she had only been able to murmur as she pleaded and wept. It moved closer still. The smell of shit was stifling despite Thyra's weakened state.

Thyra felt heat and moisture. The sensations were vague, distant. The moisture ran up her body. It dripped from her shoulders and ran up her slender, graceful neck and throat. Finally it dripped from her chin, onto her face, and trickled into her mouth. She could taste blood. Thyra became aware that it was right next to her, smiling. It spoke.

"It is on occasions such as this that I like to read some specially selected poems, to you, Thyra."

Though she could still not see well at all—it was dark, and she had blood now running into both eyes—Thyra could just make out the outline of a face inches from her own. And the voice, was it a woman, or a child? It cleared it's throat. A voice boomed.

"Brickabracka, brickabracka, sis boom ba! Thyra's got a nice rack, rah, rah, rah! Hooshamama humparama bing bang boom! On your knees, you stupid whore to meet your doom! Gimme a T!" It paused. "I, umm… I, ah, I couldn't hear you on that last 'T', Thyra. I'm a bit surprised and not just a little disappointed in you. You were usually so good at that whole yelling-out-the-letters cheer. It did a body good to watch you cheerfully squeaking out the letters as you and your little friends would jump around in what you all thought was unison. Hey, why not? It's probably the only time any of you actually felt confidently about spelling anything! Ha! Now cheer!"

It lowered its voice to a whisper, its face inches from Thyra's. Its breath was sweet, thought Thyra.

"Give…me…a 'T', Thyra."

"Mmmmhhh… hhhmmmmnn…ummmmphhh." Thyra went from crying to sobbing, and then choking from her inability to catch her breath. Her voice was still muffled by the tightly wound gag. It waited. Finally Thyra caught a little air in her lungs. Her eyes were wide open, though she could barely see. Its face seemed upside down to her. Still, it waited. "Thheeee…" said Thyra.

"Good," it whispered. Thyra began to weep softly. The face of it vanished, then, "Go! Go! Go blood, go! Thyra's such an idiot that she'll never know! Hooraaaaaayyyyy darkness!"

It was dancing, or jumping all around her now. It mocked her. As it cheered and recited the "poetry" with its little boy or girl voice, Thyra knew she was dying. Although she could not understand why and she could not remember what had happened, she knew. Thyra closed her eyes. She continued weeping. The pain in her head had gotten even worse, but then, began to subside. She prayed for death, for this to be over. It cleared its throat again.

"It's usually at this point during the recital that I like to turn over the stage to anyone with a request poem. Anyone? Anyone at all. Ah, yes, sir! You in the back. Your request, sir? ...An excellent request! Yes! An excellent request, indeed! Ladies and gentlemen, boys and Thyra, I give you a poem requested by your best friend, and your new master, Thyra, down all the way from London-town, England, and the nineteenth century, Mr. Jack The Ripper!"

A single and startling applause rang out of this darkness. It was two hands clapping, while a shrill voice cried, "Bravo! Bravo! Encore! Encore!" The venom and rage dripped from this small voice. It seemed to be all around Thyra. In her face, then in each ear, the voice would rise and fall. It at once filled the darkness and then would fall below an imperceptible whisper, or whispers. It seemed, to the dying young girl, that she knew that voice. It certainly knew her.

Thyra felt tired. She knew that she no longer had the strength to continue to fight for breath. She started to pray again.

"Whoa! Whoa, there, my little pretty!" The voice was now quite distant to Thyra. "You're not going to ignore Jack, now, are you? He came all the way down from England to entertain you! You bitch! Hey!"

Billy Werner! It was little Billy Werner's voice! For some reason, as Thyra circled the precipice of death, the identity of the voice, the identity of it, became apparent to her. She had babysat Billy for his mother dozens of times. Billy was weird, but had really seemed sweet to Thyra. He had always been so nice to her. Billy Werner?

Just before Thyra closed her eyes for the final time, she could see that Billy was standing right in front of her. He had pulled his pants down and was masturbating inches away from her face and head. *I didn't know he was old enough to do that*, was the final thing Thyra thought before she died. †

CHAPTER 6
A Clearing in the Woods

The dark was now giving way to dawn throughout the Great Woods of Littleborough. Soon the sun's rays would appear in beautiful and varied shafts of gold dancing amidst the trees, the branches, the leaves, and pine needles. The improving light revealed a holocaustic scene that was spread over the enormous clearing. The sounds and smells of the early morning wilderness seemed somehow muted here.

Inspector Dahms sent all of his men back to Deerfoot Road to help secure the area and get some equipment. He did not want anybody walking through this clearing in order to best preserve the crime scene. They returned with the gear and rejoined the inspector and Julie in the mouth of the clearing. The inspector then placed a call to Billy Pollard of the local fish and game commission. Though it was illegal to hunt wolves, the results of this attack seemed to warrant a hunt for the safety of the public. He then called the station and requested that a call be placed to the FBI. He was called back shortly and informed that they were sending an occult specialist to help. The specialist had requested that no one enter the crime scene until he arrived.

"Wait a minute," Julie said. "You're going to leave Megan and Caroline up there like that?"

"Only for a short while longer, Miss Bernard."

"You can't leave them up there, Inspector. What about their families? What about their dignity? We need to get them down from there."

"I think Miss Bernard is right, sir," Officer Marconi said. "This is pure evil. This is unholy." Officers Tubbs, Franklin, Jones and Evers all gathered around.

"We're only going to keep them there until the FBI specialist has had a look at the scene. I promise that we will get them down from there as soon as we can."

"It isn't right," Officer Evers said.

"I understand, Nick. But we need to find out who did this. As Miss Bernard said earlier, before more people get hurt or killed." The inspector then looked at Officer Marconi. "I'm sorry, Joe. Just take it easy, okay?"

"These people need their last rites administered and then to be taken down, now!" Officer Marconi said.

"He's right, man!" Officer Tubbs said. "This is bullshit!"

"You men know that the integrity of a crime scene is paramount to the success of solving the crime committed."

"It's a bunch of wolves!" Officer Tubbs said. "What the hell else is there to solve?"

"Wolves don't crucify people, Tubbs," Officer Franklin said.

"Shut up, Franklin!"

"Hey!" The inspector looked at Officer Tubbs. "Franklin is correct about that, Tubbs."

"Nobody's going to be able to discern a damned thing from this... this... shit show!" Officer Evers said.

"It's evil," Officer Marconi said. "This is evil and it has come to our little town again." Officer Tubbs turned suddenly toward Officer Marconi.

"Joe!" Officer Marconi stopped short, swallowing hard. He looked at Julie with wide, sorrowful brown eyes. Then he looked back at the inspector. A tear rolled down his cheek.

"It's evil! That's all I know! This is the devil! This is the devil and you're helping him by leaving these people up on these trees!" He pointed at Inspector Dahms. Officers Evers and Jones stepped in between Officer Marconi and the inspector, restraining Officer Marconi. "Whose side are you on? Huh? Who are you with?" He walked away muttering. "He's not one of us." Officer Tubbs looked at the inspector.

"You're wrong," he said. He went to join the others just outside of the mouth of the clearing on the path.

The inspector turned and looked at Julie, who was staring up into his eyes. He reached into his coat pocket and removed a long, slender pipe from it. He slapped the pipe firmly into the open palm of his hand to clean it out. He then reached into the side pocket of his coat and pulled out a small bag of tobacco. He slowly and deliberately took a pinch of the tobacco out of the bag and packed it into the bowl of his pipe. He put the bag back into his side jacket pocket.

"Tell me, Miss Bernard, I'm curious how you knew that Megan would be here?"

"I didn't know she was here, Inspector. I said I thought she might be," Julie said.

"I see. Earlier tonight you seemed quite certain that we would not find a pep rally here, do you remember saying that?"

"Yes, I remember."

"How did you know that, Miss Bernard?"

"I don't know. I just knew something was wrong, that's all."

"Right. Do you know of any kids at the school involved with cults or devil stuff or anything like that?"

"No! That is absurd, Inspector!" The inspector put his hand up.

"That's not what I meant. I mean someone who might have found some literature, or maybe got a strange tattoo or some jewelry? A young person who, more or less, would be an unwilling or unwitting participant. This crime scene can't possibly be from children. Or, if it is, we're all in a lot of trouble."

"No! Nothing like what is here. I don't know of any students involved in any cults at all. And in a tiny town like Littleborough, it would be something people would talk about."

"That is certainly possible."

"Now, if you're through grilling me, Inspector, perhaps we could proceed?"

The true opening of the clearing was only a few feet further into the woods on the western side of the clearing. Everyone quietly watched the beautiful pre-sunrise glow directly across from where they stood. It was obvious to Julie that none of the patrolmen wanted to go back in. With the exception of Inspector Dahms, who turned around and strode in, they all turned and slowly shuffled their way back in.

Inspector Dahms led Julie along the edge of the clearing and over to the tree to which Megan was tied and crucified. As she walked behind the inspector, Julie was careful not to step on anything that looked like a part of the crime scene. She looked down. There was an arm. It was charred and blackened by the heat of the fire and not attached to anything or anyone. The hand at the end of the arm bore a very nice ring on the ring finger and well-manicured fingernails, painted black. Julie could feel herself getting sick. The sight of this combined with the overwhelming stench of the scene itself was almost too much. It was a smell no one could get used to.

"Are you all right, ma'am?" It was the young police officer who had first met Julie out on Deerfoot Road, Officer Evers. Julie nodded her head. She was determined not to show any signs of weakness after having made that little speech to the inspector.

Officers Tubbs and Jones set up a stepladder next to the tree that Megan Streeter had been crucified on. They both held onto it, as the forest floor was quite uneven. Inspector Dahms went up first. He removed a magnifying glass from his coat pocket and looked closely at Megan's face and neck.

"I don't see anything. Okay, Miss Bernard, now you can have a look. Inspect what you need to without touching anything, if you can." Julie nodded her head. She climbed up the stepladder and looked into Megan's face.

She gently brushed Megan's hair off of her face. It was stiff and caked with dried blood. Julie examined the face and neck areas. A tear rolled down her face and fell onto Megan's sweater. Mercifully, Megan's eyes were closed. *I am going to work through this,* Julie thought. *I am going to work through this for Caroline, and for you, Megan.* Despite the grotesque nature of her death, Megan's face was still very recognizable.

"Oh, Megan," she whispered softly. Julie continued to examine Megan's face and neck. As Julie worked, her mind could not help but replay the session she and Megan had only three days ago. Megan had told her she was pregnant by her boyfriend, Sam Petrocelli. It had seemed to Julie that Megan's inclination was to have the baby and raise the child herself at home. The young girl was sure that her mother and father would support her long enough to finish high school and to get her diploma.

"Well, what about college?" Julie had asked. "Won't they help you through that as well?"

"I don't know…" Megan's voice was soft and low. She began to weep again. "How can I go to a college with a baby?" Julie took Megan's hands into hers and looked directly into the girl's large, brown, tear-filled eyes.

"Of course you can! Young, single mothers can get college degrees, doctorates, master's degrees, you name it! There are all sorts of support groups and financial grants out there for a person in your situation, Megan. And, I'm sure you can do it, with your parents' help." Megan looked back into Julie's eyes hopefully, almost smiling.

"Daddy will totally freak if I don't go to college." She sniffed. "I guess everyone else in my family did it." Julie handed Megan a box of tissues that was sitting on a coffee table. The two were sitting next to one another on the couch. Julie never sat at the desk in her office when a student, teacher, or fellow staff member came to her with a problem. No matter who was there or what was being discussed, Julie preferred to sit with, and at the same level of, whomever she was speaking with. Julie could never see herself as "authority." Megan took a tissue from the tissue box Julie handed to her and blew her nose.

"And you will, too." Julie smiled as she spoke. "But first things first. We really do have to tell your mother and father, and, also, Sam."

"Sam…." Megan whispered as more tears welled up. She could only shake her head.

"I'm sorry, Megan," Julie whispered gently, "but he has a right to know about this, too."

Megan only shook her head more vehemently than before as the tears now ran freely down her mascara-stained face.

"Daddy is gonna totally kill me!" She sobbed as Julie leaned over to hold the young girl.

"Sssshhhh…no one is going to kill you…"

This last sentence snapped Julie back to where she was and what she was now doing. Someone had killed Megan. More bile and acid crept up into her throat and choked her. Julie ignored it and inspected the face and as much of Megan's neck and throat as was possible. Weeping as she climbed down the stepladder, Julie could, again, only whisper, "Oh, Megan…" †

CHAPTER 6.66

William Chester pulled his tan Lexus around a deep bend on Fears Road, and then turned left onto Route 39. In Littleborough, Route 39 was also Main Street. It was a long, thin, winding roadway. It was a beautiful country road. The speed limit in most areas was thirty miles an hour. It had to be, due to the constant bends, blind driveways, and very few straight sections.

Farmlands were spread out all over both sides of the road. Large, sprawling fields, mostly green, but some were yellow from the fescue grasses and the marshlands, were dotted by big, beautiful barns and farmhouses. Some of these were red, some were white. Some of them were dilapidated and worn, abused by time and the wild New England weather. Some of them were brand-new homes, built during the housing booms of recent times. Most were set back with only their long driveways reaching Route 39.

Most of these lands were not marred or spoiled by fences of any kind. Instead, old stone walls ran the length and width of these fields and, in many cases, would run on for miles through the Great Woods and wild lands of Littleborough. Most of these stone walls were built in the seventeenth century. Littleborough's township was founded in 1648. The town, the roadways, the paths and wood clearings, the churches, the private schools, and the stone walls all dated back to this time.

The township of Littleborough was founded for a very special purpose: It was to be a model of how people in the new world would survive this wilderness and the natives. The founders of the town were an eclectic few; John Williams was a Christian monk from England, Shlomo Davidson was a Jewish rabbi from Palestine, and Little Eagle, a shaman of the Algonquin and Mic Mac nations. All three had led their respective followers to this place.

John had met Shlomo during a pilgrimage to Jerusalem in 1640. There the two had immediately become friends and enjoyed discussing their favorite topic: the Bible. It was also where the two found they shared another thing in common: a belief in the necessity for the separation of church and state, and a belief in the need for inter-faith tolerance.

Too often did each man witness terrible abuses by clergy in the name of their respective faiths. The abuses ranged from seizing lands, moneys or livestock, prison or death for failure to pay or donate to the church. There were even worse abuses than these. Wars were fought entirely based on the difference in faiths. Battles, tortures, slavery, starvation, poverty, and genocides were conducted in the name of these faiths.

John would speak of Jesus's response to a question concerning the payment of taxes to Caesar and the Romans, who were occupying the holy land at the time. Jesus had simply replied, "Give unto Caesar what is Caesar's, give unto Yahweh what belongs to Yahweh." For John this seemed plain enough: a separation of church and state.

Shlomo spoke of the transition of the Jews from following judges—men steeped in the Jewish faith and hence their decisions and judgments reflected that—to following kings—men mostly concerned with consolidating their power base and their legacies, but also the matters facing their nation. It was another inevitable transition to the separation of church and state.

Their talks attracted a number of people to join them and listen. These were a few Christian pilgrims and a few Jewish pilgrims. Others were local people who were attracted to the idea of such freedoms.

These views would make John and Shlomo heretics in the eyes of their superiors and peers, most notably Pope Urban VIII. This was the pope who imprisoned Galileo. When he heard of what Brother Williams was preaching in the wilderness of the holy land, he sentenced him to excommunication and death. John and Shlomo decided it was time to flee. They led their families and their followers out of the holy land to Scotland. From there they would sail for the New World and a new start.

They landed in 1647. Here they met the Algonquin and Mic Mac and Little Eagle. Both the rabbi and the monk marveled at how similarly the natives lived to what the two had only dreamt of for so long in the holy land. There would be trials and tribulations, to be sure, but they knew they had found the place to begin.

As the years turned into decades, then generations, then centuries, their descendants suffered through droughts and floods, famine and disease, hostile natives as well as hostile Europeans. The people of Littleborough learned to keep the heresy of this self-governing experiment

50

and mutual respect for other belief systems a secret. To survive, it seemed the only way.

The Algonquin allowed the new comers to hunt and fish along a narrow swath of their territory. The Mic Mac did the same. It wasn't long before a wide pathway cut through the wilderness that would later become Route 39.

St. Mark's church was on this road, along with one of the public middle schools and two private schools. Their red brick buildings dotted with dark green ivy were set back amidst rolling lawns and wide, green athletic fields. The police station was on this road, up on a hill, in the same little complex as the fire and rescue station. William Chester took it all in as he drove past.

Then there was a tiny little plaza. The Littleborough dental and medical offices were there. Right next to that were the drycleaners, then a daycare and a bank. The post office was up just one hundred feet further on Main, and from there one could see the whole of Littleborough's tiny downtown.

Here was the Olde Meat Market. Next door was Dick's, a superb breakfast and lunch diner. The Littleborough House of Pizza was across the street. It is here that Main Street ran perpendicular with train tracks and a crossing. At least twice a day a train still passed through. Across the tracks were a florist, a barber shop, and the Littleborough Pharmacy and Littleborough Insurance and Real Estate.

As he slowly cruised along, William grinned a silly, irrepressible grin too himself. It was a simple enough errand. He loved to drive. And this had served a perfect excuse to do so. So, William put on his disguise, hopped into his chariot, and cruised into town. Having completed his errand, he made only the one extra stop at the pharmacy. Though his disguise still felt clumsy around his person, William was sure that the young woman who operated the modern adding machine had taken no notice of him. She literally never stopped staring into the strange, hand-held electronic device of hers. And the older male on the other side of the store seemed too preoccupied with the mixing of what smelled to William like very powerful chemicals and addictive narcotics. William had purchased some glue, a bottle of formaldehyde, and numerous packages of Skittles, M&M's, and Junior Mints.

He turned the key to start the chariot. As he put it into drive another car drove by his car with the horn blaring and Madeline Astazio glaring at him from the driver's side.

"Learn how to drive, jackass!" she said. William could hear a concerto from Vivaldi blaring from her radio as she sped off, still yelling obscenities at him. *I think that is the fifth concerto*? he thought to himself. William began to hum it as he pulled his chariot back onto Main Street, proceeding ever so slowly over the train tracks. His grin widened. He eased the vehicle through the main section of town and up the hill past the post office.

William slowed the car as he drove past the police station, and even slower still as he went back by St. Mark's church. There seemed to be mortals all over the church grounds, particularly children. William could smell food and hear laughter. He reached over into the passenger seat of the car and patted a shoebox he had put there. The contents would have to be delivered at a different time. In it he had put his formaldehyde and candy, right next to the heart of a newborn baby. William accelerated his chariot, still grinning and humming. †

CHAPTER 7
Geraldine

Julie climbed down the stepladder unsteadily. Officer Evers gently took her by the elbow as she took the last step down. Julie smiled gratefully at him. She carefully walked around the outer edge of the clearing to the tree where Caroline had been crucified. Officers Evers and Marconi followed her. She looked up at the young girl as they secured the stepladder for her. She throatily whispered a thank-you and then she slowly climbed up the ladder. Julie carefully inspected the head, face, and neck for any markings. As she climbed down, Inspector Dahms approached.

"You hanging in there?" he asked quietly. Julie nodded.

"Yes. I guess so... I've finished up here."

"You know you didn't have to do that. I mean, examining them like that. I really didn't intend for you to spend any time here, though it is greatly appreciated."

"I wanted to at least get a look at their faces and necks, Inspector, for signs." Inspector Dahms had taken out a wooden match and had been about to strike it in order to light his pipe. He stopped and looked at Julie.

"Signs?"

"Yes. I hoped to find a signature or marking that would indicate what, or who, or even why this ritual was performed."

"Did you find any such sign, Miss Bernard?"

"No. Not on either Caroline or Megan. Was there anything painted or written on the other two people?"

"No. And there doesn't seem to be anything in the way of a signature or even literature of any kind that might clue us in here," Inspector Dahms said. He struck the wooden match against the matchbox. The flame burst and burned orange as he carefully lit the tobacco in his pipe. It smelled absolutely wonderful to Julie. He looked down at her.

"I'm sorry," he said as he waved a long, slender hand to try to steer the smoke away from Julie. She smiled.

"No, don't be. It smells good, actually."

"It's an unusual blend, but it does the trick. Were you expecting to find some kind of sign?"

"Well, not here, no. I wasn't expecting any of this." Julie looked around the clearing as she spoke, hunching her shoulders slightly and folding her arms across her chest as if she were getting a chill.

"Well, no, of course not," he said. "No person in their right mind would expect this. But, what do you mean by a 'sign'?"

"Well…I mean…a sign, or a symbol, usually left somewhere on the body of the victim. You may find a sign, or a tattoo or a piece of jewelry or something on some of the people who did…you know…this."

"You mean like a calling card, like a serial killer or terrorist group might leave?"

"Maybe, but it doesn't necessarily have to be a calling card. More often the sign indicates the actual purpose of the ritual, or a marker of who, or what, the group calls themselves. Usually, the sign indicates what it was that the participants were trying to do. But I see no sign, no name, very strange." Julie bit her lower lip in thought.

"Miss Bernard, when you say 'purpose,' what exactly does that mean?"

"This ritual was performed for a specific reason. This wasn't a basic Black Mass, or Missa Solemnis, performed by Satan worshippers. Those don't involve sacrifice. That's where this is so different."

"What, exactly, is a Black Mass?"

"The Black Mass is a parody of the Catholic Mass. It's intended to mock Christianity as much as to worship the devil. Some believe in the devil, some are atheists, some believe it is an ancient, pagan god mistaken to be the devil. The belief is generally that life is to be lived to the fullest extent; the pursuit of pleasure and luxury is the main goal.

"The descriptions vary among scholars over how these were actually performed. But the over-riding theme seems to be just a sexual exploitation of the rite. Instead of an altar, a naked woman lies down on a table, holding candles in each hand with a chalice of wine placed on her belly. Then, just like a mass, the followers ingest the 'host' of bread and the 'blood' of wine. It started around the sixteenth or seventeenth century, and is erroneously tied to witches and witchcraft."

"So, this is definitely not that, then."

"No. A ritual like this is an attempt to summon a being, like a spirit or a demon or even the devil himself, in some cases." Inspector Dahms raised his eyebrows. "Sometimes literature can be found, but I wouldn't expect to find any. To my knowledge there has only been one event like this."

"Do you know what this event was?"

"Well, there isn't even a known name for the rite, let alone its origin. It's called 'The Ball' by scholars. The theory is that the chants, dances, and the exact way of performing the rite are handed down orally from person to person, and, obviously, only among those who worship the devil."

"You mean, like that LaVey guy, and six-six-six, stuff like that?"

"No, he was actually an atheist who used the ancient Hebrew word 'Ha Satan' in its literal sense, meaning 'opponent.' 'Ha Satan' was an angel who actually worked for God, reporting back to Him on matters down on earth. The people we are dealing with worship Satan as an actual god as opposed to an archetype. They aren't atheists." As she spoke, Julie gently fingered an amulet that dangled just below her throat from a fine gold necklace she was wearing. The inspector noticed that with each question he asked her, she would look him directly in the eyes, nod her head and gently bite her lower lip.

"And the number six-hundred and sixty-six actually is a coded reference to Caesar Nero, a Roman emperor who put countless Christians to death. It doesn't refer to any devil. The number equals the total numeric value of the ancient Greek letters that spell out his name. Ancient and early Christians, like John of Patmos, who wrote the Book of Revelation, had to conceal their messages in codes and allegory to avoid being put to death, themselves."

"The Book of Revelation, that's in the Bible, right?" The Inspector asked. Julie nodded her head.

"Yes, Inspector. It's the final book in the New Testament."

"Now, isn't that the story of the end of the world, or something like that?"

"Yes, it is."

"Now, this scene here certainly seems to me to be a mockery of God, or Jesus."

"It does. The crucifixions, including the upside-down man, mock Christ's sacrifice, and the death of Saint Peter. This is pure conjecture here, but the theory goes that this is also a mockery of the story of the binding of Abraham in the Old Testament."

"Do go on," the inspector said.

"Well, Abraham was commanded by God to sacrifice his son, Isaac. So, Abraham took Isaac to mount Moriah, where the temple of Solomon was later built, to sacrifice his son. But before he could finish, an angel of the Lord stopped Abraham, telling him that his faith was pure and his obedience to God, great. And therefore, Isaac lived. Scholars believe this story was an allegory designed to stop the ritual of human sacrifice. Other scholars take the story quite literally. By murdering these people," Julie had to stop, swallowing hard, "these worshippers believe they are showing more faith, and a more powerful god. The other odd thing here is, well, the worshippers aren't all supposed to die like this."

"Mmmm, may I ask you, Miss Bernard, do you believe that the devil can be raised?"

"I believe evil can be brought out in all of us, but I don't believe in the devil, Inspector, just evil." Julie looked around the clearing again; her green eyes betrayed her shock and disbelief.

"You're right, thank you, Miss Bernard." Julie looked back up at the inspector. Their eyes locked for a brief moment.

Inspector Dahms then glanced over her shoulder. He observed one of his younger policemen, Ben Franklin, cautiously trying to fish something out of the now cooling embers of where the bonfire had raged the night before. It was the charred remains of a shoebox. It was still intact. Inspector Dahms and Julie walked over to where Officer Franklin was crouching, and peered over his shoulder to see.

"What have you got there, Franklin?"

"Not sure, sir." Officer Franklin was wearing tight, white rubber gloves. They were almost entirely covered in ash and soot from the conflagration. He handled the box gently in order to preserve any fingerprints or other evidence that the box might contain. He had a very youthful, boyish face that matched his voice. He carefully turned the box over and around so that it faced towards himself and the others. He carefully placed both hands on either side of the lid in order to raise it. A strange, scraping sound came from inside the box.

"Holy shit!" exclaimed Officer Franklin, he had instinctively pulled his hands back away from the box and held them out to the sides. He looked up at Inspector Dahms through his spectacles, which were so thick they magnified his eyes to an almost comical size. "There's something in it!"

A scream, long, shrill, and loud, pierced the stillness of the morning. Officer Franklin stood bolt right up out of his crouch and looked around, wide eyed. Everyone else in the clearing froze in their tracks and listened. Even the birds and the rest of the woods seemed to cock a collective ear and listen.

"What direction did that come from?" Inspector Dahms said.

"I'm pretty sure it came from that way, sir." Officer Tubbs was pointing to the southwest, into which the sun now directly shone across the clearing and into the dense trees and canopy.

"Jonesy, go with Tubbs and check that out. Hopefully, it's a survivor."

Officers Tubbs and Jones disappeared and reappeared alternately as they rushed into and amongst the thickly set trees and the brush, and then over to a narrow pathway that led in a south by west direction and away from the clearing.

Julie, Inspector Dahms, and Officer Franklin now turned their attention back to the shoebox. Officer Franklin crouched back down over the box. Whatever was in there wasn't moving now. He carefully lifted the lid off of the box. They all looked in. What looked back at them blinked furiously in the sudden exposure to the sunlight.

"Oh my God!" cried Julie. Officer Franklin could only blink his eyes.

It was a rat. The kind you buy at a pet shop. Someone had stapled a huge, deep purple, pointed hat to its head. The hat glittered in the sun. Julie had thrown both of her hands over her mouth in disgust. She then made her move.

"Miss Bernard," Inspector Dahms said, "you shouldn't…"

"Hey!" cried Officer Franklin, "that's evidence, ma'am." Julie scooped up the rat, along with her huge hat, out of the shoebox. She immediately began inspecting the wounds around its head. Dried blood stained its white face and head. The two law enforcement men continued their objections, but Julie cut them off.

"What are you going to do, dust her for fingerprints?" Julie held the creature to her chest, cradling it in one arm as she made sure that none of the staples had penetrated the skull. To her great relief, the wounds on the rat's head appeared to be superficial, albeit painful.

"But…" Officer Franklin stammered, now blinking his eyes as furiously as was the rat.

"But nothing. This is still a living, breathing creature, Inspector! It needs a vet right now!"

"Right. A vet." The inspector nodded. Officer Franklin simply looked over at his boss. Officers Tubbs and Jones were just returning to the clearing.

"There's nothing there," said Officer Tubbs, who was a bit winded from the running. Julie noticed that Officer Jones, who had not uttered a word yet, wasn't breathing hard at all. Then both men observed the rat nestled in Julie's arms. It still was not fully grown.

"Where did that come from?" asked Officer Tubbs.

"It was in this box," replied Officer Franklin. He then mumbled softly, "It was evidence."

"Tubbs, escort Miss Bernard out of here like a good man, will you?" Inspector Dahms looked at his watch. "And then you go home. You and

Jones have been at it since your shift started yesterday." Tubbs nodded. The inspector then took Julie's hand in his.

"Miss Bernard, I can't thank you enough for your time…" He peered down into her face. "Are you going to be all right?"

"Fine. I'm…I'll be fine," she lied again.

"I'm very sorry about Caroline Hart and Megan Streeter." Julie, who was looking down at the forest floor, nodded her head. She looked back up at the inspector.

"Who is going to go talk to their families? Has anyone contacted them?" she asked.

"No. I imagine there will be a number of calls in to the station this morning concerning a missing person, or two. The chief or I will be going to see them both shortly. May I ask why, Miss Bernard?"

"You certainly may, Inspector." They both smiled wearily. "I'm wondering if I could visit the families later, after you have spoken with them, to see if I can be of any help in dealing with this tragedy."

"That would be fine with me. I'm sure it would be greatly appreciated by both Miss Streeter and Miss Hart, too. Thank you for your considerable help in this case, Miss Bernard." The inspector extended his hand once more, and Julie took it.

Officer Tubbs held out one of his huge hands to show Julie the way out of the clearing. Julie had taken another handkerchief out of her pocket and had wrapped it around the rat, careful not to move the large hat that was stapled to the creature's head too much, as it was causing considerable pain. She then cradled the tiny rat back to her chest. Officers Tubbs and Jones noticed how quickly the rat seemed to take to Julie. Its little pink nose sniffed quizzically at her, eyes still blinking, but not as often.

With the two policemen leading the way out of the clearing, Julie stopped in the opening for a moment. Why or what made her turn around, she would never know. Though the sunshine was now brilliant, she felt an urge to look directly into it and up the east pathway that lay opposite to where she was standing. At first Julie really could not see anything. As her eyes adjusted to the light, she could see a figure standing well up the path that led East from the clearing, silhouetted by the sun.

It was a woman. She looked impossibly old to Julie. Her tall, thin body seemed quite frail. Her leonine head held a tussle of long, wild, white hair that seemed almost on fire the way the sun danced in it. But it was her eyes that held Julie. Despite the sun's glare, Julie was able to see this woman's eyes. They were black as pitch. Yet, they seemed to change to purple, then to scarlet, then blue. Julie couldn't move. Her knees felt weak. The woman smiled, or at least, Julie thought it was a smile.

"Hey, is everything all right?" It was Officer Tubbs. He looked at Julie. "Are you okay, ma'am?" he asked. Julie looked up at him. She smiled and nodded her head. When she looked back up the path there was now nothing to see. The old woman was gone. Officer Tubbs, seeing that Julie was looking east, looked too. "Did you see something, ma'am?"

"No. I thought I did, but I don't see anything now, Officer Tubbs." Julie held the rat up to her face. "Come on, let's get you fixed up and then I'll feed you. You must be starving," she said to the rat in the hat. †

PART TWO

That Remarkable Woman and Her Pink Golf Ball

"For a sorcerer, ruthlessness is not cruelty.
Ruthlessness is the opposite of self-pity or self-importance.
Ruthlessness is sobriety."
—Don Juan speaking in *The Power of Silence*, by Carlos Casteneda

CHAPTER 8
One Angry Man

Doc Robinson's place was on Southborough Road, just off of Main Street. As her Jeep Cherokee pulled onto Southborough Road, Julie looked at her little passenger. The rat was still dazed and hurting from her head wounds. Julie had tried to put her on the passenger seat, but the rat clearly wanted to remain as close to Julie as possible. She looked down just in time to see her little friend at the very edge of the passenger seat, mulling over whether she could make the jump from her seat over to Julie's lap.

"Okay, okay." Julie smiled as she scooped the creature up and gently placed her onto her lap, careful not to touch the oversized purple hat. The rat immediately settled back down. With one finger gently stroking the little rat along her back and shoulders, Julie steered her Jeep off of Southborough Road and into Doc Robinson's driveway. The building was set back a bit from the road. Doc Robinson's office was actually in the basement of his home. He lived there alone. A parking area big enough for four vehicles had been paved to the left of the property. Julie parked her Jeep there.

The house itself, brown in color and badly in need of a coat of paint, was fenced off all the way around. The fence was white and was always freshly sanded and painted each spring. The fence was to keep animals in, as well as to keep people out. Julie walked up the driveway to a gate in the fence. To the right of the gate, on the fence, was a doorbell with an intercom speaker and button. Beneath this was a wooden sign, painted white, with black lettering. The sign simply read: Ring Bell for Service. Do Not Allow Any Creatures, Great or Small, Out of This Gate!

The legendary Doc Robinson was the only veterinarian in Littleborough. He was a good vet. He loved animals and had a strict practice policy to treat any creature, domestic or wild, that was brought to his attention. What a shame, then, that he did not have quite the same feelings for people. They made him sick.

The vet employed a part-time office assistant named Michelle Floria, one of Julie's best friends in the town of Littleborough. Michelle told Julie all about her boss one night over drinks. He had been a Rhodes Scholar in school, and attended Oxford University in England. He had planned on becoming a surgeon at one of the best hospitals in the world, in Boston, Massachusetts. But the higher he climbed academically in the medical field, the dimmer his view of people became. Every fellow student he met was not in the least bit interested in curing or healing anyone, but, rather, interested only in the money. In interviews he had at every single hospital in Boston, he ran into the same attitude. These places were far more preoccupied with profits, not healing. Disgusted with the entire medical profession, he turned to veterinary medicine.

And then there was his personal life. His young wife, Belinda, assisted him as they established their new practice in Littleborough. A picture of her, young and beautiful, hung above everything else on a wall behind the counter. During a routine appointment for Rasputin, Julie had asked Michelle who it was in that picture. Michelle had whispered it was Doc's wife. Belinda was a fierce supporter of his. She, like her husband, believed that people were too selfish and self-serving for their own good. The two kept to themselves and their business.

Theirs was an intense and deeply passionate marriage. For all the wickedness that they both saw in the world, they could each see goodness only in one another. When they were not working at their practice, they would either hike together through all of New England's endless wilderness or read together in their tiny house.

Three years after they had wed, she gave birth to their only son. But, Julie was told, it was far from a happy occasion. Though the child was healthy and grew into a strong young man, the birthing had almost killed Belinda. She required constant care from that point on. Though Doc Robinson faithfully took care of his wife, her condition only worsened. Their son had just turned twelve when she died. This left Doc Robinson, already bitter at the world, enraged. At the private funeral, just father, son, and the two assistants, Michelle and Binny Moran, neither Doc nor his son cried. At the conclusion of the ceremony, a young Father Miguel Torrez overheard Doc's only words spoken on that day, as he threw a little dirt down onto the lowered casket.

"I'll see you soon, Belinda, my love. I'll see you just as soon as I've ripped God's sorry excuse for an ass apart, and flushed Him down the nearest toilet. I will see you. I love you."

Father Torrez, stunned by these words, swallowed hard as he crossed himself repeatedly, and silently prayed that God would forgive this poor, angry man for his words. As he did so, Father Torrez looked up to see Doc Robinson glaring at him. It seemed to Father Torrez as if the vet knew exactly what the Father was thinking, or, rather, praying. Father Torrez looked back down at the casket. Doc Robinson silently turned and walked away.

Upon graduating from the local high school, the son moved away. No one knew where, and no one ever dared to ask. Doc simply continued treating creatures like gold and treating people like the shit that they were, as far as he was concerned. And as for the poor, unfortunate human who crossed Doc's path when he was hung-over, well…poor Julie.

"Hello? Doctor Robinson?" Julie took her finger off of the intercom to await a response. Still wrapped up comfortably in Julie's kerchief, the little rat dozed in Julie's arms. Julie pressed down on the intercom again, waiting for the buzzer to subside, "Hello? Doctor Robinson, sir?" Julie waited.

"What!?" The word came out of the little speaker at what seemed to Julie like a thousand decibels. She looked down and saw that it had even awoke her little friend. Julie blinked her eyes several times and took a deep breath; she pressed the intercom again.

"Ummm, hi Doctor Robinson, this is Julie Bernard? I have a rat that kind of needs attention right away, please, sir." Julie waited again. She braced herself.

"A rat? Who are you calling a rat, you sons-a-bitches!" At this point Julie could hear through the intercom what sounded like something being dropped on the floor. It broke apart, whatever it was. "Fuck! Are you fucking kidding me? You fucking son of a bitch!" Outside, next to the speaker, Julie winced. "Ah, fuck me sideways on a bicycle made for two! No! Fine! No! That's fucking good! No! I don't give a flying fuck at a rolling doughnut! Jesus H. Tap Dancing Christ!"

While Doc Robinson must have been trying to pick up whatever it was, she could still hear him muttering. Julie couldn't quite make out what he was saying anymore until he suddenly shouted, "God damn it, Percival! Stop eating my notes! A fine ferret you turned out to be! Now scoot!" There was more fumbling and muttering for a few seconds more, then the intercom speaker fell silent. Then, "Fuck!" Then, it fell silent again.

Julie closed her eyes. She leaned forward, tilting her head down so that her forehead came to rest on the white, wooden gate. Without moving from this position Julie steadfastly reached over to the side and rang the intercom again.

"Doctor Robinson? I have an animal with me in need of immediate attention?" Julie hoped this tact might be less confusing to the old vet, who was soon turning seventy years old. Julie waited.

"What!" His voice boomed out of the speaker. *Well, he's almost seventy, but don't tell that to his lungs,* thought Julie. There was a pause, and Julie leapt on the opportunity.

"This is Julie Bernard, Doctor Robinson. I have a rat here in really tough shape, sir."

"Julie Bernard?" There was a pause, and Julie waited patiently. "Oh, yeah, Rasputin's mom!" The buzzer buzzed, and Julie pushed open the gate and entered, carefully closing the gate firmly behind her as she knew the vet would want. She then descended down a neat, stone path that led around the house and to the vet's office entrance in the rear. A goat grazing in the back yard picked up his head and observed Julie as she walked past, still chewing his food. Julie smiled at him. Doc Robinson was at the door, waiting. He was an enormous man. Well over six feet tall and weighing over two hundred and fifty pounds. Because of his age, and the wear and tear of a lifetime of work, Doc moved slowly.

"Hi, Julie. Sorry about all that. I didn't know it was you."

"Hi, Doctor Robinson, that's okay." Despite what she had seen and been through that morning, Julie gave him her best, wide smile. "It's a good thing it was only me at the door, and not the president, or the pope, or something."

"If it were the president, I'd still be yelling. If it was the pope, I'd still be shooting." He said. He was looking at the rat in Julie's arms as he spoke. Julie laughed as politely as she could at his little comment. She knew he wasn't joking. "Let's have a look at your friend there, eh? This way, please." He held the door open, and Julie carried Geraldine inside.

The outer office was in its usual state of total chaos. Books, magazines, and papers were scattered all over the tables, chairs, and the counter. There were boxes all over the floor everywhere. Some were opened, and the contents removed. Others were opened, but still full. The packing materials of these were spread all over the floor. As Julie and the doctor walked across the floor of the outer office, there was a cacophony of Styrofoam peanuts crackling and clear bubble wrap popping as they went. Julie suppressed her smile.

Doc led Julie into the examining room. He switched on the overhead lights, which revealed a stark contrast to the disaster area just outside. The examining room was an immaculate place. It was large and contained every conceivable modern-day instrument a vet could need. He patted one of his huge hands on the table in the center of the room.

"Now, let's see this rat of yours, Julie." Doc Robinson's breath was cut short when Julie carefully and gently placed the rat onto the table, then unwrapped the kerchief from the little rat. Julie looked up from the rat in time to see that his face had gone ashen, then an even darker shade of rage. Doc Robinson was a black man, with what one would consider a beautiful, dark ebony skin. As he looked down at Geraldine the rat, his face went pitch black. He was grinding his teeth, and Julie could see his temples and jowls were popping in and out of the sides of his head. His dark, brown eyes burned with rage through his glasses. Instead of breathing, the vet could only snort air through his broad nose. His big, bald head shook and twitched.

"Who ...did this?"

"I don't know. She was found like this in a shoebox." Julie was careful not to reveal any other details concerning exactly how she and Geraldine came to meet. "But I'm keeping her now. I was hoping you could dress the wounds, and then I'll take her home." Doc Robinson, still speechless, nodded his head.

He then turned his broad shoulders around enough to peer into a glass cabinet behind him on the wall. He grunted as he turned completely around, opened the cabinet and began to gather the instruments he would need to remove the staples and treat the wounds. Again, Julie could just hear Doc mumbling softly under his breath. She could only imagine what he might be saying now.

She gently stroked the rat as she held it still for the big vet. Geraldine audibly squeaked only once as the staples were carefully removed by Doc Robinson. He then cleaned the wounds with a gentle disinfectant. Julie marveled at his skills. Despite his enormous hands, and thick, powerful fingers, Doc had an artist's touch when it came to his profession.

When he had finished with the wounds, Geraldine looked like a new rat. Little bald spots, blue in color because of the disinfectant, were now where the staples had been. As Julie had hoped, none of the staples had penetrated the creature's skull. There were a number of very deep bruises, but no really bad swelling. Doc Robinson had pulled four staples out, all told. Geraldine, he pronounced, was a fit and healthy rat.

"Do you need a domicile for your new friend?" he said. Julie shook her head, smiling.

"No, thank you, I think I have something at home that should just do the trick."

As the vet turned away to place his instruments in the stainless-steel sink, she quickly picked up the now-removed deep purple hat up off of the stainless-steel table and put it in her purse. He turned back around. Julie took one of her credit cards out of her purse, but Doc Robinson shook his head. Julie knew better than to argue with this man. She didn't have the energy to argue, anyway. She did, however, have the energy to thank him profusely.

"I can't begin to thank you enough, Doctor Robinson. I'm so sorry to have bothered you on a Sunday morning like this. Thank you, thank you, thank you." Doc Robinson grinned. Even his stern demeanor was no match for a grateful pet owner, especially one so lovely as Julie. Geraldine was now asleep in Julie's arms.

"It's not a problem, Julie. You did just the right thing, taking her to me, even on a Sunday morning." They both smiled. Doc had walked Julie out the back door and into the backyard. Julie looked around.

"Where did your little goat go?"

"What goat?"

"When we came in, there was a little goat right over here. He was eating."

"You mean today?" Julie nodded. "You saw a goat here in the backyard today? That's strange," Doc Robinson said. "There's no goat here. I don't have any animals out in the yard at the moment because the fence was damaged last night. Are you sure?"

"I could have sworn there was a goat standing right there, staring at us and chewing grass." Julie looked uneasily around the large, fenced in backyard of Doc Robinson's. Sensing that Julie was spooked by this, Doc dutifully walked around the perimeter of the fence. Beyond the fence the entire property was all woods. Julie could see that a section of the fence had been badly damaged, as if something large and powerful had smashed into it from the forest.

"I don't see anything, Julie."

"Oh well, long night, I guess. I must just be seeing things. Well, thanks again, Doctor Robinson. Geraldine and I really appreciate it!" Julie, with Geraldine still fast asleep, walked back up the stone path and out the gate.

She climbed back into her Jeep and looked into her own tired eyes as they peered back from the rearview mirror. Julie realized that it was time to go see both Megan and Caroline's families. It was time to try to help two mothers and two fathers grieve the deaths of their little girls. A long Sunday morning only promised to get longer. †

68

CHAPTER 9
Oh, One More Thing

When Doc Robinson opened the back door entrance to the outer office, his nostrils were immediately assailed by an overwhelming stench. The entire office smelled of fresh, moist feces. On the floor, among the Styrofoam peanuts and bubble wrap, he could see what clearly looked like little hoof prints. A thin trail of brown hoof prints led across the outer office floor and into the main examining room where Doc and Julie had just been. More curious than afraid, the vet followed the hoof prints into the room. It was here that Doc Robinson came face to face with Satan. †

CHAPTER 10
Uncomfortably Numb

Father Knight had resumed his cleaning duties. The strange events that occurred at the end of the cookout replayed over and over in his mind. He could not help but feel sorry for Madeline. She had seemed so sincere when she had that outburst at the end of the service. The sorrow in her face had touched him deeply. But her warning was dire and direct. Father Knight decided to visit her later in the day, after completing his chores. It would give him a chance to walk in the brilliant sunshine and fresh, autumn air of Littleborough while checking on Madeline to make sure she was okay and for her to see that he was fine, too.

And who was that tall man in white? That encounter with him was disturbing. As Father Knight reopened the closet door in the hallway, he paused, deep in thought, oblivious to the scurrying tiny creatures in the dark corners of the closet. He consciously searched his memory as he stood, stock-still, in the mouth of the closet door.

For some reason he could not recall the tall man in white's face at all. Father Knight had an excellent memory. It had only been two and a half hours or so since that encounter. Yet, try as he might, Father Knight could not get a clear picture of the man in his mind's eye. His features had seemed to change, almost morph, as he spoke with Bishop Richter. The same was true of his voice as well. He was tall, thin, and wore white. That was all Father Knight could remember. Then, for a long moment, Julie Bernard's beautiful face and smile danced in his mind's eye and he smiled. But the lovely vision soon vanished and his thoughts returned to the tall man in white.

The whole thing had been so odd that Father Knight had forgotten to ask the bishop who the heck that person was. Bishop Richter certainly didn't volunteer any information about who it was. Father Knight regarded the old, worn duster he had taken to clean the closet with. He decided to make it a point to ask the bishop about the tall man the first chance he got.

As he thought about all the people he had met at the cookout, Father Knight carefully dusted out the cobwebs from the ceiling of the closet. As he did this, he carefully caught everything that fell from the duster—cobwebs, dust, and spiders. Father Knight was careful to avoid breathing in the dust. Once he had finished dusting the bottom of the stairwell, he carefully and very gently swept up the remainder of the cobwebs off of the closet floor.

His bucket was full of dust, dirt, and spiders. None of them were too happy, but every single one of them was alive and unharmed. Father Knight took the bucket outside, going back through the kitchen and out the back door where the garden was. Here he let the spiders go free from their momentary capture. Some of the spiders were of an impressive size, noted Father Knight. But most of them were tiny. Most important to Father Knight, however, was that God's little creatures were alive and free.

Father Knight returned to the closet to finish the job. He was smiling. He reveled in the humble task of preserving the integrity and dignity of all things created. Over the years he had been bitten by dogs, cats, snakes, a ferret named Phineas, spiders and bugs of every kind while trying to help them. He had been stung by numerous bees trying to help the darn things get out of a building or an automobile. And, of course, he had been punched, kicked, slapped, cursed at, and even spit at while reaching out to help desperately unhappy people. Often times it hurts; sometimes, one can get injured. But every time he did it made Father Knight truly feel alive. He felt he was advancing Christ's ministry. He believed he was fostering peace on Earth.

On his way back through the kitchen, he stopped and filled the bucket about halfway with water. He then took the mop out of a smaller closet in the kitchen, and went back to the hall closet to mop the floor in there. As he did, his mind could not help but search for any picture of the tall man's face. He combed his memory for anything he could find. But the more Father Knight tried, the more elusive the memory of the man in white seemed to become. He put the bucket down on the floor of the closet and put the mop into the bucket, spilling some of the water on the floor as he did so.

As he reached for the mop to start mopping the floor, he stopped. He could hear dripping sounds. It sounded as if it were coming from beneath the closet floor. Father Knight listened intently. When the sounds seemed to fade, he took the mop out of the bucket and let it drip onto the closet floor. He put the mop back into the bucket, leaning the handle into a corner of the closet. He then squatted down close to the floor and listened. Was that a voice? Amid the dripping sounds that were coming from beneath the floor, Father Knight could have sworn he heard a human voice.

The water drops sounded as if they were landing on a hard surface, well below the level where Father Knight was squatting. Having not been in the basement of the church yet, he assumed the water must be dripping through the floorboards of the closet and down into the basement. But was that a voice? Father Knight held his head cocked to one side only inches from the floor. He knew he had heard something.

Whatever it was had also attracted the attention of Ezekiel. The little old dog had awakened from a sound afternoon nap at the end of the hall by the entrance to the church. He was now right by his friend's side, just outside of the closet, listening and sniffing intently. The German Shepherd's ears stood straight up. The thick coat of fur on his back stood up, hackles raised. Father Knight petted the dog as the two looked at each other momentarily.

"What do you think, Zeke?" The dog's tail wagged slightly, but his attention to whatever was below did not waver. "Let's go down there and have a look, shall we?"

The only door leading to the basement was the bulkhead doors outside. Father Knight and Ezekiel headed out through the kitchen to the back door of the church and into the backyard. The bulkhead doors were around to the side. Not knowing the surroundings of his new parish as yet, Father Knight at first went to the wrong side of the church. Laughing out loud and shaking his head, he and Ezekiel walked back around to the west side of the church.

There were the bulkheads, two large storm doors, painted a dark forest green. Father Knight pulled one open. The steps that led down to the cellar door were clean and freshly painted gray. The door at the base of the steps was a large, heavy wooden door. It was unlocked. Father Knight pushed open the heavy, wooden door, which creaked and groaned as it swung slowly open. He and Zeke entered.

The sunlight, though fading as the sun now hovered just above the tree line, shone directly down the steps and into the doorway. Father Knight found the light switch and turned on the light. The basement seemed surprisingly small. The floor was all concrete. The walls were all brick and mortar. They looked considerably older than the floor did. There were no windows or doors anywhere in the room. Aside from one, solitary, gray metal shelf, the cellar was completely empty. The shelf was stocked with maintenance supplies, cleansers, a toolbox, extra fuses and light bulbs of every kind.

But there was no water dripping down from above anywhere to be seen. Even Ezekiel's curiosity quickly waned as the loyal dog waited by the door, ready to resume his very important late afternoon nap. Before turning to leave, Father Knight paused. No dripping water, no voices, he thought. He concluded that it had been a long, strange day. He looked at his dog.

"You and I are getting old, Zeke. We're hearing things. But that water... that has to be going somewhere. Darn strange." He patted and scratched Ezekiel behind both ears. The dog grunted his approval. Father Knight turned off the lights and closed the heavy, wooden door with all its creaking and groaning. This made him smile to himself. He ascended the steps and closed the storm door.

He and Ezekiel returned to the main hallway and the little closet under the stairs. Ezekiel slept while Father Knight finished up the last bit of mopping in the hallway and closet, all the while listening to the water dripping down through the cracks. He leaned the mop against the closet wall, squatted down, and held his head close to the floor. The dripping surely sounded to Father Knight like it was well below him. He was convinced that there was another chamber in addition to the one he and Ezekiel had just visited beneath this church. After he finished the mopping and put away the mop and the bucket, Father Knight began to search.

Using what he already knew about the building just from performing his chores, Father Knight knew that the chamber he was looking for had to be under the main chapel. The basement where he and Zeke had been was only large enough to reach partially into the main area. It covered the west side of the building, but stopped short of the eastside.

Father Knight entered the church through the front doors. As he slowly walked down the center aisle, he tried to keep track of his steps in his head. To his right were pews. Beyond these wooden benches was a narrow aisle that the congregation used when lining up for communion. The wall here was an outer wall of the building, lined with magnificent stained-glass windows depicting major figures and events from the Bible. Each one was dedicated to a former or current supporting member of St. Mark's church.

To his left were more pews. Then another narrow aisle ran the length of the church. This aisle had several doors at various intervals to its left. One door led to the choir's dressing room. One led to a storage area for prayer books, psalm books, and candles. A couple of the doors simply led one out into the main hallway and from there into the common room. And the last door led to a study, where the priests usually gathered right before a service.

Father Knight counted seventy-two steps, starting from the church entrance, to reach the small steps that led up to and beyond the altar. These nine small steps led up to three separate levels. The first level was where the pulpits stood, one on each side of the stage. The second level was where the altar itself stood. And the third leveled to where the choir sat, or stood, if they were singing. Above this last area arose a beautiful, life-sized gold crucifix with the crucified figure of Christ. Around it high up on the same wall were stained-glass depictions of Mary, the virgin mother; Mary Magdalene; Saints John, Christopher, Francis and Mark; the Archangels Michael and Gabriel; and a third Archangel, he observed. Raphael, or Metatron? He wasn't sure. There was something strange about that particular stained-glass window, he thought.

For a moment Father Knight was lost in thought, staring wide-eyed up at the window of this church. His gaze drifted back downward and he regarded the altar. It had been cleaned of the infant murder victim's blood and all the wax from the intruder's candles. He thought of Father Torrez. Every person that Father Knight had met today at the cookout had spoken glowingly of Father Miguel Torrez. This did not surprise him. But what had struck him as profound was how sincere most of them were. He had seen it in their eyes and heard it in their voices.

Father Knight looked up at the large, golden crucifix. For a moment his eyes locked onto the suffering eyes of the Christ. There the two stared back at one another in the silence. The moment then passed and Father Knight resumed his search.

He walked up and down all three aisles. He had searched every room and alcove, every nook and cranny. Still, there was no sign of a door, or even a trap door, or anything leading to another section of cellar. Father Knight thought about asking Jeb if he knew of the way into the area in question, but he wasn't sure where Jeb might be at this time, and did not want to bother him on his own time. He made a mental note to ask Jeb about it the next time he saw him.

Having searched the building with no results at all, Father Knight went back into the kitchen and poured a glass of water. He then brought the full glass down the hall and into the hall closet. Father Knight squatted down under the stairwell as far as he could fit and reached his hand with the glass of water in as far as it would go. He then poured a little water, and listened intently. Almost immediately he could hear the drops of water hitting a solid surface beneath him. And then he heard the voice—a low, hissing whisper.

"Ooooh, thank you! Soooooo thirsteeeeeeeeeeeeeee."

Father Knight froze. He stared with all his being at the blackness that was this tiny corner of the hall closet. He could see nothing. Father Knight, in one of the rarest moments in his life, had no idea what to do next. He remained frozen there, hunched down under the stairwell, in disbelief. Suddenly, something knocked the wood floor hard and loud, once, right under Father Knight's feet.

He heard it. His feet also felt it, as the floorboards beneath him rose slightly from the force. It startled him. Father Knight clumsily tried to straighten himself up, only to end up hitting his head on the underneath part of the stairwell. Ezekiel began barking and growling furiously at the closet. Father Knight, now slightly disoriented, staggered out of the closet and into the hallway, all the while trying to calm his dog.

"Sssssshhhhh…. Zeke, calm down, old boy. Easy now." Father Knight stroked the now quiet German Shepherd. Ezekiel was no longer barking or growling, but his hackles stood straight up on end. To Father Knight's concern, the dog would not look away from that closet. Still whimpering and totally on alert, the dog curled his lips, revealing his fangs. His ears alternately stood straight up, listening, then pinned straight back as if waiting for trouble to appear in that closet.

But none did. As the pain from bumping his head began to subside into just a dull ache, Father Knight attempted to gather his wits. Still clutching the now half-full glass of water in his hand, he stood with Ezekiel in the hallway. Neither man nor dog dared to take his eyes off the open closet door.

Still, nothing happened. Father Knight thought he heard what sounded like wind howling, a faint rush of air from below the closet floor. Then Ezekiel relaxed. His fine, dark coat, still discolored and ruffled, no longer stood up on end. He cocked his head slightly, still staring at the door. The dog's muscles were no longer tensed. Despite having heard no further noises, or voices, the two remained wary of the closet. Father Knight put the glass of water down on a small table nearby in the hallway. He never took his eyes off of the closet. He had observed that at least Ezekiel was less freaked now then a moment ago.

Before he could relax, however, he heard a clear, distinct voice. Though it seemed to come from the closet, it was distant. It was also human. Someone was crying for help, Father Knight realized. It was a child, or a woman. Forgetting about the strange events he had just experienced in the closet, Father Knight strode right back into the little closet and crouched back down under the stairwell.

"Hello?" he yelled through the floorboards, then waited.

"Help!" The voice was quite distant and muffled.

"Where are you?" asked Father Knight of the voice.

"I'm in a hole! A giant hole!" Father Knight furrowed his brow in thought for a moment.

"You're in a...whore...?"

"No! Goddamn it! A hole! I'm in a hole! I fell through a hole in my backyard! Help!"

Father Knight heard it fine that time. †

CHAPTER 11
The Big Hole

"Oh! Hang on, I'm on the way!" Just what way that was, Father Knight had no clue. "Come on, Zeke."

The two ran out of the hallway and through the kitchen and out the back door of the church. Father Knight slowed himself to a walk as he looked around the back area of the church grounds. He could see a white house to his right, just east of the church grounds. In front of him was his small apartment, and to his left, a path that led through the gardens down towards the caretaker's apartment. The only "backyard" it could possibly have been was this house to his right, he thought. The house itself was not set back from Main Street like the church was. The backyard, in fact, was directly adjacent to the church building itself. All that separated the two properties was the church driveway, which led to the large rear parking lot, and an impeccably trimmed and manicured hedge that ran along the property line on the other side of the driveway.

As Father Knight hurdled the hedge, with Ezekiel stride for stride, he made a mental note that the next time he saw Jeb, he would tell him how great these grounds really looked. As he and Ezekiel came into the backyard of the distressed neighbor, Father Knight signaled his dog to stay close.

"We don't need either one of us to fall in the hole, buddy."

Ezekiel slowed down his pace, and stayed close to Father Knight. Father Knight could see that the hole was almost directly in the center of the large yard. "Stay," he said to Ezekiel, who dutifully lay down. Father Knight got down on the ground and carefully belly crawled to the edge of what he thought was a sinkhole. The opening was less than two feet in diameter. Father Knight peered in.

"Well! Good afternoon, young man." Father Knight smiled as he looked down into the hole. He was relieved to see a boy who looked to be okay, despite what clearly had been at least a ten-foot fall.

"I see nothing good down here."

"No, you're probably right. Let's see what we can do about getting you back up here."

"Who are you?"

"I'm Father Knight. I'm the new priest who works next door." All Father Knight could see through the dust, dirt, and debris that now covered the child was short-cut blond hair on top of a very defiant expression. The hole, which was quite large down where the boy lay, seemed to open up into a cavern. It was too dark for Father Knight to see much of anything else other than a skinny young boy of about twelve wearing enormous shorts. Father Knight also observed that blood ran down the boy's left shin, soaking into his white high-top sneaker. "What's your name?"

"Aaron."

"Are you all right, Aaron? Can you move at all?" asked Father Knight.

"I can move everything but my leg."

Father Knight nodded. He observed that there was no real way for him to get Aaron out of such a deep hole without a ladder or ropes. He also knew that simply moving Aaron out of the hole could make his leg injury even worse.

"Aaron, we're going to need help getting you out of this hole. We're going to have to call 911."

"Just use your cell phone!" Aaron replied.

Father Knight grinned.

"I don't have a cell phone, Aaron."

"What kind of an idiot doesn't have a cell phone? That's ridiculous!"

Father Knight laughed. "Well, as a servant of God and His creation, I'm not permitted to enjoy such luxury. Now, where is your cell phone? Don't tell me you don't have one in those baggy pants of yours."

Aaron rolled his eyes skyward. "Give me a break!"

"I'd say you've already got one." The boy held his cell phone up for Father Knight to see that it had been smashed in the fall.

"Oh. I see. Wait here, Aaron." He had said it before realizing how silly that must have sounded. "I mean, just sit tight. I'm going to call for help. I'll be right back!"

"No, wait! Don't leave me alone, please." The look of defiance that Aaron wore on his face was now gone, replaced by unmistakable fear. He looked nervously around the cavern in which he sat.

"Aaron, we need help," Father Knight spoke calmly. "We have to get you out of this hole and to a hospital in order to fix that leg of yours. I will be back here in less than a minute." He looked Aaron straight in the eyes. "I promise."

"Okay, but hurry!"

Father Knight, with Ezekiel right behind him, raced back over the hedge and across the driveway. His new apartment—a small, single level structure—was a bit closer than the church itself. Though he had only been in it long enough for Father Freeman to show it to him that morning, Father Knight had seen that a telephone was on a small table just inside and to the right. He grabbed the cordless phone out of the cradle and dialed 911 as he went back outside.

"No, you stay here. I'm sorry, Zeke." Ezekiel reluctantly went back into the apartment. "There will be people and trucks and noise and other stuff you don't like," Father Knight said to his little dog, who sat down just inside the screen door.

Father Knight turned back toward the neighbor's backyard. As he did, the back door to the church slammed shut with a tremendous force. Father Knight stopped in his tracks and spun around to face the back door.

The phone in his hand clicked several times, then Father Knight heard a strange voice.

"Hello. You have reached 911. We can't come to the phone right now because we're all doing lines of coke and getting head from hookers. But if you could just leave a brief, pointless message, we'll be sure to ignore it! Fuck off and die, God-boy!" This was followed by laughter, then a dial tone. Shaking his head in disgust, Father Knight calmly redialed.

"Nine-one-one Littleborough, this call is being recorded." The voice was female.

"Hi. My name is Father James Knight. I am the chaplain here at St. Mark's Church."

"Sure! We met at the service this morning. I loved what you said, Father."

"Oh, thank you. There is a little boy trapped in a deep hole in his backyard. It's right here next to the church." Father Knight had entered the back door of the church as he spoke and was standing in the kitchen.

"The Neilson residence?"

"I don't know. I'm not sure."

"White house?" she said.

"Yes! That's the one!" Father Knight could hear at least two separate sirens wailing from down the street. He stood facing the kitchen door that led out to the main hallway and entrance to the church. He slowly reached for the doorknob.

"Okay, Father Knight? Emergency personnel are on the way. Please remain at the scene."

"Yes, ma'am." Father Knight turned off the cordless phone. He turned the knob, opened the door, and entered the main hallway of the church. There, at the opposite end of the hallway, stood the tall man in white.

"Hello, Father Knight." He smiled widely. Try as he did, Father Knight still could not clearly see the man's facial features.

"Hello," he said politely. "Who are you?"

"Who, indeed." The man's smile widened.

Father Knight heard Aaron Neilson screaming. He turned and bolted for the door behind him. He could hear the man in white laughing as he ran through the kitchen and out into the back. He hurdled over the hedge and hurriedly belly crawled back to the edge of the hole, calling Aaron's name as he did.

"Aaron! Aaron!" Looking down at Aaron, he saw that the boy was calmly looking back up at him.

"What? Dude! Chill, man, somebody get that man a valium or something."

"Yeah…"replied a winded Father Knight, "right. A valium. You had better not be able to get a valium, Aaron. I thought you screamed. I heard you scream."

"Not me. I didn't hear anything. Did you call for help, or are those newfangled, luxury telephones too tricky for you to operate?" said Aaron.

"That's funny… That's humorous." Aaron was grinning up at Father Knight now, who smiled back. They could both hear the sirens coming closer now. "I think the help has arrived. I only hope I can remember where the darn hole is… I have a very shaky memory these days," Father Knight said.

"Ha! That's so funny that I forgot to laugh."

"They're here. I'm going to go get them."

"Okay."

The sirens grew louder and louder as the emergency vehicles pulled into the church driveway. A patrolman had come into the backyard. He waved at Father Knight and then called on his radio to direct the EMTs and the rescue truck into the correct driveway. One more patrolman, two EMTs, and three firemen came around into the Neilson's backyard.

"Holy shit!" Officer Tubbs exclaimed. He had belly-crawled up to the edge of the hole on the opposite side of where Father Knight still lay. He was looking down into the hole. One of the firemen, Captain Little Joe, had belly-crawled up alongside of Officer Tubbs.

"Hi Aaron!"

Aaron looked up, squinting his eyes to better see up into the light.

82

"Hang in there, dude. We're going to get you up and out of there in no time at all." Officer Tubbs reached his big, muscular arm down into the hole and started to feel around the edge of the large cavity. He looked at Captain Little Joe. "It feels real solid right beneath where I'm at. I need a rope."

"Let's get the man a rope, Danny," Captain Little Joe said. A fireman standing at the back of his truck nodded and then disappeared behind the truck for a moment. He came back around the vehicle with a rope. Father Knight was looking down at Aaron.

"Aaron, do you see something down there? What were you staring at, son?" The boy shook his head. He looked right back at the same point he had been looking at when Father Knight had returned from making the emergency phone call. "What is it, Aaron?"

"I don't know… It's like I can hear whispers down here. Something's moving around, but I can't see a thing. And it smells!"

Father Knight looked up at Officer Tubbs, who was looking right at Father Knight. Officer Tubbs looked back down at the child.

"How big is the hole down there, Aaron? Can you tell?" Officer Tubbs was lowering the rope down into the hole as he asked this. Father Knight noticed that a third policeman had now arrived and was observing the proceedings. Aaron looked up at Officer Tubbs.

"I can't really see. But it seems to go on and…" The boy stopped short, and his eyes widened. Right at that moment, an overwhelming stench of sewage seemed to waft up out of the hole, making every man there turn away and wince. Aaron was coughing. It sounded as if he were choking.

"That could be toxic. We've got to get the kid out now!" Captain Little Joe said. He spoke with his arm covering his mouth and nose. Officer Tubbs swung his legs over the edge of the hole and jumped down into it. "Get over on the side he was just on!" The other two firemen quickly did so, lying side by side flat on the ground, both reaching their arms down as far as they could. Though coughing and choking a bit himself, Father Knight could just hear Officer Tubbs telling Aaron to reach his arms up as far as he could and that it was going to hurt a bit. To everyone's great relief, it was just enough. Officer Tubbs had lifted Aaron by the hips straight up over his head, and Aaron reached his arms out as high as he could. The firemen were able to take Aaron's hands and carefully pull the child up and out of the hole. The EMTs immediately began to look Aaron over for injuries.

Father Knight forced himself to look down into the hole despite the horrific smell. Officer Tubbs had a flashlight in one hand; his other hand rested on the butt of his firearm. He was very carefully looking around the cavern, coughing and spitting as he did so.

"Are you all right, officer?" he asked. Officer Tubbs didn't answer right away. He held the flashlight out, arm extended, swinging it slowly in an arc.

"Yeah, I'm alright." He was still staring intently at where he aimed the flashlight beam. "I don't see anything unusual down here. It's a large cavern." The odor that had permeated the area was now fading as well. "Grab the rope, all of you." There was only enough rope for the three firemen to take hold of. They were careful not to stand too close to the edge of the hole.

"Ready?" yelled Officer Tubbs.

"Ready up here!" shouted Danny.

The three men braced for the weight of Officer Tubbs. It only took him a second or two to climb up the rope and out of the hole. Officer Tubbs then got up off the ground and stretched a little. An EMT looked over from where they had been working on Aaron.

"Everything okay, Harold?"

Tubbs grinned, giving him the thumbs-up signal. "I'm good, Neil. How's Aaron?"

"He's going to be fine," said Neil as he looked back down at the boy. "A broken ankle to be sure, that's all. Right, Aaron?" The boy shrugged. Father Knight detected a slight Irish accent when the EMT spoke. The EMTs had placed Aaron carefully on the rolling stretcher. Now secured, they were heading for the ambulance. The boy's eyes widened.

"Hey! You, the guy without a cell phone, wait!"

Father Knight was about to speak with Officers Tubbs and Marconi. He smiled at them.

"He means me. I guess I'm just not cool, darn it!" The two policemen laughed. "Yes, Aaron, what's up?" Father Knight had walked around the big hole and over to where the two EMTs were about to place the child into the back of the ambulance.

"Could you please tell my folks what happened when they get home? They're gonna worry."

"I would be happy to, Aaron. I have every intention of doing just that."

"Also, we have a dog, too. Don't let my folks just let him out. He'll go right down into that hole, I just know it!" Aaron's look of concern touched Father Knight.

"Don't worry, Aaron. It will all be taken care of, I promise." Father Knight could see that the boy believed him. He rested his head back down on the stretcher as the EMTs lifted him carefully up and into the ambulance. Father Knight thanked each of the EMTs and firemen for their efforts as they departed.

"Now, you wanted to tell us something, sir?" Officer Marconi was much older than Officer Tubbs. The two police officers looked intently at Father Knight.

"Yes, I do." Father Knight paused. "I feel a bit silly telling you this. I doubt there's anything to it, really. But before I could get through to 911, I got a weird crank phone call. It was a man's voice, and he said a bunch of dirty things to me on the phone. What was strange was that he started by saying '911,', as if he knew what I was dialing."

The two policemen looked at each other.

"Where were you when you tried to place the call, Father?" Officer Tubbs asked.

"I was standing just outside of my apartment behind the church."

"And you were using the landline from the apartment?"

"Yes."

"Can you tell us if the landline in your apartment is the same as the landline in the church?"

"Well, I don't know. Probably. I didn't think of that."

"Did you see anything out of the ordinary?" Officer Marconi asked.

"Yes. As I was leaving the apartment to return to Aaron, I saw the back door of the church slam shut. So, I went in to see who was there. There was a man standing in the hallway. I saw him earlier at the cookout."

"Could you describe him for us?" Officer Tubbs took out a pen and a small notepad.

Father Knight described the man as best he could. Officer Tubbs stopped writing and looked at Officer Marconi, who was looking at Officer Tubbs. They both then looked at Father Knight.

"Father, we would like to search the church right now," Officer Tubbs said.

"Of course, you can search the church. I would be grateful." The two policemen nodded grimly. They both then turned and walked quickly back toward the church grounds.

Father Knight followed them into the small back area between the church and the apartment. Ezekiel was waiting for him just inside the screen door of the apartment, tail wagging.

"Hi, old friend. What a good dog and a good helper you were!" The dog's tail wagged even more as Father Knight crouched down and scratched him on the head and back. Father Knight walked into his new kitchen. He took a bottle of spring water out of the refrigerator and drank half of it. He had not realized how thirsty he was. He then bent down and poured a good amount into Ezekiel's water dish. The little old dog loved cold water, so he began to drink happily. It was the first calm, normal moment the two had enjoyed in what seemed like an eternity.

There was a knock at the door. Father Knight went back into the living room to answer it. It was Officer Marconi.

"Would you like to come in?"

"Thank you, no. We did a walkthrough of the church, but we didn't see anybody." Father Knight nodded, furling his brow in thought. Officer Marconi went on. "Father, we believe you saw someone. We think he's got something to do with the death of Father Torrez. So, do me a favor, if you see or hear or even think there's something wrong, call us immediately. Because whoever he is, he's bad news, okay?"

Father Knight smiled and nodded at the policeman. "Well, I certainly appreciate that."

Ezekiel had come to the door and began sniffing at Officer Marconi's leg. He stooped to scratch the dog, nodded, and then left.

Father Knight went back into the kitchen and took a second bottle of spring water from the refrigerator. He then walked back into the living room and over to a desk that had a pen and pad of paper. He wrote a note to Mr. and Mrs. Neilson. In it he briefly described what had happened and where. He emphasized numerous times in the note that Aaron was safe, and well, and where they could find him. He warned them of the big hole in their backyard. Father Knight included the church's phone number and told them they were most welcome to call or drop by if they wished. He added that Aaron seemed like a terrific kid.

He then took the note, along with some scotch tape and taped the note to the front door of the house. After all that cleaning, the service, the cookout, and then Aaron's mishap, Father Knight was looking forward to a run and a hot shower. As he reentered the area between the church and the apartment, however, something tugged at him. For reasons unknown, he impulsively turned toward the church.

He entered through the back door and into the kitchen. As he came out of the kitchen and into the hallway, Father Knight turned to his left and went through one of the side entrances to the church itself. This door was up at the front of the church, next to the pulpit and the altar. Father Knight walked past the pulpit, turned, and stood directly in front of the altar, facing the back of the church and the main entrance.

"I thought that it might be you." He sighed. The tall man in white was standing halfway down the center aisle, casually leaning back against a pew.

"It's me." He grinned, he held out his impossibly long arms. Father Knight froze. A number of children seemed to appear on either side within the wide embrace of this man. They looked awful to Father Knight. They were dirty, disheveled, and had a sickly, pale-blue skin color. Their eyes shone a pale yellow in the murky darkness that was the church. They were spread all over the pews, some sitting, some standing. They stared at Father Knight without expression. The air in the church grew colder and heavier with each and every second that passed. Each second seemed to Father Knight to be an eternity.

"Oh, do not be alarmed Father Knight. These are just a few of my… children. You see?" His grin widened. "Children, this is a well-known mortal. His kindness is legendary. He is one of those poor little lambs who became entangled in that whole magical church business!" The children all laughed. Some of them were pointing at Father Knight. "Imagine, children, that this magnificent creature is wasting those considerable talents to be a shepherd for the followers of the one called Christ!"

The laughter seemed to grow louder. It was an adult-sounding, derisive laughter. There was, to Father Knight, no innocence in their laughter whatsoever. As the laughter abated, it echoed strangely off of the pews, the walls, the raised cathedral ceilings, and stained-glass windows. In the brief silence that followed, Father Knight breathed evenly to calm himself. He then relaxed as the momentary shock gave way. He smiled warmly at the children, and then smiled up at the strange, tall man.

"I'm so sorry. Forgive me, please. It's been a terribly long day today, what with all the cleaning, preparation, a service, and then a picnic. And then poor Aaron, next door, you know," he winked at the tall man, "fell into a big hole. Were you thirsty, earlier? Perhaps you or your children would like a nice, cool drink of water?" The tall man stopped smiling and simply stared hard at Father Knight.

"You certainly have some very lovely children, sir." Father Knight took one step down from the altar. He went on, "Are they feeling okay? They seem to me to be a bit on the blue side. You do know that children need to be washed occasionally?" Father Knight slowly took the remaining two steps that led down to the main floor of the church. He was now at the same level as the tall man and the children. "It's nothing serious," he said, "but children really do need to bathe, now and again."

He took several more steps toward the tall man and his children; he wanted to reach out and try to touch one of the children. But as he drew closer, the children seemed to recoil from him and recede behind the tall man. They seemed as if they did this without actually moving any limbs, they simply floated, somehow. Father Knight blinked his eyes. He stopped walking and smiled gently. He looked up at the tall man. "You seem to know my name, sir. And what is your name?"

The tall man's face twisted in anger. "You know my name, priest."

"Oh, I do? Well forgive me, but if I did, at one time or another, know your name. I have forgotten it."

"You know my name."

"I'm sorry, but I really don't think I do." Father Knight looked right into the tall man's wide, staring, blue eyes with a sincere earnestness. The man's eyes seemed purple, now, then scarlet, now almost black, thought Father Knight. The tall man straightened himself up, no longer leaning casually against the pew. He stepped forward menacingly out into the aisle. When he did, Father Knight noticed that the children had all vanished, if they were ever even there. The tall man in white towered over Father Knight.

"You persist in denying me? You, who summoned me in The Ways of Light, now deny it? What manner of priest is this?" The tall man whirled around waving his arms as he shouted this. His voice thundered in the church. He then turned back around, facing Father Knight. His gaze then went from down at Father Knight to up above the Father's head, and directly at the large crucifix above the altar. "Tell me, Yeshua! What sort of servants do you have here? In all of Time, never have I encountered such priests! Such cowards!" His gaze then slowly moved back down to Father Knight. His voice lowered to a hoarse whisper. "I tell you now, man of God." The tall man pointed a long, bony finger at him. "Whomever among you called, I have answered. Whomever among you lies, Truth and I shall find him. Whomever among you that is in denial, he that now cowers...I shall devour."

Father Knight clearly heard this last sentence. But he found himself completely alone in the church. He remained there for a few moments, unafraid of the shadows and impervious to the silence. He then turned himself back toward the altar and looked up at the large, gold crucifix of Yeshua. Father Knight smiled at Jesus Christ. †

CHAPTER 12
Here Comes the Fuzz

Inspector Thomas Dahms walked slowly across the parking lot and up the steps of the Littleborough Police Department on Main Street. The building was at the very top of a large hill that sloped gently up and away from the street. Roughly halfway up this hill was the Littleborough Fire and Rescue building. From here any emergency vehicle could race to any point in Littleborough in a matter of minutes.

The stairs that Inspector Dahms ascended led to an all-glass façade that glinted from the brilliant autumn sun that shone through and into the building. Inside the lobby and to the right was dispatch. It was basically a large cubicle encased in bulletproof glass. Working at the computer inside the cubicle was Marge.

"Hello, Marge. Anything?"

Marge had been with the force for almost twenty years. She had spent almost every minute of it as the voice of dispatch. She was in her fifties, but did not look it. Her long hair, colored blonde, was tied back in a ponytail. She wore reading glasses that sat on her small, curved nose. These would always be in various styles. Sometimes they would be small and fancy. Sometimes they would be large and fancy, like something Elton John might wear on stage. Today they were small and pointed with a shiny violet frame.

"Inspector, this must be the quietest day in Littleborough history." She smiled at him through the thick glass.

"Thanks, Marge. I like the dirty librarian glasses."

"Thank you! I'm glad someone noticed!"

They both smiled. Marge's smile was warm and toothy and made her cheeks dimple. Inspector Dahms headed down the hall toward his office.

His office was small and sparsely furnished. There was a coffee maker on top of the filing cabinet. He strode straight for the coffee maker. The coffee pot had two cups worth of cold coffee, at least a day old. He poured some into a dirty mug that was sitting on his desk next to three stacks of books that he had requested from the Littleborough library. He sat down. It felt good to sit down. This was the first chance he'd had to sit in almost sixteen hours. He opened the top drawer of his desk and took out a bottle of aspirin. He took four of them and washed them down with the cold coffee. He then emptied what was left in the coffee pot into his mug.

Inspector Dahms leaned back in his chair. He stretched his long legs under the desk for as long as he could stand it. He then regarded the aforementioned books; each one featured the subject of demonology and devil worship. There were books about the occult, various Satanic bibles, books of rituals, and books about Voo Doo and witchcraft. The inspector rolled his eyes.

Next to the stacks of books was a thin manila folder, which contained files concerning similar cases from all over the United States. That particular stack—gathered, printed, and presented by Marge, Inspector Dahms observed—was rather small. It could only mean that there would be very little concrete information relevant to this particular case. He took the folder of case files and began to read through them.

The profile fit only four known cases. Each one of these involved four murder victims, similarly sacrificed and arranged at each of the cardinal points. There had been candles, or torches, but no conflagration had occurred at any of these others crime scenes. No literature or signs, as Julie Bernard had called them, were ever found at any of these scenes. In this case, there was no literature, but at least twenty people were dead. That made this particular case quite singular.

Inspector Dahms got up out of his chair. It creaked as he did so. He turned to face the filing cabinet. In the top drawer he had a large can of fresh ground coffee. He took this out and began to make another pot of coffee. He then took the pot down the hall to a rest room and filled it with water. He returned to his little office to find the chief sitting in front of his desk. He smiled as he walked back behind his desk, and filled the coffeemaker with the water. He then switched it on and sat back down at his desk.

The two men sat in silence for a moment. The chief was regarding the stacks of books on the desk. He heaved a deep sigh. He was a large, imposing figure. Black hair, thick and healthy, with streaks of gray running along the sides of his large head. He had dark, weathered skin. His nose was broad and prominent on his face. He was in uniform. Clean-shaven, he looked young for a man in his late sixties. His eyes were a dark brown with specks of gray. He spoke slowly and deliberately, in a deep, clear voice.

"So, what the hell happened in those woods, Tom?"

"I guess 'hell' is a good way of putting it. It looks like some sort of cult thing, Chief. Between that, and the event at St. Mark's Church, I'd say we've got some pretty serious problems here."

"Do you think these events are connected?"

"Well, I know I'm a relative newcomer to this town, but when was the last time a violent crime occurred here? In one day, we've had the two sickest things I've ever seen. I hope that they're connected, because if they aren't, then we could have twice as many psychos running around here than we previously thought."

The chief nodded, deep in thought. "That makes some sense. Did we find any leads out there?"

"Yes, we found a big cooking pot at the edge of the clearing. It has some nasty liquid in it. We'll have it analyzed, of course. But Miss Bernard informed me that the substance is undoubtedly some kind of home-made hallucinogen, acid, or something, mixed with booze and God only knows what else. We also found a good-sized mallet. It was probably what they used to drive the spikes into the victims."

The chief nodded. The tiny office began to fill with the aroma of the coffee brewing.

"No identification was found on the stranger?"

"Not yet. We'll scan for any and all missing persons reports, which will inevitably be coming in over the next few days, I imagine. Julie Bernard has some education in matters like these. She says that the true motive for stripping the victims of every item of belonging is to render the victim to be without identity. The idea seems to be to make the victim nameless, almost faceless, and devoid of any personality or existence, leaving only the soul, bare, and vulnerable, is how she put it. She says that this act is intended as an affront to God. I guess the idea being to take people who God created and basically make them non-existent? If you believe in that stuff. I don't know."

"So, she thinks that this is definitely some sort of devil worship cult, too?"

"Yes, she does. These files seem to suggest this as well. We'll see what these books have to say about it."

The chief looked at the stacks of books on the inspector's desk. "Looks like some heavy reading there."

"Mmm, indeed."

"So, is there anything else, Tom?" The chief regarded the inspector. His dark brown eyes, wide and opaque, stared earnestly.

"There is. I haven't told anyone this, but you should know, Chief. When we were at the scene, Miss Bernard searched the two girls for a sign, she called it."

"Okay."

"She was unable to find any signs on or around the two girls. Later on, however, I found a sign—this." Inspector Dahms had an opened book on his desk. He turned it around so the chief could see it. A large pentagram, or five-sided star, was sketched on the page. "It's called a pentagram, Chief. I guess it's got something to do with the devil."

"Where'd you see it?"

"It was carved into each victim's tongue. There are other, different markings carved on or around the pentagrams, but I can't figure out what they are."

The chief looked at the inspector. "Sick."

"Yes."

The chief furrowed his brow. "It seems strange to me that Miss Bernard showed up like that."

"It does. She showed me the text she had received from Megan Streeter, which checks out."

"Oh, I don't doubt her story. But it is interesting that an occult expert would accidentally be on hand for an occult crime scene."

"You've got something there, Chief. Do you know her?"

"No, we've never met. Julie isn't a townie. I think she moved here last year."

"Yes, last September. Her education and background checked out. It seems our Miss Bernard is a certifiable genius. She did mention one more thing that is of interest to the case. The blood of the victims is supposed to be collected in some sort of a cup, or bowl. We were unable to find anything like that anywhere at the scene. This could mean some person or people survived this and got away. I believe it does."

The chief nodded. "What do you think put out the fire, Tom?"

"It looked to us as if something came down on top of it. But we found nothing at the scene that would explain it. What could do that?"

"Well, that's a fair question. Was there anything else?"

"Yes, I sent you a text about the wolves?" The chief nodded. "There are some strange details about it. In the immediate aftermath of the explosion, when the bonfire was extinguished, we could all hear them growling and howling, and we could hear the perpetrators screaming as they were being attacked by what I think were the wolves. There were tracks clearly visible in the ashes and soot, as well as on the forest floor." The inspector paused. "It's impossible to say how many they were, but some of them, based on the tracks, must be huge."

The chief was silent for a moment, deep in thought. Inspector Dahms got up and poured some hot, fresh-brewed coffee into his dirty mug. He then turned to face the chief, holding the pot up towards him to offer him a cup. The chief smiled and held his hand up to say no. Inspector Dahms sat back down at his desk. He sipped his coffee and looked at the chief.

"Tell me, Chief, have you ever heard of a wolf only attacking someone's eyes, and then their heart? It's almost like that. They didn't eat any of those people, but they ripped every single pair of eyes out of their heads, and ripped their hearts out of their chests. What explanation can there be for that?"

The chief leaned forward. The chair beneath him creaked softly in the silence. The two men stared at one another.

"The only thing that comes to mind is the fact that the explosion may have caused the pack to react strangely. They felt threatened, so they attacked. They did not take or eat anybody because you and the men were on the scene shortly after that, and they had to run."

"I see," Inspector Dahms said. "That makes sense. Thanks, Chief."

"It's only a slim possibility, Tom. Because, truthfully, I have never heard of anything like that, ever. I need to see these tracks myself."

"I was hoping you'd say that." The two men smiled.

"Does Billy have his tracking party ready to go?"

"Yes, Officer Lydon texted me about an hour ago. They're tracking the wolves now."

"Good. Did the FBI send us their expert?"

"We haven't heard a thing since the original call Marge made."

"Strange."

"Yes. I don't think we can wait much longer. We need to get those victims down, Chief."

"We sure do."

"How would you feel about letting Franklin apply his training on the crime scene instead of waiting? His background and training is excellent; so is his record."

"You mean the Conan Doyle Dance? Little Fat Ben Ben is a good kid, but he is so young and inexperienced. This will be a really tough case to give him his start on, even with you there as a mentor. But I don't think we have a choice, do you?" Inspector Dahms shook his head.

"How did it go with the families of the victims?"

"It didn't," the chief said. The inspector raised his eyebrows. "There was no one at any of the residences in question. The Harts and the Streeters have vanished. Their cars, their furniture, everything is gone from their homes. Old Jed Prescott lived alone. His children, Anne and Jackson, live with their families here in Littleborough. They're gone, too, just disappeared. I've known them both since they were born." The chief shook his head.

"That explains why we have no calls for any missing persons yet."

"Yes, it does," the chief said. "I can't help wondering if these folks are now the bodies inside that clearing." The inspector nodded.

"There's something else you should know, Tom."

"Okay."

"That crime scene, that particular clearing in those woods is what's considered a place of power." The inspector looked at the chief. "It is a sacred place for the Native Americans going back thousands of years. My people visit there at least twice a year, sometimes more than that, with the tribal elders for ceremonies. My mother and my father did. Their mothers and fathers did. It traces back to the very beginnings of our people and even their ancestors. Whoever did this thing, maybe they knew this, too."

Inspector Dahms nodded his head. "Yes, sir. Thanks, Chief."

The chief smiled at the inspector as he got up out of his chair and left the little office. Inspector Dahms sat back down at his desk. He reached for the file he had been reading. The phone rang.

"Inspector Dahms, Littleborough Police Department, can I help you?"

"The chief is right." The voice was faint, barely above a whisper.

"Who is this?"

"He is a rare bird, a wise man, he is."

"Yes, but who is this, please?"

"This is nobody!" The voice broke into a shrill laughter.

"Oh, now surely you are somebody?"

"Oh, but surely there is nobody here."

"What do you know about this?"

"You must look into the shadows. It will be in the darkness, the truth you seek," the voice at the other end hissed.

"Tell me who you are."

"No, no, not ever, no. Damn me, damn me, it's too late for that." All Inspector Dahms could hear was loud, long, and maddening laughter. Then, the line simply went dead.

"Hello, hello...Hello?" Inspector Dahms hung up the phone. He picked it right back up and dialed Marge at the switchboard.

"Hello, darling, what can I do you for?"

"Marge, I need a tracer put on that last incoming call."

"What call, honey?"

"You didn't just take a call for me, and patch it through to the phone in my office?"

"No. I haven't taken a call all morning. Is everything all right?"

"Yes, it's fine. Everything's fine. Thank you, Marge."

"You got it, sweetie."

Inspector Dahms hung up the phone, deep in thought. †

CHAPTER 13
The Shadow Ghost

After getting Geraldine the rat fixed up at Doc Robinson's, Julie drove herself and the little rat back to her house. This time, she did not argue with the rat; the exhausted little creature was preparing, again, to make the leap from the passenger seat to her lap. Julie scooped her up and placed her in her lap for the drive. She wanted to get Geraldine squared away and comfortable at the house and give Rasputin, her large malamute, a chance to go outside and take care of his business. This would also give Julie some time to clean and freshen herself up a bit before going to see the Harts and the Streeters, the two families of the young women who had been brutally murdered last night. Julie parked her Jeep and started for the front door. She was covered in soot and ash from the crime scene.

As she cradled Geraldine gently to her chest with one hand, Julie fumbled with her house keys. She smiled to herself as she could hear Rasputin thumping the floor with his tail and his forepaws as he impatiently waited for her to open the door. He began to "speak" through the door to her with high-pitched whines and low-pitched groans. Finally Julie got the correct key into the lock and opened the front door.

"Hi Rass!" The large malamute began to spin in a tight circle on the hardwood floor of the entry hall, stopping to spin in the opposite direction and occasionally thumping the floors with an enormous paw. He would do this to in an attempt to avoid jumping up on Julie and knocking her over, which was something he had done once or twice when he was an enormous puppy. "Hi honey!"

Then the dog noticed Geraldine nestled in Julie's arm. He hopped up onto his hind legs and gently sniffed at the tiny rat, his ears straight up in curiosity.

"This is Geraldine, and she will be staying with us," Julie said.

She reached out her hand and began stroking his huge head. Rasputin licked her hand and went back down to all four paws and resumed his circles. Julie smiled. She looked up the stairwell, which was straight ahead and to the left of the front door where she stood. Her smile widened.

"Hi Don Juan," she said. A small cat was sitting on a windowsill on the first landing. He was jet-black in color, with wild, wide green eyes that stared down at Julie. At the mention of his name, his eyes widened, and he quickly and silently leapt from the windowsill up the next flight of steps and out of sight. Julie laughed her throaty laugh.

She looked back down at Rasputin. "Who wants to go out?" He stopped spinning and stared straight up at her with his ears straight up in the air. "Okay, big baby." Julie walked through the large hallway of the house to the back door. She opened the door and Rasputin charged into the brilliant sunlight.

Julie closed the door and went upstairs with Geraldine. For her part, the tiny rat seemed to be fast asleep. Julie went into her bedroom and walked straight to the walk-in closet. She had purchased a new pair of running shoes and had kept the shoebox in case she needed to return the shoes. She took the shoebox and lined it with some clean pillowcases and wash clothes. She gently placed the sleepy little rat down onto the linens in the shoebox and placed it on her dresser.

Satisfied for the moment, Julie began to clean herself up. She washed her hands and face, then brushed her hair. She went back down the stairs and to the back door let her large dog back into the house. She went back upstairs and began to throw on a quick change of clothes.

Rasputin, seeing Julie change her clothes, began to get excited. He started to pace back and forth in the hallway just outside her bedroom. He would look down the stairs, then back in through the doorway to check on her progress, his large tail wagging. He was speaking softly to her. Julie smiled at him.

"No, silly dog. We're not going out to play in the leaves, yet. I have to go do something that will take a little bit of time." Julie's voice was hoarse and throaty. "Then, after that, I will be all yours. And we can play and play all day!" This phrase always made Rasputin happy. When he heard this, he came right into the bedroom, tail wagging furiously.

He got so excited that he began to sneeze. "Oh! God bless you, silly dog!" Julie stooped over and scratched his large head behind his ears. Rasputin grunted his approval. Julie kissed his nose.

She then walked over to her old oak dresser where she had placed the shoebox with Geraldine inside. The little rat was fast asleep. Julie placed a saucer of water in there, along with fresh lettuce and some cheerios. But the tiny rat was not hungry or thirsty, just sleepy. Julie smiled at her newfound friend.

She walked out of her bedroom into the upstairs hall and looked at the door that led up to the attic. Julie walked over to it and opened the door, peering up the stairwell into the darkness. She reached in, turned on the light, and ascended the stairs. When she reached the top of the stairs, she had to stoop down slightly to avoid bumping her head. Julie was not a pack rat. There were only three items in the center of the room. One of these was an old, midnight blue trunk. It sat by itself, opened.

Julie walked over to the trunk and looked in. Her eyes widened and she smiled. The trunk contained old dresses, scarves, and hats that had belonged to her late maternal grandmother. Julie had been very close to her. She knelt down next to the trunk. Beneath some of these items of clothing was an old shoebox. Julie picked it up and carefully opened it. There were many small glass containers. Each one capped by a cork and containing various herbs, roots, and plant extracts from all over the world. Some of the jars were labeled, and some were not. There was a small package wrapped in old, dirty white paper. Julie took this out of the shoebox and carefully unwrapped it. She gasped. It was an old deck of Tarot cards. Smiling, she gently removed the cards from the packaging. When her hands touched this deck of Tarot, electricity seemed to run through her entire person. Memories of her grandmother began to flood Julie's mind.

Her grandmother had been a witch. The woman had kept this a secret from her husband, children, her grandchildren, and every male who knew her. Her maternal grandmother before her had also been a witch. It was a legacy that seemed to skip every other generation and went back as far as anyone could remember.

Julie recalled a day at her grandmother's house when she was five years old. She was playing alone in her bedroom, when something seemed to call out to her. She could not recognize the voice that had called her name. But call her name it did. The little girl got up and slowly walked out of her tiny bedroom and into the hallway. She looked down the hallway at the door that led up to the attic. Julie waited. Slowly and silently, the door swung open. Then the little girl heard it again, as if someone was calling out her name. It had almost sounded to Julie as if this someone was actually inside her head, because that was where the voice seemed to be coming from.

The intrepid child cautiously made her way down the hallway to the very base of the steps that led up to the attic. She looked up into the darkness. Though afraid, Julie set her chin and began to ascend the stairs. When she reached the top, she found herself standing in a large, dark room.

She took one more step into the attic. When she did, the sun seemed to burst from behind the clouds outside. It shone straight through several small windows in the attic, illuminating it in an extremely powerful way. An awesome sense of peace came over Julie. She felt at home in her grandmother's attic. That was when and where she found this very shoebox and all of its contents. She was especially mesmerized by the Tarot cards. Her curiosity and fascination peaked with the turn of every single card and the drawings on each one of them. She had gently and carefully played with them for hours and then had carefully put them back. She quietly sneaked back down the attic stairs.

Julie found her grandmother waiting for her at the bottom of those stairs, smiling. The little girl ran into her grandmother's arms. From that day forward the two would be able to communicate wordlessly. Julie knew that she, too, was a witch. Her grandmother died when Julie was only thirteen. The young girl felt an obligation to carry on the line. But after a time, she couldn't see how it was possible.

She had observed that her grandmother was forced to hide her true self, even from those she loved most. She had instructed Julie to do the same. As Julie grew up and went through school and college and into the professional world, it had become painfully apparent why; the word *witch*, in people's minds, was synonymous with evil, sometimes even associated with the devil.

So, Julie had buried the notion deep in her mind. The safest, most practical way seemed to her to simply not be a witch. It would be best for everybody, she reasoned, especially her family. Her mother and father would have never understood. She feared it would hurt them. And then there was the problem of Julie's intellect. She was brilliant. Her grades and aptitude test scores were all virtually perfect. As she ascended the world of academia, a normal, practical life seemed inevitable. As Julie now knelt in her own attic holding this shoebox in her lap, she could not help but think a normal, practical life would not be possible. She shooed this thought from her mind.

She reached into the trunk and looked beneath the clothing and found what she was looking for: an old glass case. It was heavy and required both hands to remove from the trunk. She smiled to herself as she rewrapped the Tarot cards gently and put them back in the old shoebox, then placed the shoebox back into the trunk. Julie brought the case down to her bedroom and cleaned it carefully and thoroughly. She lined it with some newspaper, and added an old sweater to one side of the habitat. She carefully placed Geraldine onto the soft, old sweater, and then put her food and water into the case. The tiny rat never opened her eyes, sleeping right through it. Julie took her purse and her car keys off of the dresser and went downstairs. She smiled at Rasputin's sweet, disapproving stare as she closed the front door behind her.

Julie drove to the residence of Robert and Stephanie Hart, parents of the deceased Caroline Hart. There were no cars parked in the driveway, so she parked her Jeep there. As she walked up the brick walkway to the front door, Julie noticed that there were no curtains, or shades in any of the windows. She rang the doorbell. There was no answer. She tried it again. There was still no answer. Julie tried knocking on the door, but as she did, it swung open slightly. She peered in. There was nothing. No people, no furniture—there was just empty silence. Julie closed the door and went back to her Jeep. She took out her phone and texted a message to Inspector Dahms, informing him that the Harts were not home.

The Streeters' residence was only a stone's throw away from the Harts'. There were no cars in this driveway, either. Julie closed her eyes and breathed in deeply. She held her breath, then breathed out slowly again. She then climbed out of the Jeep.

The Streeters lived in a duplex. Julie could see a young girl and boy playing soccer in the front yard. They smiled and waved to her as she climbed out of her Jeep. Julie smiled back, waving. She then made her way along the driveway, turning right to cross the tiny front lawn and up to the front door.

Julie rang the doorbell. While she waited, she turned back around to see that the two young children had stopped playing and were watching her. She smiled at them again, they both smiled widely. She turned back toward the front door and rang the doorbell again. There was no response. Julie had to resist the urge to start peeking through the window that was just to her left. She knew that the two little ones were watching her closely. She sighed. *I have not had a very good day with doorbells today*, she thought to herself.

Julie gave the doorbell to the Streeters' residence one more try. There was still no answer. She turned to leave and was somewhat surprised to see that she was all alone in the yard now. The two tiny children seemed to have just disappeared. The soccer ball with which they were playing was also gone. Julie looked from left to right over the small front yard. She had not seen or heard the children leave the yard. Julie found herself feeling strange again.

She knew that she was tired. She was also aware that she had been through a lot this morning and was in a highly emotional state. Regardless, she felt strange just now. Julie's intuition told her that she was being watched. It was cold that Sunday morning. Though the sun shone brilliantly just above the tree line to the east, its rays had not yet warmed the day. Julie had changed into a dark, gray pantsuit and jacket. She shivered.

That's when she heard it. It was a light tapping, or scratching, coming from behind her and above her. Julie turned around quickly so that she was again facing the house. She looked up. When she saw it, her green eyes widened, her mouth fell open, and she simply froze.

Megan Streeter was in one of the second-floor windows looking down at her. Although Julie could not hear anything, it appeared to her as if Megan was desperately trying to say something to her. Her lips kept moving, and Megan appeared to be crying. Julie could not understand what Megan was trying to tell her. That is when she saw something in the room with Megan. It stood right behind her. It was a large shadow of a man. That was all she could see. This thing seemed to be controlling Megan, and that was all Julie needed to know.

Julie began to run back toward the house. She hit the front door of the house with all she had. It did not budge. Julie staggered back and almost lost her balance entirely. A sharp pain in her shoulder flared. She stepped back up to the door and frantically grabbed at the doorknob, fumbling at it as she tried to turn it. She finally got hold of it. It was unlocked. Julie burst through the door and into a small entry hallway. The stairway was straight ahead. A loud, unmistakable thud was followed by heavy footsteps on a hardwood floor right above where Julie stood.

"Megan!"

She ran as fast as she could towards the stairs. As Julie began to ascend the narrow stairway, the noises ceased. When she reached the top of the stairs, Julie found herself looking down a long, narrow hallway that led to a closed door at the far end. Several doors to other rooms lined each side. All of these doors were open. Julie's gaze went back to the closed door at the end of the hallway. She set her chin and began to walk toward it. The first door to her left slammed shut with a force that made Julie jump.

"Megan?" she whispered softly. She went toward the now-closed door. As she got closer, she thought that she could hear whispering coming from inside the room.

"*Who is this...I don't know...I don't recognize her... Who is this... I don't know... Who are you... Who are you... Why are you here... Why have you come... Who are you...*" The voices seemed to subside as Julie got to the door. As she reached for the doorknob, Julie felt a stabbing pain in her left shoulder.

She reached for the doorknob with her right hand. As she touched the doorknob, the door to the room on the other side of the hallway slammed shut with the same vicious force that the first one had. Julie spun around to face it, crying out involuntarily as she did. She clutched her chest and stared at the door that had just slammed. When she did, the door behind her that had slammed shut first, swung slowly back open with a loud creaking and groaning. This made Julie spin around again. She backed away from the door a few feet. Julie stood there quietly for several moments.

"Megan? Megan, was that really you?" Julie could only whisper. She peered into the room through the door that was now open. There was nothing in it, not even furniture. Julie turned away from the room and looked at the door that had just slammed shut. "Megan?" Dreading what she knew must be coming, Julie inched toward the door. She expected it to burst open, or for the door behind her to slam shut, or both. "Megan? It's me, Julie Bernard. I just want to help you, Megan…please, honey."

"Who is this…I don't know…I don't know…who is she… Why has she come…Leave…leave this place…You…who are you…"

The door slowly swung open. Julie could not hear any more voices now. She could only hear the sound of the blood pounding her head with her every thunderous heartbeat. She carefully peered into this room. It was empty. Julie stepped back into the middle of the hallway. She could now feel that same feeling that she had out in the front yard. Something thumped lightly at the end of the hall. Julie turned. A soccer ball bounced down the hallway toward her. It gently came to a roll, stopping at her feet.

The door at the end of the hall slowly arced open with an audible creaking sound. Julie slowly looked up from the soccer ball and down the hall. There inside the room that was at the end of the hallway, silhouetted against a large picture window in the room itself, stood Megan. She was still crying and, it seemed to Julie, still trying to tell her something.

"Megan!" Julie started to walk down the hallway and toward the young girl. As she did, she looked uneasily from room to room and door to door. As she got closer, she could now see that Megan was, in fact, badly deformed from the terrible injuries she had received last night. Julie reached the doorway of what was the master bedroom of the house. "Megan, honey, what have they done to you?" Julie could only shake her head as she asked this. "I thought that they had killed you." She had always had an open mind, but simply could not grasp what or how she was seeing this. Is this real?

It looked to her as if the young girl was suffocating because she could not seem to speak. Julie looked through the doorway of the master bedroom. It held no furnishings of any kind. She carefully stepped into the master bedroom toward Megan. The temperature seemed to drop twenty degrees. Julie could see her breath. She looked at Megan. She could not see any breath coming from the young girl. Then Julie smelled the odor of feces. It was overwhelming. She covered her mouth and nose with her hands.

"Megan, what is it? Tell me what you need me to do. What can I do?" Julie pleaded. It was then that Julie sensed a shadow. It was behind her in a corner of the room. It glided out toward Megan. It then slowly turned to face Julie. It was a tall man. His eyes seemed to change before Julie's eyes. They were black, then scarlet, then purple, then blue, then black again. When he saw Julie, he smiled. It was a cold, humorless, and voracious smile. He ran his fingers through Megan's hair, which was still caked with dried blood. This seemed to energize Megan. For one brief moment she had the strength to speak. Julie had to tear her eyes off of the shadow man to look back at Megan. "What is it, honey?"

"Run!" Megan screamed this.

The shadow man roared his displeasure. A thousand voices began crying out all around Julie, echoing Megan's cry to run. Though Julie could still hear her screaming, Megan seemed to just vanish from sight, leaving only the shadow and Julie amidst the din of the voices. Julie turned and ran out of the bedroom and into the hallway. As she did so, she looked straight ahead. The hallway seemed to stretch out before her. It looked to Julie as if it was now endless. As it stretched, it seemed to warp before her very eyes. It seemed to grow in length and yet narrowed. It seemed to curve upward and onward, almost as if it were a spiral of some kind. *"Run! Run! Whoever you are! Run! You must run! Oh, run!"*

Julie could no longer see the top of the stairway or the railing at all. She looked back to see where the man was. He was in full flight after her. She turned away and ran as hard as she could. Her head pounded a dreadful and steady beat. The doors on both sides of the hallway were opening and slamming shut violently again and again as she ran by. *"Run! She must run! Who is she? I don't know... She must run...run!"*

Julie looked to her left in time to see into one of the bedrooms. She could see Megan, alive and healthy. She was stark naked, crying and pleading. She was bent over her bed; a man in his forties or fifties was behind her, raping her. He looked right at Julie and started laughing. The door slammed shut. Julie felt her stomach tighten. She knew she was going to be sick.

"Run!"

She looked to her right where there was a bathroom. In the tub Julie could see a woman. She was crying. The tub was filled with blood and red water. It overflowed and seemed to be flowing and splashing blood and bath water in a torrent down the hallway after Julie.

"Run! Run! You must run! Who is she? Why is she here? Why are you here? Run...you must run...run!"

Julie knew she wasn't going to make it. The hallway never seemed to end. She just kept running and running and running. Whenever she looked back, the shadow man would be right there, step for step, eyes raging and still grinning menacingly. Suddenly a shadow appeared right in front of her. Julie tried to stop herself. But it was too late.

She ran right into a large, powerful, and solid form. She collapsed flat onto her back, slamming her head on the hardwood floor of the hallway. Everything flashed a bright white and pain shot through her head. She tried to look up to see where the shadow might be, but could see nothing. Julie then felt herself being picked up off of the floor. She was vaguely aware of voices again. There were the same tortured whispers, but they were interspersed with very strong, clear-sounding voices.

"He almost had you... Who are you... We almost took her... Who is she..."

"Miss Bernard! Are you all right, ma'am? Miss Bernard, ma'am, are you all right?"

"The girl...it was the girl... She saved you... Who are you... Who was she.... Who was she?" †

CHAPTER 14
Billy Werner is a Loser

It was huge. It was purple. And, as far as little Billy Werner was concerned, it was true. Someone at some time not too long ago had taken the time and effort to spray paint these words in enormous, purple letters on an outcropping of rocks halfway up Fears Hill: *Billy Werner is a loser.* They even got the spelling right. For Billy's part, he had no idea who would have even bothered to do this. But he certainly had no doubt that these words were true.

And why shouldn't he think that it was true? He had exactly zero friends at school or in his neighborhood. He was an only child. His father had left him before he had even been born! Besides that, there was the question of genetics. Billy considered his mother, Sylvia, to be among history's biggest losers. Just one look at the parade of morons that she was constantly bringing home as "boyfriends" was all it took. They would last a week, sometimes two. Then, inevitably, Billy would come home from school to find his mother alone and in tears. Smashed on cheap wine, she would try and talk to her son about it. But Sylvia never made a bit of sense to Billy when she was drunk.

Billy stood back from the outcropping of rocks and regarded the purple epitaph. He had jogged up the pathway that ran up the north side of Fears Hill to this point. Because of the sheer size of Fears Hill, there were several different paths that wound their way up the hill. The pathway Billy used to jog up and down was the least traveled.

The rocks that formed the outcropping stood in a row along a steep embankment on the north side of the hill. This was one of the places that the high school and prep school kids in town would use for hanging out. Most of the hill itself was heavily wooded on every side except the western side. This side had an access road that came out almost to the base of the hill. There was no one on the hill except Billy at the moment. Most of the kids that used this spot to party would not get here until shortly before dark. Billy knew this. He always made sure to run here at this particular time of day. It ensured that he would be alone, or, more precisely that he would be left alone.

Billy looked around. There were probably a thousand cigarette butts lying all over the place. Crushed beer cans and broken beer bottles were cast everywhere as well. There was also a smattering of used condoms here and there to add just a little extra flair. *Yuck*, thought Billy to himself. He stretched his legs, bending down to touch his toes in order that his hamstrings would not tighten up on him too much.

Billy went running every day. He had made his school's track team last year. He found that running helped him. He felt better after a run. He felt that it sharpened his mind as well as his body. He finished stretching out and looked once again at the huge, purple letters. He laughed.

"I didn't think anyone cared," he said aloud. This was true. No one ever seemed to notice him. Billy was brilliant in school. He got straight A's. No one seemed to care. When he got in trouble at school, usually for arguing with his teachers because they were wrong so often, again, no one really seemed to care. If he won a race, as he had just three days earlier in a track meet against a rival school, the best he could get was a pat on the back from Coach Morgan. It did not matter. Even his mother was too busy screwing up her own life to bother with Billy's.

Billy was eleven years old. He was tired of being a loser. He imagined himself to be like the H.G. Wells character, the invisible man. Only he was the invisible little boy, which was even worse. Over one year ago he had, therefore, made a decision. He was going to stop being a loser.

He was going to win. He was going to do something no man in history had ever done. He was going to win a contest, a battle for the ages. He was going to leave people absolutely no choice but to notice him. They would all see that he was not a loser, but a winner. And not just a winner, Billy would be crowned as the greatest of all time. He was a young man with a plan. He saluted the large, purple letters that adorned the rock outcropping.

"Fuck you, very much!" he yelled as he began to run up the rest of Fears Hill. Billy ran harder than he ever had. He would use that writing as a motivation. Everything bad that happened to him had been used this way since he had made his decision to win.

His calves and his thighs burned inordinately as Billy put on a burst of speed along the escarpment. He raced around the edge of the rock face and resumed working his way along the path and up the hill. The path

106

wound around the left side of the rocks, then turned back, going straight up the hill. There was a small clearing that was to Billy's right that perched on top of the rock escarpment. This went back from the edge of the rocks for about thirty yards where the tree line was.

This was a known Native American holy place. In the center of this opening was an enormous, ancient tree. It was arguably the widest, thickest tree in all of Littleborough. Though it was not as tall as the beautiful pine trees and old oaks and maples that were everywhere on Fears Hill, there was majesty and, some might say, a personality, to this tree. Because of its age, which was really unknown, and the years of wild, New England weather, many of the primary branches were gnarled into impossible shapes and twists. Some of these even twisted around themselves, creating a sort of giant wooden knot.

Billy loved this tree. Every time he would feel down, or desperate, or depressed, Billy would come here and just sit under this Great Tree. Unlike his unknown father or his hopeless mother, this tree was always here when he needed it. It did not judge him. It did not expect anything from him. It never disappointed him. As he ran at top speed past the tree, Billy smiled and waved.

The forest was just as thick up here as it was in any of the other heavily wooded areas in Littleborough. Billy was forced to ease his pace a bit, as the hill he ran actually became a bit steeper toward the top. He was winded from running with so much extra pace. Despite the cool, clean autumn air he was breathing in, his lungs and throat burned from the effort he was giving. Though he had slowed himself a bit, Billy tripped over a large root of an enormous pine that grew only a few feet from the path, itself. Billy fell to the earth with a light skid and a thud.

"Fuck knuckle!" He did not know where he had heard this expression before, but it made him laugh. He could feel the familiar burning sensation of a cut or scrape on his left knee. Other than that, Billy figured he was just fine. He hopped back up onto his feet and resumed running. As he did so, he could see a very small trickle of blood working its way down from his kneecap down his shin. Though it stung a bit, Billy always thought that this sort of made him look tough. He pretended not to notice it.

He had almost reached the very top of Fears Hill. At its peak, the hill leveled off and became relatively flat. This area was surprisingly large for such a big, steep hill as this one. It was covered mostly by trees and large rocks. The size of this peak area was at least two football fields long and wide. There was, just a few feet in from that side, another clearing, an ancient Native American holy place.

It all looked so very beautiful to Billy. The path led him across the top of the hill, through the woods and right to this second holy site. At the opening of the clearing, the path upon which Billy ran widened as the clearing itself was a fairly decent size. Billy jogged across the clearing, stopping when he reached the other side.

Here was a thin line of trees that almost completely enclosed the ancient site. The path here narrowed again. It led out of the clearing and to the wide-open part of the top of Fears Hill. From this vantage point, one could look out over all of western Littleborough and points west for as far as the eye could see.

Billy stood there. He took it all in. The view, the fresh air, the adrenaline pumping through his veins from the exertion of running hard up that steep hill, all combined to make Billy feel good. He felt better than he had in a long time. He felt alive!

Which is more than one could say about poor, beautiful Thyra Lane. Billy smiled at the thought of it. It had not been perfect. He knew that. Billy had hoped that she might take a bit longer to die. After all, he had a lot more material prepared than he ended up using. The fact that she died was okay. But Billy had wanted it to be much more humiliating and frightening for her. But by the time he was really cooking, she had already pretty much bled to death. He even had to skip over the best parts so he could masturbate before she croaked! But what do you want? It was, after all, his very first attempt.

The original plan had called for an imitation of one of his all-time great heroes of evil. In a movie that Billy was not allowed to watch, a man brutalizes another man while singing a song from a musical. It was an autumn night over one year ago. Billy had been awakened by an odd noise coming from the living room. He quietly crept out of his bedroom and down the stairs toward the noises, which were becoming louder and more frequent. Billy peered through the living room door. He could now see that his mother and her "date" were creating all the noise on the couch. Billy could not quite see what they were doing, but he could certainly hear it.

But his attention was quickly called to the television screen as he heard a man half-singing and half-shouting: "I'm singing in the rain!" The man would then viciously kick another man, who just lay helplessly on the ground. "Just singing in the rain!" *Kick.* "I'm singing in the rain!" Billy was impressed. He hated bullies. He had certainly been bullied and picked on his share of times. But this bully had flair. He had style. He had…a sense of humor! Though he did not know what film that was or who that actor was, Billy never forgot that scene.

Billy had wanted to sing this to Thyra as he cut her open. The problem was the slashing, you see. Billy was new to the whole vicious, brutal-murder thing. As he had mocked the poor, young woman, he had executed a corresponding slash across her belly or up one of her sides. But it was kind of dark. Billy had dimmed the lights by unscrewing all the light bulbs in the basement, save one, to create what he hoped would be an appropriate mood and setting for the murder. The first two slashes didn't seem to really penetrate the way Billy had expected them to. This was especially puzzling to him because the knife he was using was seriously sharp.

So, Billy slashed again. But this time, he had apparently overcompensated for the first two slashes. The knife went in too deep. Billy knew it immediately because the weapon did not slash the way it had the first two times. Instead it had gotten hung up on something inside her—an internal organ, no doubt—and Billy had to exert a considerable effort to just get the knife out of her body in order to continue. As the knife was finally freed, a tremendous amount of blood flowed from the wound. Billy knew that time was running out on his plan, as well as on poor Thyra.

As he thought about his first time, Billy wondered if Jack the Ripper had struggled during his first time out. He had read that the Son of Sam had been terrible with his weapon of choice at first. It had taken several tries for him to get the hang of that forty-four. At first he had to practically empty the clip to claim the lives of his victims. At the end, only one or two shots were necessary.

Still deep in thought, Billy turned and began running back the way he had come. It was getting later in the afternoon, almost evening. The high school kids were going to be showing up soon. They would smoke their cigarettes and drink their beers. Billy didn't want to see them, or to be seen by them. He jogged back to the little clearing that sat atop Fears Hill. He continued on along the same path, back through the clearing, and into the more thickly wooded area.

He breathed in and out rhythmically through his nose. He timed this with the pumping of his arms and legs. He wanted every step to be correct and deliberate. Just like his master plan. He had taken a huge step forward in his master plan. Poor, pretty, stupid little Thyra Lane had been his first step toward ultimate victory, for an ultimate loser. Billy would lose no more. He would become the ultimate winner. He would win the ultimate victory.

Billy smiled to himself. He decided that when he got home from his run, he was going to celebrate, and do it in style! Cap'n Crunch with Crunch-Berries—the ultimate food for the ultimate winner! Billy laughed out loud as he ran.

As he neared the spot where his favorite tree stood, he looked up. Through the trees Billy could swear that he could see a man standing before the Great Tree. The man looked old. He was wearing an expensive suit with a long, black overcoat.

Billy burst out from the wood line and into the clearing where the Great Tree stood. The man in the suit turned around and smiled at Billy. He wore one of those cool hats that gangsters wore in those old, black-and-white movies that were on late at night. Billy smiled back.

"Hello there, young fellow." The man had a low, clear voice.

"Hey." Billy stopped running. He was still on the path that led down the hill. The man was standing in the long, fescue grasses of the clearing, in front of the Great Tree.

"Getting in a run, I see. That's good."

"Yeah, I run on the school track team." Billy had never seen this man before. A stranger in Littleborough was a rare thing.

"I do not wish to interfere with your exercise, young man, but perhaps you can help me. You see, I'm looking for someone, and I just can't seem to find them."

"Who are you looking for?" Billy asked this plainly. He knew everyone in town. Everyone knew everyone in town.

"Well, you see, that's the problem. I do not know who it is I'm trying to find." When the little old man said this, Billy made a face. This caused the man to smile. "I know that does not make a lot of sense, does it?"

"No. It doesn't make any sense." Billy's face was earnest. The little old man's smile widened.

"No. No, that made no sense at all. I am sorry about that, young man." He chuckled a bit as he spoke. "Yes, but you see, what I really mean is, someone is looking for me. And I'll be darned if I can't figure out just who it is."

"How do you know someone is looking for you? Why didn't they just leave a message, or something? If they really wanted to find you, they would have left their name or cell number, or something."

"Well, Billy, do you mind if I call you Billy?"

"No. That's my name." Something didn't seem right to Billy. He could not quite put his finger on it, though.

"You see, Billy, I did receive a message. It was, in my business, a very urgent message. I thought I knew who sent this message, but every single one of these people is insisting that they did not, in fact, send this message. So, I'm kind of stuck here."

"The people who left you this message didn't say who they were?"

"Exactly right. They left a message all right. Believe me when I tell you, the message was received!" The little old man shook his head when he said this, and for a moment, Billy sensed that he was angry about this. "And now, nobody seems to know who in the world it was. But it was an urgent, and, therefore, important, message."

Billy listened, nodding his head. He looked around the clearing. He looked all along the tree line and then at the Great Tree. He then looked back toward the man.

"Did you think you would find this person up here?" The little, old man burst out laughing. He shook his head and held his belly with both hands for fear of his guts spilling out. He fetched a handkerchief from the inside pocket of his long coat and dabbed at his eyes and nose. He looked at Billy, who was staring back with that earnest, deadpan look that children have when they're curious. The man went back into fits of laughter, although he tried mightily to suppress it this time.

"Oh, my heavens to Betsy! Oh, my goodness me, I'm sorry, Billy. Graciousness! No. No, young man. I did not anticipate finding anyone up here. I was simply drawn up here for some reason. So, I came."

"What does that mean? You were drawn up here?" Billy asked.

"Something told me that I should come up here. It's sort of like a little voice in my head. I thought that the cool, clean air and the smell of grasses and trees and flowers would all help me to clear my head. Then I thought I could start fresh in the morning. But now I think I know what really drew me up here."

"What?"

The little old man smiled broadly at Billy.

"You." †

CHAPTER 15
The Odor of Fear

"What happened?" The voice seemed distant to Julie. "I don't know. She was running from someone, but whoever it was is gone now."

"Is she okay?"

"I don't know."

Julie was aware that she was now outside of the house. She could feel the sun on her face and could smell the fresh air as it filled her mouth and nose and her lungs. She could smell fresh-cut grass as she felt herself being laid gently down on the ground. Julie opened her eyes. There, looking down at her with deep concern on all of their faces, were Officers Tubbs, Marconi, and Jones.

"Miss Bernard, can you hear me?" Officer Tubbs was peering directly into her eyes. Julie smiled weakly.

"Yes, Officer Tubbs. I can hear you fine." Her own voice sounded throaty and distant to her. She tried to sit up. Two of the patrolmen helped her get into a sitting position, and then gently helped her get unsteadily onto her feet. Julie held onto them both for a moment. Her head was swimming, and she felt light-headed and dizzy—and a little nauseated. Though she knew that she was safe and standing back out in the front yard of the property, she did not dare look back up at the window where she had seen Megan earlier. "Thank you," she whispered huskily. "I think I'm all right now…I think."

"Miss Bernard, did you see something or someone in there?" Officer Tubbs asked.

Julie looked up at him. "Did you see anything?" she asked him.

He shook his head. "No. No, ma'am, I didn't see anything in there. But I swear I heard…like a…like a bunch of whispers, and then heavy footsteps in that hallway. Also, it smelled like shit. But I didn't see anything. Did you see anything, ma'am?"

He waited for a moment. Officer Tubbs took Julie by the shoulders, steadying her. "It's important, Miss Bernard. Tell us what you saw."

Julie was about to speak when her eyes glanced quickly up at the window in which she had seen Megan. Officer Tubbs followed her gaze, and looked up into the window. But there was nothing to see. He looked back at Julie. Julie swallowed, and looked back at Officer Tubbs.

"I thought I saw Megan. Then, I thought I saw a tall man." Remembering this gave Julie a chill. She wrapped her arms around herself to try to keep warm. Julie looked from Officer Tubbs to Officer Jones, to Officer Marconi, and then back to Officer Tubbs again.

"You saw Megan…Streeter, ma'am?" Officer Tubbs asked gently.

"I know." Julie nodded her head and closed her eyes for a moment. "I know that she is dead. And I know that this sounds crazy." Julie looked up at Officer Tubbs. "But I know I saw her. It was her." Officer Tubbs nodded. He looked at Officer Jones, who was looking, wide-eyed, from one window to the next window then back again.

"Now, Miss Bernard, what did the tall man look like?"

"He looked like evil. He was like a shadow, or something. I'm sorry." Julie closed her eyes and began rubbing them with her hands. "I know that that doesn't make any sense." But when she opened her eyes, Julie could see the looks that the three officers were exchanging.

"Was he really thin, ma'am?"

Surprised, Julie nodded. "Yes, he was, Officer. He was tall and thin."

An unmarked patrol SUV pulled up to the property. A large man who looked to Julie as if he were in his fifties slowly eased his way out of the driver's side door and walked slowly over.

"Hi Chief," Officer Tubbs said.

"Men." The chief looked at Julie. "Miss Bernard?"

"Yes."

"I'm Chief Sam Proudfoot. Are you all right, ma'am?"

"Yes. Thank you, I'm fine. It's nice to meet you." Julie smiled up at the chief, who smiled back.

"What happened here, Harold?"

"We got that 911 call about a woman screaming, Chief. We got here and found Miss Bernard inside, running from an apparent attacker. We didn't find him, but he does fit the description given to us by Father Knight over at the church." The chief nodded, then turned and looked at Julie. Julie's eyes widened as she looked from one patrolman to the next, then up at the chief.

"Oh, my God, he attacked Father Knight? Is James okay?"

"He's fine, Miss Bernard. There was no attack, just a sighting at the church," the chief said. "Inspector Dahms has informed me of how much help you have been to us during this difficult time. Thank you, ma'am." Julie nodded her head. "You've never seen this man before?"

"No, sir. It was difficult to get a good look at his face. But his eyes were strange."

"Strange eyes, that is helpful. Was there anyone else in the house, maybe someone with him?" the chief said. Julie swallowed.

"I thought I saw Megan Streeter, up there, in that window. I know that sounds crazy. I had to go up there. I just had to see. Then I saw him, behind her. I guess I ran in after her." Julie looked up at the chief as she spoke. His large, brown eyes stared unblinking into her eyes. Julie looked away. "I know I sound hysterical," she said, shrugging her shoulders.

"No, you don't," the chief said. Everyone looked at him. "We have twenty or thirty dead people in those woods, a church being stalked by a freak, citizens like Miss Bernard being attacked. The only things that fit this case so far are, in fact, crazy things." The chief looked at Julie. "Are you sure you're all right, ma'am?"

"I'm sure." She smiled up at the chief. "A good, long hot shower followed by a good, long sleep should just do the trick, I think." The chief nodded his head.

"Okay. However, if you see or hear anything else strange or if you need anything, please let us know."

"Yes, sir."

"All right. Good. Do you want an escort home? I know that Officers Tubbs and Jones here would love to escort you home." Julie laughed as the two young police officers shuffled their feet. She shook her head.

"No. I'll be fine, but thank you."

The chief smiled and nodded. He walked along with Julie toward her Jeep. Julie climbed in, careful not to reveal the pain that was now throbbing in her left shoulder. The chief gently shut the door.

"There is just one more thing, Miss Bernard." He spoke through the open window. Julie looked up at the chief. He spoke softly. "This man as described by both yourself and Father Knight, sounds like he is what my people would call a shadow ghost. Some call them dream shadows."

"A shadow ghost?"

The chief nodded his head. "When you get home, lock all your doors and windows. And do not let in any strangers."

"I don't understand."

"Think hard, Miss Bernard. Do you remember anyone like this from a dream you may have had? It probably would have been a bad dream. You see a tall shadow, thin, and, as you say, strange eyes? Eyes that look like maybe they change size, shape, and color?"

Chills went up and down Julie's spine. She looked straight into the chief's deep, dark brown eyes, with his earnest expression. Julie closed her eyes. Waves of exhaustion came over her.

"I'm sorry, Miss Bernard. Please forgive me. You've been through a lot this morning." Julie opened her eyes. "Just, please, lock up?" Julie smiled and nodded.

"I promise." As she drove away, Julie waved.

The chief then looked at his three patrolmen. "There's a chance that the tall man was waiting here for Miss Bernard to show up."

The three police officers exchanged glances. The chief looked at his watch. "You will all drive by and observe Miss Bernard's residence continually until this thing is finished. I'll inform the other shifts the same. We got her into this mess; let's not get her killed for it. Do you understand?"

"Yes, sir."

"Good." The chief watched the three men climb into their patrol cars and drive away. He then turned and looked up at the windows of the small duplex. He closed his eyes and he sniffed at the air. He breathed in deeply, and held it in. He breathed out slowly, and then smelled the air again, and again. Miss Bernard had told the truth. He could smell it. The chief opened his eyes. There was the scent of rage and desperation, murder and deception, and the odor of fear. †

CHAPTER 16
When Rage Meets Rage

"What do you think you're doing here?" Doc Robinson said.

"I would have thought you would be happy to see me." The devil smiled his most charming smile.

"Do you ever stop lying?" Doc Robinson turned his back to the devil and began to wash and sterilize the instruments that he had used to heal Julie Bernard's rat.

"Not if I can help it. How is the little rat, anyway? Is she going to pull through?"

"Yes. No thanks to you, dirt bag."

"Oh, come now, you don't really think that I would have anything to do with something like that, do you now, Doctor?"

"No, I don't. But I do think that you enjoy it."

The devil laughed. "Now, now, now, you're only saying that because it's true." He continued to laugh. Though the devil often laughed, and laughed hard, it was always somehow empty and devoid of any humor. Doc Robinson did not respond to any of this and simply continued washing his instruments. "That Julie Bernard is really something else, hmmm? I mean, she is so very beautiful—loves animals, too. She was very kind to me out in the backyard. She smiled, said hello. She is a very refreshing mortal, don't you think, Doc?"

"Yes. For once, you've got something there," Doc Robinson replied. He thought for a moment, then added, "Well, I guess even a total loser is bound to get some things right when they are around for an eternity. It's probably by accident, no doubt."

The devil had stopped laughing. His look was serious. "No doubt. I wonder if we could return to the business at hand."

Doc Robinson had finished sterilizing his instruments. He reached up to open the cabinets above the sink and put the instruments away. He then slowly turned his massive frame around and faced the devil. "The business at hand? What business could we possibly have left to do? You've taken everything. There is nothing left." Doc Robinson could now feel rage welling up in his chest. He began to advance toward the devil menacingly. "I'm surprised at your pure stupidity to come here and start shit with a man who literally has nothing to lose. You're a fucking idiot."

The devil began to grow in size right before Doc Robinson. He was now an enormous goat with a human head and face. "I'm the idiot? How does that work, exactly, Doctor? Am I the one who signed the soul of his first born away? Hmmm, let me think... No. No, you were the genius who did that."

"Yes. That's right. I made that mistake. I made that one mistake. But make no mistake now, our days of doing business are over." Doc Robinson stood right in front of Satan, his face inches from the devil's face. "You are not welcome here, little angel. Do you hear me? Not welcome. Whatever horseshit reasons you thought you had to come and bother me are pointless. Just like you."

At this, the devil spun into a rage. "Pointless? Pointless? I created you! I created all of this! With Him! We created you, all of you! Every last, worthless mortal being! I sat next to Him! I sang for Him! I wrote poetry for Him! I helped Him create all things...including you! I was His favorite! I loved Him more deeply, more purely, and more completely than all of you miserable, puny mortals combined! You! What have you created? You animals speak of meaning in your lives, as if we somehow owed you that too. Well, how about life itself, on this rock in this universe we built for you all. Huh? How about it, Doc? How about the true miracle? The miraculous, physical plane, the miracle of mortality? Yes, that's right, Doc. Death is the miracle, the miracle of that True Creation in which we helped. What's the matter, Doc? That's not meaningful enough for you? Do you really think He owes you some sort of explanation?"

"Yes!" Doc Robinson's voice thundered. "Yes, He does owe me that! He owes Belinda that! He owes everybody that! He took my Belinda. She was a good woman. She was a healer, a real healer. And she loved Him. More than you ever did, Devil. Because, unlike you, she did not love herself first! It was God and His pointless creation that she loved first! So, He poisoned her, made her sick, and made her suffer beyond description. Then, with a whole lot of help from you, He took her. Just like you took my boy! So how about it, Satan? Huh? Can you feel that? Can you? That's hate. Hate! Hate! I've got lots of it here. All for you, and for Him. Because you are both pointless! Just like me. Not like Belinda. Neither one of you could ever shine like she did. So, get over it, asshole. Get over yourself. And the same goes for You!" Doc pointed up at the sky as he roared, "Fuck you all!"

The devil drew in a deep breath. He breathed it out slowly. As he did this, he began to change, little by little, from a large goat into something else. When he had finished, he looked up at Doc Robinson.

"Wow. Graciousness, that was terribly exciting. My goodness me, you sure do have a temper, Doc. When you die and get sent down to me, I'll make sure you get a good job." He laughed his empty, bitter laugh. "There is, of course, no pay. But oh, the benefits! Oh, my mercy me!" The devil looked at his wristwatch. "I do not wish to be rude, Doctor Robinson, but I do have another appointment by a tree on a hill I have to keep. So, here's the deal." Doc Robinson stood in the doorway leading back out to the main hallway of his office. "I will release your boy from my grip. He will be free to die and to join his mother in the hereafter. I just need you to help me when the time comes."

"When what time comes?"

"That time will come soon. I'll contact you. If you don't come when I call, the boy stays with me, okay?"

Doc did not answer. He glared at the devil as he walked past him and out into the hallway. Doc Robinson watched as he walked down the hall and through the reception area, with the sound of the peanut Styrofoam bits all over the floor crackling and snapping as the devil walked out of the office door and into the backyard. He no longer looked like a large goat. He had now taken the form of an ordinary person: a little old man. †

CHAPTER 17
Instant Replay

"I don't know about this, I really don't." Officer Evers said.

"I do. This is wrong," Officer Marconi said. He removed a white sheet from a long, metal table that ran the entire length of the wall and handed it to Officer Franklin.

"Come on, you guys," Officer Franklin said. "He's just as shocked as we are. He's trying to find out who did this the best way he knows how." He and Officer Jones folded up the sheet.

"Leaving those kids' bodies up like that? Well, it's the wrong way, Franklin," Officer Marconi said. He shuddered at the thought of it. Rage, sorrow, and revulsion mingled in his puppy-dog brown eyes.

"What do we even know about this guy?" Officer Tubbs said. "We got a name. That's it. When the chief hired him, all he would tell us is that the guy had a shit-ton of experience. He never said where he's from or where he worked. Nothing."

The patrolmen were prepping the Littleborough lab for the removal of the bodies from the crime scene. The lab was no afterthought when the new facilities for the police, fire, and ambulance were being constructed. Back in the late autumn of 1960, there had been two terrible fires. A dormitory at a private school had caught on fire around ten o'clock at night. Within about an hour of that, a dormitory for a girls' school less than a mile away was burned to the ground. Over a dozen children lost their lives in the two tragedies. . Both blazes were lit, investigators later found, with kerosene and a match. The arsonist was never caught.

Because the facilities available at the time of the tragedy were limited, the charred remains of the children had to be laid out in a small basketball gym at the high school. Each child had to be placed carefully on a canvas tarpaulin and then covered with a nylon one. Teachers, neighbors, and school administrators all helped the small, beleaguered volunteer fire and rescue team to sift through the burned-out dormitories to find the kids. It was a night that the residents of Littleborough would never forget.

As a result of that terrible tragedy, the new lab in the basement was state of the art. Adjacent to it was a large, empty room specifically designed for such unfortunate events. It was in this room that Littleborough's coroner, Jacob Miller, would perform the autopsies with the help of the FBI.

"I think we should give him a chance," Officer Franklin said.

"We just did, numbnuts," Officer Tubbs said. "We all watched him decide to leave four murder victims nailed up onto trees over night for the FBI. That was his chance and he chose wrong."

"Tubbs, the FBI told him to leave the crime scene as-is. He didn't decide anything."

"Yes, he did," Officer Evers said. "He didn't have to do it. He could have told the feds no and just done the right thing. Right is right."

"Amen," Officer Marconi said.

"Has anyone even seen any FBI show up?"

"Not yet, no."

"Are they even coming?"

"Of course they're coming."

"How do you know?" Officer Franklin looked at Officer Tubbs.

"What?"

"Do we even know if Dahms even called the fuckin' FBI?" Officer Tubbs said. There was a silence.

"Well, they're clearly not here. I know that much," Officer Evers said.

"He doesn't care. He isn't one of us," Officer Marconi said.

"What does that even mean?" Officer Franklin said.

"I'm only saying that we don't know this guy from Adam."

"Which proves nothing. People always fear the unknown. You don't know him, so you don't trust him."

"How can anyone trust a man who can do what he just did?" Officer Evers said.

"Franklin, you went to college." Some of the patrolmen snorted and rolled their eyes. "You probably took all those pointy-headed investigative courses, huh? Why don't you just take a little look into the good inspector's background? Let's find out what's so fuckin' secret about this dude." Officer Franklin licked his lips and looked around the all-white, brightly lit room at the other patrolmen, who were all looking right at him. He turned around and removed the last white sheet from the last metal table.

"I don't know if…" As he turned, he saw that the other patrolmen were looking toward the lab entrance. Inspector Dahms was standing in the open doorway. There was a long, awkward silence that followed.

"We haven't heard back from Virginia. I don't know why. Marge is still trying to get back in touch with them." He looked straight at Officer Franklin. "Franklin, the chief tells me that you took quite a few of the advanced courses in crime when you were at college."

"Yes, sir. I took advanced criminology and crime scene courses in college."

"Do you think you can process the crime scene?"

"I think so."

"Franklin, are you kidding?" Officer Tubbs said. "You couldn't stop crying the whole time we were at the scene. How the hell are you gonna see anything?"

"It's called education and training, Tubbs. And thanks for the vote of confidence, too, by the way." Officer Tubbs shook his large head.

"Thank you, Franklin. I'm aware of your outstanding background from your file. You have my vote of confidence." The inspector looked at Officer Tubbs. "In this case I think we have no choice but to proceed. The sooner we do, the sooner we can get the victims down and clean up the crime scene."

Everyone looked at Officer Franklin. Officer Franklin looked up at the inspector while still holding the half-folded sheet. He licked his lips and blinked his eyes through his thick spectacles.

"'Kay," he said.

Inspector Dahms drove Officer Franklin and Officer Tubbs back to the scene of the crime. The two young men had to conceal their amusement when he pulled out of the rear garage of police headquarters in his old, 1979 Buick station wagon. It was lime-green in color. Officer Tubbs sat in the front, suppressing a smile. Officer Franklin climbed into the back seat with an outright grin on his face.

Inspector Dahms steered the old station wagon onto Deerfoot Road and down and around the deep bends in the road to where the path was. He parked on the right side of the road on the shoulder behind Officer Lydon, who had parked his SUV there as well. He had been watching the path and the entrance to the woods here to make sure no one would take it and find what was in that clearing.

The three men got out of the car. Inspector Dahms nodded to Officer Lydon as he strode across the road, down the embankment, and into the woods. The two young patrolmen followed him along the path. As they walked the mile or so through the Great Woods of Littleborough, Officer

Franklin could feel his stomach muscles grow tighter and tighter with each step he took. It had all seemed so easy in college. *But this is real,* he thought. Instead of a grade in a class, lives were at stake. He licked his lips again. They were as dry as a bone.

Inspector Dahms stopped at the mouth of the clearing. Already it looked completely different to him. Though he had left this place just a little over an hour ago, it now seemed like weeks or months. The weeds and undergrowth seemed taller, thicker, and greener. Brilliant sunshine shone through the lush, green canopy, dancing amidst the trees and the leaves. A light autumn breeze gently caressed the leaves and branches all around the clearing. They swayed and sang softly with the silent shafts of sunlight in an ancient intercourse. The crime scene was still in its original state. It was a truly beautiful day in hell.

The three men spent several gruesome hours collecting evidence from the scene. Inspector Dahms and Officer Franklin collected samples of flesh from each body and body part in order to send them to a state lab for DNA analysis and, hopefully, identification. They gave each sealed bag to Officer Tubbs, who then brought the evidence back to Officer Lydon, who waited in the SUV cruiser. They took a small sample of the black, sticky fluid that was in the large black pot at the clearing's edge. They removed several remnants of the long, red robes that had been worn and a piece of what appeared to be bongo drums, although it had been badly charred in the fire. They also were able to find three of the theatrical masks in decent enough condition to examine as well.

The inspector, Officer Tubbs, and Officer Franklin then went over the crime scene once more with a fine-tooth comb. They examined and measured the footprints and paw prints in the ashes on the clearing floor. They collected samples of fur believed to be from the wolves. They examined the enormous tree limbs that had been broken and fallen from the canopy. They took pictures of everything as it was; the entire clearing, the forest floor, the masks, the cauldron, the drums, and all the victims and remains were documented and photographed. Finally, they examined the victims of the crucifixion—the sacrifices, as Julie Bernard had called them. Inspector Dahms did not reveal to his patrolmen what had been carved onto each victim's tongue. Then it was Officer Franklin's time to apply a special technique.

"Are you sure you want to do this, Franklin?" Inspector Dahms said.

"Yes." Officer Franklin licked his lips and swallowed hard. He looked up at the inspector and then at Officer Tubbs. The three men stood in the mouth of the clearing. Officer Franklin looked out from the mouth. He took a deep breath, then walked past the Inspector and Officer Tubbs straight into the middle of the clearing where the bonfire had been. His light blue eyes burned through his glasses with a mix of horror and curiosity.

"So, this is it." Officer Franklin swallowed hard. He took some deep breaths, blowing out the air slowly, puffing his pudgy cheeks out as he did so. He looked around the clearing. Staying right in the center of it, he turned his body slowly in a 360-degree turn. His arms were held down tightly to his sides and his feet shuffled as he moved. Black soot from the ashes of the bonfire wafted around him and now covered his shoes and socks and went partway up the trouser legs of his uniform. But Officer Franklin was oblivious to it. Inspector Dahms could see his lips moving. It was as if he were reciting something. He couldn't hear what it was the young man was saying, though.

Officer Franklin looked straight up into the sky. He began to walk in small, tight circles in the center of the clearing. He appeared to the inspector and Officer Tubbs as if he were marching in a parade. His arms stayed down by his sides as he marched. He held his head high and tilted back, still gazing upward. As he walked the circle a second time, he widened it just a little bit. He did a third and then a fourth circle, each one a little larger than the last. He left behind him a slight trail in the soot and ashes that began to take the form of a spiral working its way outward and away from where the bonfire had raged. He continued this outward march while examining the treetops and limbs that partly enclosed the clearing itself. Officer Franklin stopped marching. He turned to his right and was now facing the tree on which the body of Megan Streeter was. His gaze slowly shifted from up at the sky down to the very base of the enormous, old tree. His eyes rose up the tree slowly and then focused right on Megan.

"Oh, Megan," Officer Franklin said. His face had gone blank. He stared, expressionless. His normally rosy red cheeks were now sheet-white. He walked straight toward the tree, stopping about five feet from the base. He spread his arms out, as if preparing to embrace someone or something. His lips were moving again, but he made no sound. Inspector Dahms and Officer Tubbs watched on in silence.

Officer Franklin spun around in a sudden jerking motion. The innocent look in his eyes was now replaced by a wild, almost primal look. He half-skipped and half-danced straight across the clearing, nimbly avoiding bodies and body parts, right back through where the bonfire had been and to the tree on the opposite side of the clearing where the body of Caroline Hart was. He moved with a purpose. His child-like face had transformed into a look of intensity and willful intent. He stopped several feet from the base of this great tree. His gaze slowly moved up to where Caroline was held by the ropes and spikes.

"Caroline," he whispered. Again, he held his arms out to either side.

Then Officer Franklin began to emit a low moan. He spun around. Inspector Dahms noticed that despite his heavyset build, Officer Franklin was light on his feet. Again he danced and skipped his way through the center of the clearing, this time veering off toward the tree upon which old Jed Prescott had died of a heart attack. As Officer Franklin danced and skipped and jumped, ash and soot arose around him and trailed behind him. He stopped right in front of the tree. He then put his hands on his hips and looked from side to side.

"Oh! Come on! You have got to be kidding me!" He continued looking from side to side for a moment. He then shrugged. "Carry on! Carry on anyway!" Officer Franklin yelled this out to no one in particular. He spun around to face the upside-down man who was held to a great tree on the north side of the clearing, then froze. The young patrolman stood absolutely still for several moments, staring at the unidentified man held upside-down on that tree. He pointed a pudgy finger at him.

"You! It's all down to you!" Officer Franklin then broke into a headlong sprint across the clearing toward the upside-down man. He'd gotten halfway across when he tripped on something at the edge of where the large bonfire had been and fell face first into the soot and ash. There was a loud thump as he hit the ground. An enormous cloud of soot and ash rose up, obscuring the view of the center of the clearing momentarily.

Officer Tubbs took one step into the clearing, but hesitated. It seemed to Inspector Dahms that the patrolman was torn between helping Franklin get back up and not interrupting this bizarre display for fear of interfering with the "investigation." The inspector thought about Officer Franklin's sterling academic record as he watched him flop around in the ashes. His glasses had fallen off of his face.

After a minute of frantically searching around blindly, Officer Franklin fished them out of the soot and had gotten himself back up onto his feet. As he cleaned his glasses off with a handkerchief he had taken from his pocket, Officer Franklin blinked his eyes furiously amid the risen dust and ash. His incessant blinking reminded Inspector Dahms of a rat he had seen here just a few short hours ago.

Officer Franklin's face and body were covered in soot and heaven only knew what else. He coughed, hacked, and spit a few times, and worked his tongue frantically, trying to remove some of the ash from his mouth. As he did so, Officer Franklin peered out from his black, soot-covered face at Officer Tubbs and the inspector with a bright blue-eyed innocence through his now-cleaned spectacles. He spat and blinked once more, then turned to face the tree to the north.

He resumed his sprint across the clearing. A cloud of dust and ash wafted after him slowly. He stopped just a few feet away from the great tree and the poor man held upside-down. He then bent sideways, looking at the man while holding his own head almost upside-down.

At this point, Officer Franklin burst back into his strange dancing. He went around the fire several times. First, he moved clockwise, then counter-clockwise. All the while he was dancing, leaping, and spinning, his light, singsong voice could be heard. He was, at times, talking, and at other times ranting. His round face was flush from all of the exercise. Officer Franklin was getting winded, but this did not seem to slow him down at all.

"Dancing round and round we go…dark, dark, dark, dark, dark, dark, dark, dark! Very dark! Ooooh, hot, hot, hot, hot, heat! Burning fire! Crackle, crackle, crackle! Sssssinge me! Yeeeooowww! That's a hot mamamamamamamamamamamama!" Officer Franklin stopped at one point, staring down at a spot in the undergrowth outside of the area that had been the fire. He looked sideways at it, and then pointed down at it.

"There was oral sex right here….whoooaaa…." He flung himself back down on the ground, and then got back up again just as suddenly. He looked up, waving his arms about wildly as if trying to fend off something swooping down from above. He ducked back down. He then rolled away, laughing out of control as he did. "Ha! Missed me! You missed me! Whooooooooooooooooooooooo!"

Officer Franklin then resumed running in a circle around where the fire had been. As he did, he made what could only be described as a siren-like noise. Wailing, like a small boy playing cops and robbers. "Woooo, woooo, woooo,woooo, woooo,woooohablehmmmmmnfffff!" He had fallen, again, much harder than the last time.

He lay still for a moment, panting. Inspector Dahms and Officer Tubbs watched on. This time both men were sorely tempted to go in and help the young man get back onto his feet. But before they could, he was up again. As he arose, Officer Franklin pointed down at where he had fallen. "You are dead!" He yelled this. "That is just! You have disturbed my resting place! I should just…" He trailed off for a moment. He was looking around, as if actually seeing the people who, just the night before, had danced to their deaths. "Mmmmmm. Look at all the people to eat! Oh yeah!" And Officer Franklin immediately began to strut around the scene like a rock singer. He then resumed his strange, wild dance.

Again he stopped at the four cardinal points where the four main "sacrifices" had been offered. At the first two, where Megan and Caroline had been found, he smiled broadly. He put his thumb up high in the air.

"Nice one!" he yelled both times. When Officer Franklin got to old man Jed Prescott's tree, he frowned. "Bad show! Bad show, all 'round! Really, old man! That is going to be a problem! Big problem! Not at all a good thing, old bean. Bad show all the way 'round!" Officer Franklin then spread his arms out to either side, and like a child pretending to be an airplane, "flew" across the crime scene to the upside-down man.

"Rooommmrumrumrumrumrooommmmmmrumrumrum!" There, he stopped one more time. He stared at the cross. At this point, Officer Tubbs and Inspector Dahms noticed a hush seem to come over the forest. It was as if the woods and all its inhabitants were waiting to see how this final little scene would play out.

Officer Franklin stepped closer to the tree. He knelt down on one knee and put his face inches from the tree and the man who hung upside down on it. He then turned his head so as to see the man upside up. Although they could not hear what he was saying, Officer Tubbs and Inspector Dahms could see his lips moving. He was whispering something to the victim. Officer Franklin then shook his head gently and started to weep.

Officer Tubbs and Inspector Dahms then looked at each other. Both men seemed to be thinking the same thing. They entered the clearing and walked over to where Officer Franklin was. They helped him to his feet. Officer Franklin seemed surprised to see other people. He looked up into Inspector Dahms's face as they steadied him. His face was almost totally black from soot. Only his bright, blue eyes that peered through his thick spectacles and the tear streaks down his pudgy cheeks weren't completely black.

Officer Franklin slowly turned his head the other way, looking straight up into Officer Tubbs's face. He smiled. He reached up, touching Officer Tubbs's face.

"Hey, I know you," he said. Officer Tubbs nodded.

"Yes, you know me. Now, come on. We've got to get you cleaned up."

"I don't want to have a bath."

"Of course not. Don't worry about that right now."

"Okay."

They had managed to get Officer Franklin to the mouth of the clearing. Inspector Dahms and Officer Tubbs could see that he was still out of sorts. They gently turned him away from the crime scene.

"The car is this way, Officer Franklin. Okay?"

Before they could lead him away, the young patrolman planted his feet as firmly on the ground as he could. He grabbed Inspector Dahms's arm.

"He's here, you know. Right here, right now, watching us."

Officer Tubbs looked at Inspector Dahms, and then looked back at Officer Franklin.

"Who is here? The person that did this? Where? Where are they, Franklin?"

But Officer Franklin was shaking his head. "No. No. Not the person. We're not looking for a person. It is a thing. A thing did this. And he's laughing, I can hear him!" Officer Franklin raised his voice as he spoke. "I hear you! I hear you!"

"Okay, that's it." Inspector Dahms took Officer Franklin by one arm, and Officer Tubbs took him by the other. They managed to get him turned back around, and started walking him away from the crime scene.

Officer Franklin closed his eyes, and went almost completely limp. His head rolled from side to side. He then opened his eyes, and looked straight up into the sky. He whispered, "There, where within dwells no soul, he reigns." Officer Franklin's head rolled weakly from side to side. He looked up at Inspector Dahms and said, "He rules over us, dead man." He closed his eyes, but only for a moment. When he reopened them, he seemed to be completely under his own power.

He looked up at Inspector Dahms, then up at Officer Tubbs. Officer Franklin smiled at them, his white teeth gleaming from out of his black, soot-covered face. He took a deep breath and looked once more at each man.

"Right, good, I think I've got it. Let's go get something to eat." †

CHAPTER 18
Julie Meets Her Match

Julie steered her Jeep Cherokee off of Route 39 onto a large, shady shoulder that sat between a cemetery and one of the town's reservoirs. She was heading to the coffee shop on Main Street from the Streeters' residence, thinking about what had happened inside that house. Her memory played out every detail of the event while her mind searched for logical, rational explanations for the things she heard and saw and felt. Everything had been okay until about a minute ago.

Then, anywhere and everywhere Julie looked, all she could see was Megan Streeter's face, contorted, dying, pleading, warning. It would then go away for a moment, only to return in more detail and clarity. Though she knew that these pictures were only in her head, Julie could not concentrate on her driving. She put the Jeep in park and switched off the ignition. There, she sat in silence and let her mind play out the terrible memories of the morning.

The shoulder here afforded her with a beautiful view overlooking the reservoir. This enormous body of water was almost entirely surrounded by thick woods, with only a few small openings where one could see a house or a favorite fishing spot. The late morning sun sparkled and skipped on the water's surface. A light breeze playfully danced and splashed from west to east. But as she stared at all of this, Julie did not see any of it. The visions of what she had just been through were still quite vivid. But the shock was finally starting to wear off and the truth was beginning to sink in.

Julie felt dirty. She was shaking her head now. She knew this meant that tears were coming. They came. They ran down her face. Julie dabbed at her eyes with a tissue. She blew her nose and continued to stare out over the reservoir weeping softly. She took out her cell phone and looked at it. She scrolled through her contacts to the one that read simply; *Dad*.

Julie put her thumb on the call button and bit her lower lip. She closed her eyes. She set her chin and pushed the call button. Nothing happened. Julie looked closely at her cell phone; there was a signal. She tried it again, but the call did not go through. *What is going on here*? Julie wondered.

She scrolled back down to her father's phone number. Julie hesitated. *Please*, she thought. Before she could press the button, her cell phone began to play "Walk the Line" by Johnny Cash. It startled Julie into almost dropping her cell phone. She shook her head and smiled. It was the ring tone for her dad.

"Dad?"

"Hey there, Tiger! What's hot?" He had called Julie "Tiger" since she was nine years old. She was playing on a basketball team that was called the Tigers. Julie had been furious to learn that they weren't called the Lady Tigers. Her father had thought that that was the greatest, and the nickname stuck. "Hey, are you crying? It sounds like you're crying, sweetie. Is everything all right?"

Julie started to speak, but as she did so the cell phone signal seemed to stop working.

"Hi Dad! Dad? Dad, are you there?" Julie stopped talking and looked at the phone. The signal seemed to return and Julie could still hear her father.

"Julie? Hello? Hello?" Julie's heart sank, and she had to bite back the tears.

"Dad? Dad? Oh God, please, Dad?" Julie could hear her father as plain as day.

"Julie? Damn these infernal things. Modern technology, my ass." Julie could now hear him talking to her mother. "I don't know, it sounded like she was crying. Yes, of course I'm going to call her back." Then, the signal went dead. But the cell phone did not ring. Through her tears, Julie clenched her teeth and kept trying to dial her father back, but the call just would not go through. She tried again and again. Julie looked up and out her windshield for a moment; she closed her eyes and drew in a deep breath, then waited. *Maybe Dad will be able to get through to me*, she thought.

The silence inside the Jeep Cherokee seemed to close in all around Julie. After what she had seen today, after what she had just been through, she did not dare open her eyes. There was still no call. Julie held the cell phone up to her chest; her eyes were still closed.

Julie breathed in deeply and held it, as she had been taught to do when meditating. She concentrated on her breath and her balance. She ignored the pictures in her head, and the sounds that she seemed to somehow still hear. While in this state, Julie prayed for strength and began to feel better. She opened her eyes again, looking into the brilliant sunshine and the now-serene waters before her. That was when she could sense it and see it. Julie could only just make it out in her furthest peripheral vision that someone was standing next to her Jeep. Their face was inches from Julie's. She could hear and feel their breath. She stifled a scream and spun halfway in her car seat.

It was a woman. She was smiling a toothy smile at Julie. Julie looked closely at her eyes. Each iris had specks of blue, green, gray, and brown. Julie had never seen eyes like that. They held her. The woman straightened up and Julie could see that she was quite tall and slender. She looked older but appeared to Julie to be quite beautiful. The woman was wearing golf attire. Julie realized that the woman was holding a golf club casually across her broad shoulders.

"If I keep hitting golf balls over here, I might as well just take up fishing!" she said.

Julie smiled politely. She remembered that just across the street from where she was parked was a tiny nine-hole golf course. Her smile widened.

"Oh, did your ball land over here somewhere?" Julie asked.

"Yes, it's right there, Julie." The woman pointed into the Jeep. Julie turned and gasped. There, sitting right in the center of the passenger seat, was a bright pink golf ball. Julie's jaw dropped open. She turned to look back at the woman. "What's the matter? You don't like pink on a golf ball? You think it's too showy, huh?" The woman nodded. "Maybe you're right. It's just that they're easier to find if you end up in a hazard, you know, like a Jeep or something." The woman waited while Julie stared. Then the woman smiled gently. "My ball, please, Miss Bernard?"

"Oh, I'm so sorry. Right, right, your ball… Here you go." Julie handed it to her.

"Thank you." The woman began to turn away, then stopped and turned back and faced Julie. "By the way, a very dear friend of mine asked me to give you a message: You have plenty of strength; next time, pray for wisdom." Chills went up and down Julie's spine. She stared into the woman's earnest face and she felt like crying.

"Who are you?" Julie said.

"That sounds like something you should be asking yourself, doesn't it?" The woman stared directly into Julie's eyes.

"What do you mean?"

"Why didn't you tell the inspector about your dream last night?" Julie looked into the woman's eyes. Her mouth dropped open. She could not speak for a moment or two as her brilliant mind raced and scrambled to make sense out of what was happening here.

"How do you know about my dream?"

"What, do you think you're the only one who has dreams?"

"No, of course not, no, but how do you know?"

"Because, unlike you, I know who I am, Julie." The woman bent down so that her face was inches from Julie's face. She never blinked. Her gaze held Julie frozen in her car seat. "I know what I am. I know that I am. I might even know what is. And maybe I know what should never be. I know who I am. I know what I am." The woman then lowered her voice to a whisper that was barely audible to Julie. "And I know who and what you are." Julie thought her heart was about to explode out of her chest with fear at those last words.

"Please, who are you?"

"No," the woman straightened herself up, still staring, "who are you?"

"Please, how do you know me? How do you know my name?" The woman stared down but did not answer.

"How could you know about the dream I had?" Julie stared up at the woman. Her wide, green eyes searched the woman's striking eyes. "Please, who are you?"

"No one of consequence. Now, call your father. I had to take a two-stroke penalty to see you." The woman muttered this as she strode across the street to resume her golfing.

Julie looked on, speechless. She watched as the woman clambered up a steep embankment on the other side of the street and out of sight behind a line of trees and brush that ran along the little golf course.

Julie dialed her father and the call went right through. She and her dad talked for fifteen minutes about nothing and everything. She admitted that she had been crying, but was able to be vague about why in order to keep her word to the police. Her dad voiced his concern for her, but Julie assured him that she was fine. By the time they said good-bye, Julie felt better. She looked at her watch. She was late for coffee with Father Knight at Dick's. But as she started her Jeep Cherokee and pulled the vehicle back onto Route 39, all Julie could think about was that remarkable woman and her pink golf ball. †

134

PART THREE
The Terrible Truth and The Beautiful Lie

"We want cattle who can finally become food;
He wants servants who can finally become sons."
—C.S. Lewis, The Screwtape Letters

CHAPTER 19
The Coffee Break

Julie steered her Jeep Cherokee into the parking lot of Dick's. The parking lot was full, as usual. She drove through the parking lot into a back lot directly behind the coffee and breakfast stop, which overlooked more woods and wildlife of Littleborough. Though she was late, Julie took some time to fix her makeup and brush her hair. She applied a little lipstick, looking at herself in the rear-view mirror. Her eyes were still a bit puffy from crying. There were dark circles under those puffy eyes, and no amount of makeup was going to hide that. Julie smiled into the mirror.

Figures, she thought, *coffee with the sweetest man I may have ever met and I look like I just walked off the set of a bad zombie movie.* Julie climbed out of her Jeep and hurried across the parking lot to Main Street and the entrance to Dick's.

Everybody in the town of Littleborough, Massachusetts, loved Dick's. It was a clean, well-lit place. Natural sunlight streamed through the many windows into the dining area. It was warm and very much more like a large living room with tables and chairs in it than a coffee and breakfast shop. There was a fireplace at the far end, next to where the cooks worked feverishly over two large grilles behind the counter.

The counter ran the entire length of the dining area, lined with very comfortable stools except for where the register and a large newspaper stand were positioned near the entrance. The walls were adorned with pictures of various trains and train stations. The building itself was right next to the train tracks that led through Littleborough. In the 1950s, 60s, and 70s, it was a train stop. The food was superb; the coffee was even better. The waitresses were all universally beloved in the town and Dick was as true a gentleman as there ever was.

Julie walked into the bright coffee shop. She smiled as she held the door open for an elderly couple that was just leaving. They smiled at Julie as they slowly walked past her and out the door.

"Julie! Hi!"

Julie smiled widely. "HI Michelle! How are you?" She threw her arms around her friend, who had thrown her arms around Julie.

"I'm doing great, sweetie. How are you?" Michelle smiled up into Julie's face. Her smile froze. A look of deep concern came into her deep brown eyes as she looked at Julie. Julie took her hands in hers and gently squeezed them.

"I'm doing fine, girl. No worries." Julie smiled. "It has, I will admit, been a crazy couple of days. I'm pooped, but good."

"Crazy like drinking and smoking late into the night and then being ravaged by a sex-crazed hunk of a man, that kind of crazy?" Both women laughed. Michelle nodded her head. Long, raven black hair tousled over her shoulders and halfway down her back. Her smooth, China white complexion dimpled when she smiled or laughed. Julie shook her head.

"I wish. I'll fill you in at our next evening of bridge." Michelle giggled. Julie and Michelle used the term "bridge" for whenever they were planning to have drinks and sometimes smoke pot. "I'm actually here to have coffee with James."

Michelle's mouth dropped open. "Oh my God, that's right. You texted me that! Ooh, he's so cute!"

Julie nodded. "I know. He's super sweet, too."

"Not too sweet, I hope. I loved what he said at the service this morning."

"Mmm. Speaking of texts, I got your text about your dreams. Are you still having them?"

Michelle nodded her head. "Yes, I am. They're totally erotic, Jules! They're awesome!"

The diner went silent. A number of heads turned to look at Julie and Michelle, but only for a moment. The men all smiled. The ladies all smirked except Bea, who burst out laughing. Julie and Michelle looked around the room for a moment, and then burst out laughing as well.

"Sorry!" Michelle waved her hand to everybody. "I know, too much information!" She and Julie giggled as everyone there resumed their breakfast or lunch.

"You texted something about a wolf?"

"Mmm-hmm. I think it's his spirit animal that's coming to see me in my dreams. He's this huge, bad-ass wolf. It's terrifying and totally orgasmic, girl."

Julie chewed her lower lip for a moment, deep in thought. "Michelle, you have to promise me something, okay?"

"Of course! Anything. What?"

Julie hesitated. She squeezed Michelle's hand in her own. "Just be careful, that's all."

Michelle peered into Julie's weary, green eyes. She furrowed her brow, then nodded her head. "Okay, I will be careful. I promise—if you promise to get some rest."

Julie smiled. "It's a deal. I will rest, I promise you that."

Michelle smiled. "You liar." They both burst out laughing. "I have to go to work, I'm late again! Good luck with James."

"Thanks." The two hugged once more before Michelle went out into the parking lot and the bright day outside. As Julie turned away from her friend, the smell of fresh-brewed coffee, honey maple bacon, and fresh baked bread mixed with the brisk autumn air filled her senses.

"Well, hello there, Julie."

"Hi, Dick." Dick was standing at the register behind the counter. He was a tall, elegant man. His hair was still black, despite his age of sixty. He wore old-style thick horn-rimmed glasses. He was always smiling.

"Gee whiz, Julie, you look like you're frozen stiff."

Julie smiled widely at Dick. "I hope this weather isn't a harbinger of things to come."

"Now, you've lived up here long enough to know that we're doomed." Julie laughed. "We're doomed, Julie, to another frigid snowy winter."

"No, please!" Julie said.

"Hi Julie." Bea, the most beloved of Dick's waitresses, had come over. "Is he threatening you with bad weather again?"

"I was merely giving Julie a stern warning," Dick said.

"Well, I've got a stern warning for you, scaring our customers like that. Dick, you're incorrigible!" Bea took Julie by the elbow as everyone who was in earshot laughed. "Come have a seat, dear."

"Thank you, Bea," Julie said still smiling. She looked around the room for Father Knight. He was sitting at a small table along the back wall, smiling at her. "I'm actually here to meet with Father Knight."

"Oh, you lucky duck!" Bea said. "He's cute and so sweet. Been that way since he was a baby. Good luck." Bea jabbed her elbow into Julie's rib cage as she whispered this. Julie laughed.

"Bea, you're so bad."

"It beats being dead, honey. I'll get you guys some menus."

"Thanks." Julie turned around in time to see her friend, Richard, a waiter at Dick's, approaching.

"Hi Julie." He gave her a gentle hug and kissed her lightly on the cheek. Julie kissed him back.

"Hi Richard. How are you?"

"I'm doing good, doing good. How are you, dear?" A look of concern came over his face as he looked at Julie. "You look tired, hon."

"I'm fine, thanks, Richard. I am a bit tired, but fine."

"You're here to meet with Father Knight?" Julie nodded, smiling. "You lucky little bitch. He's so hot, yum." Julie laughed her throaty laugh. Richard smiled. "Good luck, dear."

"Thanks. Let me know when your next recital is." Richard was a brilliant pianist. He gave her the 'thumbs up' as he returned to work. Julie walked over to where Father Knight was sitting. He stood his slender frame up as she approached. "You don't have to get up for me."

"I wanted to," James said. He stepped out from behind the table and gave Julie a hug.

"Mmmm," Julie rested her head on his shoulder and closed her eyes for a moment. "I could stay here for hours." Julie realized then how exhausted she was. She had to open her eyes for fear of dozing off.

"Oh dear, I don't think Dick's stays open that long." Julie smiled. They sat down.

"Here we go, kids." Bea arrived at their little table with napkins, silverware, menus, and glasses of water.

"Can I get you something to drink, coffee, tea?"

Julie looked at James, who shrugged. "Would you like something, Julie?"

"I'll have a decaf tea, please, Bea."

"All right, and for you, James? You ne'er do well, you stinker, asking Julie out instead of me. I saw you first, you know. You men of the cloth are all the same. You come in singing 'Hallelujah, hosanna in the highest,' and other sexy expressions. Then you have your wicked ways with the women of your choice, and zoom! You leave in a puff of robes and wafers because you're late for a mass. How do I get in on that action? Now," Julie, James, and half of the folks in Dick's were all laughing out loud, "coffee or tea, hon?"

"I'll have a decaf tea as well Bea, thanks."

"You've got it." Bea left to make the tea. Julie was still laughing. James could only stare into her green eyes. Her smile, white teeth and full lips with just a light hint of lipstick, and the way her cheeks dimpled made her seem so genuine to him at that moment. James couldn't be sure, but he suspected that at this moment he was falling in love with Julie Bernard. He reached his hand across the little table and took Julie's hand.

"Here we go." Bea arrived with two steaming decaf teas in clean, white mugs. "Now, how about food?" James looked back at Julie. Julie looked up at Bea, shaking her head.

"I'm not really hungry right now, Bea, thanks."

"The tea will be just fine," James said.

"Well, okay, lovebirds. But your children are going to turn out skinny like you two if you don't eat! Dingbats!" Bea shuffled off to clean off an empty table before seating several people who had just entered. She was still smiling.

Julie and James resumed looking at each other. Julie smiled. James smiled back. They both could only gaze at each other in silence. Time stopped. It was as if all the people in Dick's faded away for a moment. Then the breakfast and coffee shop seemed to fade with the people. Slowly the world followed suit, followed by the sun and the moon and the stars, and finally all of Creation. All that remained, and all that ever was, was James, Julie, and two cold cups of tea on a little table. There was that moment. And then life faded back in and everything returned.

"So, have you lived here all your life?"

"I was raised here. I've been away at seminary for several years, and college before that. But old Littleborough is pretty much the same as it was before, you know, small." Julie smiled.

"I think it's beautiful here," she said.

"Oh, so do I. I only said that in hopes of you smiling at me one more time." James smiled broadly at Julie. "What about you? How long have you lived in our humble borough?"

"This is my second year here and at the high school. The job is okay, though God knows I love the kids and not the administration." James laughed. "But I love it here. It's like, I don't know, it's like I totally belong here or something. You know what I mean?" Father Knight nodded his head. "I know the townspeople don't see it quite that way."

"What do you mean?"

"Well, you know, they're sweet, warm, kind, generous, and incredibly secretive."

"Oh, that. Yes." Both burst out laughing. Father Knight shook his head.

"Do you know, they won't let anyone not originally from here to attend any town meetings or even to have an audience with the Town Elders?"

Father Knight nodded. "Yes, I know." He smiled at Julie. "I left, so I have a seven-year waiting period myself before I can attend such a meeting."

Julie's eyes grew round and wide. "But you're our priest, for heaven's sake. That just doesn't make any sense."

"I guess from the outside, none of it makes much sense."

"It's so mysterious. I think it backfires more than they think. All I ever hear are these crazy rumors about the town, the people, how it was founded, and by who or by what."

"I think you might be right. Secrets never seem to accomplish what they're intended to. That much I do know," Father Knight said. Julie smiled.

"You're right," she said. Father Knight nodded. Julie regarded James. His eyes were perpetually smiling. His skin was light and smooth in contrast to his dark brown hair and soft brown eyes.

"Yes, let's talk about you, Julie Bernard." Julie smiled again. "Where are you from originally?"

"I grew up in Westport, Connecticut. It's a very well-to-do town with mansions, yachts, and golf courses. I went to school at New York University and got my doctorate at Columbia. I spent those years working as a volunteer at the Emily Carey Elementary School, in Harlem. It was a great experience for me. It was challenging, but I learned so much. Or, I think I did anyway." Julie smiled.

"Is your family still in Westport?"

"Yes, they are—my mom and dad, my two younger brothers, who are both two feet taller than me now, and a sister who is the youngest. They're the best." James smiled as Julie said this. "What about your family, James? Are they still here in Littleborough?" James shook his head and his smile vanished. Julie noticed that a cloud seemed to pass over his eyes when she asked this.

"No, my parents moved up to Rye, New Hampshire, when Dad retired. I had an older brother, but he died about fifteen years ago in an accident."

"Oh, I'm so sorry, James. I didn't mean to bring up something so painful or personal."

"No, that's okay, Julie. Really, it is. You could not have known. And it was a long time ago."

"It still must hurt." Julie's eyes searched his.

"Yes, it does. John and I were very close. He was a bit older than me, but he always found time to do stuff with me. We used to go fishing a lot." James smiled as he remembered this.

"Anyway, I'm happy to say that my family is also quite close. I'm very lucky." Julie smiled.

The two sat in silence for several minutes in Dick's, smiling at one another. Julie gazed into James' soft, brown eyes. They seemed to her to be honest, almost pure, and sad, she thought. Julie felt something in her belly. It was as if it had flipped, or done a summersault. Julie wondered if she was falling in love with Father James Knight.

The sound of Stevie Wonder came softly from Julie's purse. James could not suppress his smile. Julie smiled back and mouthed the word "sorry" as she retrieved her cell from her purse. The text was from Inspector Dahms: *several follow up questions for you-can meet anywhere anytime thx.* Julie responded with *ok will let you know.* She put her cell back in her purse and leaned forward.

"You know, I just want to say, James, I mean, I know I already told you this, but I thought that what you said at the memorial was so beautiful." James smiled. "It really meant a lot to all those people." James nodded.

"Well, thank you. I hope so."

"Is Madeline okay? She was so upset."

"She's fine. Father Freeman walked her home after the picnic. They stopped at Willy's on the way and he bought her a couple of bottles of her favorite wine. I was touched by the way you went to her when she started freaking out." James smiled at Julie as he spoke. "You try to help everyone, don't you?" Julie smiled back.

"Don't you?" she said. He took her hand, again. A look of concern came over Julie's face.

"Is something wrong?" James asked.

Julie's eyes searched his. She had told herself that she wasn't going to ask. She had thought about it on the way over, and felt it would be better left alone. But she now realized that she had to know. She was worried about James, and what the tall man might want from him.

"Did something happen at the church earlier, I mean, that involved the police?"

"Yes, how did you know?"

"The chief mentioned it earlier today." Julie hesitated, biting her lower lip.

"Well, there was an accident next door to the church. A little boy fell into a large sinkhole in the backyard of his parents' house. The EMTs think he may have broken his ankle. But other than that, he should be fine."

"Oh."

"Why do you ask?"

"Oh, nothing. The chief didn't say anything about a boy falling into a sinkhole. He had mentioned an incident at the church and that you had described a tall, thin man."

"Oh, him." James rolled his eyes up toward the ceiling and then looked back at Julie. "Yes, I did see a tall, thin man in the church. And I don't mind saying he is the strangest person I have ever seen," James said. Julie's eyes grew wide. A look of concern came over James's face. "Why, do you know who this person is or something?"

"No, I don't know him. I saw him, too. And when I described him to the police, they mentioned that you had seen him. But I never got a good look at his face. It was weird…"

"I couldn't get a good look either. It is weird…"

"Yeah, it was almost like, like…"

"His face seemed to change constantly, like…"

"Yes, it did. His eyes totally seemed to change."

"You're right. They did," James said. Hearing Julie say this seemed to jog his memory a bit. There was a pause. James looked at Julie. "He certainly doesn't seem to be very nice." There was a heartbeat of silence. Julie burst out laughing. "What?" James watched as Julie just kept laughing harder and harder. "What?"

"Nothing, I'm sorry. It's nothing," Julie said, still laughing.

James smiled despite himself. "What did I say?"

"It wasn't what you said, James, but how you said it that was so funny to me. I'm sorry." Julie could not stop smiling.

"Well, don't be sorry. I could watch you smile or laugh until the end of days."

Julie smiled and reached her hand across the little table and took his hand. There the two sat silently for a few minutes as their decaf tea grew ice-cold. Father Knight furrowed his brow.

"Wait a minute, where did you see this man?"

Julie's smile ran from her face. She swallowed hard as she tried to think of what she could say. James could see that Julie was reticent to say anything about it. "Hey, it's okay if you don't want to tell me. Whenever you feel like telling me, then tell me. It's okay."

Julie smiled wearily at James. "You are so sweet," she said. "I promised the chief and the inspector I would not say anything about it to anyone. I'm just not sure if that should apply to you since you've seen this man too." James nodded. Julie looked down at her untouched mug of decaf tea. She closed her eyes and breathed in and out slowly. She looked up at James.

He was smiling at her.

"You look very tired, Julie Bernard." Julie smiled and nodded. "Come on. Let me walk you to your car." They both stood up. James left Bea some money on the table next to the untouched decaf teas.

"This is too large of a tip, padre!" Bea called out as they approached the door.

James and Julie waved, and then left Dick's. The sunshine was brilliant, making both of them have to shade their eyes with one hand as they walked across the parking lot. Julie shivered.

"May I?" James put his arm around Julie's shoulder.

"Thanks." Julie leaned into him. When they got to the Jeep, Julie turned around to face James. Her smile had vanished. Her look was serious. She put her arms up around his neck. James put his arms around Julie's waist.

They kissed. At first they both kissed lightly, their lips barely touching. James was awed at how soft Julie's lips were. They began to hold each other more firmly, pressing themselves together as closely as they could and warming each other in the cold autumn air. Their lips still barely touching, their tongues gently danced. The sensation of Julie's tongue on his own sent an electric shock through James. This same sensation raced through Julie, making her entire body tingle all over. James's heart thumped in his chest. His temperature began to rise, and he began to get an erection. Finally their lips met more firmly. They each became breathless and they had to stop. Neither of them was cold any more.

Julie sighed and looked up at James. He was staring at Julie. A slight rattling noise came across the parking lot from the back of the little breakfast and coffee shop. Julie and James looked over just in time to see most of the townspeople inside Dick's quickly moving away from the back windows, pretending that they had not, in fact, been watching Julie and James kissing.

They turned back to each other, smiling. Julie burst out laughing. James shrugged, shaking his head. They smiled into other's eyes and said good-bye. James knew he was in love. Julie waved as she pulled her Jeep out of the parking lot. He was walking back to the church. They had agreed to have dinner tonight at seven. Both smiled all the way home. †

CHAPTER 20
Pigs in Blankets

"Me? I didn't draw anybody up here. I run up and down this hill every day." Billy was looking at the strange man when he said this. The little old man smiled. His eyes seemed to dance and shimmer when he smiled. Billy looked sideways at him. This made the strange little old man begin to laugh. "What's so funny?" Billy said.

"Not you, Billy. I'm not laughing at you, son." Being called *son* hit Billy like a thunderbolt. He had never been called that before by anyone, ever. He swallowed hard. The man looked up at Billy, his smile vanished. "Are you all right, Billy? You look like you were struck by a thunderbolt."

"What? No. I'm fine."

"I really wasn't laughing at you, Billy. I was laughing at this strange circumstance." The man began to chuckle again. He was shaking his head.

"I still don't see what's so funny," Billy said.

"That's partly why I was laughing so hard. You see, Billy, when something funny happens, and someone there isn't laughing because they do not think it was funny, and they look terribly serious, well, that can make it seem even funnier. That's all." Billy appeared, to the little old man, to be thoroughly unconvinced. The little old man thought for a moment. Then, he looked back at Billy. "Have you ever made your mother really angry? But you thought it was funny? So, you're trying very hard not to laugh? But you do laugh because she's so angry? Then she sees that you are laughing, and so she gets even angrier, and you laugh even harder?" Billy was nodding his head now, smiling.

"Yeah! Yeah. I remember when she was dating this pothead. He was a total dick. So, one day I flushed his pot down the toilet. Dude, she had a baby cow! I never laughed so hard in my life!" Billy was delighted to see the effect that his story had on the little old man. He doubled over with laughter. His hands were on his stomach as if he feared his sides might split open. Billy also noticed that this little old man's laughter seemed to carry and echo all around and above him. It reverberated beneath his feet and almost seemed to shake Fears Hill itself as it thundered through the forest and woodlands. Billy smiled broadly at the little old man as he once again took out his white handkerchief and dabbed at his eyes with it.

"Oh my, mercy me! You flushed his pot down the toilet... ha-ha-ha-ha!" The little old man went off on another fit of laughter. Billy waited. After a bit, he finally seemed to get a hold of himself. He looked at Billy. "That was an outstanding thing to do, Billy. Really, that was topnotch! Bully for you, young person!" The little old man was still laughing a bit and shaking his head slightly as he spoke. A moment passed.

"I hate bullies," Billy said. The little old man stopped and looked at Billy. He then fell onto the ground at the base of the great and ancient tree, laughing uncontrollably. Billy watched this spectacle of a very well-dressed little old man roaring with laughter and rolling around on the ground amongst the tall, yellow grasses, and the large, gnarled roots of the great tree with a mix of confusion and fascination.

The little old man slapped the ground with his open palms and then rolled onto his back, kicking his legs in the air. He curled up into a little ball with his arms folded across his stomach. Billy honestly thought that this little old man was going to puke. Though his laughter was now muffled, he could hear that it had changed into a strange and very high-pitched sound. It almost sounded like he was crying. At one point, Billy thought the little old man was saying something, still while laughing, speaking straight into the ground with that same, strange high-pitched voice.

Finally, this strange, little old man began to calm himself down. He rolled back over onto his back, trying to catch his breath. He reached into his coat pocket for his white handkerchief. Billy rolled his eyes, looking skyward.

"Why don't you just staple that thing to your face? It would save a lot of time," he said. The little old man, who was just sitting up, immediately went back into convulsive fits of laughter. This made Billy laugh too. And there, the two laughed out loud for several minutes. Billy helped the little old man get back up on his feet. He then picked up his hat off of the ground and handed it to him.

"Thank you, Billy." The little old man smiled at him. He held his hand out toward the pathway that lead back down to the base of Fears Hill. "Shall we?"

They began to make their way down Fears Hill. On the way down, the little old man had explained to Billy what he had meant by "bully for you."

Then Billy asked him what he had meant when he said that he had been "drawn" to that spot.

"Maybe we can talk about that over some pancakes and sausages."

"What?"

"I'm asking if you would like some pancakes and sausages, my treat. Oh, I realize it is, in fact, suppertime for most mortals in this neck of Creation. But I do find that the best meals are made up of the stuff of breakfast, don't you, Billy?"

Billy looked at the little old man earnestly. "I love having breakfast for dinner too!"

The little old man smiled. "Well then?"

"That sounds so good. But my mother is going to wonder where I am. I probably should have gotten home by now, if I had kept running, I mean," Billy said.

"Is she home from work yet?"

"No. I haven't seen her since yesterday morning. She's been seeing this really weird dude. He's really tall, really creepy, and he's always wearing black, with all kinds of jewelry and stuff. Sometimes she goes to see him straight from her work. She usually calls me at the house if she's going to get home late, but she must have forgot last night. I don't have a cell phone. I'm like the only guy on earth who doesn't have one." Billy was shaking his head as he said this.

"Well now, Billy. You're not the only one." The little old man was smiling his broad smile.

"You don't have a cell phone in that fancy coat? All you have is that white hanky, huh?" Billy smiled mischievously when he said this. The little old man laughed.

"I actually have my car keys and my wallet in here, too. It's up to you, Billy. But if you would like some pancakes and sausages—or whatever you like, really—it's my treat! You don't have to worry; I'll explain to your mom if she gets mad." Billy smiled, and nodded emphatically. "Grand!" The little old man smiled. "My car is this way. I parked over on the other side of the hill."

"That's cool."

The sun had almost set behind the trees to the west. It created a beautiful orange and yellow sky just above the tree line and reflected those same glorious colors just below a bank of white puffy cumulus clouds.

"Where are we going to go get pancakes and sausages?" Billy asked. The little old man smiled.

"Why, the International House of Pancakes, of course!"

"Yes!" Billy pumped his fist. The little old man laughed.

"It's my favorite too. I mean, speaking quite frankly, Billy, if the International House of Pancakes isn't your favorite place to eat, then sir, may your soul be damned for eternity."

"Amen!" Billy shouted as the two rounded the bend and into view of the little old man's car. A tan Lexus chariot waited for them. Driving a modern chariot was a new and awkward experience for the little old man. But he drove slowly and with great care so as to avoid any issues with mortal drivers.

It was several miles west on Route 39, which was his favorite road, and just over a series of railroad tracks and presto! Right there by the tracks was that heavenly bastion known as the International House of Pancakes. The two new friends found themselves being seated by a pleasant and slightly plump little waitress named Beatrice.

"Coffee, hon?" she asked the little old man.

"Oh, yes please." He smiled warmly at her as she poured the freshly brewed coffee into a clean white mug on the table in front of him.

"How about you, dear?" Beatrice smiled at Billy. Billy was looking out of the window at the train tracks, which ran along parallel to the building. He looked up at the smiling waitress.

"You don't drink coffee do you Billy?" the little old man asked.

"No!" Billy made a face. This made the little old man start laughing.

"Would you like some hot chocolate?" Beatrice asked.

"Yeah!"

"Sure! I'll be right back." Beatrice went back for the cocoa. The little old man held his clean white mug of coffee up to his face and he smelled the rich aroma of the brew. His eyes closed as he did this. Then he sipped it. He breathed out a contented sigh. He opened his eyes and looked at Billy, smiling.

"My goodness gracious, that is so very good, I must say." He took another small sip. He then placed the mug back down on the table and folded his hands.

"Here you go, dear." Beatrice had returned to their table with a clean white mug filled to the very brim with steaming hot chocolate. Layered on top of the hot chocolate was a good-sized dollop of whipped cream. The little old man smiled up at her.

"Thank you, Beatrice."

"Yeah, thanks," Billy said.

"No problem, dear. Would you like menus?" The little old man looked at Billy. Billy was looking up at Beatrice, nodding his head.

"Yes, please," he said. Beatrice pulled two large laminated menus from the back of her apron and placed them down on the table in front of Billy and the little old man.

"Thank you," they both said this at the same time. Beatrice smiled.

"You take your time and just call me over when you have decided." She moved toward the entrance of the dining area to seat several more people who had just come in. Along with Billy and the little old man, there were only a couple of other tables that were occupied.

There the two lost souls sat in silence. The little old man looked over the menu, quietly pondering what he should eat. Billy continued to watch the train tracks to see if any trains might go rumbling by. After a little while Beatrice had made her way back to their table.

"Have we decided yet?"

The little old man looked at Billy. "What do you think Billy?"

"I'm ready to order if you are."

"Splendid!"

"Can I have the pigs in blankets?"

"Sure!" Beatrice wrote down Billy's order.

"And for you sir?"

The little old man was smiling broadly at Billy. He then looked slowly up at Beatrice, still smiling. His eyes held her. Lights seemed to almost dance wildly in the large pupils of his eyes. They were like some sort of window into another world, or time, or both, she thought. Beatrice looked closer at his eyes. They were multicolored! She could see green and blue, gray and brown! His eyes seemed to her at that moment to be so deep, and the way they shimmered! Beatrice thought for one moment that she could just lose herself in this little old man's eyes forever and never come back. He spoke gently and this released her from his gaze. She caught her breath.

"I have absolutely got to try the pigs in blankets, myself. That positively sounds to me like the ultimate soul food!"

Beatrice laughed as she wrote down his order. She then took their orders back to the kitchen. She returned immediately to freshen up the little old man's coffee.

"Thank you, Beatrice." She smiled warmly.

"Not at all, it's my pleasure." She made her way to another table.

"What a magnificent creature."

"Who, her?" Billy turned around to look. "She is?" The little old man smiled at Billy and nodded his head.

"Yes. Her." He deeply inhaled the aroma of his freshened coffee as he held the clean white mug up to his nose. Then he sipped it and sipped it again before putting it down. He smiled as he observed Billy doing the same with his cocoa. Billy put his clean white mug down on the table and looked across at the little old man.

"Why do you think she is magnificent?"

"Well, consider the facts, Billy. Here is a person who has every reason to be bitter or even angry at life. Once, she was happily married with at least two children, maybe more. Now she is divorced and forced to raise the children alone. Her job is a tough one. She is on her feet all day. And naturally she is expected to be pleasant to everyone who she waits on. It is not a high-paying job. It must be very difficult for her to make ends meet.

"Her life is hard. And every day she wakes up, she is afraid for her children because she does not know what will happen to them if something should happen to her. Her life, and by extension, her children's lives, are day to day. Her life is lonely. She carries on all by herself. In the end, she knows that for her children to survive this world, for them to have just a glimmer of hope to thrive in this world, all depends upon her. And only her. There is no one else. That is stressful. That is a tremendous amount of pressure on her. She lives under this pressure, on this lonely path. She goes to bed each night with those same thoughts weighing on her mind. And she wakes up with those same fears and worries. Yet, she never fails to love her children. Through it all, she somehow manages a brave face that is tender, loving, and nurturing. And here she is, Billy. Serving us these delicious drinks and soon a delicious meal. And she is as kind and sweet to us as if we were her own family. She remains positive. Therefore, she is magnificent." With that the little old man picked up his clean white mug in both hands and sipped contentedly at his coffee.

Billy drank his hot cocoa as he thought about what the little old man had said. "You noticed all that, huh?"

The little old man nodded. "I can see it in her eyes."

Billy looked sideways at the little old man, almost making him laugh. "Her eyes?"

"Yes. It has been written that the eyes can be the window to the soul. But there is more to it. The eyes are a conduit to and from the soul." Billy furrowed his eyebrows. The little old man just smiled.

There was a period of silence during which Billy was deep in thought.

"Do you do that sort of thing all the time?"

"Yes."

"Why?"

"It's fun."

Billy thought for a moment longer. "What do you see in my eyes?" The little old man smiled at Billy. Billy smiled back, nervously.

"Well, the problem there, Billy, is that since we met, you and I have been walking around and sitting around chatting. So, I have been able to learn a great deal about you because of the many things you have told me about yourself, your mother, and your life." Billy nodded his head. The little old man went on. "Now, when I first saw you as you came running out of the woods, there it was clear to me—and anyone else, mind you—that you are in good physical condition. You don't mind pain. Or, at the very least, you're able to block it out of your head. I could also see that you are angry."

Billy was listening intently to the little old man. "I'm not angry," he said.

But the little old man only shook his head, then continued. "I mean you are very angry at the world. You think that your mother is weak and stupid. You think your teachers and coaches and fellow students are also stupid and cruel." Billy laughed nervously when the little old man said this. "And your father is somehow not in the picture. You are certainly angry with him." The little old man paused, then asked, "How am I doing?"

"That's perfect. I can't believe you could tell all that just from seeing me."

The little old man held his hand up, stopping Billy. "Well, don't be too impressed, Billy. I'm sure that some of those conclusions that I have drawn are deduced from subsequent conversations that you and I have had since first meeting. For example, your mom. You told me about the time you flushed her boyfriend's drugs down the toilet." The little old man laughed a bit as he said this; Billy laughed too. "That is how I came to the conclusion that things aren't perfect for you and your mother, and that your father is gone. It wasn't just from my seeing you. Do you know what I mean?"

"Yeah. I guess I do." Billy looked back out of the window at the train tracks.

"Still, it must be very hard for your mother to be so all alone." Billy swallowed hard, and looked down at the table momentarily. He then looked back up at the little old man.

"You mean, like this waitress lady here." The little old man smiled and nodded his head gently.

"Exactly, Billy. Life is brutal and frightening for all warriors."

"Warrior? She's just my mother."

"Mothers are warriors, Billy."

"Here we go!" Beatrice had arrived with their food. "More coffee for you, dear?"

"Oh my, yes please." The little old man smiled.

"Right." Beatrice smiled back as she went to get Billy's milk. The little old man looked at Billy. Billy was busily spreading butter all over his pancakes, which were each rolled around a sausage. The little old man did the same. He then observed as Billy poured hot maple syrup all over his pancakes and sausages. Again, the little old man did the same.

"Here you go, dear." Beatrice placed a tall, ice-cold glass of milk in front of Billy.

"Mmmm, ffthank you." Billy's mouth was full of pancakes when he had said this. It made Beatrice and the little old man laugh.

"And more hot coffee for you, hon."

"Excellent. Thank you, Beatrice."

"You are very welcome. Let me know if I can get you guys anything else, okay?"

The little old man smiled at Beatrice and nodded. He looked at Billy. "Well Billy, how are those pigs in blankets, then?"

"They're awesome!" Billy barely stopped eating long enough to take the breath to answer the little old man. The little old man smiled. He then devoured a little pig himself, with some maple syrup. It was good, he thought. And so, the two newfound friends sat and ate their pigs in blankets and watched as no trains went by. †

CHAPTER 20.20
Last Call

After the cookout at St. Mark's Church, Father Freeman drove Bishop Richter back to St. Anne's Church in the little town neighboring Littleborough. The fifteen-minute drive was made in silence. Both men's thoughts drifted. The subject of their thoughts was the same. Father Freeman pulled his old blue Chevy truck into the driveway of the church and parked.

"Can you come in for a drink, Pat?"

The bishop nodded. "There's something I'd like to talk with you about as well, my friend. I have a feeling we are on the same page of the playbook." Father Freeman nodded and they climbed out of the truck.

The two men of God slowly walked along the rear walkway and up the three steps leading up to the screen door of the back entrance of the church. They entered and walked down the main hall and into the office where they had been just the day before with Father Knight. Father Freeman went straight to the little cabinet that he kept his scotch in. He poured two drinks and put the bottle down on the desk. They both sat together in the cushioned chairs in front of the desk. They drank in silence. The bishop refilled their glasses and then eased back into his chair with an audible grunt. He lit a cigarette.

"Lucifer popped by for a visit after the cookout today," he said. Smoke slowly exhaled through his nostrils. Father Freeman nodded.

"I saw him walking into the back door of St. Mark's while I was cleaning off the grill. We exchanged the customary 'one-finger' salute." Now the bishop was nodding his head. He leaned over and reached for his glass, then sipped it thoughtfully.

"He seems to think that we summoned him," the bishop said.

"He thinks we challenged him?"

"That's what he was implying."

"Did he say anything about what happened to Miguel?"

"He certainly mocked his death. He mentioned his heart attack. But strangely, he didn't take any credit for it. And he never mentioned the holy water, either. Strange."

"It is peculiar." Father Freeman said. "It makes no sense. Lucifer must be mistaken." Father Freeman paused. "But to think that he has already taken the life of an infant, stained our holy water with the child's blood, and took Miguel… It's too late to avert a confrontation." He took out a cigarette and put it in his mouth.

"I'll bet he's harassing Father Knight as we speak, "the bishop said, swallowing hard. Father Freeman looked at him. He was holding a lighter up to light his cigarette. He took the cigarette out of his mouth, shaking his head.

"Poor James. He's never going to understand this." Now the bishop looked at Father Freeman.

"Why not? The child surely believes." Father Freeman nodded his head at this, and lit his cigarette. He blew the smoke out straight up in the air.

"Oh, James believes in God, all right," he said. "But he's young, Pat. He is definitely of the new-age mindset. You know, the Bible is allegory, the modern scholarship that concludes there is no sufficient proofs or tests as to the existence of God, Jesus, a soul, an afterlife, the devil, or hell, or even evil for that matter. To James, evil is simply the absence of love or light. Only the truly insane do evil." The bishop had been nodding his head as he listened. He looked at his friend.

"Yeah, I'm sorry to have to say this, but I do know what you mean." He sipped his scotch. "I meet many modern scholars, students, professors, and young priests, like us." The two men laughed. "They all think this way, with precious few exceptions. And don't get me wrong, like you, I know that these kids are brilliant. They have access to one thousand times the amount of information and data we had access to. The archaeological leaps we are making due to the advancements in technology really does make the past seem as if it were right at our fingertips. But in a strange way, the search for truth seems to be leading us away from truth."

"I agree." Father Freeman finished his glass of scotch. He refilled both glasses.

"You're worried about young James?" the bishop said.

"Yes. It's tough to fight something you don't believe in," Father Freeman said.

"That's true enough," the bishop said. "You were quite close with his father?"

"Joseph and I were childhood friends here in Littleborough. We grew up together, schooled together, we chased girls together. We played high school football and tennis together. We smoked our first cigarette and drank our first beer together. We got caught by Joe's mother drinking and smoking, and subsequently were grounded together." The two men of God laughed. "Joe was a doctor in Littleborough for years. I was at St. Mark's Church, as you know. I baptized all of his children."

"I seem to remember that the oldest son died mysteriously," the bishop said. Father Freeman nodded his head, sighing.

"That was fifteen years ago. It was one of the toughest funerals I ever had to do. John was his name. He drowned in one of the ponds on St. Mark's school property. He had gone fishing by himself, slipped on a steep bank, and hit his head as he went into the water. James took it very badly. John was his hero. For a while James's behavior was a concern. He got into some trouble at school, you know, drugs and alcohol. But he worked it out."

"You were there for him then as now, John," the bishop said.

"James's mother, Marie, was a pillar of strength. She was faithful, resilient, so strong. I guess now James really is on his own."

"Well, not entirely. The church is sending a Judge to help us through this situation." Father Freeman raised his eyebrows.

"A Judge, huh? I've heard of them, never met one, though. Have you?"

The bishop shook his head. "No, never. I've heard that there is only one actual Judge, not a group of them. But who the hell knows for sure?"

"Have you ever asked the Teacher?" Father Freeman asked.

"No. I don't know of a single Bishop who has." The bishop chuckled. "Not one of us has had the guts to ask much of anything from the Teacher." Now Father Freeman laughed.

"Understandable enough. I wonder what she'll be like."

"I'm told she's their best." The bishop shrugged his thick shoulders as he spoke. "Maybe she is the only one we have. She's probably already here, gathering information. We'll meet with her later, I'm sure, when she's good and ready to meet us." He lit another cigarette.

"I hope so. I've always wondered if they were real. And, if they were real, I've always wanted to meet a Judge. Do you think she would answer some questions, if we asked her politely?" Father Freeman looked over at the Bishop, who shrugged his shoulders again. "Very politely?"

"Maybe. I don't really know what they're allowed to say and what they may not be able to say to us low-life priests." He smiled mischievously at his friend. Father Freeman smiled back.

"Yeah, we're humble, all right." The two men of God burst out laughing. The bishop stubbed his cigarette out in the tiny ashtray on the desk. Their smiles faded from their faces. The bishop spoke.

"Hell, between the Judge being here and Satan being here, I would say James is in for a bit of an education, then."

"More like a rude awakening, I think," Father Freeman said. †

CHAPTER 21
Over Easy,
and Don't Turn Them Over...

Inspector Dahms entered the old and beloved establishment known as Dick's. Officer Tubbs and Officer Franklin followed behind him. The inspector smiled and nodded at Bea. The three policemen had agreed to meet here exactly one hour after they had returned to the station from the crime scene.

Inspector Dahms had needed to update the chief on things and had hoped to get a report from Billy Pollard on the tracking and hunting of the wolves. Officer Tubbs, who was the shift supervisor, had needed to make out his shift report. Officer Franklin had needed to take a bath. He had not, however. He went down to the first floor of the headquarters and into the men's locker room with the express intent of showering and cleaning himself up. He found himself sitting alone on the bench in front of his closed locker door. In his hands he held several files that the inspector had given him to read over. Without a single thought, he showered. In the shower he could only stand under the tepid water, staring. He did not wash himself. He could only let the water run down his entire body as he stood there, cold and naked. He dried himself and dressed. He then sat back down on the bench in front of his locker, holding the unopened files in his lap. He hadn't even realized he had bathed until Officer Tubbs had finished with the reports, which took the full hour, and had then come down to get him. Officer Franklin was still sitting there. Staring. What was extraordinary to Officer Franklin was that he hadn't been thinking, or processing, or anything. He had simply sat, stone cold still and silent, for almost an hour.

"Hey Ben, you okay?" Officer Tubbs had asked. He could only nod his head as he got up and followed Officer Tubbs out of the locker room.

"Well, hello, Tom." Bea smiled up at him through her glasses. "This table's clean and ready if you want it, hon." When Bea turned toward Officer Franklin, she stopped short and her mouth dropped open. "Good heavens, young man, just look behind those ears! Benjamin, you're positively filthy!"

Officer Franklin hung his head. "Yes ma'am."

Bea clucked and shook her head up at him. She stood barely five feet tall and the policemen all towered over her. Her hair was cut severely short. A very handsome person, she wore no makeup, ever. She was heavyset, her lower body was extremely powerful from a high school and college career in field hockey and then waitressing at Dick's for thirty or so years. She then turned her pale, round face up at the inspector with a smile. Her beady, blue eyes smiled warmly.

"Tom, where did you take this poor young man to get that dirty? Don't try to tell me that you didn't have a hand in this." The inspector and Officer Tubbs both smiled. "The restroom is right back there, dear."

"Thank you, ma'am." Officer Franklin walked behind the long counter toward the rest room to try and wash the remaining soot and ash. Cooks and waitresses scattered in every direction as he passed so as not to get filthy themselves. They all were suppressing their laughter.

"Thank you, Bea, that's perfect."

The inspector and Officer Tubbs both sat down at a table in the back corner of the dining area. Bea poured them both some hot coffee.

"I'll be right back to take your orders."

The inspector and Officer Tubbs sat in silence for several moments. They both looked at each other. Officer Tubbs shook his head. The inspector drank some of his hot coffee. He then looked back at Officer Tubbs and smiled a tired smile.

"Well, that was a very interesting performance."

"What the hell was that?" Officer Tubbs said.

"Well, Officer Tubbs, it's a proven method of investigating complex crime scenes. Initially, of course, you do what we did. Go through and record the entire crime scene and reconstruct the exact events based on the physical evidence and what we each witnessed last night. Based on that reconstruction, Officer Franklin re-enacted the whole thing in order to gain insights into those events we wouldn't otherwise have. That's why it was so emotional for him, I think."

The door to the restroom opened and a much cleaner Officer Franklin emerged to the applause of the wait staff and cooks. He smiled his wide boyish smile and blushed. He nodded at the two men as he took his seat opposite them.

"Coffee?" Bea asked him.

"No, Bea. I want the biggest breakfast you guys have."

"One 'beat the house,' three eggs, three pancakes, toast, home fries, and your choice of bacon, sausage, or ham." Officer Franklin's wide blue eyes lit up through his thick glasses.

"I'll have that."

"Okay, bacon, sausage, or ham?"

"Yes please."

Bea laughed. "Okay. How do you like your eggs?"

"Fried, sunny side up, please."

"Anything to drink, hon?"

"Can I have a glass of milk and a glass of orange juice too?"

"Of course, you can! I'm just going to refill the inspector's mug with more coffee…No more for you, dear?" Officer Tubbs smiled and shook his head politely. "All righty then, we'll get your order in right away."

Officer Franklin was beaming now. "Thank you, ma'am!"

As Bea walked away, he looked at Inspector Dahms and then at Officer Tubbs, still grinning. Officer Franklin patted the table with his open palms as if playing the bongo drums. His small delicate hands and pudgy little fingers went *thumpity-thump-thump* a few times.

He smiled again, and then looked at Inspector Dahms, and then at Officer Tubbs, and then back to the inspector. Both men stared in silence. Officer Franklin stopped his drumming and licked his lips.

"You guys probably want to know what I found out, huh?"

"Here we go dear, one 'beat the house' special with bacon, sausage, and ham." Bea placed two plates that seemed to be holding an impossible amount of food on them in front of Officer Franklin. She then placed a large glass of ice-cold milk and a large glass of orange juice next to the two plates. "Does anyone need anything else?" The three men all shook their heads. "Okay. I'll be back with more coffee for you in a few minutes, Tom."

The inspector smiled at Bea. "Thank you, Bea."

"Yes, thank you, Bea," echoed Officer Franklin, his mouth was already full of eggs and pancakes.

"My pleasure!"

Officer Franklin ate as if he had not eaten once in his lifetime. Inspector Dahms calmly drank more of his coffee. Officer Tubbs glared impatiently at Officer Franklin. It did not take long for the young man to finish. The two plates were practically clean. Officer Franklin washed it all down with the cold glass of milk. He then sat back and collected himself for a moment.

"Boy, was that good!" he declared. "Anyway, I have good news, bad news, and unbelievably bad news. The good news is, we have the people who are responsible for the deaths of Megan Streeter, Caroline Hart, Jed Prescott, and the unknown victim. They are all dead, lying in that clearing in the woods. In fact, the only actual victims of murder here are the four people who were crucified. The rest of those people were all involved in the ritual; they were all complicit in the thing. So, you were right about that, Inspector.

"The bad news is, at least one worshipper, probably the leader, did escape, somehow. He must have because whatever was used to collect the blood of the innocents is missing and none of the remaining bodies at the crime scene match the size of his feet. So, you were right about that, too, Inspector.

"The unbelievably bad news is that whatever that thing is that killed all those other people, the worshippers, is still out there somewhere in our woods." Officer Tubbs looked at Inspector Dahms for a moment. The inspector nodded.

"Thing? What do you mean thing, Franklin? It's a pack of wolves. You heard the howling."

"Yes, Tubbs. I heard the howling. It was one animal. It was one really loud and really big animal, but only one."

Inspector Dahms's cell vibrated its low tone. It was a text from the chief: *tracking crime scene now. one big animal. any word from hunting party?* The inspector responded: *no word be careful. keep in touch.*

"Sorry, go on, Franklin."

"Yes, sir. I guess the most telling things that we found were the absolutely huge branches that were ripped off the tops of some of the trees along the canopy around the clearing. The fact that they were only a little bit burned during the fire burst proves that they came down just after the burst, seconds after. The odor of burnt hair at the scene is worth noting. The seemingly impossible extinguishing of the fire is the central question, and so is also what gives us our answer.

"I also agree that whatever put out the fire came from above. It is what ripped those limbs downward as it descended. It landed on top of the bonfire causing the fire to burst out in all directions and then suffocating it completely out in a matter of seconds. What could do that, Inspector?"

"The only possibility I have been able to think of is that the people responsible for this ritual somehow rigged something above the bonfire that they planned to use to put it out. Maybe a huge tarp or some other kind of fireproof fabric was used. And maybe it accidentally dropped during the ritual. Though I am aware we found no evidence of a tarp or ropes or anything like that."

"That's right. So, think back to last night. The moment the fire went out is exactly when we heard the first really loud, horrible howl."

"That is true, Franklin," Inspector Dahms said.

Officer Tubbs shrugged. "So?"

"So, it seems to me that the timing of the howl and the smell of burnt hair is suggestive."

"Suggestive of what?"

"It suggests that whatever it is that came down onto the bonfire got burned by the fire and howled. It is so large, it somehow fanned the flames outward, and then almost immediately after that extinguished the fire. It then proceeded to tear everybody there apart!" Inspector Dahms gently touched Officer Franklin's arm as a signal to lower his voice in the coffee shop. Several elderly men sitting at the counter had turned and were glancing over at their table nervously.

"Sorry, Inspector. I'm just a little hyped up, you know, from the crime scene and then the yummy food."

"I understand. But listen carefully, now. Wolves don't climb trees. There are no known animals here in Littleborough that can do what you think this thing has done. Not one."

"But Inspector, you saw the paw prints."

The inspector nodded. "Yes, I saw them, Franklin. But the chaos in that clearing, coupled with many tracks that could have been enlarged by the rear paw stepping just behind and inside the print left by the fore paw as the animals attacked can trick even an expert eye into thinking the print is enormous. I, therefore, couldn't be sure."

"I see what you mean," Officer Franklin said. The inspector's cell vibrated. It was the chief: *animal came from tree tops. headed towards doc robinson's place.* He replied: *ok.*

"All right, Officer Franklin, Officer Tubbs, I should tell you now that the chief thinks it's only one animal as well." Both patrolmen were silent. "I would like to hear what you found from your reenactment now."

"Yes, sir. This was a sophisticated group of people. They prepared and performed this thing in a way that makes this case quite singular, I think." Officer Franklin glanced at the inspector nervously. His gaze returned to his empty plate and he went on. "All of the people there were specially chosen by the leader. They chose the location very carefully.

"We can divide the crime scene into two. The first part was this ritual. The participants file silently through the woods from all four paths that lead to the clearing. The leader is there, waiting. From the length of his stride, I'd say he was probably tall, like your height, Inspector. He is probably a charming, charismatic, and attractive man. He probably has some money and a high station in life.

"The victims are already tied up onto the trees. A broth is imbibed by the participants. It is also probably forced on the victims. Toxicology should find a powerful narcotic and a hallucinogen present in the bodies.

"They surround the leader, kneeling. He probably speaks or reads from their bible; I don't know if they're prayers or whatever. Then five of them start drumming, bongos, congas, and kete' drums. They all dance around the bonfire, first clockwise, then counterclockwise. There is chanting or singing. I assume they simply repeat what the leader chants. Sex seems to occur spontaneously. Then, one by one, the victims are each killed, sacrificed, and their blood is collected into some sort of vessel, a cup or chalice. There are more incantations or whatever after that in order to appease and summon the being."

"All right, wait a minute," Officer Tubbs said. "What do you mean by 'summon a being'?"

"The being in question I would presume to be the devil, Satan, Lucifer, or whatever name you want to call it."

"Yes, that's right, Officer Franklin," Inspector Dahms said. "The evidence certainly points to a ritual to raise a devil."

"So, we are looking for devil worshippers, then, as we try to ID those bodies?" Officer Tubbs said. The inspector nodded.

"Inspector Dahms gave me these case files." Officer Franklin handed them to Officer Tubbs. "The first case is from a small town in New Mexico. A police chief and two of his patrolmen responded to a similar crime scene back in 1928. They found one survivor, a worshipper named Claire. Before she died, she whispered two words: the Ball. She was stark-raving mad, though.

"There's no known literature of any kind on it anywhere in the world, only several legendary occurrences and then cases like this where the law gets involved. According to the report, she would laugh hysterically, scream a long, piercing scream, then burst into tears and sob uncontrollably. She was wearing a satanic pentagram necklace and had a tattoo of Baphomet, another name for the devil, on the small of her back. And tattoos weren't as common back in the twenties.

"They found a broth laced with peyote, which is a powerful hallucinogen. There was a fire that people had danced around and there were four murder victims at each cardinal point. Their throats had been cut and the blood collected into some type of container, again, probably some ornate chalice, or cup. Whatever was used was never found, like in our case."

"But they were all caught?" Officer Tubbs asked.

"No, not everyone. All the participants died during or right after the ritual of a heart attack or pure fear and madness. Claire died five days later. The police found twenty-one bodies. But the leader, the Reverend Jedidiah Edmund B. Choate, got away." Officer Tubbs was nodding his head as he looked through the files.

"Jesus, there's only three cases for reference?"

"Yup. That one is from a late nineteenth century case just outside of London, England, and an early seventeenth century case in a village in France. The eyewitness descriptions and accounts seem quite similar, and the reports were confirmed by local authorities."

"You did quite a bit of research in that one hour, Franklin."

"Thanks, Inspector. Believe it or not, I mostly just sat at my locker and stared for that hour. Weird. Anyway, did you know there's also incidents in Egypt and in Ethiopia that are supposedly written in ancient Egyptian and Cuneiform that sound almost exactly like this?"

Inspector Dahms smiled. "Yes. Of course, you did."

"So, that's it, then?" Officer Tubbs said.

"Not quite," Officer Franklin said. "Inspector, this ritual was botched, which is why everyone there died." Officer Franklin looked at the inspector. "It kind of makes me wonder if something similar happened in New Mexico, where everybody died in that incident. Well, everyone except the leader, that is. Just like this case. Maybe they screwed up the ritual somehow? Or maybe the leader actually expects this to happen and all of the would-be worshippers are just dupes, patsies who were the target of the leader all along? Anyway, something went wrong and the victims weren't properly sacrificed. This is incredibly bad, apparently."

"First of all," Officer Tubbs said, "what do you mean by the phrase 'properly sacrificed'? Why is that bad? What possible difference does that make?"

"Well, in this case, it was the difference between four people dying and thirty or forty people dying, because whatever it was that they summoned killed them all, just like in New Mexico."

"Except that the deaths of the worshippers in New Mexico were found to be from natural causes, heart attacks or panic, mostly, and not a huge creature like the one we're apparently dealing with," Officer Tubbs said.

"That's true. But, well, I mean…it makes you wonder what it is they all could have seen to make everybody there die of pure fright. Supposedly they're expecting the devil; instead, whatever they summoned was something even scarier than that? What in the world is scarier than the devil?"

"What? What do you mean 'whatever was summoned'?" Officer Tubbs hissed.

"Officer Franklin, is that what you're suggesting, that these people somehow raised the devil and that he killed them all?" Inspector Dahms and Officer Tubbs both leaned forward in their chairs. Officer Franklin shook his head.

"No, no, no, that's not what I'm saying at all. There is no data at hand to indicate any sign or proof of the devil."

"Okay, good," Officer Tubbs said, leaning back in his seat.

"No, the physical evidence at the crime scene leaves me no doubt that what came through that doorway is a giant, flying demon wolf."

"A what?" Officer Tubbs's voice cut through the coffee shop like a razor. The popular breakfast and coffee shop fell silent as everyone turned to look at the police officers huddled around the back-corner table.

The inspector calmly finished his coffee. "Let's leave," he said.

They paid for their breakfast and hurried out of Dick's into the crisp, sobering autumn air. †

CHAPTER 22
The Baptism

Upon returning to St. Mark's Church after tea with Julie, Father Knight found the police there. Jeb had called them to report his daughter missing. The man had sounded utterly distraught when he spoke on the phone with Marge at the police station. He told her he had searched the whole of the church grounds to no avail, including all of Sandra's favorite hiding places. But there was no sign of little Sandra anywhere to be found. So, he then called the police. Inspector Dahms and Officer Franklin had only just arrived when Father Knight walked up the driveway to the church.

"Hi, can I help you?" Father Knight said.

"Yes, I hope so. I'm Inspector Dahms, and this is Officer Franklin."

"Yes, we met at Father Torrez's memorial earlier." The men shook hands.

"I really liked what you said at the service, Father," Officer Franklin said.

"Oh, well, thank you."

"I'm sorry I could not attend, Padre. We're a bit busy these days."

"Oh, that's perfectly all right, Inspector. Now, what can I do for you?"

"We're here to speak to your grounds caretaker. Jeb Choate, that's his name?"

"Yes, that's right. Is something wrong?"

"According to him, his daughter is missing."

"Sandra is missing?"

"You know her, Padre?"

"Yes, I met her this morning just after the service."

"I see. We're organizing a search party, looking for volunteers if you're interested."

"Well, I am. Count me in, Inspector."

"Excellent, thank you. You didn't happen to notice what she looks like, what she was wearing, that sort of thing?"

"Yes, she's blonde, with pigtails. Blue eyes, I think, and she was wearing a pink dress with blue on it, and had pink ribbons or bows in her hair. She's about five years old and stands only so high." Father Knight held his hand out to indicate her height as best as he could remember.

"Now, you've only just met this caretaker, is that right?"

"Yes, that's right. But I…"

"When did he start working here, do you know?"

"Well, I believe in the last year or so."

"Where did he come from, Padre?"

"I don't know, Inspector. Why do…"

"Very good, thank you, Padre."

As the inspector was speaking, Jeb had come around the corner of the church and walked over to where Father Knight and the police officers stood.

"Why, hello there, Inspector, Officer, and Father Knight, we meet again, sir. Thank you kindly for coming so quickly."

"Not at all, sir. You are the father of the missing child?"

"Yes, sir, I am." Father Knight noticed that Jeb and the inspector were both roughly the same height. They both towered over him and Officer Franklin.

"Now, I have your full name as Jeb Choate," the inspector said.

"Yes, sir."

"That is an interesting name. Jeb is your actual, true first name?" The inspector looked at Jeb, who hesitated before responding.

"Why, yes sir. That is truly my God-given name."

"Hmmm, I see. Do you have a police record, sir?"

Father Knight looked up at the inspector, and his brown eyes widened when the inspector had said this to Jeb. He then looked at Officer Franklin, who had also been looking up at the inspector with a wide blue-eyed expression. Officer Franklin then looked at Father Knight.

"Hey, hey, Inspector, what is this? I thought you were here to look for Sandra?" Father Knight said.

"We are, Padre, we are. I'm just curious, is all. Now then," Inspector Dahms regarded Jeb, "you were about to answer me, sir?"

Jeb was looking back at the inspector. A smile crept slowly across his face, revealing very white teeth. His cheeks dimpled deeply as he did so. "Why, no, sir. I do not have a police record, as you call it. Now, about my daughter, sir?"

"Right. What is your daughter's name?"

"Sandra Choate, sir."

"Okay, Mr. Choate, when was the last time you saw Sandra?"

"Why, it was only this morning, in the church, just after the memorial for Father Torrez. Father Knight was there, and so was the Bishop. I had some cleaning up to do after the picnic and then some chores around the grounds. When I went inside to make us some supper, I found that she was gone."

The inspector nodded. "Was there any indication that she was abducted? Did you see anything that looked as if there had been a struggle?"

"No, sir, no, sir, it really seems as if she just got herself a notion and those little legs of hers got restless and away she went. It does worry me. She's wandered off from time to time before, I mean. Sandra gets to pretending sometimes, she has a good imagination, but she's never done anything like this."

"That's okay, Jeb." Father Knight gently put his hand on the tall man's shoulder. "Children do this as they get a little older. They become more adventurous. We'll find her."

"Thank you, child." Jeb smiled at Father Knight.

"Mr. Choate, I'm going ask you to stay here, in case she returns home." The caretaker creased his brow in deep thought for a moment, and then reluctantly agreed. The inspector handed him his card. "You can reach me here any time. Please do let us know if she does come home, okay?"

"Yes, sir, I shall," Jeb said.

The search parties were formed, and everyone agreed to split up into pairs. The inspector wanted everyone to begin searching near the woods and fields around the church property. Father Knight was sent across the street from St. Mark's. He went alone.

He wandered through the heavily wooded area around the church grounds for about an hour or so. He stayed mostly on the many paths that ran all over the entire woods of Littleborough. The path he ended up on led him away from the church grounds toward the grounds of the school of the same name. He crossed over some of the school's athletic fields.

Here, Father Knight found a faint, barely used path that led down from the athletic fields and away from the main school property. Two old stone walls crossed right here. Though in disrepair from centuries of neglect, they still somehow stood relatively intact and clearly demarked the forest into seemingly random sections. He stepped over one of the old stone walls and made his way toward the thicker woods and wild lands, and toward the Great Woods of Littleborough and Fears Hill.

"Sandra!" Father Knight stopped and listened. His voice carried across one of the two small ponds he was standing between. He turned toward the other pond, on the northerly side of the path. "Sandra!" He looked around. There was no sign of the little girl.

Father Knight walked out of the woods and onto a small road that led between the two ponds on the St. Mark's school campus. The little road forked just ahead of him. One fork curved to his right and up to a large dormitory of the boarding school. The other road continued for only several hundred more feet before ending at more athletic fields. These fields were surrounded entirely by the Great Woods. Looming above it all was Fears Hill.

"Sandra!" Father Knight knew these grounds well. As a child he had fished these ponds with his older brother, John. In the winters they would play ice hockey on the larger of the two ponds. It was in this pond that a young schoolteacher had found his brother's body. Father Knight swallowed. It occurred to him that he had not been down in this area since the tragedy. It had been a long, long time. His mouth went dry. Father Knight opened his bottle of spring water and sipped from it. It tasted strange to him. He looked at the bottle; the water looked quite clear and clean. "Sandra!"

He began to walk along the little road toward the athletic fields. As his eyes scanned across the fields, Father Knight could see a small group of townsfolk just beyond the fields in a wooded area just south of Fears Hill. Since there were people searching out there, he decided to walk into the woods and search along the perimeter of the two ponds. Father Knight started with the smaller of the two.

"Sandra!" He entered the woods along the very western edge of the pond. The sun was still quite high in the sky. The sporadic shade amidst this thinly wooded area made the air a bit cooler. His sneakers made an audible squishing sound with each step in the damp, marshy area.

"Sandra!" Father Knight stopped and listened again. But he heard nothing. He was about to walk further on into the woods when he heard it. It was soft, but it was an unmistakable low, primal growling.

The hairs on the back of Father Knight's neck stood up and he froze. *What could that be?* he wondered. Then he heard it again, only this time it had sounded like it came from behind him. He turned himself around, but there was nothing to see.

He looked out across the athletic fields to see if, perhaps, the people searching over there had heard what he thought he'd heard. There was no sign of anyone over there. They had all seemingly vanished. Father Knight smiled and rolled his eyes. He turned back around and continued to make his way through the woods. By now he had come about halfway along the southern edge of the small pond.

"Sandra!" He waited. This time something answered his call. It was a roar. Though it was something in the distance, it was loud and seemed to fill the whole of Littleborough's forests. The silence that followed was palpable. The roar had sounded like a lion or a tiger, or a bear. *Oh my,* thought Father Knight as he smiled to himself again. *Now is not the time to let my imagination run wild,* he thought. His head began to ache slightly. "Sandra!"

Father Knight continued on. He had circled the first pond and was standing on the little road looking at the larger pond. He sipped some more water from his bottle. The taste made him shudder slightly. Both ponds and the little road in between them seemed much smaller than he remembered. The smell was the same. The dark, pungent odor of the muck from the ponds and his shoes brought childhood memories flooding back to him. He smiled. Father Knight started toward the western edge of the large pond. He felt light headed and a little breathless. For some reason, he was seeing and sensing constant movement in his peripheral vision. Lights and colors danced in his eyes, only to vanish whenever he would turn and try to see what was there. He blinked his eyes and shook his head. He realized that he could not stop smiling.

"Sandra!" This area was lightly wooded, but the ground was firm and dry. "Sandra!" A large cluster of cat-o'-nine tails stood just inside the pond, bathing in the late afternoon autumn sunlight. Father Knight made his way around the southwestern edge of the pond and began to walk north. "Sandra!" Here, Father Knight could see that there was something floating in the water. It looked pink in color and floated eerily on the top of the pond water. His stomach flipped with red-hot fear. He broke into a run.

He ran along the bank of the pond until he reached the northwest corner, where the pink garment was. As he ran, Father Knight felt as if he was losing his balance. The ground beneath his feet seemed as if it was moving, as if it was spinning, as he tried to navigate it. When he reached the spot where the garment was floating, he tried to stop himself. His head felt as if he was still running. He turned himself clumsily toward the pond. He could see that the garment was just out of his reach in the water. Father Knight looked around frantically for a stick or a fallen branch that he could use to fetch the object out of the water. As he searched, he noticed that everything in his peripheral vision—the lights, the colors—seemed to be spinning around him as well, disorienting him further.

He found an old branch at the wood's edge and dragged it to the edge of the bank leading down to the pond. He dropped his water bottle on the ground and carefully stepped as close to the edge of the pond as he could. He took the branch with both hands and slowly and carefully swung it out over where the garment floated. He lowered the branch into the water right on top of the pink form. The branch stopped and rested on the surface, as if hitting something solid that lay beneath the pink cloth. His heart began to pound in his chest. Father Knight licked his dry lips. He could not believe how dry his mouth was. The pain in his head began to throb. His head felt quite heavy and the dizziness seemed to be getting worse. The dark waters in front of him seemed to be swirling all around the pond.

Father Knight shook his head and refocused. He carefully tried to manipulate the large branch in a way to draw the object closer to where he stood at the very edge of the pond. It seemed as if it had become snagged with something else beneath the surface. He could not move it. He realized he was going to have to go into the water if he was going to find out what or who this was. He was not sure how deep these waters were. It was something he and all his friends growing up around here never really knew. Nobody ever swam in these waters. The water was too dark and muddy, and besides, a healthy population of snapping turtles living in these ponds was deterrent enough. Father Knight took a deep breath and then stepped toward the dark, frigid waters.

As he was putting his foot down into the water, he slipped down off of the embankment and landed, chest deep, in the pond. The jolt of ice-cold water mixed with a thick mixture of the sediment in the water was both exhilarating and repulsive. He spat some water out that had gone into his mouth. All he could smell and taste was the powerful and pungent muck of the pond. He could feel his running shoes sinking into that muck at the bottom of the pond. It was slippery. As he carefully angled himself toward the pink cloth, Father Knight softly stepped one step closer. His feet felt as if he were sinking into the muck itself at the bottom of these waters. He had to actually work his feet free of the muck with each step, careful not to lose a sneaker as he did so. He reached out his hand but could not reach the pink dress. He steadied himself in the water and took one more step. Father Knight kept his eyes fixed on the pink dress.

One more step, he thought. His foot slipped, soaking him right up to his neck. Father Knight tried to steady himself and regain his balance with his arms, which splashed the dark water in all directions and covered his face and head. He spit more water out of his mouth as he steadied himself. The cold water on his face made him feel a little bit better.

He was finally able to reach out and take hold of the cloth with both hands. He wrested it free from whatever it had been snagged on, and carefully pulled it back to the edge of the pond. It felt light to Father Knight. It felt too light to be Sandra's body, thank goodness. He felt, in that moment, an awesome sense of relief. The most difficult part for him was getting out of the pond. There was very little to grab onto along the banks of the pond to use to pull himself out, and his shoes kept slipping on the muck at the bottom. Worst of all, the headache and dizziness had both come back with a vengeance. It took Father Knight several minutes before he was able to gain a foothold and pull himself out of the dark waters.

He breathlessly crawled up the bank on his belly, bringing with him the stench of the pond. The green and yellow grasses on the bank were turned a dark greenish black where he now knelt. Father Knight looked at the cloth, which still floated at the water's edge. It was a small dress—bright pink, with blue. *What are the odds?* he thought. His head pounded. His heart pounded. He was strangely out of breath. He reached over and grasped it with one hand. He then pulled on it to try to get it up onto the bank. It was heavy, now. He couldn't get it out of the water.

Suddenly, the dress seemed to pull itself back into the water, almost pulling Father Knight back into the pond with it. He let go of the dress just in time, landing on his belly facing down the steep embankment of the pond. He lay there for a moment and regarded the garment. He shook his head and blinked his eyes. He drew a deep breath and reached his hand out for the dress. He couldn't quite reach it. He stayed on his belly and eased himself further down the steep embankment toward the dark waters. Once more, he reached out his hand for the pink dress.

There was a loud rush from beneath the surface of this pond. The water in front of him seemed to explode, as if something enormous had hit the water. More ice-cold, filthy pond water splashed all over Father Knight and straight into his face. He cried out as he quickly pulled his hand back and straightened himself up. His soft, brown eyes were as wide as saucers. He watched on, helplessly, as the small, pink dress raced across the dark waters to the opposite side of the pond, leaving an enormous wake. The waves from the wake slapped the steep banks of the pond with a dull, squishy thud in the following silence.

Father Knight spit more pond water out of his mouth and staggered clumsily up onto his feet. His every move was accompanied by a squishing sound as he was soaked to the skin from head to toe. Still, he could not take his eyes off of that dress. It had crashed into the far bank with a whoosh of pond water. Father Knight stood, mesmerized. The dress then submerged silently until it was out of sight. The pond surface gradually grew still. Father Knight could only stand, soaking wet, and stare in amazement.

Little blonde pigtails, tied with two pink bows, slowly came to the surface in the dead center of the still pond. Dread filled his body as little Sandra's blue eyes emerged from the depths of the dark waters and peered at him from just above the water's surface. Her head, and then her body, in her muddy, pink dress, slowly rose out of the water and up over the surface of the pond. Her blue eyes and her smile gleamed from behind her muddy face. Father Knight felt light headed again.

Her head tilted to one side. Father Knight thought he could hear what sounded like whispering. Though he tried to concentrate, to focus on it, he found that he could not understand any of what was being said. His eyes closed. He had to exert an enormous amount of energy to reopen them. When he did, he saw that Sandra was gone. At least, he thought so. His vision was obscured by the dancing lights and colors that had now left the safety of his peripheral vision and had moved into plain sight. Somewhere he could hear a little girl laughing, then, it faded. He wondered if Sandra had ever even really been there.

Father Knight tried to turn away from the pond and walk back to the little road. He could not keep his balance. His head felt heavy and the forest and ponds seemed to all be spinning around him rapidly now. He collapsed onto his back. He tried to keep his eyes open. He looked up into the bright blue sky. A shadow passed over his eyes. A tall, rail thin form appeared over him. A shock of wild, white hair on top of this form blew in the breeze.

Father Knight thought he could hear laughter. A wet, warm sensation came over his chest. There was an overpowering odor of urine. He could no longer keep his eyes open. Father Knight prayed that Sandra would be okay. It was the final thing he thought before losing consciousness on the bank of the large pond. †

CHAPTER 23
The Obligatory Shower Scene

Julie wasn't sure, but there was a very good chance that she had never felt worse in her entire life. Tea with James had been wonderful. But her brain and her body were both hurting. She was exhausted. A comment made by a college roommate occurred as she slowly drove her Jeep Cherokee home from Dick's: "I feel like I was just screwed by a malodorous, six-hundred pound, sexually crazed African mountain gorilla, twice an hour, for a week." This was following a night of drinking at a fraternity party at the end of a semester. Both Julie and her roommate had then spent the next day taking turns alternately laughing and throwing up in the bathroom of their dormitory. She smiled wearily at the memory.

Julie could not wait to get home. There would be no sit-ups, or running, or yard work today, she had decided. She was going to go home and hug Rasputin, walk him, feed him, and feed Geraldine and Don Juan. Then, Julie was going to take the longest, hottest shower she could stand, followed by a mug of hot tea and a book in bed under all of her blankets. Julie knew that she was dangerously close to the limits of her endurance—physically, mentally, and emotionally. She pulled into her small driveway and parked the Jeep.

The cool, fresh air filled her lungs as Julie walked up a tiny stone pathway that led to her front door. As she fumbled the keys on her key chain to get a hold of the door key, Julie could not help but smile a tired smile. Just inside the front door she could hear Rasputin doing his *thump* dance.

"Hi Rass!" Julie had gotten the door open and, squatting down, threw her arms around his furry neck. "Hi! Who's my big boy? Oh, who? Boy, it's good to see you!" *Thump, thump, thump!* She kissed him right on his nose. *Thump, thump, thump!* Julie looked up the first flight of stairs to the windowsill on the first landing. Don Juan the black cat stared down at her silently. "Hi Don Juan." Julie smiled up at him. His green eyes widened and he bolted out of sight. Julie laughed her throaty laugh. It was truly good to be home.

She looked at Rasputin. "Now, who wants to go outside for a minute?" *Thump, thump!* Julie let the big dog out the back door, which was straight down the main hallway from the front door. Rasputin wasted no time in doing his business and coming right back into the house. He followed Julie up the stairs, sniffing and panting with excitement, his tail still wagging.

Julie walked straight over to her dresser where she had left the glass habitat with Geraldine in it. She looked down and smiled. Geraldine was still sleeping. She lightly stroked the rat's back. The tiny rodent's eyes opened and blinked momentarily, sniffing at Julie's fingers. The rat in the hat then resumed her nap.

Julie had put on a dark gray pantsuit in order to look as professional as possible for her meetings with the Streeters and with the Harts. She peeled it off quickly, flinging each item onto a chair she had in the corner of her bedroom by the walk-in closet. Julie then walked into the bathroom and over to the tub. She started the shower, putting the water up to hot. As the water warmed, Julie then looked at herself in the mirror. There were dark circles under her eyes. Her jaw and her neck ached from all the crying and terrible tension that she had undergone that morning. Julie took two aspirin.

She looked at herself one more time in the mirror, this time directly into her own eyes. She stared hard. *What did you just witness? What was that?* Her green eyes seemed for just a moment to be someone else's eyes, the eyes of a stranger, staring, searching, questioning her own sanity. A chill went down her spine. *Who are you?* But no answer came.

She stepped carefully over the side of the tub and into the shower. The water hit her body and, at first, stung from the high temperature. Julie forced herself to allow it to cascade all over her. Soon she had acclimated herself to it and it felt wondrous. For several glorious minutes she stood perfectly still under the steaming water and let it run playfully down her body. It loosened up the tight, tense muscles in her back and her neck. Julie began to feel better.

She took the bottle of shampoo from the stand in the corner of the tub and began to wash her hair. She leaned back into the stream of hot water and let it rinse her hair and head clean of the morning's horror. Julie then put the conditioner in her hair. While she let the conditioner sit in her hair, she picked up a bottle of body wash and squirted a bit of it into her cupped palm and began to wash her face. It felt to Julie as if she were cleansing away an eternity of grime, mixed with blood, soot, and tears.

She breathed out a slow, contented breath through her nose as she rinsed her face, her eyes closed, at rest. Julie then began to wash her body, and this energized her further. She leaned and stretched her sore muscles as she did this. It felt good. *Thump, thump, thump!* Julie froze, her eyes now wide open. *Thump, thump.* There it was again.

"Rass? Rasputin! Come in here for a minute would you, big boy?" Julie waited. The water bounced off her tense body. Despite the water's hot temperature and the steam that had filled the bathroom, the air around Julie now felt ice cold. "Rass?" Julie quickly rinsed the soap off of her body, all the while listening intently for any more noise. She had left the door that adjoined her bedroom with the bathroom open. She had a clear view from where she was in the shower, through the doorway and into the bedroom. She could see her bed, her bedside table on the far side, and a mirror that hung at the head of the bed.

Julie kept her eyes fixed through the bathroom door. But she saw and heard nothing. Her heart pounded in her chest. Quickly she tilted her head back into the water stream to rinse the conditioner out of her hair. She tried to keep it from running into her eyes, which were still fixed on the door. *Thump!* Julie nearly jumped out of her own skin and cried out. She covered her mouth with her hands. This one sounded much closer than any of the previous ones.

"Who's there?" Her hair rinsed, she shut the water off and listened, but all she could hear was the pounding of her own heart and the blood rushing in her head.

Julie stepped out of the shower and quickly grabbed a towel off of the rack and began to dry herself. As she did this, she slowly made her way over to the bathroom door and peered into the bedroom. There was nothing there. Rasputin wasn't in the bedroom and Julie could see that Geraldine the rat was still nestled in her habitat. Julie wrapped the towel around her torso, clutching it to her chest, and walked over to the bedroom door that led out to the upstairs hallway.

"Rasputin?" She listened. Julie could hear the light jingling of her dog's ID tags and license that were on his collar coming from the bottom of the stairs in his usual response to her voice. Julie breathed a sigh of relief. "Darn it, you big, naughty boy, you scared me half to death!" Julie went back into the bathroom and finished drying herself off. She threw on her old jeans and her favorite nightshirt. She then started her hair dryer and began to blow dry her hair. *Thump, thump, thump!*

Julie turned off her hair dryer and rolled her eyes up skyward. *Thump, thump, thump!* Julie now knew it was Rasputin. She could hear him sniffing and grunting as someone scratched his back just out of her sight in the bedroom. Julie took one step toward the bedroom door when she saw the reflection of an unmistakably tall, thin shadow glide across the mirror by the head of her bed. She cried out, dropping the hair dryer onto the floor with a plastic cracking sound and a clatter. Her hair still half wet, Julie took one more step toward the door. This time the shadow came straight back across the mirror the other way.

Julie could only see a tall blur go by. She entered her bedroom in time to see the shadow glide straight out of the room and down the hallway, down the stairs and out of the house. Julie looked over at her dresser. Geraldine and the shoebox that Julie had left right next to the habitat were gone. Julie then heard the back door to her house slam shut. She couldn't be sure, but Julie thought she could hear a low, throaty laughter coming from her backyard. She slipped on her running shoes, grabbed her cell phone and purse, scratched Rasputin and kissed him, and raced down the stairs and down the main hallway to her back door.

As she opened the back door, there was a knock at her front door. Rasputin went over to the door and began to sniff and bark, his tail wagging. Julie looked out into her small backyard. There was nothing. She turned and looked at her front door, which was straight down the main hall from the back door. The knocking continued, as did Rasputin's barking. Julie bit her lower lip. She turned and looked back into her backyard. A young girl who looked to Julie to be about five stood at the edge of the woods smiling at her. Julie could not see her very well in the shade of the forest. The girl was wearing a pink and blue dress with a bow in her hair.

"Hi, what's your name?" Julie said.

The little girl did not answer. Her fierce, piercing blue eyes stared straight in to Julie's green eyes. Her stare was mesmerizing; it held Julie there, frozen in place. Julie could feel herself being observed, inside and out. The child was looking straight through her eyes, into and throughout her entire being. Julie could sense her strength, defiance, independence, and fierceness. But there was so much more. Julie could feel the little girl's power. It was awesome, almost overwhelming.

A shadow moved in the darkness of the forest behind the little girl. Upon sensing this, Julie felt a dread and fear burning in her stomach. Julie looked as hard as she could to see what it was. Though she was unable to get a good look at it, Julie could, again, sense something profoundly powerful and ancient. The person at the front door knocked again.

"Miss Bernard? It's Inspector Dahms. Are you all right, ma'am?"

Julie looked at the little girl. Rasputin kept barking. After a moment, the child seemed to recede into the shadows of the forest. Julie closed her back door and went to answer her front door.

"Inspector Dahms, hi." Julie smiled.

"Miss Bernard, I'm terribly sorry to have disturbed you." The inspector stooped down to scratch Rasputin behind the ears.

"No, not at all," Julie said. She glanced at her back door.

"Is something wrong?"

"Well," Julie smiled and rolled her eyes, "I thought I saw someone in my backyard just now, but they're gone, I think."

"It wasn't a little girl, was it?"

Julie looked into the inspector's face as he straightened up and her eyes widened.

"Yes, it was a little girl. She was wearing a pink and blue dress. That was all I could really clearly see. Well," Julie grinned, "that, and her blazing blue eyes. Please, come in."

Inspector Dahms entered the main hallway. Julie led him to the back door of the house. "What happened, Inspector?"

"Her father reported her missing about twenty minutes ago. He's the caretaker over at St. Mark's Church. He said he thought she had run away to play. She apparently has a vivid and wild imagination, and loves the woods."

"Oh no, she's out there with all those wolves that we heard last night?" Julie opened the back door and Rasputin plunged into the backyard. Julie and the inspector both followed him into the bright sunshine.

"I'm afraid so. We have all our people and half the town out looking for her." The inspector had walked to the edge of the lawn and peered into the forest. "Where about did you see her?" Julie pointed to the section of woods that she had seen the little girl standing in. He strode over toward the spot and peered into the woods. As he did so, he called dispatch and informed all parties of the recent sighting. Julie still had her purse and cell in her hands. She put Rasputin back inside her house, along with her purse, closed the back door, and started making her way into the woods. "Miss Bernard."

"Yes, Inspector Dahms?" Julie stopped and turned, smiling up at him.

The inspector hesitated, smiled, and shrugged. "Nothing," he said.

They left the sunlight for the shadows. †

CHAPTER 24
Chasing the Bat
Who Took the Rat

Julie and the inspector headed straight into the heart of the forest. The woods here were thick and the underbrush even thicker. It sloped gently downward for almost a mile before leveling off at the ponds and large athletic fields of the school and, beyond that, the base of Fears Hill. Julie led the inspector to where she knew there was a path. This path skirted the ponds, the fields, and the marshlands, and ran in a north by northwest direction. They walked quickly. The inspector was still speaking on his cell phone to Marge back at dispatch. Julie looked for any sign of the little girl or Geraldine. She knew the young girl that she had seen in her backyard was too short to have cast the shadow that she saw in her bedroom. Besides, she had a sneaking suspicion of who had taken her rat.

"All right, that sounds good. Thank you, Marge." Inspector Dahms put his cell in his jacket pocket. "It appears we're heading in the right direction, Miss Bernard. Sandra has been sighted down by the ponds on the St. Mark's school property."

"Her name is Sandra?"

"Yes. With any luck, we'll have her back with her father within the hour."

"I hope so. This is no time for a little girl to be wandering around these woods. My goodness, devil worshippers, wolves, and God only knows what else is running around here."

"Mmm, that's the truth. So, tell me, Miss Bernard, as a woman of science, what attracted you to also study the occult? The two seem incompatible to me."

Julie, who was in front of the Inspector, turned and smiled up at him. "I think it was just curiosity, you know? I consider myself to be a practical woman. I'm comfortable with science and logic and proofs. But I also believe in God. I guess a part of my scientific mind wants to remain open to other possibilities. Faith in such things is impossible to prove, but equally impossible to disprove."

"That's true. Never thought of it like that."

"I guess that's why I chose psychology as my 'science.' It just seems to me that the mind is where the two disciplines seem to collide. I guess you could say it's the front line where the physical meets the metaphysical."

"That makes a lot of sense." Inspector Dahms and Julie walked in silence along the narrow path for several minutes. "Tell me, what do you know about the reverend Jedidiah Edmund B. Choate?"

The name was familiar to Julie. She didn't know why, at first. She took several more steps along the narrow path when she felt her stomach flip. An ice-cold bolt of lightning went down Julie's spine. She stopped walking on the narrow path and turned herself around, looking straight up at the inspector, her wide, green eyes searched his hard, gray eyes. Her jaw had dropped open. The two stood there for a moment.

"Oh my, that's a name I haven't heard in a forever." Julie pursed her lips. She shook her head, her dirty blonde hair waved and shined in the filtered sunlight of the woods. She turned back around and continued to walk briskly along the path. The inspector followed. "From what I can recall, he was a Baptist minister in Arizona in the early twentieth century. He was a cruel and truly evil man. If a person from his congregation sinned or broke a law, they were beaten, or whipped, and locked in a closet he had specially built down in the cellar of the church. Some scholars have suggested that he would visit those locked up in the night and rape them. But there's no actual evidence of that.

"He was excommunicated. No one knows why. The church authorities never told anyone what had happened. But it had been rumored that in the basement of that church he had erected an altar to the devil. He disappeared for a short period of time. He reemerged as a priest of Satan and had formed a satanic cult. They all moved into that old church. Within several weeks, every follower there was found dead in the desert."

Julie gasped. She lost her breath for a moment. She stopped and turned back to face the inspector. "It's just like what we saw this morning!"

He nodded. "That is the incident referred to as 'the Ball'?"

"Yes." Julie bit her lower lip and began walking again.

"Because one woman was still alive when law enforcement officials came upon the scene, and before she died, that's what she said?"

"Yes."

"I see. But other than committing mass murder, what do these people think they are accomplishing?"

"Well, as you know, the basic precepts to most religions, Christianity included, is that one needs to live a good and holy life in order to be rewarded in the afterlife. A righteous person will go to heaven, or be reincarnated as a person with a higher station in life, that sort of thing. The belief here is the opposite; its that one is rewarded for their faith and service to the devil, or whatever, on this earth in this lifetime. The most widely accepted theory is that the worshippers are raising the devil to gain wealth, power, and even immortality, in exchange for their souls. But so little is known about the 'Ball,' these are guesses. I can't believe we may have actually seen one." Julie swallowed, still in thought. "Some scholars think that the ritual must be completed within twenty-four hours, by adding one more sacrifice. The congregation brings a child to the same place where the original ritual was held. They must repeat the incantations and kill the child with a knife, as Abraham was ready to do to his son, Isaac. The blood of this child is then mixed with the blood of the four original sacrifices, and sipped by each member."

"Charming."

"Mmmm."

"So, there is a chance that the leader of the group may return to finish the deal?"

Julie stopped again and turned around to face the inspector. Her eyes searched his. "I thought the leader died with everyone else at the clearing."

The inspector shook his head. "I believe he survived, somehow."

The two stood in silence for a moment. Julie turned and began walking again. "We've got to find Sandra."

They resumed walking along the path. Within several minutes they had reached a point where the path branched out into three separate directions. One seemed to lead back toward the school, one went straight on ahead, and the third went off to their right. An old stone wall crossed with another old stone wall here. Both walls ran on in each direction for as far as the eye could see in the thick woods of Littleborough. Something tugged at Julie to take the path to her right. The inspector headed straight for the path that led down toward the two ponds.

"I think I should just scoot along this path, Inspector."

"Are you sure, Miss Bernard? I think this path will lead us right to where the child was last seen."

"I know. But this is not a very long path, and we could cover twice as much ground this way, you know, just in case Sandra should come back up here."

The inspector hesitated. Julie smiled up at him. "Inspector Dahms, I promise I won't be long. I just want to be sure. I'll call you if I find anything, and if not, I'll meet you down by the ponds."

He nodded his head. "Yes, that does make sense, Miss Bernard. I'll call you if we find her. Good luck."

"Thanks, you too."

The inspector strode down the path toward the ponds and Fears Hill. Julie quickly made her way along her chosen path. When she was out of sight of the inspector, she broke into a full run. She knew this was not a short path. She also knew this was the right way to go. She did not understand how she knew this. She ran hard.

Julie stopped running when she reached the edge of the woods looking out across an athletic field on the grounds of the St. Mark's school. The sun was still quite bright and high in the autumn sky. Across the field were more woods. Fears Hill loomed up and over the Great Woods of Littleborough. Julie knew that Sandra and Geraldine the rat had crossed this field and entered the woods over there.

"Sandra!" She began to walk across the field. She kept her eyes fixed on the tree line ahead of her, looking for any sign of movement. Having crossed the athletic field, she entered the next section of woods. "Sandra!" Again, the pathway forked off in three different directions. One of these led back toward more school grounds. That left her with just the two options. Straight ahead of her were thick woods. To her right were thick woods that also went up into a steep hill. It looked dangerous. Julie knew that this was the correct direction. It just had to be. She sighed.

"Sandra!" She started to walk slowly up the hill. Julie had hiked all over Littleborough and was familiar with the woods, the ponds, the reservoirs, and the streams. But something was different. The woods seemed to breathe an uneasy silence. She could not hear one single bird. Julie noticed there weren't even any squirrels or chipmunks scurrying in and out and up or down the trees. She had reached the top of the steep, rocky hill. "Sandra!"

The path she was following led down the other side of the hill. This side seemed to be even steeper than the other side. Rocks appeared to jut out at various, sharp angles. Julie looked at her watch. It had stopped. She looked at her cell phone. No signal. A howl, long, guttural and loud, filled the forest. Julie froze for a moment, the hairs on the back of her neck rising. There was a slight echo that seemed to sound all around her as it subsided. She could not be sure from which direction it had come. At least it sounded as if it were somewhat distant, and not too nearby. She sighed again, looking around carefully from her perch on top of the small hill. Satisfied, she began to carefully make her way down the other side of the steep hill.

"Sandra!" Though the rocks that cropped out of the hill looked jagged and dangerous, they were all very firmly fixed into the hillside. Julie was able to get herself down to the base of the little hill fairly quickly. "Sandra!" She looked carefully around from her new vantage point at the bottom of the small hill that was adjacent to Fears Hill. Fears Hill loomed above her, to her left, and obscured the sun and the entire western sky. The path seemed to follow along the very base of Fears Hill in a northerly direction. It wound and weaved its way around the trees and the brush. "Sandra!"

Julie could still see the smaller hill from which she had descended behind her, but only just barely. There was still no sign or sound of life anywhere. She also noted that she no longer seemed sure where to go. *See? You don't have any powers or psychic abilities, after all,* Julie thought. That's when she saw it.

She only caught a glimpse of it out of the corner of her eye. It had startled Julie. She involuntarily cried out softly when she saw it, covering her mouth with one hand quickly to stifle herself. It seemed very tall and black. It flashed across the top of the hill from which she had just descended, from left to right, and disappeared back into the woods. Julie stood there for a moment, her mind trying desperately to piece together what she had just seen. But she could not imagine what the heck that could have been. She could now only think of Sandra, so, she began to run. Julie ran along the path back toward the little hill where she had seen the whatever-it-was. Her mind raced to process what it was she was seeing.

"Sandra!" She reached the base of the small hill. Despite its steep incline and the sharp, jagged edges of the rocks everywhere, Julie raced up to the top of the hill as fast as she could go. "Sandra!" Her voice seemed to echo strangely all around her; it seemed to travel everywhere in the woods, disorienting her.

"Ahhh, ah aaaaah, haaah!" The sound seemed, to Julie, to come from right behind her. She turned around, expecting to be confronted by something right there on top of the hill. But there was nothing on the hill with her. She looked down at the base of the hill from which she had just raced up. She cried out again as the tall, rail thin form now raced across the path at the base of the hill where she had just been. It seemed to have a mane of long, white hair. It clutched something in one of its long, bony hands: Geraldine's shoebox.

"No!" Julie screamed. She half ran and half fell back down the hill after this thing. The creature had disappeared into the woods again. She reached the bottom of the hill in a tumble of arms and legs. She was vaguely aware that she had fallen quite a way down and was bleeding from several places. But Julie's attention was firmly fixed on that thing. She painfully pulled herself back up onto her feet and crashed into the woods at the point she believed the thing had entered. But it was nowhere in sight.

Julie waited and listened. Her heart thumped in her chest and the blood pounded in her head, making it difficult for her to hear anything. She looked back at the path in time to see a shadow race back the other way toward the little hill. Julie took off after it. The creature continued its strange laughter as it led Julie further into the woods. With a burst of speed, Julie was just able to catch up. She tried to grab at the shoebox with one hand. As she did, the creature stopped and turned, gripping the shoebox with one enormous and bony hand. It stooped down to tug at the box at the same time that Julie reached in with her other hand. Julie's head collided with the leonine head of the creature. Both Julie and the shoebox fell to the forest floor at the feet of this creature.

Julie saw a flash of white light for a moment. Pain seared through her head and she could swear she heard a ringing sound. She put her hands up onto her head and tried to gather herself. Her head began to throb. She looked at her hands and saw that she was not bleeding from the blow. Julie looked up in time to see the person she had been chasing. At first her eyes had difficulty focusing. The ringing sound faded and as she blinked her green eyes, her vision returned. An impossibly old woman regarded Julie. Julie stared back, transfixed, breathless. She could not even scream. She could only stare, her eyes wide open in total disbelief.

The witch held Julie with her own withering stare. She towered over Julie, who thought to herself that this thing must be seven feet tall! Her gown was long and black. It covered the old woman from her neck right down to the forest floor. The dress looked like canvas. It hugged the old woman's rail thin body tightly. Her wild, white hair was tussled and windblown. A wide and unsettling smile spread slowly across her long, thin, wrinkled and weathered face, led by thin black lips that revealed sharp yellow teeth.

The witch bent down and scooped Geraldine out of her shoebox and into her arms. She held the little rat up for inspection, looking at her carefully and sniffing her all over. She then began to howl with laughter. She held her head up high and arched her back slightly as she laughed. The witch then looked down at Julie with what almost seemed like approval, her pitch-black eyes piercing, but somehow softer. *Are they changing color?* Julie wondered. The witch picked up the shoebox and turned and fled into the forest, cackling as she went.

"No!" Julie staggered to her feet and plunged further into the woods after her. It was then that Julie noticed this woman wasn't moving, she wasn't running, she wasn't walking. She was somehow gliding over the forest floor. It was almost as if she was flying. Julie realized that this must have been the person she saw on the path at the crime scene. She was tall, thin, and had that shock of white hair. After all, she came back for Geraldine; she's probably the bitch who stapled those staples to Geraldine's precious, tiny head!

A twinge of anger burned in Julie's belly at the thought of this and she ran even harder through the woods. Though she still could not see the witch or Geraldine, Julie somehow knew that they had come this way. She saw another path over to the right. It was heading east, toward Fears Hill. Julie was familiar with it and instinctively angled herself to the right toward this path. She began to run at almost full speed as she gained the path.

Within several minutes Julie had reached Fears Hill. The hill and the trees all rose up above her and seemed to cast a foreboding shadow. Julie started up the hill. She had not gone very far when she heard a branch snap. The sound had seemed to come from her right. Julie silently made her way toward the sound.

"Hah. Hahaha, menthemmenthemdadada aaah." The voice was old and deep. It almost had a rhythmic, singsong quality to it. It seemed to be coming from directly in front Julie, who was still in the woods, probably ten yards off of another path. She could see the witch was now on that path. Her back was turned toward Julie. She was crouching down, doing something with the earth at the base of a large, elm tree. Julie could not see what it was that she was doing.

She took one step toward the witch, and then another. As quietly as she could, Julie crept out of the woods to the very edge of the path. She took one more step toward the witch. All of a sudden, out of nowhere, came the *Sound of Music*. Julie Andrews's beautiful voice filled the woods. It was the ring tone Julie had selected for when her friend, Richard, called her cell phone.

The witch whirled around, straightening herself up to face Julie. She towered over her. Julie pulled her cell phone out from the back pocket of her jeans. Still staring up at the witch, Julie answered the call, holding the phone up to her head.

"Richard." Julie could only whisper.

"Hi, hon, are you searching for Sandra, too?" As Richard's voice came out of the tiny speaker in the cell phone, the old woman's head tilted slightly as she observed the curious little box Julie was holding in her hand. The witch seemed to chuckle to herself. "Jules, are you still there?"

But Julie was not there. She looked up, wide-eyed and with her mouth dropped open, into the old woman's eyes. They were black in color. Or, were they purple, or scarlet, or blue?

The old woman regarded Julie. Her stare held Julie fast. Try as she might, Julie could not move from that spot. A smile slowly crept across the creature's face. Her blackened lips, yellowed teeth, a dark, almost black tongue leered down at Julie. She then held out one of her large, bony hands with the palm held up and open. It looked to Julie like there was dirt and bits of what looked like moss and mushrooms in the palm of her hand. Then, with no warning or hesitation, the old woman blew the mixture straight into Julie's face, her eyes, and her mouth.

Despite her reaction of immediately shutting her eyes tightly and trying to spit the mixture out, it was far too late for Julie. The mixture was light and fluffy. It all went straight into her eyes and up her nose as well as into her mouth. Julie put her hands up to cover her face. Her eyes burned slightly. She began to sneeze violently and was having tremendous difficulty breathing. She fell down onto her knees. She sneezed once more, then began to fall forward so she put her hands down onto the ground. Her tongue had gone completely numb and it felt like it had swollen to double its size.

Julie could still hear the old woman with her low, throaty, singsong speech, standing over her. Her head began to feel impossibly heavy. She had stopped sneezing violently now. Her nose was as numb as her tongue and mouth. She could no longer hold her head up. Her head pulled her downward and then hit the ground between the witch's long, slender black boots.

Julie was no longer struggling for breath. She was able to breathe deeply now. She was distantly aware of herself being rolled over onto her back. She could not move. Despite the terrible mix of fear and pain, she tried one last time to open her eyes. As she did, Julie thought she could just faintly hear Julie Andrews' singing again. "The hills are alive…"

The old woman was now standing directly over Julie. She seemed to be peering down into Julie's face. The witch began to pull her long, black dress up her legs to just above her knees. She straddled Julie as Julie looked helplessly on. Julie could then sense a warm, wet sensation spreading slowly over her chest and abdomen. She could smell the urine. It was a very powerful odor. The old woman stepped over Julie. Julie could now only close her eyes. She could hear the witch speaking her singsong patter. She seemed to chuckle again. Her laughter echoed in Julie's head. Julie felt her ankles pulled together by one of the witch's powerful hands, and then her legs lift up. The witch began to drag Julie into the woods and up Fears Hill. *No,* Julie thought as she passed out into unconsciousness. †

CHAPTER 25
A Shadow of a Man

Inspector Dahms had been called back to the station during the search for Sandra as missing-person reports began to pour in. As he walked back to where his old Chevy was parked back at Julie Bernard's place, he received a text from the chief: *trail leads directly to doc robinson's place-the animal knocked his fence down-still no word from hunting party but they did come through here.* The Inspector texted back: *will go talk to doc robinson.*

The talk with Doc Robinson was predictably brief. Inspector Dahms eased his station wagon into the driveway. Officer Lydon was waiting in his police SUV. The two men nodded hello silently. Officer Lydon followed the inspector across the small parking lot. They made their way into the woods where the front corner of the white fence surrounding the property met the driveway and the Great Woods of Littleborough. Here the forest floor sloped sharply downward below where the property stood. The two men descended the slope and slowly walked along the perimeter of the property to where the backyard was. They had to climb up a steep bank for just a few feet to see the yard. When they reached the top, they could see what the chief had been referring to.

Two full sections of the white, wooden fence, which stood almost seven feet high, were lying flat on the ground in numerous splintered pieces. Officer Lydon and Inspector Dahms looked at each other in silence for a moment. The inspector took out his magnifying glass from his jacket pocket and squatted down. He began to inspect the fence where it had been broken and smashed. Doc Robinson walked out of the door that led from his office and into the backyard.

"What do you think you're doing?" he said. Inspector Dahms continued examining the fence. He then reached over and picked up one of the broken pieces off of the ground and stood back up. He studied the splintered wood very closely.

"Hey, I just asked you what you think you're doing?"

"Just having a look, Doc." The inspector did not look up.

"Without my permission?"

"Yes."

"Get off my property."

"We will." The inspector didn't move, however.

"Now."

"Right." Inspector Dahms had reached into his jacket pocket and produced a small set of tweezers and a clear, plastic baggy. He deftly took the small tweezers and very carefully removed hairs—brown and black, some white, or gray—from in between the slats that had once made up the white, wooden fence.

"Hey asshole, I mean it! Get out of here!" Doc Robinson took a step toward the two policemen.

Inspector Dahms put the sample of hair into the baggy, and then put the tweezers and the baggy back in his coat pocket.

"I know you mean it, Doc. We're just leaving. Quick question for you: Did you happen to see what did this?"

"No, I saw nothing."

"You must have heard it when the fence came crashing down, though?" Doc Robinson stared at the inspector, who stared back at the vet. "Yes?"

"No. I didn't see anything. I didn't hear anything." He shrugged his massive shoulders. "Too bad, huh?" Doc Robinson turned abruptly and walked out of the backyard and back into his office. The inspector looked at Officer Lydon, who chuckled softly.

After returning to the station, Inspector Dahms quietly walked up to his tiny office. He took the dirty coffee pot and mug to the washroom and rinsed them out with cold water. He filled the pot almost to the top and walked back to his office. He filled his little coffee maker with the water and put the coffee into a clean filter and then switched the machine on. He quickly checked his messages as his office filled with the aroma of cheap coffee. When the coffee had brewed, he filled his mug and sipped it. He reached across his desk and grabbed the stack of papers that Marge had left for him on his desk. He began to read through all the reports that had come in.

Two cups of coffee later, he had read all of the reports. There was a great deal of information for him to process. He got up from his desk and stretched himself. He smiled grimly at the sounds of his bones, joints and cartilage snapping and popping as he did so. He then went down to the basement of the police headquarters. Here is where he would come to smoke and to think. It was dark, it was quiet, and there was plenty of room down here for him to pace back and forth. He had always paced. It helped him to think. It helped him to sift through inordinate amounts of information efficiently. In the silence, there was clarity. Deep in thought, he puffed gently on his pipe.

The list of missing people was getting much longer than he had expected. A young woman named Thyrra Lane had been reported missing by her parents. Sylvia Werner had been reported missing by her employer, and no one seemed to know where her only son, Billy, was. Bartholomew Heimerdink, whose picture matched the unknown victim at the crime scene; his two cousins and their spouses; and his brother, Roger, and sister, Sarah, were all reported missing by Bartholomew's mother.

Old man Prescott's son and daughter and their spouses were missing, too. The entire families of both of the young girls who had been brutally murdered, Megan Streeter and Caroline Hart, had vanished. The homes in which they had lived right up until yesterday, as far as anybody in any of the families and the communities knew, now stood completely empty. The people, the family pets, and every last belonging of these families had vanished. No one had seen or heard a thing—no movers, or moving trucks, no packing or loading, no good-byes, no forwarding addresses. They all had apparently taken great pains to leave no clues as to where they were going or of what they were doing. It was as if they had never existed at all, ever.

The inspector frowned, creasing his brow as he thought about this. He puffed on his pipe only to discover that it had burned out. He put his fingers around the bowl of the pipe. Strangely, it was ice cold, as if it had never been lit. He headed for the stairs leading up to the first floor of the police headquarters to rejoin the search for Sandra when he heard what sounded like a scratching sound. Inspector Dahms stopped and listened. *Did I just hear that?* He was sure a noise came from somewhere down here in the basement.

The room he was standing in was an almost perfect rectangle of concrete walls and a concrete floor. The room was divided into two large sides by a row of massive metal supports that lined the very center of the basement. It was very well lit when the lights were switched on. The lights were not switched on. The inspector preferred them off. The only light this allowed for was prisms and shafts of sunlight, deflecting and diffracting through the small, rectangular windows that went around the entire foundation of the building. Each support cast a large shadow along the concrete floor and the walls of the large basement.

There was no furniture of any kind. By the stairs there was a little nook that turned a corner into a smaller room in which the central heating and cooling system and the boiler for the hot water were kept. They were both large and fairly new. Inspector Dahms could not see into the boiler room. He listened intently. There it was again. It was a soft, high-pitched scraping sound. He peered around the nearest support to see the opposite side of the basement from where he had been standing. There was the light echo of his footsteps that pattered around the large basement. Still, there was nothing to see. Then he heard it again. This time it went on for several, unmistakable seconds. A long, pronounced scratching sound, like a blade, or a claw, being dragged over stone.

Inspector Dahms turned himself around quickly this time. His gaze went straight toward the basement stairwell and the boiler room. It was then that he could smell it. It was a rotting smell. It was the odor of decay, feces, and death. The stench seemed old, almost ancient. It was as if something had rotted, then decayed, then rotted again, and was now decaying again.

Inspector Dahms sighed. He reached into his long coat pocket and withdrew his tobacco. He filled the ice-cold bowl of his pipe, which he was still holding, with the smooth mixture, taking his time to do so. He put his tobacco pouch back into his coat pocket and withdrew a box of wooden matches. He took one out and lit his pipe, all the while keeping one eye trained on the boiler room doorway.

He puffed well on his pipe for a moment or two. Satisfied that it was lit to perfection, he walked closer to the door that led into the little boiler room and peered in. It was pitch dark. There were no windows in this room. The smell emanating from the boiler room was overwhelming. Inspector Dahms had to step back one step, still puffing on his pipe. He took a deep breath and then stepped back into the doorway and felt around the walls on either side of the door for a light switch. He found it on the left side and switched it on. No lights came on. The inspector rolled his eyes upwards and sighed, blowing out a blue puff of smoke directly into the darkness of the boiler room where it disappeared from sight.

"Suppose you just come on out and say hi?" His low, gravelly voice cut through the silence of the basement. He calmly puffed on his pipe. "Please, I should like very much to meet you."

Time seemed to come to a stop. There was no sound, not even ambient noise. The boiler room was silent. The basement was silent. The world outside was gone. It was as if all things were somehow muted, here and now. The smoke from the pipe swirled slowly and silently in time and space. The moment passed. A distinct chill filled the entire basement and the inspector realized that he could now see his breath. He became aware that someone, or something, was moving in the boiler room.

"Oh, but we have already met, Thomas." There was a vague familiarity in that voice, Inspector Dahms thought, but he could not immediately place it. It was a deep, clear, and resonant voice. A strange, dark shadow seemed to move along the far wall, from one side of the boiler room to the other side, nearer the stairwell. As it moved, the familiar scratching and scraping sound returned. It seemed to get louder. This shadow was so dark that it appeared to the Inspector to be darker than the pitch black of the room it was in. As he watched this strange thing creep across the wall in the shadows, he could see that it somehow cast its own reluctant shadow that followed in the darkness.

A tall, thin form emerged and began to take shape. The creature was spindly in appearance from head to toe. Its arms and legs seemed impossibly thin. It was impossible for the inspector to tell where the elbows or knees were, or if there even were any. It manifested in front of Inspector Dahms just inside the boiler room doorway. Though he could not see a face on this person, the inspector could somehow sense a malicious grin leering at him from the shadows.

"Do you recognize me now?"

"No. I cannot say that I do recognize you, though I thought that I might have recognized your voice. So, who are you?"

"Why, Thomas, I'm positively hurt that you don't know who I am. After so many years of wonderful marriage, and…intercourse, I was your best friend, Thomas."

"Well, I'm sorry if I've hurt your feelings, but I don't recall anyone, ever, I considered a friend. So now that we have established that fact, why don't we try again?" Inspector Dahms smiled pleasantly up at the tall shadow. It clearly was much taller than him. The inspector slowly exhaled tobacco smoke out through his nostrils. His gray eyes never once left the shadow's form. "Who are you?" Inspector Dahms spoke gently.

"But Thomas, I was your best friend and truly your protector." The voice had been deep before, but it now seemed to almost hiss at Inspector Dahms. "You say that you recognize my voice? This is because we have conversed, you and I. Many, many times we spoke. Intimately, Thomas, so intimately."

"I am sorry. I have no recollection of such…intimate conversations, as you put it."

"Oh, but you do, Thomas. You do. But it is deep. So deep." As the shadow said this, a loud clicking sound seemed to come from it. It had sounded almost like very low-frequency static from a radio, or like an underwater electrical shock might sound. The inspector observed that the dark shadow seemed to vibrate physically when it made this sound. At least, that was how it looked to the inspector. The voice of the shadow returned to its deep, clear voice. "You see, Thomas, it was in your dreams that we would meet, you and I. And you would talk with me. We spoke so often in your dreams, Thomas. Are you beginning to remember? Are you beginning to see? That was where you would go to think, Thomas, while you were dreaming. You came to me. We would sit and we would think and we would speak. Remember, Thomas? Remember?

"What made you safe on all those dark nights, deep down in the lowest, darkest depths of the great structure shaped to suit you and me to a T? Oh, Thomas, you know, where there was fun and games, and torture and death. Remember? It was the mind against the mind, us against them, good versus evil, with the whole of the Earth at stake, no? Our way of life was being threatened! Our way! We were a team back there, defending our way of life…safe…defending our way, in the shadows. Remember? You do remember, Ice Man! Remember!"

As the shadow spoke this last word, the word *remember*, the voice seemed to rise in pitch to match that of a woman's voice. It rose suddenly into the shrill screaming of a woman in agony. It was a voice Inspector Dahms instantly recognized. The voice broke into a bitter and loud laughter. The rage, despair, and vitriol in that laughter spat out at the inspector with a palpable force and was followed by an overwhelming odor of rotting flesh and death. The inspector stood stock still, regarding the shadow as it clicked and buzzed. For a split second, Inspector Dahms thought he could just make out a face—at least the eyes, he thought. They were black. But before they vanished back into the shadow, they had seemed to somehow change into purple, or were they blue?

"Yes," the inspector said. "I am ice man. I'm sorry, but I still don't know your name? I really must insist on your name, sir?"

"My name is important to you? What's in a name? It is what is in the soul that tastes…I mean, that counts, Inspector Colonel. What is in your soul, do you think? Shadows…shadows are we. You and I, we are brethren, we are legion, you and me, so delicious, mmm, yum yum! Know me by my name, in the shadows."

"No, but thank you, anyway." Inspector Dahms stepped toward the shadow in the boiler room doorway. "I really need a name for the arrest forms, you see. You have been very, very naughty and you are in need of a bath. I know you were at that crime scene. I recognized the smell. I also have eyewitness reports concerning you assaulting Julie Bernard. I'm just going to take you for a little walk upstairs…" As Inspector Dahms spoke, he observed the shadow recede back into the boiler room. As it moved back along the boiler room walls, he could hear the same scratching sounds he had heard before. This time, however, they were fading away.

"Do you know where you are, Thomas? Know you this place? You know me; you know my name. There is no name. No name. We are one, Thomas. I reside, deep down, where there is only distance, and emptiness. You must find where you are, Thomas, in order to find me. Then we'll be together again, forever…"

Inspector Dahms stepped into the boiler room, turning on the light as he did so. This time, the lights came on. He found himself alone, with no shadow but his own. †

CHAPTER 25 OR 6 TO 4
A Hallmark Moment from Hell

The little old man drove Billy back to his mother's house after their pancake supper. The tan Lexus smoothly pulled off of Pequot Road and into the little driveway in front of a small ranch-style house with a tiny front lawn. The house and the entire property were bathed in darkness. A lone street lamp at the far corner of the property shone dimly in the naked and pale full moonlight. There was no car in the driveway.

"I thought that your mother should have been home from work by now, Billy." The little old man looked over at the young boy.

"Yeah, she should be. She's probably out drinking with that orangutan boyfriend in black."

"Do you have a key to get in the house?" the little old man asked, chuckling.

"Yeah, I think so." Billy and the little old man got out of the car. Billy began to check his pockets for his house key. The little old man was looking at the house. He slowly walked away from his car and into the tiny front lawn to a point several yards away from the front door.

Though it was terribly dark, Billy could see well enough in the moonlight that the little old man seemed somehow transfixed on the house, staring. He watched in fascination as the little old man seemed to start swaying, ever so slightly, with his face tilted slightly upward, as if sniffing at the night air. Billy wondered what he was looking at. And what was he smelling?

"I found my key!" Billy walked toward the little old man holding up the house key in his hand as he did.

"Splendid, Billy." The little old man smiled.

"Do you want to see my room? It's wicked cool!"

"Oh, I would love to, young man. Thank you. I would hate to miss out on anything that was wicked." Billy turned and inserted the key into the lock and unlocked it. He opened the door and led the little old man inside. Billy reached to his left and switched on a light that illuminated a living room. The furniture was old and dilapidated. The room was dimly lit and gloomy. A wide-screen television stood silently in the corner. The two walked through the living room. The hardwood floors creaked and groaned under their footsteps.

Billy led the little old man through a doorway that came into a small hallway with equally creaky, old hardwood floors. At the very end of this hallway was a door. It was closed. There was a second doorway to the left that led into the kitchen. To the right, the hallway opened up a little bit and ended at the foot of a staircase leading up to the second floor. Billy flipped another wall switch on and an overhead light dimly lit the hall and the staircase.

"My room is up here," he said. But the little old man did not seem to hear Billy. He simply stood frozen, staring at the closed door at the end of the hall. Billy followed the little old man's gaze to see what he was staring at. When he realized what it was the little old man was staring at, a chill bolted up and down his spine. He was staring at the door that led down to the basement. It was the door that led to the body of Thyrra Lane.

Billy looked back at the little old man. He had closed his eyes and seemed to be sniffing at the air again. Whatever it was he could smell, Billy observed, he seemed to really like it. The little old man half smiled, keeping his eyes closed and slightly rolling his head and neck from side to side as he continued to inhale deeply through his nose.

Blood was rushing through Billy's body and straight up into his head with an almost deafening roar as he now stood, frozen, watching the little old man. The overhead light in the hallway seemed brighter than normal to Billy. It burned hot on his skin, like a spotlight. The silence was unbearable. For a brief moment in time, Billy Werner was sure that he was about to be caught. All of those brilliant plans of his would be wasted, his ultimate victory snatched away, because he had forgotten that he had a body hanging upside down in the basement.

Billy stared alternately at the little old man standing in the hallway, and then back at the closed cellar door. He then heard a noise. It sounded to Billy as if it had come from the basement. It had sounded like a woman coughing, or choking. *But Thyrra is dead. I know she is!* Billy thought desperately to himself. He looked back at the little old man to see if he had heard the sound, too. But the little old man was looking right at Billy, smiling widely.

"Now Billy, let us see this 'wicked cool' room of yours, eh?"

Billy hesitated, then awkwardly nodded his head and pointed the way up the stairs. The little old man began to ascend the old, hardwood staircase. As he followed him up the stairs, Billy could swear that he heard that same sound again coming from the basement. He looked nervously back at the door that led down to the basement as each stair groaned in protest.

The stairs led up to a hallway which led to several rooms on the second floor. To the right was a full bathroom and across from it, on the left side of the hallway, was Billy's bedroom. At the end of the hallway was the master bedroom. Billy led the little old man into his room. He flipped on a light switch to reveal a small, single bed, an old, wooden dresser, and a desk and chair that at some point in time had been painted white. Textbooks and notepads sat neatly stacked on the desk. The little old man noted how neat and organized Billy's room was compared to the rest of the house. The bed had been made, no clothing lay anywhere, and there were no toys or anything strewn about the room. Everything was in order here.

Billy showed the little old man all of his most treasured belongings. He had a small collection of knives, each of them "borrowed" from here and there. The little old man chuckled at this. Then Billy showed him his secret stash of books. Some were biographies of all the great serial killers from all over the world. Others were investigations into the identities of unknown serial killers. It was clear to the little old man that Billy's favorite was H. H. Holmes. Billy kept these in a duffle bag stuffed all the way under his bed. The little old man could not help but admire these, and was struck by Billy's knowledge concerning the topic.

The two then descended the stairs down into the hallway on the first floor. At the base of the stairway was a small table with a small mirror hanging on the wall above it. There were several pictures on the table that appeared to have been taken by a digital camera. The little old man picked up one of these pictures and stared at it. It was a picture of a man and a woman. They were both posing and trying to look sexy for the camera.

"Yup," Billy said. "That's Mom with her new boyfriend. Man, is he ever a puke." The little old man started to laugh, and shook his head. "Oh, no," Billy said. "You're not gonna roll around on the floor here laughing again, are you?" Billy was smiling broadly as he asked this. The little old man was still chuckling softly. He shook his head.

"What's so funny?" Billy asked this earnestly.

"Nothing is funny, Billy. I simply have had a splendid day and I owe it all to you."

"Me? I didn't do anything."

"Oh, but you did, Billy, you did. You see, my fine young man, you have helped me to find those that summoned me. And thanks to you, I can now conclude my business here."

"You can?" Billy looked surprised. The little old man nodded his head, smiling. He then placed the photograph carefully down on the table, face down.

"I must go now, Billy. But don't you worry, we'll be seeing a great deal of each other in the days and years to come, I promise."

"Okay!" Billy was genuinely pleased. This delighted the little old man! "Can you find the front door, okay? Cause I have to go to the bathroom before I piss my pants."

The little old man smiled. "I certainly can, Billy. And thank you, young man." The two shook hands.

"You're welcome, I guess. Oh hey, thanks for the pigs in blankets!"

"You are most welcome. Good-bye."

"Bye." Billy turned and ran through the kitchen to the small bathroom that was just off of the kitchen. As Billy unzipped his fly and began to urinate, he breathed out a long, slow, sigh of relief. He then smiled from ear to ear. Billy really liked that little old man; he was cool. Though he did not fully understand what the little old man had meant when he said that they would be seeing a lot of each other, he liked the idea of it. After all, this was the first man that Billy had ever met who seemed to care about Billy. But that was going to have to wait, Billy thought as he zipped up his fly. *Right now, I have a body to dispose of.* He flushed the toilet and looked at himself in the bathroom mirror. *I look older,* he thought. He smiled to himself. *This should be fun.*

As Billy walked back through the kitchen, he stopped short. The same ice-cold chill he felt go up and down his spine before had now returned. The door to the basement now stood wide open in the hallway. Billy listened intently for any sounds coming from anywhere, but he could not hear anything over the sound of the blood rushing to his head. He looked over at the kitchen counter he was standing next to. A wooden block sitting on the counter held an array of carving knives. Billy drew the largest of these knives, the very same knife he had used to kill Thyrra, from the wooden holder.

He then carefully crept out into the hall, and the old, hardwood floor creaked under his weight as he did. He stepped into the open doorway of the basement and looked down the stairs. He could see that someone had turned a light on down there. The dark, stained concrete floor at the base of the stairs was lit by the one, naked light bulb in the basement ceiling. The old, wooden floorboards in the hallway creaked again as he stepped towards the top of the basement stairs. Billy began the descent. He closed the hallway door behind him. *Whoever was down here,* Billy thought, *is never coming back up.*

"Oh, yoo-hoo, dead man! Heeeeere little dead man!" Billy's voice seemed to boom in the quiet and confined basement. "Come out, come out, wherever you are!" Billy reached the bottom step, and then he softly and carefully took the final step onto the concrete basement floor. Straight ahead of him was the corpse of poor Thyrra Lane. She was still bound, gagged, and dead. Dried blood still clung to her body and had coagulated into an impossibly large pool on the cold, hard basement floor directly beneath where she hung. Thyrra's long hair, still shining, almost touched it. But there was something different, Billy observed.

At first, he couldn't quite place what it was that was different. Confident that he was alone in the basement, Billy put the knife down. He walked around the corpse of his first-ever victim. He could now see the huge gash that he had clumsily made that had hastened her death. Billy smiled.

"Oops!" He said this and started laughing, but he stopped short. For a moment, he had lost his breath. Resting in one of Thyrra's bound hands was a note addressed to "Mr. William Werner, Esquire." Billy took it from Thyrra's hand. "Thank you, Miss Lane." He said this with a mischievous smile as he opened the envelope and removed the letter. It read:

Billy, my dear young boy. Do forgive me for prying into your affairs without asking you first, but I simply could not resist seeing your artwork first-hand. Rest assured, I think it to be a masterpiece! Bully for you, young William, bully for you! My goodness me, here I thought that you were a smashing young man with great potential, when all along you are a smashing young man who is living up to his potential! But, alas, there is the bad news, Billy. Well, I say "bad news" in a very relative sense, of course. There is something I now know that you must know, now. Your mother will not be returning to you, Billy. She has died, son. I am sorry, my young friend, but I am quite sure she is gone. The man in the photograph I saw upstairs in the hallway caused her death, and he, too, is dead. Below, you shall see a name, and a phone number, Billy. I would very much like for you to call that number and ask for that person. Simply tell them your name and inform them that you are the son of William Chester. They shall take good care of you, Billy. So, too, shall I. Very truly yours, W.

Billy was surprised when a tear dropped from his face onto a corner of the note.

"Oh no," he whispered softly as he quickly tried to dry it before it spread to any of the text. He sniffed loudly. For the second time in a day, Billy had been called "son" by a man he looked up to. He very carefully put the note back into the envelope. He would keep that letter for the rest of his life. Billy had stopped crying now.

He turned back around to look at his "masterpiece," grinning ear to ear. He had won. The world's biggest loser was no more. He had won his first real victory, and the taste was beyond sweet. Billy felt like savoring it. The light in the basement was still on, but Billy didn't care anymore. He was free. He walked over to Thyrra, smiling broadly. He felt as if he towered over his helpless victim. Billy pulled down his pants and began to celebrate. †

CHAPTER 26
A Rat Trap

Julie tried to open her eyes. She blinked her eyes several times and tried to focus them, but she could not. She could not see. Her vision was blurred and clouded. Her head felt heavy. She tried to pick her head up but to no avail. She had the vague sensation of movement. She could just barely hear the sound of leaves and sticks and brambles lightly crunching and cracking. The sounds were so distant and seemed somewhat muted. She closed her eyes and tried to focus on the sounds and sensation of movement.

After several moments of listening intently, she deduced that her body was sliding across the cold, rough forest floor, and that this was the sound she had been listening to. Julie could feel the vice-like grip of the witch's hand wrapped around her ankles, pulling her effortlessly through the underbrush of the Great Woods of Littleborough and up Fears Hill. She tried to open her eyes once more. The sunlight danced in and out of her clouded vision as it caromed through the canopy of the forest above and into her eyes. The trees seemed, to Julie, to be peering down at her with a sympathetic cold dread as the witch dragged her through the woods.

The witch stopped. The old woman released her grip on Julie's ankles, dropping her legs to the ground ruthlessly. Julie watched the tall, gaunt shadow of the witch reach downward with her enormous hand toward her head, taking Julie by her hair and sitting her up. The witch then pulled Julie forward and onto her knees, and then forced her head down onto the ground. Julie could feel the ground beneath her give way. The forest floor opened wide. It was as if the earth were swallowing her whole.

Julie frantically reached out her arms as she fell, trying to get a hold of anything to prevent herself from falling. She crashed right through the brush and the brambles. As she fell further, she hit solid earth. Julie made an audible grunt as the wind was knocked out of her. Her head hit the solid earth. She cried out weakly and fell forward. Julie could see a dark, earthen surface appear beneath her. She braced herself for a hard landing.

She rolled as she hit the ground to lessen the blow. A sharp, terrible pain in her right ankle shot up her leg. There was even more pain in the shoulder she had injured earlier in the day. When her head hit the ground, everything flashed a blinding, brilliant white in Julie's head. This was accompanied by searing pain.

She laid twisted half on her back and half on her right side. With some considerable effort, she rolled herself squarely onto her back and tried to open her eyes to see where she was. The knocks to her head seemed to help clear her vision. She could see the hole through which she had been dropped, illuminated by the remaining sunlight in the forest above. She watched helplessly as the old woman covered the hole back up with branches and brush, blotting out the sun. The old woman's laughter echoed in Julie's head. *Please stop*, Julie thought, as she closed her eyes. *Please, please stop.* The sound soon faded to silence.

Julie opened her eyes. She had no idea how much time had passed since she had passed out. A tall shadow stood over her and seemed to be looking down at her. A dark face slowly descended downward toward Julie. She felt a surge of helplessness and fear. She was pinned flat on her back and could not move at all. Finally the dark face came into her view as the shadows gave way to light. Julie could see that it was the woman with the pink golf ball. Her face emerged from the shadows, mere inches from Julie's face. The woman was staring directly into her eyes. Her look was serious and unblinking.

"Well, well, well, well, well, then, there, now, little witch, what have you gotten yourself into?" The woman smiled menacingly into Julie's face. Julie was mesmerized by the different colored specks in the iris of both of this woman's eyes. The woman's voice was low. She spoke clearly into Julie's head.

"I'm not a witch." Julie's voice was hoarse and soft, barely above a whisper.

"No. You're right, there. You're not even close to being who you are. I said 'little witch,' not witch." The woman nodded her blonde head toward the darkness. "Her, now that is a witch, maybe even a witch and a half."

Julie tried to shake her head. She struggled to speak. "She's evil. She kidnapped a little girl, Sandra." The woman began shaking her head. "I saw her do it." Julie tried to raise her voice, but only ended up coughing. The woman put her hand over Julie's chest, her long fingers splayed out widely. The coughing subsided immediately. Julie looked up, wide-eyed, at the woman.

"You look, but you do not see. You listen, but do not hear. You think, and therefore do not understand," the woman said.

Julie regarded the woman for a moment. "What does that mean?" she asked.

"Don't worry about it right now," the woman said.

A scream, loud and shrill, emanated from somewhere in the darkness. The woman with the pink golf ball looked over her shoulder into the pitch darkness, then looked back down at Julie.

"I saw her with Sandra in the forest."

"Yes, but you don't know why she did it, do you, Julie?" Julie was silent. "How did you know to take the upper pathway to Fears Hill?"

"What?"

"What told you to do that?"

"I don't know." Julie shook her head slightly.

"Why did you go up into your attic, Julie?"

"Wait, how did you know...?"

"What was in that shoebox?"

Julie lost her breath for a moment. "How could you possibly know...?"

"That is three times in one day that you have denied your true self and heritage." As the woman spoke, Julie was, again, trying to shake her head as tears formed at the corner of her eyes. She looked up at the woman with wide, green eyes. A tear rolled down the side of Julie's face.

"I could never be like that...that woman," she said.

"No, you're right, there. But then again, you don't have to be. I'm not saying you have to be any specific kind of person or thing. But for Christ's sake, Julie, be who you are, not what you think you should be."

Julie had closed her eyes. Her head throbbed with pain. She opened her eyes and looked up at the woman. "I'm not a witch."

"Uh-huh."

"There's no such thing as witches or magic spells, only science."

"Don't tell it to me, tell it to her." The woman's menacing smile returned. Her white teeth gleamed in the darkness of this underworld. Julie set her chin.

"Where are your golf clubs?" Julie asked.

"I almost lost that match so I could meet you there."

"How do you know me?"

"I could've lost as much as fifty cents, even a dollar!"

"No, please, really, who are you and how do you know who I am?"

"Of course, my opponent went straight into the water on the next hole and that evened it up."

"Why are you doing this?"

"I birdied the next two holes."

"Why won't you tell me what is happening?"

"But he was good. He was good. I only took him for twenty-five dollars. He put up a game little fight, for a man. You don't golf, do you, Julie?" Julie did not answer. Her green eyes sparkled. "What a pity, you'd make a fine caddy."

"Who are you?" Julie asked.

"Right now, I'm only a dream."

Julie opened her eyes. The light, though there was very little of it, made her head hurt so she closed them again. The vivid dream she had just had still lingered. For a second Julie thought that she smelled lilies. The scent was soft and warm, almost loving. It faded, then vanished. Her face was inches away from a dark, moist, earthen wall. The powerful odor that permeated the air and the walls returned. Julie realized that she was becoming acclimated to it.

She kept her eyes closed and listened for the presence of the old woman. A loud roar came from directly above where she lay. The earth beneath where she lay and all around her shook and vibrated violently. The howling died down, picked up, and died down again. All was quiet again. Julie continued listening intently. Though soft and distant, she knew she could faintly hear the strange murmurings of the old woman coming from somewhere down in this...*Whatever it is*, Julie thought.

Despite the throbbing pain in her head, Julie tried to look around. It was dark and shadowy. She could see that her fall had been at least thirty feet. She tried to lift her head up off of the earthen floor. When she did, nausea and dizziness instantly came. She put her head back down and closed her eyes. She concentrated on her breathing. She kept as still as possible until it all passed.

Julie reached out her left hand and touched the wall. It was cold and moist and rough. She carefully and painfully rolled herself toward the earthen wall and onto her belly. Using the wall to help herself get upright, it took several painful minutes for her to get up onto her knees. It took several more minutes for her to get up onto her feet. Still leaning against the cold, damp, earthen wall, she opened her eyes and looked around. She could now see that she was where she thought she was: in a deep underground cavern beneath the Great Woods of Littleborough. The walls, the floor, and the ceiling were all earthen. The only light source seemed to be from a solitary candle mounted high on the right side of the passage in front of her. It flickered only slightly. Julie carefully turned her head and looked behind her. The passage seemed to go on indefinitely in that direction. It was unlit and pitch dark. Julie turned herself back around to face the passage lit by the single candle.

The cavern was very narrow where Julie stood. She stared hard to see into the shadows beyond where the single mounted candle burned high up on the wall. She thought she could just see where the passage appeared to open up into a larger space. It also appeared to be dimly lit by candlelight. The cavern looked to be at least fifty feet away from where she was. It also sounded as if this was where the old woman might be. Julie could still just make out the strange, almost rhythmic speech of the old woman.

She looked down at her ankle. It had swelled up to twice its original size. She could not be sure if it was broken or badly sprained. Still leaning on the earthen wall for support, Julie tried to put a little bit of weight on her ankle. Pain shot through the ankle and up her leg. Julie bit her lip. She tried again. This time Julie angled her foot differently to see if this would help to ease the pain. Though it still throbbed, she was able to move a little in this way, albeit with a pronounced limp.

Julie began to hobble her way down the dark, earthen passage toward the larger opening of the cavern. She took great care so as not to alert the old woman. She knew she was physically no match for this person, especially since she had injured her ankle and shoulder.

Surprise was Julie's only weapon; she wanted to keep the advantage. She inched her way along the passage, still leaning heavily on the walls of the cavern. There were more sounds coming from the opening ahead. As Julie drew closer, she could hear what sounded like crying and pleading, and a forlorn wailing. She could sense an unmistakable despair in the voices. It tugged at her heart.

She reached the point in the passage where she was directly beneath the mounted candle. Julie was just a few feet from where she would be able to look into the opening and see whatever may be there. She glanced up at the candle on the dark earthen wall, and then back toward the opening. After one more awkward step forward, she looked back up at the candle. It was mounted, somehow, inside the open jaw of a human skull. Julie's eyes widened.

"Okay," she whispered.

A loud clatter startled Julie. She tore her eyes off of the skull and candle to look down the passageway toward the noise. It sounded as if it had come from somewhere deep inside the cavern. Julie could hear the old woman laughing somewhere in that darkness. From this right side of the passage she had only a partial view into the space ahead. It opened up even further on the right. The singsong sounds of the old woman had grown louder now. The pungent smell of earth and fire, smoke, and the forest had also grown stronger.

Julie edged her way along the earthen wall and peered into the larger part of the cavern. Due to the flickering of countless candles, it took her a moment for her eyes to truly adjust to the light in the Great Cavern. A great multitude of these candles were mounted up high along the walls on what she was sure would be more human skulls. Julie could now see the entirety of the underground cavern. It was enormous and it was alive. Julie felt as if she were being watched, observed by someone or something unseen.

She could not see the wall, if there was a wall, on the opposite side from where she stood. The cavern just seemed to go on and on, forever, into the shadows. Huge, towering oak shelves ran along the two walls that Julie could see. They were packed with impossibly old books, some of them quite large, Julie noticed. There were also boxes, crates, and jars of every size, type, and description, spread everywhere on the earthen floor around and on top of these great oak shelves.

Large, long, oak tables were spread randomly in the wide-open areas between these gargantuan shelves. More large, old books sat on these tables. Most of them were opened. There were many more boxes, baskets, and jars of every size and of every conceivable shape on or around these great oak tables. Numerous candles flickered and danced on every large, oak table and every large, oak bookshelf.

A snapping and crackling sound came from somewhere off to her right. Julie looked in the direction from where it had come. Through the darkness and shadows of the large, oak tables and the large, oak bookshelves, Julie could see a flickering light. It was all silhouetted by an enormous fire raging inside a huge hearth. Darkness draped down each side of the hearth and the flames. Though quite large, Julie could only just see it as she stood hundreds of feet away from the hearth and the fire. There was what appeared to be a tall, thin silhouette that seemed to be moving around where the enormous hearth stood. Julie assumed this to be the old woman.

When Julie had first entered the Great Cavern, she had sensed that she was being watched. It had honestly felt like whatever was watching her was everywhere, all at once. It felt so strange. Now Julie began to sense that whatever had been observing her had decided that she was not a threat. She began to sense, then hear, and finally, see movement. Everything down here appeared to be moving to Julie, somehow. She looked more closely. Then she realized that the large oak tables and the giant oak bookshelves, the earthen floor, and the earthen walls and the ceilings were alive with bugs, spiders, moths, mice, rats, bats, cats, weasels, skunks, squirrels, chipmunks, ferrets, frogs, snakes, and heaven only knew what else. They all collectively seemed to be resuming their busy day after having been briefly interrupted by Julie's presence.

The ceiling was at least sixty or seventy feet high and earthen, like the walls. Large cobwebs shone and shimmered in the candlelight across the ceiling and in every corner of the cavern. Gigantic roots from the trees above that made up the Great Woods of Littleborough hung down from the ceiling like huge, gnarled hands reaching down into the very soul of the earth.

As Julie's gaze went from these ancient roots of these ancient trees back down to this ancient place she now stood in, she found herself feeling a strange numbness and a buzzing sensation. She looked around herself but could see no logical explanation for why or how she was feeling this way. Julie now faced the front of the Great Cavern and the large fire that raged in the enormous hearth. The flames that she could just make out on the far side of the cavern danced in her green eyes. She sensed that she could somehow see all around herself. There was no pain. She felt for one moment as if she were looking down upon herself and her surroundings. She felt a supreme awareness she had never felt before. She felt totally alive in that moment. She felt power fill her entire being. An intense familiarity overcame her. It was as if she had been here before. But Julie knew that this could not possibly be true. As she thought about this, her feelings of power and self-awareness began to dissipate. The throbbing pain in her head and her ankle returned.

There were symbols etched deeply into these earthen walls, these great oak tables and these great oak bookshelves. In the center of each earthen wall was a candle-lit symbol, a letter or character of some kind. Julie was unfamiliar with most of these symbols. Even in the condition she was in, these symbols piqued her boundless curiosity. There was an unfinished pyramid with an all-seeing eye etched into the wall directly above the giant hearth where the large fire burned. The detail of the etching was breathtaking.

There was a pentagram carved into the earthen wall to Julie's right. Opposite the pentagram etching was a hexagram etched into that earthen wall. Around these large etchings were many smaller symbols. Julie was able to recognize some of these. There was a symbol that resembled the ying and the yang. There was the sun. There was a shooting star. There was a cross, a crescent moon, a full moon, an eagle, a bear, a rat, and a wolf.

Julie looked up. The dark, earthen ceiling sparkled and twinkled in the candlelight. As she examined it, Julie began to recognize various constellations and the solar system. The planet Venus was above the pentagram. The constellation of Orion was above the hexagram. The constellation of the Pleiades was directly above the pentagram.

Julie turned herself around as carefully and quietly as she could. The back area of the cavern, the spot from which Julie had entered, was the darkest area. The light from the huge fire and the mounted candles barely penetrated the blackness. There was just enough light for Julie to make something out on the back wall, facing the hearth and the fire. It was a large etching of a face. Julie stared at the face. It was a woman's face. She was beautiful, thought Julie. The face stared silently, powerfully, over the entirety of the large cavern. Chills ran down Julie's spine. She had seen this before, somewhere. She couldn't place it, though.

Below and to the right of this face was an etching of a serpent devouring itself, forming a perfect circle. An etching of what looked to be the Earth was to the left and slightly below the woman's face. Julie had to tear her eyes away from the beautiful face of the woman etched into the earthen wall and, again, slowly and carefully turned herself around to face the fire.

She thought she saw something move on the floor a scant few feet away from where she now stood. She looked closely. There was a cage against the wall to her right. Someone, or something, was curled up tightly in a fetal position inside that cage.

Julie took one more step, and then another. As she moved deeper into the cavern more and more of it was now in her view. She simply could not believe its size; it seemed to go on endlessly. She could see that countless candles were, in fact, mounted in human skulls everywhere. They were up on the walls and they were mounted on the enormous oak bookshelves. Many of the candles were spread all over the large oak tables. As they flickered, the shadows danced around the cavern and up and down the walls as if they had a life of their own. They danced, intertwining with the firelight and the shadows it cast, as if it was all part of an eternal Ball.

A surprising number of these long oak tables were spread out all over the cavern. Each had bowls and jars of every conceivable size and shape on them dispersed among the skulls with candles. The large books, some opened and some closed, lay flat on many of the large oak tables. Julie peered down at one of the open books. It was hard for her to see what was on the brown-yellow pages in the strange candlelight. The characters seemed totally unfamiliar to her.

Candles burned amidst the old and worn looking books that lined the shelves. In between these shelves were more symbols carved into the earthen walls, each lit by a specially mounted candle. Julie could see the old woman now. Or, more specifically, she could make out the tall, rail-thin silhouette of the witch. She was tending the enormous fire that burned inside the huge hearth at the far end of the cavern, still murmuring and cackling. There were dozens of round wooden crates that had been made from small branches woven tightly together dispersed all over the cavern floor amidst the large oak tables. Some of these crates were stacked one on top of another. The rest were spread out randomly. The overwhelming smell of earth—dank, deep, and primal—and smoke filled Julie's nostrils.

It was too dark for Julie to see what was in these crates. She decided to try to use these as cover to see if the person in the cage was still alive. Julie lurched painfully across the cavern towards the cage, never taking her eyes off of the old woman. She crouched down onto her hands and knees, being careful to keep her swollen ankle from taking on any unnecessary weight, and crawled the last few feet over to the cage. She looked inside the cage. Hot fear flared in her belly; it was a person!

She took the person's hand and felt for a pulse. The hand was tiny. The pulse was surprisingly strong. Julie peered into the darkness of the cage. In the flickering light she was able to just see light-blonde hair. Julie gently felt around the edges of the little cage until she could feel a cloth-like material. She maneuvered herself as quietly as she could to get into a position where she could see just a bit better. She looked closely at the cloth-like material in her hand; it was pink in color. It was a pink dress. It was Sandra! Anger flared in Julie's belly. The young child was asleep, or unconscious. Julie carefully peeked over the stack of wooden crates to see where the old woman was. She was still tending her fire inside the hearth. Julie regarded the hearth. *Oh my God*, she thought, *could that be a giant oven?* She returned her attention to Sandra.

"Sandra," Julie whispered, "Sandra, wake up, honey." Sandra did not stir. Julie tried to gently shake the child. "Sandra, Sandra, wake up, please, honey?" The little girl did not budge.

Julie looked around the massive cavern for a way out. But it was too dark and shadowy to see much of anything along the dark edges of that Great Cavern. The old woman was still busily tending to her fire, cackling and speaking her singsong speech to no one in particular. Julie left the cover of the stack of crates for one of the large bookshelves just a few feet to her right. She knew the way out must be where the witch was. She kept her eyes wide and unblinking, fixed on the old woman by the fire. Using the shadows for cover, Julie began to inch toward the witch. †

CHAPTER 27
The Secret Passage of Secrets

Father Knight opened his eyes. It was dark. His head ached and his mouth was dry. He was not sure where he was. He stretched his sore body and realized he was in his own bed. Ezekiel was fast asleep at the foot of the bed. Father Knight could hear the small dog's steady, rhythmic breathing.

He listened to the sounds of the night, trying to remember what had happened earlier. He did not remember changing and going to bed. He remembered water and…Sandra. Father Knight sat bolt right up in bed, but dizziness and nausea overcame him and he quickly lay back down and rested his head on the pillow. His head still felt quite heavy. He could still smell the muck from the pond and the powerful odor of urine.

Father Knight lay still and tried to remember. His thoughts were interrupted when something made a *thump* that reverberated throughout the little apartment and his bedroom. Ezekiel wearily picked up his head and cocked it to one side, his furry ears standing straight up at attention. Silence followed.

Father Knight pulled the blankets and sheets off and swung his legs over the side of the bed. His head swam. He turned on the bedside lamp. *Thump.* There it was again. He could feel it through the floor under his feet. It sounded like it was coming from somewhere just outside the tiny apartment. Father Knight sighed. He waited for the dizziness and nausea to pass. Though his head still felt heavy on his shoulders, he got up and put on his sandals and a bathrobe. He patted Ezekiel on his backside, took a bottle of water from the fridge, and went outside to have a look.

The cool night air was refreshing. Father Knight took a big drink of his water. He began to feel better. He looked up into the night. The clouds raced across the starry sky. Some of these would briefly blot out the full moon entirely only to have it return as quickly as it had gone. Father Knight walked out into the small lawn area in between the apartment and the church. He breathed in deeply while he got his bearings and his eyes adjusted to the dark. He listened for the sound he had heard. But now there was only silence. The only sound he could hear was the wind as it wound its way through the treetops and the bell tower above.

Thump! This sounded to Father Knight like it was right behind him. He turned quickly to see what was there. But there was nothing. It was still just him, by himself, in the back lawn of his new parish in the middle of the night, in his pajamas. Father Knight smiled to himself. *Heavenly Father,* he thought, *what have You in store for me?*

Thump! Right after this last *thump,* Father Knight was sure he heard a curse word. It sounded like someone had said "shit." A flicker of light caught his eye. It was coming from the Neilson's backyard. He walked across the driveway and peered over the hedge.

An eerie light dimly glowed from down inside where the sinkhole in the center of the yard was. He sighed a deep sigh as he swung one leg, then the other, over the neatly trimmed hedge. He knelt down on all fours in his pajamas, his sandals, and his bathrobe, and carefully belly-crawled to the edge of the sinkhole and looked down.

There were two light sources emanating from opposite sides down inside of the hole. Curiosity gripped Father Knight. He could just make out the bottom of the sinkhole from the light of the full moon. He swung his legs over the side of the big hole and made the jump. He landed on his feet with an audible grunt, bending his legs enough to absorb the hard landing. He straightened himself up and looked around the cavern. It was an old crypt. The lights were dim. They each came from two distinct doorways that were facing one another at each end of this tiny crypt.

Father Knight walked through the door that led back toward the church and entered a short, earthen hallway. He followed it to an opening where the light source was coming from. He walked through the opening. Here, he found himself standing in the basement of the church, behind the large, metal shelf. The shelf was somehow attached to the basement wall and could be swung open or closed easily. It sat silently in the open position. A lone candle burned on top of the shelf.

Father Knight walked back through the secret opening in the basement and into the earthen hallway. He made his way along the hallway and back to the crypt. He walked over to the other doorway and peered through the door and into the passage leading away from the church. He was surprised at how large it was. Though it was very dark, there was a hint of candlelight flickering from somewhere further along the passage. Fully in the grip of curiosity, he entered.

As he walked through the darkness, Father Knight felt the passage gently slope downward, deeper and deeper into the earth. The passage was easily six feet wide. The "ceiling" was high, maybe ten or twelve feet. It was hard to judge because the passage way was so dimly lit. The floor was smooth beneath his slippers. The walls in here felt rough and earthen. The passage had a damp, clammy feel to it. The smell of earth was heavy.

Father Knight stayed to the right of the passageway, feeling his way along the wall with his hand. The passage seemed to slowly bend to his right. After several minutes he could no longer see the crypt behind him. There was darkness behind him, and darkness ahead. Hot fear flared in his belly. Father Knight shook his head and smiled to himself. He continued to slowly make his way along the passage.

Finally he reached the end of the long bend in the passageway and now stood where it apparently straightened out. Father Knight could see that it led on for hundreds and hundreds of yards. Where it led would be anybody's guess. Though still dark and shadowy, someone had lined this section of the passageway with lit candles mounted at roughly ninety-foot intervals. They were mounted up high on what appeared to be gold mounts that gleamed and glistened eerily in the shadows. These were somehow fixed into the earthen walls.

Father Knight began to walk along the straight passageway. It went on and on. The further it went, the more incredulous he became. More than once Father Knight found himself stopping, and turning around to look back from where he had come, just to see if he had made any progress at all. Finally he felt he had reached the end of the long, straight section, as he could see a faint light ringing around the shape of a doorway up ahead.

As he drew nearer, the doorway appeared to Father Knight to be made up of a large, dark cloth or curtain. There were no sounds coming from behind it. He quietly walked up to the doorway. The curtains were scarlet, purple, and black in color. They were quite large and very heavy. They were beautiful. The doorway was large and wide. It towered over Father Knight. He carefully pulled the thick, heavy cloth to one side of the doorway and peered in. What he saw took his breath away.

The entire room was well lit by innumerable candles. Father Knight needed a moment for his eyes to adjust to the light from the darkness from which he had emerged. He waited patiently for a moment, blinking his soft, brown eyes. He could see that it was an ancient and incredibly beautiful tiny chapel. It was circular in shape. He was standing at the top of a set of stairs that led down several steps to a landing. Many small wooden benches and chairs were placed around the center of this chapel along this level. In all, Father Knight counted twelve such levels of stairs, landings, and wooden benches and chairs. At the very bottom of the room was a stone floor with various symbols etched into it. These symbols surrounded a circular altar with a circular pulpit surrounding it in the center of the room. The ceiling here was quite high, he observed.

Hanging at equal intervals of the chapel were three other long and dark maroon, scarlet, purple, and black tapestries or curtains. More stairs led down to each landing from these doorways as well. The walls looked as if they had been plastered many years ago. There were carvings and paintings and frescos on these walls with inscriptions beneath them. The inscriptions were beautifully handwritten in Latin, Greek, English, and Hebrew. There were other inscriptions, too, of which Father Knight did not recognize the script.

There was a striking portrait of Christ after He had risen. It took Father Knight's breath away. He stared at it for several moments. His gaze moved down to an etching beneath the inscription—a perfect triangle.

He turned around and looked at the portrait directly opposite this and froze. It was a stunning portrait of a woman. It was just her face; there was an elegance about it that took Father Knight's breath away again. The artist had somehow captured grace and intelligence, strength and perceptiveness in just those eyes. There was a symbol etched beneath the inscription here, too. It was a hexagram. It was the Jewish Star of David. Inside each space was a corresponding dot. Then it came to Father Knight; it was Solomon's seal.

Before entering, he crossed himself. He then walked around the wooden bench that was in front of him and down each set of steps and each landing to get to the altar. There were books laid out around it. There was a New Testament that looked impossibly old to him. It was opened. Father Knight looked at it closely. He could see that it had been written in ancient Greek. Next to it was another very old book. It was the Torah, the Old Testament. This was written in ancient Hebrew. They both had been meticulously handwritten. In the center of these was another ancient-looking work. But Father Knight did not recognize it. He could not make out the language it had been written in. The letters, or symbols, were meaningless to him. They were the same characters that were up on the walls under the artworks.

"Why James, you son of a gun, you wrecked the whole surprise!"

Father Knight jumped at the sound. He turned to see Father Freeman coming into the tiny chapel through the same doorway he had come. Father Freeman grinned at him, but something seemed very odd about how he looked to Father Knight. "Ah! I see you're interested in the old book, hey?"

"Yes, I am," Father Knight said.

Father Freeman slowly descended the stairs to the altar area and walked around several of the small, wooden benches and sat down heavily in one of the small, wooden chairs near the altar where Father Knight stood.

"Father Freeman, what is this place?"

"It's a chapel." Father Freeman shrugged.

Father Knight shook his head. "No, John. It's much more than a chapel, and I think you know that." He sat down in a small, wooden chair facing Father Freeman. "What is this place?"

"A chapel," Father Knight sighed.

"Okay. If you say it's a chapel, then I guess it's a chapel," he said. Father Freeman looked at his young friend for a long moment. Then he nodded his head. He raised himself up wearily from his seat and went to the altar and regarded the old books for a moment.

"What do you think this place is, James?"

"I wish I knew."

"Take a guess."

Father Knight frowned. He glanced around the chapel for several moments. He studied the portrait of Christ. Then his gaze turned to the portrait of the woman's face. He swallowed hard and turned back to face Father Freeman.

"Do you know who the woman in that portrait is?"

"Who do you think it is, James?"

"Would I be asking if I thought I knew?"

"Do you recognize the symbol beneath her?"

"Yes, I do. It's the seal of Solomon."

"That's right, James. That seal was imprinted on a special ring given to Solomon to combat and control demons."

"Yes, that's what I understand it to be. But Solomon wasn't a woman, John. So, who is that woman?"

"Who do you think it is?"

"Never mind, John, forget it." Father Knight rose from his seat and began to pace the tiny chapel. His head still hurt from the day before.

"You give up too easily, James."

"No, John, I don't. Playing childish guessing games seems to me to be a bit of a waste of time. If you don't want to tell me, then don't. But I'm done guessing."

Father Freeman shrugged his shoulders. "Okay." He lit a cigarette. "You got the seal part right. That's something."

"No, actually that's nothing, John. It's meaningless. A symbol for controlling demons is not real. It's just a symbol used by well-intentioned but frightened and superstitious people. It was probably just Solomon's royal seal and nothing more. The demonology stuff was all made up much later, you know that."

"Do I?" Father Knight looked at Father Freeman.

"That's what they taught me at Seminary."

"So, that's it then, huh?"

"Sure seems that way to me," Father Knight said.

Father Freeman nodded. "Okay, James, take a look at the old book for a minute, would you?"

Father Knight looked at the small altar upon which the three holy books rested. He sighed. "Fine." He walked over to the altar and gently opened the old book. On the inside cover was a portrait of a woman's face. It was the same exact portrait of the same exact face that was prominently displayed on the chapel wall.

"Now look at the inside of the back cover," Father Freeman said. Father Knight carefully closed the book and reopened it from the back cover. He froze. Father Knight felt nauseous. He felt hot and cold all at once, breaking into a chilled sweat. His skin crawled. There, inside the back cover of the old book, was a portrait of a man—a tall, thin man with pure evil and malice in his eyes. Father Knight gently closed the book and turned to face Father Freeman.

"Who is this?" he said. Father Freeman smoked his cigarette. "I've seen this man twice, now. He spoke to the bishop at the picnic and then later visited me in the church. He is clearly pictured in that portrait. Who is he, John?"

"I think you know who it is, James. You just don't want to acknowledge that he exists."

"That who exists?"

"Lucifer, the Morning Star."

"Lucifer? John, you surely don't believe—"

"Oh, come on, James. For Christ's sake, and I mean that literally. What do you believe? There was just God, then man? God never really made angels? Do you actually think that Michael and Gabriel are the same as the Easter Bunny and the Great Pumpkin? They are not fictitious, James. Lucifer, Mephisticles, Belial, and the Satan are all one and the same and real.

"The War of Souls is the Eternal struggle. It is true and real. What about the scriptures, James? Do you really actually think that a handful of superstitious morons just made it up because they couldn't explain their world any other way? Give me a break!" Father Knight smiled to himself. Father Freeman began to pace around the tiny chapel. He lit another cigarette and then continued to speak.

"You kids, and your science and technology make you think that you're smart and that the people in the past were idiots. The only reason you, me, and every other jackass on this planet is still here today is because our ancestors were able to survive. And the reason they were able to survive is that they were able to accurately and truthfully observe their world. They weren't as backward as they are made out to be.

"James, I know that you believe in God. But do you seriously think that that's it? Everything else to you is just some story that someone made up to either illustrate a moral point or to coerce the meek into staying in line? The temptation of Christ happened, James. Lucifer tempts man, every man, every day. For some people this is a neat story that was invented by New Testament authors to address issues of their time. For others it is a literal story. For them it is a matter of faith, but not for us, James." He sat back down in the small, wooden chair.

"You and I are guardians, young man. Faith is the comforter for the flock, James. We priests do not merit such comfort. Knowledge of the Truth is the cold, awesome burden we bear. There is no doubt. We can't hide behind the fabric of faith. We must, instead, stand up and face the beast armed with the Truth and armed with His Love. You better believe it, buckaroo."

"John," Father Knight looked at Father Freeman, "what are you talking about?"

"Well, James, I was going to let you get some rest, give you a chance to sleep. But since you found us on your own, I may as well tell you now."

"I heard these loud thumping noises. I thought it might be…well, you know."

"Yes, I do know. That's all right, James. What you heard was me and the bishop accidentally dropping Miguel's body a couple of times. Pat's closing the secret entrance right now, as we speak, so that you won't find it."

"Father Torrez's body? John, what are you doing with that?"

"We need it."

"The police were going to do an autopsy on his body."

"They already have, James. He died of a massive heart attack. But we took back his body because we're really going to need it."

"Oh, my…you…what do you mean 'need it,' John?"

"I'll explain later."

"Okay…okay…you'll explain why you stole Father Torrez's body from the police later. Great." Father Knight started to laugh as he said this. Father Freeman looked at him. Father Knight shrugged his shoulders. "What is this place, John?"

"This is a holy place. It was constructed twenty, thirty, maybe forty thousand years ago. It was buried twelve thousand years ago beneath what Native Americans today call a place of power, O At Ka; a clearing in the woods. They believe that spirits can enter and leave our world, or plane of existence, through a clearing way up above us if the time and circumstances permit. We also believe this. You're in the center of a labyrinth of passages that lead to other holy places."

"It was buried? Why?"

"That's a long story for a different day, James."

"Right, naturally."

"Uh-huh, anyway, you and I came from St. Mark's Church, from the south. The passageway that leads to the east leads to the chapel and crypt that are beneath the St. Mark's school. The great tree of wisdom over on Fears Hill is to the west, and so it can be reached by walking the western passage. The north passage leads to a labyrinth that represents the underworld."

"A labyrinth?"

"Yup."

"Wait, don't tell me. A story for a different day?"

"Yup." Father Freeman lit another cigarette. Father Knight nodded his head. For a moment there, he almost wished he smoked cigarettes.

"What is that...old book, as you called it? And what language is that?"

"There is no known name for it. The work is so ancient it is believed to be the very first written language in the world. The only people who can actually read, or speak, the language are called 'Judges.'" Father Knight looked at Father Freeman.

"Judges?"

"Yup."

"You mean the Judges that our seminary teachers would sort of whisper about but then never answer a single question about it after that?"

"The very ones."

"Have you ever met one?"

"Nope."

"Oh."

"Sorry. Bishop Richter says he's never met one, either. But who knows?"

Father Knight was deep in thought. "But surely the first writing was the cuneiform tablets, the Sumerian language, in what is today Iraq," he said. "There are only rumors of an earlier text that supposedly came from what is now Ethiopia. No one has ever actually found anything to prove that, though."

"Yes, that's true. No one but us privileged few actually know about this older text. This old book was brought here from Southeast Africa, right around where Ethiopia is today, as you said. Some scholars believe that the place where these books came from is now under the gulf of Amman, but again, who knows? Holy men scripted copies of the original for every place of power in the world, or so it is believed. These copies, like this one, were then sent to their appointed destinations all over the world by these holy men."

"But John, they couldn't have known that North America even existed at that point. How could they have made a copy of this book and sent it along to a place that they did not even know was here?"

"Oh, but you see, they did know, James. They simply didn't look at things the way you or I would. They didn't know whether it was a continent, an island, or even a spot on the ocean. They only knew that there was a point here created by God that they had to protect. So, they did."

"Protect?"

"From evil. The shadows, James. That's why Lucifer has come here. That's why he visited you." Father Knight rolled his eyes up at the ceiling.

"You mean that strange man? John, the man I keep seeing does not know why he's here."

"What are you talking about, James?"

"The man—the tall, creepy guy, who you obviously think is Lucifer— has absolutely no idea who called him out, as he puts it. He came to visit me in the church after the picnic. He was very angry with me and with God when I made it clear to him that I did not understand who he was or what he meant. I think he believed me when I told him that I did not call."

Father Freeman arose from his seat and began to pace back and forth around the tiny chapel again. "But the fact remains that he is here. And he thinks that we have somehow called him here to do battle."

"To do… battle? What battle? What is this, the *Exorcist*? That's ridiculous! John, Bishop Richter said that Father Torrez died of a heart attack. And now you say that the autopsy proves that. I can't imagine what it must have been like to find a baby's heart in the holy water; that would scare the daylights out of anybody. But that's not a supernatural event, John. I'll admit that this tall man is strange. Maybe he's even the sick person who put the infant's heart in the holy water. But he hasn't done anything to convince me that he's somehow a fallen angel or the devil himself."

"Then who the hell is he, James? The infant's heart did not just magically appear in the holy water. Who do you think that creature is, then?"

"I don't know who that is, John. But a mortal human is most certainly capable of a horrible and depraved act like that. I will admit he does look exactly like the person in the portrait. And he seems like he is capable of such a thing. But it is not a supernatural event, John."

"This doesn't change anything, James," Father Freeman spoke gently. He sat down in his small, wooden chair. "I know that your belief is predicated on the Truth, and the power of Love. So is mine! These things still hold true. But in order that we puny, little human beings have at least a modicum of free will, there then must be the dark side. And unfortunately this darkness must be as ancient and as powerful as the Light on this physical plane."

"But John, that struggle is something inside of us. That's entirely different than some terrible angel who wants to fight us. What's the point?"

"That is the point." Father Knight and Father Freeman turned and looked up to face the southern entrance to the Tiny Chapel. The voice came from behind one of the large, deep maroon curtains that adorned the tiny chapel's four entry points. Bishop Richter entered the tiny chapel. He had come down the same passageway as Father Knight and Father Freeman had come, from the St. Mark's Church. He smiled as he entered the chapel. "Hello James." The bishop looked at Father Freeman. "Well, you were right, John. I guess this is a little hard for James to swallow. Have we heard from our friends on the other side recently?"

"No, Pat. But we'll surely be hearing from them soon," Father Freeman replied. The bishop had walked down the small flights of stairs toward the altar and sat in one of the small, wooden chairs with Father Knight and Father Freeman. "James did mention something earlier that you must be told about now, though, Pat."

"Okay, what?"

"Lucifer apparently still does not know who called him out either."

"Are you sure, my boy?" James nodded. The bishop looked at Father Freeman, who shrugged. "Well, I'll be damned. And of course, I mean that literally." The bishop and Father Freeman both smiled. "So, we do not know who challenged Lucifer, and Lucifer does not know who challenged Lucifer. We do not know who has challenged us, and Lucifer does not know who has challenged us. Quite the conundrum, isn't it?"

"Bishop Richter," Father Knight spoke softly, "what exactly is it that makes this man believe that someone has challenged him, as you call it. Since he now knows it wasn't us, why wouldn't he go back to where ever it was he came from?"

"The reason is that someone has challenged him. And Lucifer knows this because he is here. He would not have come to this place for any other reason. Eternal spirits don't just travel around as they please. They are called or drawn to a place. They often do not know why they were drawn to a place until they have arrived." The bishop chuckled, shaking his large, bald head. "For Lucifer, this must be exasperating." He smiled a big smile at Father Freeman, who was also smiling. "Gosh, it's a darned shame." Both men were now laughing.

"Yes, it really is too bad," Father Freeman said. "Life just isn't fair sometimes." Father Knight looked from the bishop to Father Freeman and then back at the Bishop.

"How can you both think that this is funny?" he said. "Father Torrez surely died as a result of this challenge, and so did an infant. Bishop Richter, forgive me for speaking out of turn, but I do not understand how…"

"No," the bishop interrupted Father Knight. "I know that you don't understand any of this, James. In fact, it would appear that you do not even believe in the devil or his domain. Is that true?"

"Yes, yes, sir, it is true." Upon hearing Father Knight say this, Father Freeman rolled his eyes.

"How can you not be sure if you believe in someone when you have already met them? Jesus, James!" The bishop put up a hand to calm his old friend down.

"James," the bishop spoke softly to Father Knight, who now looked right at the Bishop. "Who do you think that was that visited us at the end of the cookout?"

"You said that you did not recognize him. I honestly do not know who he was; he never gave his name. And at that first meeting he didn't even acknowledge me. When he and I met in the church later, he did call me out. But I had no idea what he was referring to. This seemed to only anger him even more. But he never told me who he was." Bishop Richter smiled warmly at Father Knight. Father Freeman shook his head.

"So, who do you think that actually was then, my boy?"

"I don't know."

"Ask yourself this, James. What was his demeanor when he brought up the subject of Father Torrez? How did he know to refer to the word *heart*? Did he seem like any of our other parishioners to you?" Bishop Richter then leaned forward, his face just inches from Father Knight, but still looking at the young priest directly into his eyes. He spoke in an even softer tone. "Do you actually think he had come to mourn the death of Father Torrez, James?" Bishop Richter asked. He then slowly sat back in his small, wooden chair.

"No, sir, I don't."

"Okay, good. Now, James, I get the distinct feeling that you have no trouble believing in Christ, or God, or the Holy Spirit, on mere faith. But when it comes to the others, on the dark side, you need proof. Is that right?"

"Yes. Yes, that's right, Bishop. I honestly think that the devil is a product of early religious leaders attempting to explain why bad things happen to the righteous in a monotheistic faith, and, in some cases, to coerce obedience from the masses with the use of fear.

"There really is no mention of a devil in either the Old Testament or the New Testament with the exception of the Temptation of Christ and The Book of Revelation. There is a serpent in Genesis, but it is never referred to as the devil or Satan. The Aramaic, Greek, Hebrew, and even the Coptic versions do not ever say the serpent is the devil. We know from Jewish tradition that Satan was actually a messenger to God. His job was to observe humanity and to report back to the Lord. The ancient Hebrew word, Satan, can mean 'opponent.' It doesn't mean devil.

"And the word *Lucifer*, as you both know, means 'bringer of light' in Latin. It is a reference to the planet Venus. Ancient man viewed Venus as the sign in the night sky that the sun, and daylight, is coming. It's a harbinger of hope.

"As for Hell, I do not believe that our all-loving God would ever damn any of his children for eternity. It simply is not consistent with the Holy Father as described and worshiped by Christ, or with the Christ himself."

Father Freeman had stopped pacing back and forth, and was now seated back in his small, wooden chair. He spoke much more calmly. "That is a very logical and valid concept of God, James. But it is not entirely accurate. The descriptions of the Creator are highly complex, very much like us."

"But, Father Freeman, Bishop Richter, are you then suggesting that God is having His own internal struggle between right and wrong?" Father Knight asked this question innocently.

The bishop shrugged. "That's not for any of us to know, James. But it's possible that the Morning Star, Lucifer, is a reflection of just such an emotion or feeling of Yahweh's. Perhaps each angel He created represents a different aspect to the Creator, and to Creation itself.

The creation of man takes place, and Yahweh loved this being that He had created, called man. He instructs His angels to serve man. Only His favorite angel says no. He tells Him that he will serve only Yahweh. He will love only Yahweh.

"This defiance angers God. A number of the angels side with Lucifer in this conflict. Michael and many other angels banish Lucifer and his followers out of heaven. This banishment was a conscious decision made by Yahweh. Those who were banished fell down to the earth. Satan and the fallen ones work tirelessly here to tempt, divide, and destroy mankind." The bishop leaned forward in his small, wooden chair as he spoke. His light, blue eyes were fixed on Father Knight, unblinking, burning intensely through his spectacles. He spoke softly, but each word was breathlessly choked with emotion.

"We of the cloth are not only blessed to have this knowledge; we are entrusted with it. We are burdened with it. The only reason the Dark One is not directly named in the Good Book is because it is the Good Book. There is no place in the Word of God for such blasphemy as the names of the true serpent. Nothing unholy can be put in the Holy Book. The fact that Satan bears the name 'bringer of light,' or Lucifer, can also be a harbinger of evil on this world. My child, if the planet Venus were to not appear one terrible night, no daylight can follow. It would be eternal night. It would be eternal darkness." Father Knight listened carefully to Bishop Richter. He had learned this story in Seminary.

"So, you both believe this story to be true?" Father Freeman and the bishop nodded their heads solemnly. "You both believe in the Devil?" They nodded again. "Oh," Father Knight said. And there they sat in silence, each man pondering the terrible truth and the beautiful lie. †

PART FOUR
Her Eyes

"Convictions are more dangerous enemies of truth than lies."
—Friedrich Nietzsche

CHAPTER 28
A Coven in the Oven

Julie never got close to the old woman. Peering from behind two stacked crates that contained something that smelled very much like manure, she watched the witch seemingly glide across the worn cavern floor without making a sound. She then glided straight through the large fire that burned in the oven and then vanished out of sight. Julie was sure that she had not clearly seen what happened. She shook her head and blinked her eyes. Though the fire still burned, raging inside the giant hearth, the witch was nowhere to be seen. *Did she really go straight into the fire?* Julie couldn't be sure. She turned back toward the cage that held Sandra.

"Sandra, wake up. Please, honey, wake up. Wake up, Sandra." Julie spoke this in a low, clear tone directly into the little girl's ear. She shook the little girl gently. Sandra opened her eyes. She quickly closed her eyes and tried to stretch herself inside the tiny cage. She opened her eyes again and quietly sat up. She did not seem interested in Julie at all. She looked around the large cavern before finally regarding Julie from inside her cage. Julie smiled at the little girl and put her forefinger up to her lips to encourage her to be quiet. But she could see that something was not quite right with Sandra.

The young girl's eyes were jet black and wild. She would only look Julie in the eyes briefly before looking away and casting her wild gaze around the cavern. Julie whispered her name once more and she finally looked back at Julie. She stared straight into Julie's eyes. A low, primal sound seemed to emit from the little girl, like a wild animal growling. Sandra bared her teeth at Julie. Her growling became louder and more menacing. She regarded Julie with a wild-eyed look, a mixture of rage, fear, malice, violence, contempt and…hunger. Julie felt chills running down her spine.

"Shhhhhh, Sandra, please," Julie pleaded. She looked over her shoulder and back at the roaring fire to see if the witch was returning. Sandra managed to get herself on all fours, still staring at Julie. The little girl began spinning in violent circles inside her cage, emitting her low, menacing growl. She would stop, suddenly, and regard Julie. Then, just as suddenly, would crawl in a violent circle in the opposite direction inside her little cage. The cage shook, rattled, and clanked loudly, filling the huge cavern with noise. Julie straightened herself up and stepped back from it.

"She's possessed."

Julie spun around, crying out involuntarily, her green eyes wide. She covered her mouth to stifle the sound. Pain shot up her leg from her ankle. The voice that startled her had come from inside another, larger cage mounted at eye level on one of the large bookshelves right behind her. She could not see who had spoken those words. She cautiously limped a bit closer to the shelf and peered into the darkness of the cage.

"Richard!" The sound of her own voice carrying throughout the cavern startled Julie. She lowered her voice. "Richard. Oh my God, Richard, what happened?" Julie could barely see his face. He struggled inside the small cage but was able to reach his hand out. Julie took it and squeezed. "Richard, what did she do to you? Are you all right?"

"Ssshhh," Richard said. "Believe me, Jules, you do not want that thing to hear you and come back here and stuff you into one of these things." He swallowed hard and licked his very dry lips. "She puts the 'bad' in badass." Julie had to stifle a laugh when Richard said this.

"But what happened, Richard?" Julie said.

"We all volunteered to search for Sandra, the whole town was there. We were all in the woods near Fears Hill when that thing showed up. We were all spread out all over the side of the hill. I thought I saw the little girl behind a tree. When I walked over to it, that bitch just came out of nowhere. Next thing I knew, I woke up in here. Since then, I've watched her drag every last one of us down here and stuff them into a cage." Richard's voice was hoarse and barely above a whisper.

Julie looked around the cavern. Her eyes had adjusted enough for her to see that there were a lot of these cages. Most of these had been placed onto the bookshelves. Every cage appeared to have someone in it. Not one of them stirred, or made any sound at all.

"Richard, we've got to get everyone out of here." Julie began to feel around his cage to try to find a latch. "How did she trap you?"

"I think she drugged them all, somehow. When I saw her I just fainted. I woke up in here." Richard paused for a moment. "What is that awful smell?" Julie stifled a laugh.

"That would be me. Our new, elderly friend peed on me after she drugged me."

"Kinky."

"Mmmm."

"You always get the good action." Julie and Richard each smiled. For the first time they could both see each other's face in the candle-lit cavern. Their eyes were swollen, their faces and bodies battered, dirty, and bruised. Their clothes were in tatters. Their eyes sparkled from the multiple candlelight.

"I can't find any latch to this cage," Julie said.

"Probably because you're thinking about it," Richard said.

"What?"

"You're thinking about it." Saying this made Richard cough and choke softly. He tried to spit, but his mouth was just too dry. Julie looked around the cavern, scanning the large, wooden tables that were dispersed all around the room for anything that looked like it might contain water. She guessed that she had dropped her bottle of water when she had encountered the old bat back in the Great Woods of Littleborough. She couldn't make anything out in the dim candle-lit cavern that looked like it could have water, however. She looked back at Richard, their faces mere inches apart.

"What do you mean?"

"Well, let's face it, Jules, why aren't you in a cage like the rest of us?"

Julie thought for a moment. "I don't know."

"I think that you do know."

"What are you talking about, Richard?"

"Don't think, just do," he said. "I can't believe I just said something so corny. My God, what am I, Yoda? Sweet Jesus, Jules, I'm gay Yoda."

Smiling at his comment, Julie grabbed hold of two bars on top of the cage, one in each hand, and pulled on them with all the strength she could muster. She was surprised how easily the cage slid off of the shelf and she lost her balance. She almost fell over onto her behind. Julie covered her mouth with both hands and watched, wide eyed, as the cage crashed and clattered onto the worn earthen floor. As it landed, the top of the cage popped open with another loud clatter. Richard let out a long, low-pitched groan.

"Oh, my God, I'm so sorry, Richard," she whispered. She helped Richard get himself up, slowly and stiffly, and out of the cage.

"Ow," Richard said.

"I'm so sorry, hon. Are you okay?"

"I'll be fine." He looked around the Great Cavern. "Well, that's bound to get that old bat's attention," Richard said.

Julie looked back at the fire burning in the oven. There still was no sign of the witch. A voice seemed to wail from somewhere deep in the labyrinth. They both knelt down behind two stacks of wooden crates that sat almost directly in the center of the great cavern.

"I think I know where there's an exit," Julie said. "We'll grab Sandra and everyone else and then try to get out of here." Julie peeked over the top of the stacked crates at the oven again. A shadow stood in front of it. Richard peeked, too.

"What is that?" he said.

"I don't know," Julie said. But as she spoke, the shadow slowly turned away from the fire and faced them. It was Sandra. Her eyes had returned to their normal, fiery blue. They seemed to flicker like the fire that raged behind her. Her tiny silhouette was framed by the illumination of her light pink dress. Julie glanced over to see that the cage that held Sandra was, in fact, empty.

The little girl seemed to now be staring straight back at Julie. Julie tried to allow her eyes to focus a bit more, but as the little girl slowly turned herself all the way around, their eyes met. Somehow, despite Sandra's dark silhouette against the raging fire, Julie could clearly see her eyes as they shone and shimmered in the gloom of the lair. They held Julie frozen to the spot where she knelt. She felt something shift in her belly.

Richard could tell by the look in Julie's eyes that something was wrong. He peeked over the stacked crates in time to see Sandra gliding slowly and silently toward them. He cried out involuntarily and ducked back down behind Julie, covering his mouth with both hands as he did. As she glided effortlessly across the cavern's earthen floor, Sandra's neck, arms, and legs grew longer, and then longer still. Her head tilted on her long, slender neck to the right, slightly. She was smiling humorlessly at Julie.

Sandra thrust her right hand out, clenched in a fist. She opened her hand, tiny fingers splayed out, to reveal her palm. The two stacks of crates that Julie and Richard knelt behind burst apart with a loud cracking sound. One stack seemed to fly across the cavern to the right, hitting the earthen wall with a tremendous force. The other stack did the same thing to the left side. Julie and Richard both cried out and clumsily staggered to their feet.

"I don't think we're going to be able to grab her," Richard said. Sandra tilted her head slightly left and regarded Richard. He whimpered softly and hid behind Julie. Julie stooped down slightly, so her head was level with the little girl's head. She smiled her sweetest smile at Sandra.

"Hi Sandra, my name is Julianna. My friends call me Julie. And this is my friend, Richard."

"Hello." Richard smiled his best smile.

"We're here to help you, honey. Your dad is very worried." Despite the desire to not show any fear to Sandra, both Julie and Richard began to slowly back away as the little girl advanced upon them. Sandra spread her arms wide as if to embrace them, her hands and fingers seemed to grow in length. As she came nearer, they could see that Sandra was still smiling. It gave both Julie and Richard chills. Her eyes appeared to be changing in color. They went from her normal, fierce light blue to a deep purple, then scarlet, then a black that was as dark as pitch. Her eyes then slowly returned to their normal light blue. Sandra tilted her head back to the right at a slight angle. The blaze from the large fire behind her seemed to dance in her blonde pigtails.

"Aaaaahhhhhahahahahahaha!"

Julie's heart sank. The witch had reappeared behind Sandra in the same way that she had left, gliding straight through the fire that still burned in the oven.

"Maahhhahahahahahahahahahahammmm-maaaaaahahahahamemenemenem...hmmmmmaaaahh!"

In one of her long, bony hands, she held two backpacks. She tossed them onto the nearest of the large, wooden tables as she glided noiselessly over to where Sandra stood. Julie watched the backpacks as they came down with a dull, squishy thud. She then noticed a familiar-looking shoebox at the far end of that particular large wooden table. Julie noted that and looked back at the witch.

The witch turned and regarded Richard. His feet were frozen to the ground; his brown eyes stared at her in wide terror. Richard began to weep as she glided toward where he and Julie stood. Julie's green eyes sparkled. She stepped in between Richard and the witch and braced herself for another confrontation that never came.

The ground under their feet and the walls that surrounded them began to shake as if there had been a volcanic eruption or an earthquake. A wind seemed to rip through the cavern with a deafening howl. It brought with it a suffocating stench of shit, decay, and death. All of the creatures—the birds, the bats, the bugs, the cats, the weasels, the chipmunks, the spiders, and rats—scattered in every direction. Julie and Richard both fell to the earthen floor of the cavern as it shook. Dust, dirt, and debris filled the air from the ceiling downward, and carried through and then out of the cavern on the howling winds like a small sandstorm.

Sandra stood quietly by the witch, unfazed by it all. Pinned flat on her back by the force, Julie could distinctly hear her name being whispered on the wind. The torment, rage, and raw hunger in that voice made her close her eyes tight. Then, as suddenly as it had all started, it stopped. There was a momentary silence, followed by a deep, primal growling, and then back to silence.

"What on God's green earth was that?" Richard asked. He was still flat on his back.

"Aaaaahhhhmememememememaaaahbaaaabaaaayyyy......ahhahahaha haaaa......aaaaaah.........memaaaahbaaaabaaaayy.....maaabaaaaabaaayyyy."

"I don't know, honey." Julie stiffly got herself up onto her feet, pain shot through her leg and her shoulder as she did. She helped Richard get to his feet. The witch resumed advancing toward Richard and Julie.

"No, please, no, don't put me back in that cage." Julie was still in between the witch and Richard. She faced the witch. "No! No! Please, I don't want to be back in there!" Richard was screaming now.

The witch stopped right in front of Julie, towering over her. But she did not look at Julie. She simply stared at Richard. Julie turned in time see that Richard had fallen back down to the ground onto his hands and knees. "No! No! No!" As he screamed, Richard crawled back inside the cage and closed the lid over himself. "No!" As the metal latch clicked shut, he began to weep softly.

Julie looked up at the old woman. Anger flared in her belly. The witch seemed to be smiling. She laughed and shook her leonine head. Her eyes were now green. They were wide, clear, naked, and piercing. They were human, thought Julie. At that very moment, looking into this person's shocking green eyes, Julie felt something deep inside of her shift again. Her heart pounded, a sharp pain shot through her head, and her stomach felt as if it had literally flipped over. Helpless, Julie stood frozen, rooted to the earthen floor. She looked down at the ground.

The witch glided around her and lifted the cage that held Richard back onto the large wooden bookshelf with one hand. Richard wept and murmured incomprehensibly. The old woman was now outright cackling. Sandra was beaming and giggling as the old woman patted her head and face, still mumbling her strange, singsong speech. Sandra's eyes had returned to their normal blue. Julie looked at Richard.

"Don't worry, Richard, I won't leave you here. I'll get you all out somehow."

"No, don't. Julie, please, just leave me here. Just go. Go, honey. Please. I don't want her to be angry with me. I don't want her to hurt me. Please, just go. Just go." Richard's voice dropped off and he resumed his murmuring.

The old woman stood between the large wooden table and the great fire that burned inside the great hearth. Her tall, thin, menacing frame appeared as a silhouette. Her eyes burned a dark blue and purple. She beckoned Sandra with one long, bony finger. Sandra smiled and walked toward the old woman. The witch bent down to speak to her face to face. Sandra turned and looked into the oven and at the raging fire inside it. Julie could not hear what was being said. *I probably wouldn't understand a word of it, even if I could hear it,* she thought to herself.

After the witch finished speaking, Sandra turned back to the witch, smiled, and nodded her head. She threw her arms around the neck of the old woman, who hugged her back while laughing and talking in her singsong speech. Sandra then turned back around and marched her little legs toward the oven and the fire that raged within. Julie's eyes widened in horror. As Sandra stepped over the threshold of the furnace, Julie screamed. "Sandra, no!"

Despite the terrible pain in her ankle and shoulder, Julie charged at the old woman. The old woman turned. One of her long arms shot out like a lightning bolt toward Julie and with one, enormous, bony hand, stopped Julie in her tracks. The witch had seized Julie by the throat. Julie grabbed the old woman's wrist with both hands and twisted with all her might. She could not break free of the witch's grip. Julie looked up, wide-eyed, at the witch. She then grabbed at the witch's hand and fingers that were clasped around her throat. The witch was far too strong for Julie. The witch forced Julie down onto her knees. Julie looked on helplessly as the witch reached out her other hand.

She held up a large, black mushroom cap in her long, wrinkled and weathered hand. The witch stopped choking Julie, instead moving her hand over Julie's face where she applied tremendous pressure on Julie's jaw, forcing her mouth to open. Julie desperately tried to close her mouth, but the witch was just too powerful. She put the mushroom cap in Julie's mouth and then held her mouth closed with the same brute force. It tasted truly awful. Julie tried to spit it out, but the witch's hands kept her mouth closed. She then forced Julie to chew it. It was mealy and the taste made Julie's entire body shudder. Her eyes watered. She gagged and began to choke again. She knew she had to give in. Julie finished chewing and then swallowed the mushroom cap.

The old woman released her grip on Julie, turned, and glided effortlessly into the large oven and through the flames. Still on her knees, Julie finished swallowing everything that was in her mouth. Her head felt so heavy, and Julie felt dizzy. The weight of her head pulled her forward and down onto her hands and knees. Still spinning, Julie gently laid her head onto the cavern floor. She rolled over onto her back. She looked one last, desperate time for Sandra. But Sandra was gone. Darkness came. †

CHAPTER 29
The Challenge

Father Knight, Father Freeman, and the bishop sat quietly together, each man of God alone with his own thoughts. The bishop and Father Freeman were drinking from a bottle of scotch that Father Freeman had produced from inside his robe, along with two glasses. The two men also smoked one cigarette after another, Father Knight observed. The smoke from the cigarettes swirled, slowly and silently, straight up into the candle-lit air toward the darkness and flickering shadows of the chapel ceiling.

The three men of God all looked up as one of the large, deep purple, scarlet, and maroon linens swished aside. A man entered the chapel through the west doorway. He was small in stature and somewhat elderly. He looked to Father Knight as though he could be the same age as the Bishop. He was smartly dressed in a gray pin-stripe suit with a long, dark overcoat. He held a shoebox under his arm. He smiled at the holy men as he closed the curtain behind him. Still smiling, he nimbly descended the stairs that led down toward the altar, removing his hat and overcoat as he did so.

"My goodness me, Bishop Richter, but it is so nice and warm in this place." The little old man rubbed his hands together. "It's becoming frightfully cold outside with that howling wind, I can tell you." As he spoke, the little old man gently placed his overcoat over the back of one of the small, wooden chairs, and then placed his hat carefully on the seat next to the shoebox. Father Knight looked at Father Freeman and the bishop to see their reaction, but they both were simply sitting stoically in their seats, smoking their cigarettes. The little old man looked down at Father Knight and his smile widened.

"Well, hello James! You know, I've heard so much about you, I feel like I could be your brother." Father Knight froze. The word *brother* had jolted him. His soft, brown eyes widened as he looked up at the man. Father Freeman spoke up.

"Hey, why don't you cut the crap and get to the point, Loserfer."

"Oh, how terribly clever that is, John! It is sadly typical of a man of the cloth—utterly quaint, and yet distinctly pointless at the same time. Because, you see," the little old man turned himself back toward Father Knight, "James is the point. And we have heard sooooo much about this young lamb…" He paused, smiling broadly at Father Knight. "I mean to tell you, good sirs, he's almost a legend down around our little neck of Creation. Yes…he…is." The little old man sat down in one of the small wooden chairs. His striking pale blue eyes with specks of brown and green and gray never left Father Knight's brown eyes. He continued to smile. Father Knight could only stare back at this strange man.

Silence reverberated in the chapel. Father Knight began to feel cold. His hands, his feet, and his nose were all freezing. As soon as he had noticed this, Father Knight then observed that he could see his own breath in the air. He looked back at the little old man, who still sat, staring and smiling. He did not look cold. In fact, he looked very comfortable. A strange energy seemed to emanate from this person. Father Knight looked closely.

He could sense a searing hatred, a burning rage, from inside this man. His mouth smiled, his eyes did not. For all the elegance that the man possessed—the sharp suit, the shined shoes, the London Fog fedora—and for all his manners, his eloquence and grace, pure menace and malice oozed beneath that veneer. It was those eyes, Father Knight thought to himself. They belied a depth of rage and anguish no man, woman, anyone, or anything could ever imagine.

This creature existed outside of the realm of God's love and grace. Father Knight now knew with absolute certainty that he was staring into the eyes of Satan, whose eyes were staring straight back into his own.

"So, you are Satan?" Father Knight asked this earnestly.

"Yes, James. That is one of the names you people use to refer to me." The devil nodded as he spoke. "Your mentor and the bishop usually call me by that, and Lucifer, as well."

"I see." Father Knight looked down at the floor for a moment in thought. He looked back up at Satan and asked, "But, then, what is your real name?"

The devil smiled. "To know that is to know me, and you shall find out only too soon, lamb."

Father Knight shrugged and nodded his head. "Was that you, then, who spoke with me in the church?"

Again the devil smiled and nodded. Father Knight continued, "You looked so different." Father Knight then looked down at the floor again, furrowing his brow as he paused. "Then, who were those poor children?"

This seemed to anger Lucifer, but only for a moment. "Oh, just a few… lost souls, my boy. No need to worry." His smile returned as he said this. He kept his eyes fixed on Father Knight. "Yes, men of the cloth, James is very definitely the point. I do apologize for not having recognized you earlier, my boy. Heaven knows, I was not expecting to find such a lamb as you in a den of lying wolves such as this. Lucky for you I came when I did, young man. Chin up, hang in there, no need to fuss now, I shall save your soul from them." Lucifer smiled into James's eyes. The silence returned.

Another one of the large, deep purple, scarlet, and maroon curtains was gently tugged aside. Everyone turned to see a large, powerful-looking man awkwardly backing his way through the doorway from the east. The man then turned around slowly to face the four individuals who were all sitting in front of the small altar. In his arms was the now-stiff, decaying, recently autopsied, dead body of Father Miguel Torrez. Doc Robinson's dark brown eyes burned out of his large head with what truly struck Father Knight as murder.

"Ah, very good, Doctor, just take it through there and wait for me, please. I won't be but a moment."

"Hey," Bishop Richter spoke up in a loud voice, "what the hell do you think you're doing with Miguel's body?" The bishop had risen quickly to his feet as he spoke.

Father Freeman had also risen from his seat. He was pointing at Satan and yelling. "What kind of bullshit is this? You put him right back where you found him, dick-head."

Satan looked truly surprised by their protests. He looked left and right, alternately, from the Bishop, to Father Freeman, and then back at the bishop in astonishment at this sudden outburst from the clergy.

"My dear, fellow warriors, I am merely taking something that is already mine."

"Already yours?" The bishop was now slowly moving toward Satan as he spoke, his voice was rising. "That was never yours, and never will be yours. You've been too long in the shadows, Lucifer. It's softening your brain. There is no way in heaven, hell, or on earth that Miguel's soul is yours."

"Yes, it is!" Satan screamed this and burst from his small wooden chair up onto his feet. "He called me out, and I won by rule. He died while making the challenge, and so he is mine!" The devil shouted this in a deep, clear, and resonant voice that did not match the body from where it had come. Father Knight sat frozen in his small wooden chair. He was not sure now if he should stand up like everyone else. He was not sure he even could stand up if he tried.

"Miguel died when he found what you left in our holy water, you jack-ass!" By now, Father Freeman was standing right next to the Bishop. Both men of the cloth were face to face with Satan in the center of the tiny chapel. "A baby's heart was placed, by you," Father Freeman pointed at the devil, "in our holy water! That's really smooth, Lucifer. Gosh, that's so fucking original, don't you think, Pat?" The Bishop, his light blue eyes glaring, nodded along with Father Freeman. But the devil was shaking his head impatiently.

"No, no, no, nonononononono no!" The face of Satan, in the guise of the little old man's face, had turned a bright red. He held his arms out, his palms up, in exasperation. "You liars. You liars! You are such unbelievable liars!" As the devil exclaimed this, he whirled around in a small circle, his arms held out as if he were being crucified. He stopped short, suddenly grinning at the bishop and Father Freeman. "I say, do either of you have handy a spear, perchance?" Satan put his hand and wrist across his forehead in a dramatic fashion. "Oh, Father, why hast thou forsaken me?" His mocking smile vanished as he screamed, "Why hast though sent me these lying cowards of the cloth?"

"We're liars? We're liars? John," the bishop turned slightly to look at Father Freeman, "I guess you'd better fire up the pumps because Lucifer is cutting some fine crap." The bishop lit a cigarette, blowing the smoke straight into Lucifer's face, which made the devil blink his blue eyes once or twice. "You seem to be forgetting a small matter of an infant's heart in our holy water. You challenged us, Lucifer. You came to us, sweet pea, now let's get on with it."

"Get on with what? It's over, Pat. I won, Pat. You...called me!" Before either Father Freeman or Bishop Richter could respond, the devil held up his hand as if to ask for a moment. "Ah, ah," he said over his shoulder as he nimbly moved back up the few steps to where his coat and hat were. "If the infant's heart that you both so lament about came from me, then why, in creation, would I still have this?" The devil held up the shoebox, opened, and inside the blood-smeared box the priests could see the tiny heart of a newborn baby.

At the sight of this, Father Knight immediately felt sick to his stomach. He had to tear his eyes away from the tiny heart in the shoebox and looked down at the earthen floor of the chapel. Despite being freezing cold, he broke into a feverish sweat. His head was swimming; the chapel seemed to be spinning. His hands and feet, his arms and legs felt clammy and moist in his pajamas.

"You sick, sick puppy! You're a fucking disaster of an angel, Lucifer!" It now appeared to Father Knight that Father Freeman and Bishop Richter were both vying with one another to get at the devil. They both shouted at him, and the devil, for his part, shouted right back.

"I'm a disaster? How am I a disaster? I answered your damn call, didn't I? Well, didn't I?"

"You made a call and now you're trying to weasel out of it, which is typical of a horseshit pussy like you, you pedophile!"

"Pedophile?"

"Yes!"

"Pedophile?"

"Yes!"

"Oh, that's funny coming from a priest!"

"You probably do think it's funny you warped, sick little pig!" the bishop shouted.

"Who are you calling a pig? Don't you dare call me pig! The only pigs here are you two God-sycophants, and that littlest piggy of them all, Miguel. That's right, little piggies, liars, Father Torrez is my little piggy."

"Like hell he is! Listen carefully, ass face, Miguel is a sweet, innocent, little piggy. You are a walking, talking, gas-passing, windbag of a fucking little piggy!" Father Freeman shouted this.

"Wind bag?" The devil paused. "Hmmm, I like that one, John. And it suits you quite well, naturally." Satan had turned away from the two priests as he said this. He seemed to be dismissing them entirely as he began walking around the altar and the small pulpit of the tiny chapel, muttering.

"What makes you think Father Torrez challenged you? He dropped dead of a heart attack when he found...when he found that. The coroner left no doubt about that." The bishop swallowed hard at the thought of the tiny little heart that his dear friend, Father Torrez, had found two nights ago. He then shuddered at the reality that two infants had lost their lives in this odd and terrible confrontation. Satan had stopped muttering and was regarding the bishop thoughtfully.

"How do you know that he was not summoning me? The heart attack does not indicate motive or circumstance, Patrick. The good Inspector Dahms found blood on Miguel's hands. His hands, Patrick."

"So what?" the bishop replied. "That only shows that Miguel put his hand in the holy water, probably to see what you had put there."

"Except that I did not put it there, you dumb bastard!" The devil raised his voice when he said this, but did not shriek. The bishop paused.

Father Freeman spoke up. "Sorry Lucifer, but as a reliable witness or source of information, you don't exactly fill anyone with a sense of confidence. Know what I mean, buckaroo?" He lit a cigarette and handed it to the Bishop, who accepted it gratefully.

"Wait a minute, how would you know Inspector Dahms?" The devil smiled when the bishop asked this.

"He is…very well known to all of us. He is a hero of sorts. He is a truly…delicious sort of man. And by the way, he is known to Miguel, and to his sister."

"What the hell are you talking about, Satan?" Father Freeman asked. But the devil smiled and shook his head.

"Ask the good inspector, who we should be seeing very shortly, I suspect."

"Sorry Satan, it's still not good enough," the bishop stated flatly.

"So, you shall not desist?" Satan asked this of the Bishop.

"We shall persist."

"It's a challenge I find impossible to resist." The devil turned to leave, hopping up each step and each landing of the tiny chapel. He put on his dark long coat and London Fog fedora.

"Don't forget your fucking shoebox, douche." Father Freeman's brown eyes glared at Satan. The devil laughed.

"Oh my dear me, no, I will not forget that." There was the slight British accent again. "And do not worry, John, neither will little Nicholas Tewksbury, born yesterday, gone today, thanks to Miguel." Satan turned to exit the tiny chapel behind the same deep purple, scarlet, and maroon curtain and through the west doorway that Doc Robinson had taken the corpse of Father Torrez.

"Nice. We're happy for you, Lucifer. What a truly proud moment this must be for you in your glittering career as an asshole." Bishop Richter and Father Freeman started slowly up the small steps after Satan. Father Freeman turned back to signal to Father Knight to wait where he was. Father Knight nodded his head, but he could not hide his utter bewilderment at what was taking place.

He looked at his mentor. Father Freeman smiled grimly at him and winked. Then he and the bishop followed Satan, disappearing behind the large, deep purple, scarlet, and maroon curtain. And there Father Knight sat alone in the awkward and deafening silence of the tiny chapel. †

CHAPTER 30
The Ascent

Julie opened her eyes. Still lying flat on her back, she started coughing violently. She rolled over onto her side. When she had finished coughing, she hacked and spit. She laid quietly for a moment and collected herself, drawing in several deep breathes. All she could taste and smell was that mushroom cap. Her entire body shuddered on the cold cavern floor.

Julie slowly got up onto her hands and knees. She eased herself back into a kneeling position. She rubbed her throat with both hands where the witch had choked her. She coughed, hacked, and spit again. She slowly and stiffly got up onto her feet. She walked back to where Richard was and peered inside the cage. She was surprised to feel no pain in her ankle or her shoulder.

"Richard, Richard, honey, are you okay?" But Richard could only stare back at Julie from inside his cage. Julie looked back at the fire that raged in the oven, then back at Richard. She was again surprised to feel no pain in her shoulder as she took hold of his cage and pulled it off the shelf. As before, it clattered to the ground and the door sprang open. Richard groaned.

Julie made her way around the entire lair and pulled out every single cage she could find among the large wooden bookshelves, freeing its prisoner. There were firemen, EMTs, plumbers, landscapers, several golfers, selectpersons, and many townspeople who had all volunteered for the search for Sandra.

Richard had groggily gotten himself up. "Oh, God. No. Jules, what are you doing? If that woman comes back, she's going to kill you. Shit, she's going to kill me! You know you can't beat her. She's a freak show. She already almost killed you."

"True, but she didn't. For some reason, I think she needs me to be around." Julie looked at Richard in the gloom and candlelight of the great cavern. "You were right, Richard. I do think too much. For some reason that old bat won't kill me off. That gives me leverage as far as I'm concerned."

"Are you going to tell her that if she comes back?" Julie smiled at Richard. He shrugged and smiled back. "Okay, that was a stupid question." He was cut off by a deafening howl that seemed to come from directly above them. Again all the creatures in the lair scattered, scampered, or flew in every direction, screeching and squealing. It sounded as if something enormous was stamping its feet on the ground above. Dirt, dust, debris, and many, many spiders wafted down from the roof of the cavern.

A deep, primal growling came from everywhere all at once. The earth shook violently all around, throwing everyone to the ground. Despite the din, Julie heard her name being called. The desperation in the voice tore at her heart. Its hunger overwhelmed her. She threw her arms over her head and tried to block it out. *Please stop*, she thought.

It stopped. There followed a silence.

"What…the hell…is that thing up there?" Richard said. Julie laughed.

"That's a good question, for sure." A fireman, Danny Gavin, had walked over to Julie and extended his hand to help her up. "Are you all right, ma'am?"

"Yes, thank you, I think I'm okay." The fireman helped Richard up with an audible grunt.

"Thank you, Danny. Whew, I've only dreamt of being saved by a big, strong fireman."

"Bloody hell," Danny said. He turned toward Julie. "Cheers for getting us all out of those cages," he said. She detected an Irish accent.

"Yes, thank you, Julie," Selectperson Bert Snodgrass said.

"Leave it to a woman to save us all, naturally!" Selectperson Barbara Wordsworth said.

"It was a woman who put us all in those cages, Barbara," Captain Little Joe said. He pointed toward a dark corner of the lair. "That's the way she brought us in. That's the way out. I'm thinking we should get away from here before whatever that thing is up there finds us down here."

"Not to mention that old battle-axe coming back," Richard said.

"Good God, Richard, shush!" Bea said. She looked around the cavern uneasily.

"Let's go," Captain Little Joe said. Julie nodded her head.

"Oh, I think that makes sense," she said. "Lead the way, sir." The group, which numbered almost forty, filed out of the lair. Julie waited at the end of the line.

244

"What are you doing, dear?" Richard asked.

"Um…Richard, I need you to go with them. There's something I have to, umm, check, before I can leave. I'll only be a minute, I promise. I'll catch right up."

"I'll wait if it's only a minute."

"No, really, umm…no, I need you to go, honey. This could be a bit longer than a minute. Just go, okay? Before you-know-who comes back."

"Right, Jesus, I forgot about her…I'll see you outside, honey." Richard hastily joined the others as they exited the lair.

Julie walked back to the large, wooden table by the oven where she had seen the shoebox. She picked it up carefully and opened the lid; Geraldine the rat was not inside the shoebox. There were rat droppings and pee spots. Scattered in and among the poop were more of the black mushroom caps. Julie reached in and scooped them out, thrusting them into her jeans pocket. She had no idea why she did that. She just did it.

She turned and faced the fire in the large hearth, or oven. The high flames licked and danced in her green eyes. She took a deep breath and walked straight into the flames. The sorrowful cries and distant screams that reverberated throughout the cavern faded. The mice, the cats, the birds, the bats, the bugs, the snakes, the spiders, and rats all gradually returned to the comfort of the witch's lair.

Julie entered a pitch-black passage that seemed to go on a gradual incline. Her eyes seemed to her to adjust unusually well to the darkness. She could sense heat all around her and behind her from the entrance of the large oven, and she could feel cooler air in front of her as she walked on.

Julie found herself able to breathe more deeply than she ever had before in her life. The air seemed so fresh, cool, and exhilarating. It filled her with energy. The intense, throbbing pains in her back and shoulder, her ankle, and in her head were all gone.

Her senses were sharpened. Her awareness heightened. Julie knew her perceptions were somehow altered by the mushroom cap she had been forced to eat. Despite this and the obvious danger ahead, she also felt a sense of calm. The lightest touch of a dew-covered leaf at the end of a low-lying branch brushed her cheek. It was very cool now.

Julie realized that she was in the woods. It was dark. Night had fallen. There was time, but not much. She broke into a run. †

CHAPTER 31
The Date

Julie breathlessly entered her home through the back door. Rasputin was waiting for her. She held the door open as he bolted into the backyard. She followed him back outside to try to catch her breath. She stretched her legs and her back as she watched the large dog sniff intently at the point where she and the inspector had gone into the woods earlier in the day to try and find Sandra. The cuts and abrasions on her body burned as hotly as her muscles.

She tried to process everything that had happened since she had left the house with Inspector Dahms to search for Sandra. She had found Sandra. Julie knew that much. But God only knows where that little girl was now. Sandra seemed to know the witch. She certainly trusted her. What was the witch trying to do with Richard and everybody else? Julie wondered. She shook her head.

The cool autumn air energized Julie after her long run back to the house. The sweat all over her body cooled in the light evening breeze. Her body tingled. Julie noticed that there seemed to be little lights dancing in the periphery of her vision. She had thought she saw them when she ran through the woods. They sparkled and shone brightly only to disappear when she turned to look at them. She could smell the autumn in the air and it was exhilarating. Julie could not believe how she felt so truly alive after everything she had seen and been through today.

She reentered the house with Rasputin close behind and walked over to a beautiful full-length mirror that hung in the main hall. She burst out laughing. Her hair was tangled with leaves, sticks, and pine needles. Dark circles hung under her eyes. Julie was covered in dirt, leaves, pine tar, and God only knows what else. There were scratches and bruises on her forearms and neck. She felt the acute burning of cuts and throbbing bruises up and down her back and her legs. And there was that smell, of course. The powerful odor of urine from that crazy old bat peeing on her chest. Rasputin had smelled it immediately on her, making him drool. Julie turned from the mirror and looked at him.

"Oh my God, look at what happened to your mama!" she said. He wagged his tail. Julie sighed, still smiling. Rasputin looked different to her. He seemed to somehow be shining, almost glowing. She realized it was his aura. It shined a reddish brown. The red would be his natural instinct of protectiveness, she knew. The brown was his attachment to the earth and the natural world. She could see his thoughts and feel his feelings. Julie knelt down and he lowered his huge head into her arms. "You were worried," she said. His tail wagged once as she stroked his neck and back. "I'm sorry I worried you, you big, furry baby. I was worried, too, Rass. I'm home now, big boy. I'm going to try the whole shower thing, again. Then I will feed you, okay?" He licked her face. This always made Julie laugh. She laughed out loud.

She reached into her pocket and took out her cell. It was dead. *No wonder it's been so quiet*, she thought. She put it in the charger and went upstairs to take a hot shower. As she went up the stairs, she stopped on the first landing and looked up at the top of the stairs into the darkness. She could see Don Juan's beautiful green eyes staring at her. The black cat had vanished by the time she reached the top step. She had an hour to get herself ready for James. He would be arriving around seven for dinner. She smiled to herself at the thought of possibly dating a man who did not own a cell phone.

As before, the shower had felt exquisite despite the cuts and bruises. Unlike before, it was not interrupted. Julie was surprised at how easily she was able to shower without thinking of what had occurred earlier. She threw on an old pair of blue jeans and a tight, light green sweater. It was seven o'clock. Julie came down stairs to feed Rasputin. There was a knock at the front door. Rasputin started barking and went to the door. Julie shushed him and opened it.

"Miss Bernard, I'm glad to find you here. We were getting worried."

"Hi Inspector, please come in." Julie smiled as Inspector Dahms stepped into the hallway. "I'm so sorry to have worried you like that. My cell died at some point."

"That's all right, Miss Bernard." He stooped his tall frame down to pet Rasputin.

"Any luck finding Sandra?"

"None, I'm afraid. Can't figure how she gave us the slip. We're still trying to reach everybody to suspend the search until morning light. I haven't heard back from anybody in quite some time."

"Oh, I'm sure everybody will be fine, Inspector. I got back just a little while ago, myself. Can I get you something to drink?"

"Not unless it's coffee," Inspector Dahms said. He smiled.

"Great." Julie smiled up at him. For a moment the space between her body and the inspector's seemed electric to Julie. She took his coat and his hat and hung them by the front door. She could see his hair was cut short and as gray as his moustache. "The kitchen is this way. I need to feed the big brave doggie anyway." Inspector Dahms smiled and followed Julie into the kitchen.

"So, where did you go off to?" Inspector Dahms asked. He leaned his tall, thin frame against the doorjamb of the door leading into the kitchen. Rasputin wagged his large tail and watched every move Julie made intently as she prepared his food.

"Oh well, I thought I saw Sandra on a path on the side of Fears Hill. I followed, but the woods seemed to just swallow her up. I'm not even sure if it was her." Julie turned to Rasputin with his large dish of food. He began eating before she had actually put it down on the tile floor. She looked at the inspector. His aura burned a dark red all around him. *That's masculinity and leadership,* Julie thought, *with some anger and his considerable will power as well.* Inspector Dahms smiled. Julie smiled back as she went over to a cabinet and took out some coffee grounds.

"You really don't have to."

"I want to. Besides, don't you want to ask me any more questions?"

"Oh, now I hope you don't think I'm, what did you call it, grilling you, Miss Bernard?"

Julie laughed. She had a natural, throaty laugh. She shook her head. "No, that's not what I meant at all. I was thinking more along the lines of the occult, Inspector. I still haven't had a chance to pull out those old books and do the research I promised."

"Well, it's been a bit of a busy day, today, hmm?"

"Yes, it has." They shared a smile. Julie led Inspector Dahms into the living room. He sat on a large couch. He marveled at how soft it was. She walked over to one of two large bookcases that stood opposite to each other in the large living room. The shelves of each were lined with countless books on psychology, education, religion, the occult, and many novels and biographies. Julie pulled out several of these books and placed them in a stack on a dark oak coffee table sitting in front of the couch. The inspector took the book on top and held it up for examination. *The Satanic Rituals*. It was written by Anton Lavey. He looked at the next book, *The Church of Satan*, by Michael Aquino. Beneath this book was *La-bas* by Huysmans. The fourth book surprised the inspector: *The Jewish Encyclopedia*. Julie returned from the kitchen with a steaming cup of black coffee for him.

"Thank you, Miss Bernard."

"Please call me Julie, Inspector."

"Okay, thank you, Julie. And please, call me Tom." Julie smiled. She had poured herself a glass of red wine. She took a sip. Wine had never tasted better. The flavor danced on her tongue and she could feel it warm her entire body. Julie sat down on the large, soft couch next to the inspector. Rasputin had finished off every last morsel of his dinner. He had followed Julie into the living room, and climbed up onto a large easy chair. He curled his enormous body up on it and fell right to sleep with an audible grunt of contentment. Julie laughed out loud and the inspector smiled.

"Julie, before we start, there's something I'd like to show you."

"Okay." Tom removed a piece of paper from his jacket pocket and unfolded it. He placed it down on the coffee table. Julie picked it up and peered at it. It smelled like his tobacco.

"What are these symbols? They look like letters, or ancient symbols or characters of some kind," Julie said.

"I was rather hoping that you might be able to recognize them."

Julie shook her head. Her shoulder length, dirty blonde hair waved around her shoulders.

"No, I'm sorry, but I'm not sure what they are. They're symbols or characters or letters from something, I'm sure. I can see what looks like a pentagram, or maybe a hexagram that makes up some of these symbols. I would need time to research it."

"Fair enough. Thank you," Tom said. Julie smiled.

"May I ask where you found these?"

Tom hesitated. He breathed out slowly as he considered the question. Julie could see his aura change slightly, from the dark reds to a lighter red, with pinkish tinges, as he thought. Slowly but surely, his aura returned to the dark reds.

"I found one symbol for each of the crucifixion victims. They were carved on the victim's tongue."

"Oh my God!" Julie covered her mouth, wide eyed. Her stomach flipped.

"I know. I'm sorry, Julie. I shouldn't have told you. It's horrible."

Julie grabbed her glass of wine and drank a large gulp, shaking her head. "That's why you didn't find any signs on Megan or Caroline. They were hidden." The two sat in silence for several moments. Julie breathed as evenly as she could. She remembered herself telling Megan that she would work through this. She set her chin and looked at Tom.

"Okay, let's see." She looked over the books on the table. "That's odd, I thought I had grabbed the...oh!" Inspector Dahms held up *The Jewish*

Encyclopedia, smiling. Julie laughed. "I guess we're on the same page, Inspector...sorry, Tom."

"So it appears." He handed the tome to Julie.

"Thanks." She opened the large book and began to flip through the pages.

"So, what are you looking for, Julie?"

"Something old, I think. This is something that strikes me as being more 'Old Testament' as opposed to 'New Testament.'"

"I see." Inspector Dahms sipped his coffee thoughtfully. He had taken out his notepad and pen. "Well, that makes sense. I had a chance to research some of the names and book titles you had mentioned this morning at the scene. You were right; that Lavey guy was an atheist." He was reading from his notepad now. "You also said theistic Satanism only goes back a few centuries, right again. And the 'how to make a pact with the devil' instruction books don't involve murder."

"You're referring to the Grimorium Verum and the Grand Grimorium?"

"Yes."

"No, they don't."

"Assuming the people performing these rites think that they worked, were there ever any reports to suggest that they actually did work?"

"All we have are reports from antiquity." Julie sipped her wine, then gently bit her lower lip, deep in thought. "Let me see, now. There's one in Scotland in 1591 at a place called Auchinleck House in which a Ritchie Graham and a John Boswell supposedly raised the devil. The ancient rite may have been what was called a 'Taghairn.'"

"A taghairn?" Inspector Dahms furrowed his brow. Julie laughed.

"Yes."

"Okay, what's a taghairn?"

"Originally, it was believed to be a way for people see into the future. A person would wrap themselves up in the hide of a castrated male cow and sit by a waterfall, or a cliff's edge, and then ask their question aloud. They would meditate and apparently the answer would come."

"Well, it sounds ridiculous, but that doesn't make it satanic."

"No, it doesn't. In the case of John Boswell, who lived at the Auchinleck castle, he was notorious for his interest in witchcraft and sorcery. Richie Graham was considered to be a wizard by the people of his day. Maybe they embellished the ritual and believed they saw something. What happened isn't exactly known. What is known is that the Privy Council—sorry, the authorities—found out about it and John Boswell fled Scotland never to return."

"I see. Hmmm, that's interesting"

"It is, isn't it?"

Julie and Tom shared a smile. He could smell her perfume. It ,was beautiful, like flowers. Julie could smell him. He smelled like the forest mixed with his pipe tobacco. It was a dark, primal scent. She had noticed Tom's aura when he had entered the house. She regarded it now as he smiled at her; there was the dark red around his body—masculinity, will power, leadership and calm under fire, she surmised.

She realized she was noticing it again because more colors were forming within his aura. One of these colors was a lighter red, which signified a vitality and sexuality. She could also see the very outside fringes had a faint orange mixing with the red; this, Julie knew, meant desire. She could feel his desire in her mind and body, as well. She refocused herself on the subject at hand.

"Then there's Aleister Crowley, who was a notorious occultist. He claimed to have been contacted by a messenger from an Egyptian god called Horus in 1904 while in Cairo, Egypt. Some scholars have surmised that he may have used an ancient Egyptian rite to do this. He also claimed to have raised a preternatural being named Lam while in New York City some years after that. He was a prolific occultist who claimed that he summoned many different beings over many years. The problem with him is the fact that he imbibed every drug known to man throughout his entire adult life, so, who really knows what was going on with him?"

"Mmm, good point, there."

"There are also incidents in which a demon is summoned inadvertently; the Native Americans believe that to say the name of an evil spirit, like a shape-shifter, can invoke it. The same beliefs can be traced back to India, Africa, and the Aboriginal tribes in Australia.

"In the book *Histriomasticx*, from 1632, I think, William Prynne wrote that at a performance of *Doctor Faustus*, which is a play by a man named Christopher Marlowe about a man who sells his soul to the devil, real demons appeared on the stage, driving several actors and patrons into madness. I guess now I can see why they all went mad."

"Maybe he just didn't like the play," Inspector Dahms said. Julie burst out laughing.

"You're probably right. Can I get you more coffee?"

"Yes please." Julie put the *Jewish Encyclopedia* on the coffee table, got up, and went into the kitchen with his mug. She returned with the coffee and her bottle of wine. She poured herself a little more wine. They smiled at each other as she sat down on the couch.

"Thank you." He sipped his coffee. "You have some very interesting pictures up on the wall there." Julie followed his gaze to three print copies of paintings that hung on the wall opposite from where they sat.

252

"Oh, thank you. Yes, I love these pictures."

"That one on the left there looks like Joan of Arc."

"Yes, that's right. That's a print copy of a miniature depiction of 'Joan de Arc.' The original dates back to around 1450 AD. The artist's name is unknown."

"Who is on the right, there?"

"That's a depiction of Lilutu, or Lili. She is an ancient Sumerian and Babylonian goddess of storms and nature. The Hindus of ancient India mention her as Lila. These spirits have power over nature and can be associated with witches. It's where the name Lilith comes from, in ancient Jewish mythology." The Inspector nodded. "The one in the middle is a print of a mosaic of Mary, Jesus's mom, by Sosos of Pergamon."

"They're striking paintings."

"I think so, too." They both smiled. As she regarded the print, it occurred to Julie that this was quite similar to the portrait of the woman she had seen earlier today in the witch's lair. *It can't be*, she thought. Julie picked up the large encyclopedia and placed it in her lap. "So, where were we?"

"*Histriomasticx*?"

"Right, thank you. That brings us to the Bible, which has numerous stories about demons. In the New Testament, Jesus exorcises demons a number of times. There is, of course, his confrontation with Satan in the wilderness in which the devil tries to tempt Jesus. When Jesus performs one of his exorcisms, he invokes the name of King Solomon as someone who was also able to exorcise demons.

"King Solomon had a ring that supposedly had the true name of God on it. This ring allowed him to be able to summon and master evil spirits. He used these spirits to build his great temple in Jerusalem."

"And that's in the Bible?"

"It's actually in an ancient text called the Testament of Solomon, which is here." Julie pointed to the top of a page in the *Jewish Encyclopedia*. "King Solomon supposedly wrote it and, like so many Biblical texts, it was copied again and again over the centuries. But there's no proof that Solomon actually wrote it." Julie shrugged.

"So, the information on this stuff is scarce, and what little there is seems vague?"

"Yes, I'm afraid so. When it comes to this aspect of demons, a face-to-face encounter is a rare thing. Demonic possession tends to be the way demons become a part of life on this physical plane. So, even if they should choose to appear and be seen, it would be in the guise of something, or someone else." Julie had been flipping through the pages of the *Jewish Encyclopedia* and came to a page that had several sheets of paper folded in it. They had been there for a long time, the inspector observed. The papers had yellowed with time.

"Okay, I was hoping I still had these notes."

"What notes are these?" Julie handed them to the Inspector.

"These notes were taken in one of the best classes I ever took in college. I really should go through all my old books and collect all the notes from that class, someday."

"This is at Columbia University?"

Julie paused, looking at the inspector. "Yes. How did you know…"

"I checked you out. I'm sorry, but I had to."

"Oh, don't be. I don't know why I'm even surprised." They both smiled.

"Now, this particular class was part of your post-graduate education?"

"Yes." Julie's eyes returned to Inspector Dahms's gaze.

"This wouldn't by any chance be the class that had no name, only a number assigned to it?"

"Yes, oh my goodness." Julie started to laugh. "I'd forgotten all about that!"

"Why is there no name or description for this class?"

"The subject matter was too eclectic for an apt description. That class was amazing!"

"So, we are talking about the same class, then? This was taught by a Dr. JoAnna Plischenko?"

"Yes, that's right. JoAnna was also my advisor and a good friend to me while I got my doctorate." The inspector nodded.

"And this specific class was part of the curriculum?"

"Yes. There was no classroom for this class, Inspector. It was designed by Dr. Plischenko and her brightest students. It is expensive. To take the class costs almost the same as tuition for a whole semester." The inspector raised his eyebrows. "We traveled all over the world. We would literally observe the spiritual practices of whomever or wherever we went. We went to Tibet and observed three separate types of Buddhism. We went to the American southwest and worshipped with the Hopi tribe and the Yaqui. We would actually participate in the rituals and ceremonies, if the people and their spiritual leaders would allow it." Julie smiled as she remembered.

"Did this include devil worship, Julie?"

"No. And looking back on it, it was strange."

"What was strange?"

"Well, Dr. Plischenko is well known in academic circles around the world. She's a genius. She's a published author and is a guest speaker at various universities all over the world. She is famous for her skepticism.

She is an avowed atheist. Her rigor for the facts and hard, provable, and measurable data is also legendary." Julie smiled at the inspector. "I'm sorry. I guess that's a long way of saying that she is not a superstitious person. But every single year since she has offered this course, she has refused to include any kind of thing involving the devil."

"That is interesting. It sounds like one hell of a class."

"Mmmm, it was."

"You're considered a genius in the occult field and psychology, as well, aren't you?"

Julie blushed. "Well, I think that's going too far, Tom." She looked down at the coffee table.

"I don't." Tom was reading the notes Julie had handed him. Julie sipped her wine. It tasted even better than before. She felt warm and her limbs seemed to tingle every time she moved. "Okay, this is interesting."

"What is?"

"Jedidiah Edmund B. Choate."

"Oh, him."

"Yes, him. So, you learned about him in this class?"

"I think so. If the notes are from that class, then it must have been. Do you still think that's what we saw this morning?"

"I don't think there's any doubt about it." Tom said. "This is the fourth time that name has come up today."

"The fourth time?"

The inspector nodded. "Yes, I saw it in an old police file taken from a data base out of New Mexico. I asked you about it in the woods and you recognized his name immediately. And then one of my patrolmen, Ben Franklin, found it too."

"He was a monster."

"Yes. But you, your professor, and your classmates never witnessed any sort of devil worship ritual performed?"

"No, the subject of Satan was one of the few things we examined in the campus library and not in the field."

"I see." Inspector Dahms went to sip his coffee. The mug was empty.

"Oh, would you like some more, Tom?" He smiled.

"No, thank you, Julie. May I ask, do you remember what, if any, conclusion or ideas your class had concerning the purpose for this ritual?"

"It should be in these notes," Julie said. She leaned over and reached into his lap for the papers. Inspector Dahms could smell Julie's hair. It was fresh and natural. There was unmistakable warmth, like summer, in that smell that matched the radiant color. "Here we go." Julie gently tugged one sheet out from the rest and began to read it. She stayed where she was, leaning slightly over his lap. Julie felt drawn to the inspector. He put his arm around her shoulders. She leaned into his side and read aloud.

"According to these old notes, not a single one of us, I think there were twelve in the whole class, had any clue what it was for. I know I didn't. Dr. Plischenko said at the time, here it is, right here—it's ancient. It goes back to the time of prehistory, when there was no writing or record keeping of any kind. So, really there were just symbols, and words for these symbols, usually carved on cave walls. Both the word, and the symbol itself, contain tremendous power for these people.

"So, she reasons here that the only visible, physical symbol is the circle in which the ritual takes place. The circle can represent eternity. Sometimes it's represented as the cycle of life and death. The people can dance around the center in an ever-increasing circumference, like a spiral. Spirals can also represent eternity. The four murders are, therefore, the truly horrible price in blood for the participants to achieve eternal life." Julie looked up at the inspector. He was reading the notes along with Julie. He looked at her.

"I see. I'm sorry, but how does Solomon fit into all this?"

"I think that the man you're looking for wears a ring that has the seal of Solomon engraved on it. And possibly a name for the devil engraved on the inside of it." Inspector Dahms looked at what Julie was pointing to; it was a drawing of a ring bearing a hexagram with corresponding dots in each triangle within the symbol.

"And the purpose is to cheat death?"

"That's what Dr. Plischenko thought at the time, and I'd have to agree. It's logical enough."

"It's insane," Inspector Dahms said. Julie burst out laughing.

"No, no, that's not what I meant, Tom. I'm speaking from the standpoint of the participants; the evidence at hand does logically point to that."

"Yes, I see now what you're saying. Please accept my apology, Julie." The inspector was grinning now. Julie was still laughing.

"Perception is the key to so many disciplines, Tom. It certainly pertains to what you do. And you really are deeply perceptive. It is also central to psychiatry. We have to consider the perceptions of our patients seriously before diagnosing a thing. And as for all things spiritual, religious, or faith oriented, perception underlies every facet. It's why we tried to fully participate with as many different faiths as we did. The idea was to see it through their eyes, 'glimpse it through the lens of their perception' is how JoAnna used to put it. It included taking the mind-altering substances for some of the braver in our class."

"Did you ever participate like that, Julie?"

"I participated in all of the rituals we were allowed to, but I never dared go that far. Sometimes I wish I had, Tom. But I was scared to at the time. You know, the stigma of drug use made me nervous, I guess." The irony began to set in. *I'm on mushrooms right now,* Julie thought. She had to suppress her laughter. She could not suppress her wide grin.

"Would've scared me, too," the inspector said. Julie smiled and looked at him. Tom was smiling back at her. He leaned his tall, thin frame down until their faces were inches apart. Julie's breath was sweet like the red wine she was drinking. He put his hand gently on the back of her head and kissed her. Julie lost her breath. Her lips tingled with an electric charge. His hand felt huge and powerful on the back of her head. It drew Julie in.

Her hands fumbled with his belt and his hands fumbled with the button on her blue jeans. They could not stop kissing. Each could barely breathe. Julie slowly leaned back onto the large, soft couch. She stretched out her legs as straight as she could as he pulled her blue jeans off of her. Her sweater rode up her belly, revealing her stomach and her naval. Tom removed his pants and underwear and mounted Julie. They began kissing again.

Julie felt a tingling over her entire body. She smiled and tilted her head back, writhing beneath his weight. He kissed her throat and the side of her neck. She smelled so good, he thought. She smelled like flowers and nature. His breath was cool to her skin, which ran red hot. She opened her legs and welcomed him in. He immediately began to thrust up and down over her with a rhythm that was primal, breathless, frantic.

Julie suddenly cried out, arching her back and wrapping her legs around Tom's back. Her head went forward and down and she shuddered beneath him as she climaxed. Her toes curled tightly until they cramped. Julie laughed her throaty laugh. They were both drenched in sweat now. They rolled over together as Tom lifted Julie up as he settled down on his back on the couch. Julie mounted him and could feel him swelling inside her. The nipples on her small breasts felt as if they might explode. She arched her back and writhed over him.

Julie looked down at Tom and gasped. The colors of his aura ran that same deep, dark red and seemed to be rippling outwardly. She reached her long, slender arms down and began stroking his chest. He was muscular and powerful. The hairs on his chest were a salty dark and gray. Julie could see bits of her own aura as she moved over him. Pinks and a very light red color rippled around her like water. The colors represented erotic passion and femininity.

Tom sat up and rolled Julie over onto her belly. She got onto her hands and knees as he mounted her from behind. Julie's beautiful figure, the small of her back, her elegant neck, and beautiful hair drove him to near madness. It took only a few minutes of wild, violent thrusts. Julie bent down as he climaxed. Tom's entire body shuddered and he grunted audibly several times. And it was over.

They dressed quietly. Each checked their cell for messages. *Strange,* Julie thought. She had not heard at all from James. He should have been here hours ago. Inspector Dahms had several messages. He had to get back to work.

"Julie, I want to thank you for a very illuminating evening."

Julie smiled back at him. "Me too, Tom. Let's do it again, under not-so-similar circumstances, though, hmmm?"

He laughed. "Right. Good night."

"Good night." †

CHAPTER 32
The Descent

Father Knight had been alone in the tiny chapel for what seemed like an eternity. He sighed. How could time ever tick in an ancient and holy place such as this? he wondered. He looked around at the tiny chapel. It's simplicity and symmetry, with its stunning artworks, the pulpit and altar, was breathtaking. Then, there were those ancient texts! Father Knight hoped that the bishop would allow him to examine this chapel and those texts and research its history sometime. He wanted to know everything that the bishop and Father Freeman knew.

First things first, however, James, he thought to himself. *There is this "challenge" business.* He went to the altar. He took the Old Testament and New Testament and set them side by side upon the altar. Father Knight knelt and prayed deeply and intensely. He prayed to God that He would give James the strength and courage to do His Will during this time. He prayed to Jesus Christ that He would protect him and that He would help and inspire him when the time came. He found himself in a truly deep, meditative, almost dream like state.

He never knew for how long he had been lost in prayer, but after a spell, Father Knight sensed there was someone with him in the tiny chapel. There was a presence with him in this place right here and right now. He could feel it. Still kneeling at the altar, he opened his eyes slowly. They took a moment to adjust. The tiny chapel had grown dimmer, somehow. It appeared as ethereal and dreamy, he thought. The candles that all lit the room seemed now somehow to be more distant. They appeared as stars in a dark night sky.

Time and space no longer seemed to be in order in this place. Father Knight looked up at the altar before which he knelt. There, looking straight at him from the opposite side of the altar, was Satan. The devil was kneeling, as if in prayer. But he was not in prayer. He was staring at Father Knight, smiling. He appeared now to James in his true and most ancient form.

Satan glowed an ancient, shadowy white. He was an unholy mix of stardust and dark matter. His face appeared to look just like James's face with a surreal luminescence. At times it seemed identical to James's, except his eyes. They were black, then they seemed to change into a deep purple, then a scarlet. Then, they looked like a pale blue. They would darken back into a midnight blue, go purple, and finally back to black.

Father Knight watched Lucifer's eyes with a mix of fear and fascination as the two stared at one another across the great altar in the tiny chapel. And then he realized why those eyes seemed so familiar to him. Father Knight recognized that these were the very eyes of the strange, tall man. They seemed to reflect his own, somehow. Father Knight could see himself inside them, as if he were trapped in them. He felt like he was being consumed by them. He swallowed hard, but continued to look Lucifer straight in the eyes.

"You look different than you did before." As James spoke these words, they at once seemed to echo and die in the tiny chapel. The devil did not respond at first. James smiled at Satan. He was still not completely out of the deep, meditative state in which he'd been in while at prayer. It tugged gently at him. There was safety back there, deep in prayer; he knew that.

But James was intent on obeying the will of God. He did not want to let down Christ as he had once let down his brother. He slowly arose from the altar. As he did so, he observed as Satan effortlessly raised himself up. He spoke to James. His voice was clear and crisp, almost singsong.

"Forgive my earlier embodiments, James. We of angelic creation are at the mercy of conditions in your physical plane, just as you mortals are. We try to appear as we might be expected to appear in order that we can be known or recognized. But here, in this holy place, James, you see what is made up of me." Lucifer smiled at James. "Walk with me."

The two began to walk away from the altar. Father Knight noticed that the tiny chapel seemed to dissipate before his very eyes. He found himself walking along a dark, endless passage, which descended deeper into the earth at a steep angle. The devil walked alongside him.

"I know what it is you wish to say to me, James. So sweet, so sweet, so sweet, you are, lamb. You would say if it is a fight you wish for, then, let us fight! You would say that you shall forgive me as I devour you. Like the One I knew from the Galilee, the Teacher. You would turn your cheek as I took your life. And you are pure, James. To that, all of Creation would attest." Satan moved closer to James, his white-light face mere inches from his. "It's the purity of the mortal, of the combatant, or sacrifice, that truly matters in such matters, you see. And yours is for the ages, James. Though I am who you think I am, I am not what you think I am."

The two continued walking. The passage opened into an enormous chasm. Giant, razor-sharp stalagmites hung down from the roof of this cavern. A strange, unnatural light seemed to come from somewhere down in the depths of the chasm. The long shadows from the stalagmites twisted downward, as if they were long, bony fingers reaching for one's very soul. Satan led Father Knight along a narrow pathway that led across the great chasm. The path seemed to become visible with each step. It would then vanish, only to reappear with the next step.

"It is they who have lied to you, James, not me. We need not fight, you and I. Remember, James. Remember your intended ministry? It was to be a ministry of peace, through truth, lamb." Father Knight looked at Satan, who smiled, nodding his head. "Yes, yes, James, I was there at your ordination. A ministry of peace, you intended. And yet, here you are, being marched off to battle by the very church that was founded in the name of the Teacher who was teaching the opposite way! A mortal would say that this is…ironic, no?"

As Satan asked this, they had arrived at the far end of the chasm and entered a different section of the passage. It was cold and damp. Somewhere Father Knight could hear what sounded like rushing water. The passage began to decline more steeply. Father Knight could see his own breath faintly in the darkness of the passage.

"Do you truly wish to fight me, James?" Satan stared unblinking as he awaited James's answer.

"No. I do not wish to fight anyone. But when the soul of an innocent is at stake, fight I must." James looked up at Satan now. "Surely you can understand that?" To James' surprise, the devil nodded his head.

"Yes, I can. It would seem that the one who I had thought challenged me was innocent. So, you see, again they lie to you, while I tell you the truth. The lamb called Father Torrez is no longer under my claim. We need not fight, you see, James? Do you see?" Father Knight looked hard at Satan for several moments, thinking frantically. The devil smiled at him, and then shook his head, and said, "No. No tricks up my sleeve, or loopholes, is it? Yes, that is it. Loopholes. There are no loopholes, James, no tricks. No lies."

The two walked in silence for a while. Father Knight's mind raced. The roar of the water was becoming louder and louder. Despite the size of the chasm, the sound seemed to echo and carry endlessly around the two as they walked. It was deafening to James and he struggled to clear his mind. Finally they came upon a break in the passage. A large river of dark waters raged by with a torrent of foam and mist. James could just barely see the dark passage continue on the other side of this river. As the two approached the riverbank, the deafening sound subsided.

James closed his eyes for a moment and breathed in deeply, then held his breath. He breathed out slowly and opened his eyes to see the devil staring at him.

"So, Father Torrez did not challenge you, as you put it?" James said.

"No, he did not. The act in question was performed by a very old and dear friend of mine. He is a priest, of sorts. But nothing like you, James." The devil reached into the water and pulled out a bell. He rang it. Father Knight looked into the black water as it roared past. A form loomed out of the darkness of the foam and the mist. The shrouded silhouette of a hooded creature rowed a large rowboat toward them.

"All aboard." Satan smiled. The two clambered aboard the boat. It was old and rotted. It creaked under their weight and Father Knight was sure that the churning waters would splinter the craft into many tiny pieces any minute, and he, the devil, and the shrouded figure would all be swept away to heaven only knew where. But it did not splinter apart. Despite the raging current, the shrouded figure effortlessly rowed the boat across the river. The foam and mist parted as the boat cut through the black waters.

"But, then, why did your friend challenge you?" Father Knight asked.

"Oh, that was no challenge; it was…a welcome-home gift."

"I see. Then, if we are not meant to fight, where are we going?"

"I assumed you men of the cloth wished a confrontation anyway when I discovered you in preparation in the chapel."

"You mean, when I was in prayer?"

"Yes, of course, why else would you remain in the chapel?"

"No one told me anything. I simply wished to serve God."

Satan laughed a bitter laugh. "Then your God, your Bishop, and your mentor have sent you off to sea on a ship of lies. Like a lamb to slaughter, they sacrifice you for the sake of pride."

"What do you mean?"

"That is an explanation better given by your own people than by me. Ask your Bishop, or your mentor, if they haven't run off to hide, yet."

As the devil spoke, James could see the bank on the other side of the river looming in the darkness and shadows. The rest of the boat ride was made in silence. The black-hooded boatman docked the old rowboat along the bank, and Satan and James disembarked and continued walking along the dark passage. The sound of the rushing waters faded as they made their way into the next passage. Silence waited here. Father Knight felt a gratitude for it. They walked in a golden silence for several minutes. A scream broke the stillness. It was long and filled with an agony James could never have imagined.

It was followed by a howl, and then crying. As the devil and James walked toward these sounds, even more voices began wailing. James could hear people pleading and screaming. They came to the end of the passage. There was no opening or high ceiling here. There was only a hole. It was from here that the screams were coming.

"What is this?" James asked.

"This is a portal to hell and my domain."

"I thought we were going to talk about the truth."

The devil smiled and pushed James over the edge. "Truth, indeed." †

CHAPTER 33
Need a New Game Plan

"I don't know how much more of this I can take," Officer Marconi said. He choked back tears and spoke through gritted teeth. His chubby-cheeked face was still pale and sickly. His large, puppy dog brown eyes belied the shock. Officer Tubbs nodded and patted him on the back.

"Hang in there, man. This is almost done."

"At least Dahms let us take the damned bodies down," Officer Evers said. He was washing his large hands and thick, muscular forearms in a large, white sink basin on the west wall of the large lab in the basement of the Littleborough Police Headquarters. It had taken the entire Littleborough police force and fire department hours and hours to clear the crime scene of bodies and body parts. Even then, no one could really be sure that they had found everything or everyone.

It was decided by the chief and Inspector Dahms to leave the remaining trace evidence in place for further investigation: the large, black pot with the sticky fluid, the few remaining fire charred masks, a mallet, the bongo drums and the conga drums that were found along the clearing's edge. It was still unclear how many people actually had lost their lives in those woods that night. The number for the death toll, everyone knew, was over forty, though.

For their part, the patrolmen were exhausted. They had all cried themselves out as they worked. No one had been able to eat a single thing that day, except Officer Franklin. Officers Marconi and Evers were still gagging and occasionally vomiting pure stomach acid.

"Any word from the search parties on finding the little girl?"

"No. The inspector radioed to Marge to tell us not to join the search until tomorrow morning. He wants us all to go home and get some rest," Officer Tubbs said.

"Is he out of his mind?" Officer Marconi said.

"That's what the message says."

"With a huge, rogue wolf out there, he wants us to go home and rest? I may never be able to sleep again!" All the patrolmen were nodding.

"I hear you, Marconi. But that's what the man is telling us. Doesn't mean we have to, though."

"I'm gonna start searching just as soon as we've wrapped it up here," Officer Evers said.

"Me too," Officer Marconi said.

"Where's that little puke college boy, Franklin?" Officer Evers said.

Officer Tubbs put his finger up to his pursed lips. "He's upstairs on the computer Marge uses. He's checking out you-know-who."

"Good."

"About time." The men had finally finished. The bodies and body parts had been removed and, identified or not, tagged. They had then showered in their locker room to wash the day's horror off of their backs. The locker room went silent. Officers Jones and Lydon came out of the showers wrapped in towels. They both sat down on a long wooden bench in front of their respective lockers. There they sat, slack jawed, staring blankly at nothing at all. The light foot falls of Officer Franklin could be heard as he hastily descended the stairs down to the locker room. He breathlessly came through the open doorway of the locker room. All the patrolmen turned to see him.

"Hey you guys, I've finished researching the inspector's background."

"Sssssshhhhh!" Officer Tubbs's eyes widened as he addressed Officer Franklin. He shot a nervous glance toward the locker room door. "Damn it, Franklin, you want get us fucked? The chief will kill us if he finds out what you did."

"Sorry," Officer Franklin whispered. His face contorted slightly in thought. "Hey, wait a minute. What I did? This was your idea, Tubbs."

Officer Tubbs shrugged and nodded. "Whatever. You know what I mean. It's our asses if we get caught."

"Well, I got the scoop."

"And?"

"He's a national hero, Tubbs."

"Then why have we never heard of him, Franklin?" Officer Tubbs said.

"Because he was a spy." Officer Lydon laughed softly, shaking his head.

"A what?" Officer Marconi said.

"A spy, for us. At least that's what it looks like."

"Really?"

"Yup, it's all in here." Officer Franklin was holding a thin manila folder and carefully handed it to Officer Tubbs.

"Where'd you get this?"

"I took it from the chief's files. So, you guys need to read it and then give it back so I can put it back before the chief finds out what I did."

"Why, Benjamin, you sneaky little bastard." Officer Tubbs was grinning. "I didn't think you had it in you!" Officer Tubbs slapped Officer Franklin on the back of his head.

"Ow!" Officer Franklin put his hand up over the back of his head where he had been slapped. "I don't have it in me, Tubbs. I'm literally crapping myself as we speak, so please, just read it and let me get it back in there so I can have a shower."

"Make sure you wash behind those ears, Franklin," Officer Marconi said. All of the patrolmen except Officer Franklin burst out laughing. Officer Franklin looked at Officer Tubbs.

"You told them?"

Officer Tubbs shrugged, still smiling. He opened the folder he was holding and began to read. He furrowed his brow.

"He also told us all about the big, bad flying demon wolf, Ben! So, look out!" Officer Evers said. There was more laughter. Officer Franklin blushed, his face turning a rosy red. He could not look at any of the other patrolmen. Officer Tubbs was reading the file.

"Franklin, there's nothing here. Nothing that tells us he's a cop," Officer Tubbs said. Officers Evers and Marconi peered at the file over his shoulder.

"That's right, Tubbs. Look at the military record."

"I did! Nothing! No branch is mentioned, no rank, no serial number, just these awards."

"Exactly. The awards. The fact that there is nothing in there to suggest what he was strongly suggests it was covert. Whether he was CIA or NSA or whatever is irrelevant. His service and those, those medals, tell me all I need to know."

"Not me," Officer Marconi said. "We still don't know who the hell this guy is. Those records could be forgeries for all you know, Franklin."

"Forger...forgeries?" Officer Franklin looked up at the ceiling and threw his arms up in the air. "You guys asked me to check him out and I did! The same exact record that you hold in your hands is also in our system. They're identical!"

"Ssshhh! Jesus, Franklin," Officer Tubbs said.

"Oh, who cares?" Officer Franklin said. "You guys wanted the information, I got you the information. You don't like the information, so now you don't want the information? So, you say it's fake information. Let me tell you this; it is the last time I do anything like this for any of you, because, well, what's the point if you're not even going to believe it?"

"No, it's cool, Ben. It's cool," Officer Tubbs said. He held his hand up to try to calm Officer Franklin down, and to quiet him down. "You came through for us, man. Unfortunately, they're hiding who this guy is from us."

"Exactly. He isn't one of us," Officer Evers said.

"Whatever," Officer Franklin said. He took the file back from Officer Tubbs and walked to the locker room doorway. He looked up the stairs, to the right and then the left. Seeing no one around, he raced back up the two flights of stairs to return the file to his boss's filing cabinet just as fast as he could. As he got to the top of the stairs to the second floor he could see the chief's office straight ahead. There was no sign of the chief, or anyone, anywhere.

Officer Franklin sprinted his wide, frumpy frame down the hall and into the chief's small office. As he had before, his tired, pudgy body broke into a cold sweat. His breathing was labored as he went over to the filing cabinet and opened the top drawer as quietly as he could. He could hear his own heart pounding with every beat as he ran his short, pudgy fingers through the personnel files. He placed the file back into the drawer carefully and closed the drawer.

Though he no longer needed to, Officer Franklin raced out of the office of the chief, back down the hallway and down the two flights of stairs to the men's locker room. He burst through the door to find all his fellow patrolmen standing at attention. They all turned when he came in. The chief was addressing them.

"Ben, glad you could join us," he said.

Officer Franklin looked uneasily around the locker room at his fellow patrolmen. He swallowed hard.

"Yes sir." He said.

"First of all," the chief looked his men directly in the eyes, "I want to thank you all for holding yourselves to such a high standard today. I know it wasn't easy. That crime scene was the worst thing I've ever seen in my whole life. I'm sure it was for you as well. Thank you, men, and great job. Here is where things stand at the moment. Our animal is asleep, or resting. I tracked him around Fears Hill until well after dark. The sound and scent stopped somewhere almost a mile up on the western side of the hill.

"We have still not found Sandra. There have been sightings all over Littleborough, but they don't add up because they place her everywhere at the same time. We have received a number of missing person reports now. The inspector is dealing with those upstairs.

"We haven't heard from Billy Pollard or anybody from his hunting party in quite a while. We can't reach or find anyone of the town's volunteers who were searching for Sandra. And there is still no sign of the FBI expert they supposedly sent."

"What the hell is going on, Chief?" Officer Tubbs said.

"I don't know. I do know that since last night at the crime scene my cell service has been in and out."

"Mine too," Officer Franklin said. The rest of the patrolmen were nodding their heads in agreement.

"So, that may have something to do with it, I just don't know."

"Right," Officer Tubbs said. "What are we going to do about Mr. Mystery Man, that peachy inspector of yours, huh? Who the hell is he, Chief?"

The chief sighed. He looked at each one of his men in the eyes with his wide, opaque brown eyes. "He is the best man for this job right now, Harold. I understand you're suspicious of him. He's not from here and so we don't think of him as one of us. Right now, he's all we've got. Just be patient, okay? For right now, I want you all to go home and get some rest."

The patrolmen all spoke up at once.

"I can't do that!"

"Get some rest? How? That's ridiculous!"

"Are you out of your mind?"

"You want us to go home? We've got fifty fucking people lost in those woods right now! No way! No fucking way!"

The chief was holding his hands up to quiet and calm the men. "I can't force you to go home, of course. If you feel you need to resume the search, I would understand that. But every one of us is exhausted. We've all been under a ton of strain. You guys should get some rest and start fresh first thing tomorrow morning."

"Nope," Officer Tubbs said. He had changed into a fresh uniform. They all had, except Officer Franklin. They began filing out of the locker room. "You coming, Franklin?"

"Ummm..."

"You and Ben are coming upstairs with me," the chief said. "We're going to go over a few things together, if that's all right with you?"

"Yeah, okay," Officer Tubbs said. He looked at Officer Franklin, who was staring wide-eyed back at him.

"Take a shower, Ben. I'll see you upstairs in my office when you're ready."

"Yes, sir."

The chief turned and walked out of the locker room, followed by Officer Tubbs, leaving Ben alone. The sound from the door closing reverberated around the locker room. Officer Franklin hung his head and sighed. He stripped off his dirty clothes and went into the showers. †

CHAPTER 33.3

Colonel Thomas Dahms of the CIA entered the elevator alone. He stood in the center of the elevator for a moment. He did not move. He could only stare at the warped reflection of himself created by the cold steel frame of the elevator. He slowly exhaled, then turned himself around to face the elevator door. A single light shined on the panel next to the door: LEVEL 13- TOP SECRET CLEARANCE ONLY.

The hallway from which he had come was long and narrow. It was not well lit, but rather shadowy. *A fitting lighting scheme for a building such as this,* he thought. He reached into his coat pocket and removed his pipe and tobacco. He began to clean the pipe by thumping it into the open palm of his hand several times. He then filled it with the tobacco and packed it down. He put the tobacco pouch back into his coat pocket and pulled out a box of wooden matches. He removed a match and struck it against the box. It lit with a light *whoosh* of flame. The flame danced in his gray eyes. His eyes stared, unseeing, down the endless corridor of shadows.

The screams of the woman were still ringing in his head. The visions of her tiny, helpless body writhing in agony on the metal table burned their way into his mind and memory. He knew better than to try and shut these pictures off. They would keep coming, like all the other things he had seen and heard while in the Middle East and while he was here, deep inside the Pentagon.

The orders to arrange a trap for a terrorist swam before Colonel Thomas Dahms's eyes. This terrorist had vital information that could potentially save tens of thousands of Iraqi and American lives, it said. His trap worked to perfection. He could see the interrogation of the terrorist begin immediately in his mind, as clear as day. He could feel the pinprick the captured terrorist had felt as he had been drugged. The man began to babble and the words jumbled and echoed in the colonel's head. The man seemed to look right at the colonel. He spoke in clear English, "Double agent, we call, Mata Hari."

Colonel Dahms could hear the Americans who were interrogating him speaking in hushed whispers. The agent in question was a CIA interpreter. She was an MD herself, so, her cover was that she worked as a Red Cross doctor. The only agent they knew of that fit this description was Anna Torrez, older sister of Father Miguel Torrez. That name rang in the colonel's head over and over and over. Anna Torrez.

Colonel Dahms could hear his own voice speaking. His persistent insistence that the information was bogus, and that Anna was a loyal and valuable CIA asset, fell on deaf ears. His voice was somehow muted, as if he were speaking underwater. He could still see the orders come in from Virginia; the order to seize Anna and bring her back to the United States was issued. The man given the order was Colonel Thomas Dahms. He could now see her in his mind's eye; she was bound, gagged, and drugged. She was flown back to America,

The men who were assigned to interrogate her were all CIA, and believing her to be a double agent, were highly emotional and brutal in their approach. The colonel knew these men. He could see them clearly now; he closed his eyes. But they all looked different to him. Their eyes were of a different color. Their voices were different. As they tortured Anna, the colonel could not understand a single word any of them spoke. It was not English. It was not Arabic.

Anna seemed to understand, though. But Anna would not crack. She steadfastly refused to admit to any of the charges that were being leveled at her. It was toward the end of the fourth day of "questioning" that cracks began to show amidst the interrogation team. Several members began to have serious doubts about Anna's guilt. They reported their doubts.

Colonel Thomas Dahms had been ordered to return to the United States and oversee the interrogation himself. But by the time he had returned and arrived at the lowest level of the Pentagon, Anna was too far gone. He walked into the room in which she was being held. The overhead lights blazed a white, soulless light down onto her. She was strapped to the metal table. Her arms, her legs, and her head were strapped down as well. He had never met Anna. He walked over to the table and looked down upon her. She was resting. It was the first sleep she had been allowed to have since being taken.

Her eyes opened and fixed her gaze on the colonel. A smile slowly crept across her face. Her dark brown eyes, beautiful, oval shaped and very feminine, turned jet black.

"Why, hello, Thomas," she said. "We've been waiting for you." Her eyes changed back to brown. Tears rolled down the sides of her head. And there Anna Torrez died. Colonel Dahms looked at the physician who had been tending to her. He nodded his head solemnly at the colonel.

"She's gone," he said. "I didn't know you knew her. I am sorry."

"I didn't," the colonel said. He walked out of the room and back down the long, shadowy corridor toward the elevator.

He lit his pipe in the elevator and puffed deeply on it. He reached out to press the button for the ground floor of the Pentagon, some thirteen stories up. The elevator doors slid silently shut. The elevator began to move downward. The colonel furrowed his brow. He looked at the control panel, but all the lights and buttons seemed to be pressing themselves and lighting up and then going off alternately. The elevator picked up speed as it plummeted far below the depths of the Pentagon building. He tried furiously to press any and all of the buttons to try and stop the fall but nothing worked. It was when he stopped trying to press the buttons that the elevator seemed to come to an immediate stop.

Colonel Dahms stood in the center of the elevator, his pipe still smoldering in his hand. He looked back down at the control panel. There was only one button where there used to be at least twenty buttons. The word next to the lone button read HELL. There was a clicking sound on the other side of the elevator door. The colonel looked at the door. It clicked one more time. Then, it clicked again. Slowly, the elevator doors slid silently open.

Standing just outside the elevator door was a tall, thin, and gaunt figure. The colonel could only just make out its form in the shadows of where it was standing. The figure raised its head and regarded the colonel. It was the body of a man, with the head of an enormous goat. Antlers protruded wildly from its head. Jet-black eyes stared into Colonel Dahms's gray eyes. It smiled at him.

"Now, did that ring a bell, Colonel?"

Something, somewhere, was ringing. Inspector Dahms opened his eyes. It was the phone on his office desk. He sat up in his chair and stretched. He reached for the phone and answered it. It was the chief asking if he could come up to his office.

"Be right there, Chief," he said. †

CHAPTER 34
The Gravity of the Situation

The hot shower had made Ben feel much better. It also made him feel sleepy. Waves of exhaustion came over him as he slowly made his way up to the chief's office. The two flights of stairs he had raced up and down twice only fifteen minutes ago felt like Mount Kilimanjaro now. Officer Franklin didn't know how he knew, but he knew that the chief had figured out what he had been up to. He hesitated before walking into the office.

"Hello, Ben."

"Hi, Chief." Officer Franklin stood just outside the open door staring wide-eyed and awkwardly at the chief.

"Come in, sit down. Harold had to go to the bathroom."

"Okay." Officer Franklin sheepishly shuffled into the tiny office and sat down on the small wooden chair in front of the desk.

"This will only take a minute," the chief said. He was shuffling piles of paper and folders on his desk in an attempt to create some semblance of order. He looked up. "Harold." Officer Tubbs was standing in the doorway. "Come in, take a seat."

"Yes, sir." Officer Tubbs sat next to Officer Franklin in the only small wooden chair left. Officer Franklin did not dare to look at his partner. For his part, Officer Tubbs's face was quite ashen from being so angry.

"There, that's a little bit better." The chief looked up at the two patrolmen. "You both look tired."

"I'm tired, sir," Officer Franklin said. He looked at the chief. "I'm kinda wondering how you do it, I mean at your age. I…hmmm, sorry about that." The chief laughed.

"Don't be. You get to a certain age and sleep doesn't come so easily, I guess. I'm afraid I've spent more nights awake than I have asleep in my adult life. I don't think I'm really missing anything." Officer Franklin smiled. "Ben, I don't want you to feel you can't go home for a while and get some rest. You too, Harold," the chief said. Officer Tubbs did not speak. He simply shook his head.

"I don't know, Chief." Officer Franklin looked down at the floor. "What are you going to do?"

"We're here to determine that," the chief said. Officer Franklin quietly breathed a sigh of relief. The chief regarded Officer Tubbs and Officer Franklin. The three sat in the small, brightly lit office in silence. Only the light hum of a long fluorescent light could be heard in the entirety of the building.

"The inspector just told me about some interesting theories you had about our animal out there. What was it you called it, a flying, demon wolf?" Officer Tubbs snorted. Officer Franklin shot a glance at him.

"Yes, Chief, that's what I saw at the crime scene."

The chief regarded his young patrolman. His deep, almond-shaped brown eyes stared, unblinking.

"Franklin," Officer Tubbs said. "We're the police." He leaned forward slightly and spoke softly. "We're not the paranormal experts. I don't know what you saw at that crime scene that I missed, but I'm looking for a human or humans. They are the ones that did this. And we are looking for a wolf. Albeit, I admit it sounds like one hell of an animal. But it is just an animal."

"What did you see, Ben?" the chief said.

"Well, the clearing itself is what is known as a place of power."

"A place of...oh come on, Franklin! We're looking for real people, places, and events here. We're not looking for a 'place of power.'"

"No. That's true, Tubbs. We are not looking for a place of power because we already know where it is. You guys, I'm telling you that these things are real. I have always wondered, but now I have physical evidence. This isn't superstition. If it were, we wouldn't have had to pick up all those dead bodies and body parts off that clearing floor!" Officer Franklin had to stop for a moment. He swallowed hard.

"Take it easy, Ben," the chief said.

"Look, the dead people are real enough; the scene we all saw was real enough. If you guys don't want to believe that it is a place of power, then don't believe it. But know this, the people who held that ritual believed it. You had better believe that."

The chief nodded his leonine head.

"Yeah, that's a reasonable conclusion to draw about the cult worshippers. My own people have believed that clearing to be a portal between our world and the spiritual world since the beginning of time." Officer Franklin nodded his head. Officer Tubbs looked at the chief.

"Really?" he said.

"Yup."

"That's right." Officer Franklin felt energized by the chief's acknowledgment of the place in question. "The original Native Americans, your ancestors, Chief, who settled here thousands of years ago realized that it was a special place. Clearings in forests, caves, certain mountaintops, plateaus, or hilltops, special trees, or rocks, and anywhere else where very important events take place are all places of power. There's a bunch of reasons behind this; some are faith based, others are based on actual events. Some of it is science. And some of it is just a feeling people get when they're in such a place.

"You guys know that the earth has its own electro-magnetic field. In some places, like Stonehenge, for example, the electro-magnetic field is more pronounced, more powerful. This is a scientific fact. The same is true for good old Littleborough." As he spoke, Officer Franklin fished several pieces of paper folded together out from the inside pocket of his uniform. They were covered in soot. As he carefully unfolded them, more soot and ash fell down onto his clean uniform. "Shit." He handed the papers to the chief, who placed them on his desk. All three men leaned over the maps.

"I looked this up online when we got back from the first look at the scene. The electro-magnetic fields are actually reversed here, and the readings are simply off the charts. See? Look at this area in particular; the St. Mark's Church, a chapel over at St. Mark's school, and several areas over by a Fears Hill, which includes our little clearing." Officer Franklin looked up earnestly at Officer Tubbs, then at the chief. It was an extremely detailed series of satellite photos of most of Littleborough, with the areas of interest highlighted. Superimposed over the photos were charts showing the directions and measurements of the electro-magnetic fields. "Off the charts," Officer Franklin repeated.

"I see. Where is all this information from, Ben?"

"A couple sites on the Internet," Officer Franklin said. "The satellite pictures are from a high-tech company that the inspector knew about, and the measurements for the electro-magnetic grid were taken and published by a group from Columbia University, a Dr. Pleshenko. It was the inspector who found them, too."

"Very good, Ben, go on," the chief said.

"Okay. Well, someone in the cult, most likely the leader, obviously knew of the significance of that clearing. So that's where they opted to perform the ritual. The rite is simple enough. Four sacrifices are required. They cannot go willingly. The idea behind all this seems to be to somehow create a doorway, or portal, between our physical world and either other dimensions or time/spaces. Like maybe hell?"

Officer Tubbs looked up from the maps and held up his hand. "Okay, wait a minute. Now, are you speaking literally, or are you just talking from the standpoint of the people involved in performing the ritual? Because I do not believe in a doorway to or from hell."

"Look, you believe or don't believe whatever you want. All I'm telling you is the facts. That crime scene back there leaves no doubt. It renders us only one, inescapable, conclusion: that the point of that ritual was to literally raise the devil."

"Only something went wrong," the chief interjected, calmly trying to keep the young patrolman focused on the explanation.

"Yes, that's right. Something went very wrong. You see, the people in the group performing the rite aren't supposed to die. They are supposed to live through the ritual and see the devil, or whatever. But obviously something hit that fire. There was the conflagration. The fire knocked everyone down, burning some of them quite badly. But in almost the same instant the fire is then extinguished. The trouble is, as you already know, there were no accelerants present. There does not seem to be any physical explanation for the fire to burn out of control like that, and no way for it to have been put out.

"Therefore, my examination of the crime scene leaves no doubt that whatever caused the fire to swell also caused it to go out. Finally, my examination of the body parts at the crime scene indicates that whatever it was, stayed around long enough to kill and partially eat everyone there— their eyes, lips, throats—and it removed and probably ate their hearts. The serrated edges of its huge teeth are present on every corpse and body part," Officer Franklin had to stop short and swallowed hard for a moment, "we have downstairs. So, what happened?"

"What happened? What happened? Damn it, Franklin, you're supposed to be the fucking expert here, you and that Mr. Mystery spy. Why don't you tell us what happened?" Officer Tubbs's voice remained low, even, and calm, but his dark brown eyes blazed. Officer Franklin had recoiled from the sound of the curse word. As he did, he subconsciously took his thick glasses off and began to fiddle with them with his pudgy fingers. His wide blue eyes remained fixed on Officer Tubbs's eyes. He blinked hard twice.

"Well, you don't have to swear, you know." He closed his eyes tightly as he spoke. "And besides, I don't want to tell you because I can already tell that you don't want to hear it."

The chief had put his glasses on in order to see the charts that Officer Franklin had produced. They rested on his broad nose as he regarded the young patrolman through them.

"Ben," he said.

"Okay, here it goes. A group of people go to a place of power on a special night at a very particular time. The enormous fire in the center and the ring of fire along the outer edges of the clearing creates the physical, earthly door, lit for all on this plane to see. The brutal deaths of these innocent people at the four points in the circle seem to create a rip or tear in the fabric of our plane of existence, within the same circle of fire. This completes the doorway, and the chants and the blood apparently draw the demon to enter our world from his. These people had to be serious in order for the thing to have even half-worked." Before Officer Tubbs could stop him, Officer Franklin held up his hand.

"I know, I know, I know. How does it work? Right now, you think it's all mumbo jumbo, superstitious nonsense, right? Don't answer, don't even answer, because I already know. But in your minds, privately now, you don't have to answer, but ask yourselves this: Do you believe in God? You don't have to tell me, it isn't important that I know, just ask yourselves, you know." Officer Franklin paused, licking his lips.

"Now, if you do believe in God, there must then be a soul, and a place where souls go, and all that jazz. But also, if you believe in God, you believe in good. And you simply cannot have good here on earth without good, old-fashioned evil. So, we have good, we have evil, we have good souls, we have evil souls. We have God... What does that leave out?" The chief and Officer Tubbs looked at each other. Officer Franklin went on.

"What's truly important to the leader of this cult, and to the ritual, are the sacrifices, the timing, and the location. Remember, if you truly believe in God, then you truly believe that the souls of these innocent people ascend to heaven after death. Now, what must that entail? It requires the transformation or transfiguration of the soul from the mortal, earthly body to the immortal plane of God.

"In other words, a ripple, or opening, in the time-space continuum, this is when our physical universe merges, albeit very briefly, with that higher, or lower, plane. This is only a theory, but current theoretical quantum mechanics and astrophysics, things like 'M' theory, and String theory, are giving it more credence every day. Because of the truly hellish nature of the particular ritual in question, pain, fear, terror, torture, and death imposed on purity and innocence, a rite like that is bound to attract evil souls, spirits, or demons.

"The inspector and I did all this research together. Because of the anomalous electro-magnetic fields all over Littleborough, the possibility of a vortex forming is highly likely."

"What the hell is a vortex, Ben?"

"The way the inspector and I interpreted it, a vortex is anything that spins around and around, Harold. A tornado is a wind vortex. A whirlpool is a water vortex. The way our solar system rotates around the sun is also a vortex. There are scientists studying the phenomenon now and not a lot is known. But it may form a vortex of energy, positive and negative particles vibrating or colliding in a giant whirlpool of wind or whatever, I don't know.

"It's a confluence of factors, the place of power, with its unique and powerful electro-magnetic field, where many spiritual rituals, most of them positive, have taken place over thousands of years. There's the time, and the date, which is Halloween. There's a full moon. And, finally, the fact that things simply did not go as planned."

"What was planned, Ben?" the chief said.

"The proper sacrifice of all four of the cardinal victims, apparently by means of crucifixion in this case, was the plan. But only three of the four victims were found to have died this way, as you both know. The first two sacrifices, Ms. Hart and Ms. Streeter," Officer Franklin swallowed hard as he mentioned the names of the two young women whose corpses he had examined, "went correctly. They had been brought there unwillingly, then tied up, drugged, and murdered." He swallowed again. "But the third point, or sacrifice, old man Prescott...from the patterns on the forest floor, I was able to deduce that no attention was paid to him, or the unknown victim. Old man Prescott, therefore, probably died of a heart attack."

"So, Ben, what you really mean to say is that these people messed up this ritual because old man Prescott died before they killed him?"

"Yes."

"Okay, but other than reducing the charges of murder by one count, how does this show you anything other than a botched ritual with an admittedly mysterious fire? I don't see any evidence of demons or of ripples in the time and space continuum." Officer Tubbs waited, staring.

"It's really quite simple. As I've told you, the forest floor clearly shows that the worshippers found that their third sacrifice had already died. But they never made it to the fourth sacrifice point. Only the leader got that far, and the fourth victim was still alive to see it, albeit upside down." The chief and Officer Tubbs both looked at each other, then back at Officer Franklin. Both men asked him a question at the same time.

"What do you mean by 'see it,' Billy?"

"How do you know that the fourth victim was still alive at the time?"

"The inspector pointed this out to me. The fourth victim's bowels let go right about the time the leader got there; therefore, he was still alive. His fecal matter is clearly inside of one of the leader's footprints, made when the leader stood right next to the upside-down cross. His toes and the balls of his feet seem to dig in there, maybe he was bending down to see into his final victim's eyes. But that's when all hell must've broke loose."

Officer Tubbs had waited impatiently for Officer Franklin to stop speaking.

"What was it you meant by 'see it,' Franklin. What is it you think the fourth victim saw?"

"I told you what it was he saw, Tubbs."

"But, then, I still don't see why you think this demon is running all over town, Ben. This looks all too human to me." Officer Tubbs's wide, brown eyes stared earnestly into Officer Franklin's face.

"It's elementary. There simply is, at this time, no other earthly or human explanation for three events that we know to have happened: one, a bonfire quintupled in size and intensity with no discernable accelerant; two, that that same huge fire was then completely extinguished within seconds after that; and three, something incredible survived this conflagration and mauled everyone present. The giant wolf tracks leave no doubt. And what could've caused of all those broken treetops and the huge limbs to fall everywhere?

"This thing descended from above the clearing. All those broken tree tops surround the whole clearing, it must have huge wings. It must have landed on the fire; the wings fanned the flames and then extinguished them. Then it attacked the worshippers. These people screwed up their ritual, and summoned a different creature, the wrong demon. It sounds crazy, but when you can eliminate every other possibility, whatever you're left with, no matter how improbable, is the truth. That's a quote from Sherlock Holmes, by the way, but it also happens to be true."

The chief's cell vibrated on the surface of his small wooden desk. It was a text from the inspector: a photo of a drawing in a book of a large bejeweled ring with an engraving of a serpent devouring itself. A second text soon followed with a picture of the sign of Solomon's seal. Beneath the photo the inspector had typed one word: *tonight*. He looked at his two patrolmen.

"Okay, thank you, Ben, Harold. Both of you go home and rest for a couple hours. Be here and ready to go by eleven thirty tonight."

"Eleven thirty tonight?" Officer Tubbs said.

"We have somewhere to be around midnight tonight."

"Okay, where?"

"The clearing in the woods."

"The crime scene? Why?"

"We believe the leader of that group will be returning to finish what he started."

"What makes you think that?"

"You do."

"Me?"

The chief nodded. "Yes, Ben, you. If I remember correctly, you pointed out that what we think is irrelevant. Whether we believe that the devil can be raised is not the question. But that the answer is that this individual does believe it."

"But if he does believe it, he probably figures the whole thing is botched and by now is getting himself gone."

"Maybe. Maybe not. The inspector did a little extra research on that old case out of New Mexico. There is a subsequent police report filed by the same investigating officers. It was filed the very next morning after the discovery of the original crime scene in the desert."

"Okay." The chief handed Officer Franklin the file. "A missing baby?"

"Yes, a new born baby was snatched out of the hospital during the night, sometime between four and six in the morning. The baby was never found." Officer Franklin swallowed as he read the report. He handed it to Officer Tubbs. "The investigating officers did not link the two events together."

"But you think there's a connection?" The chief nodded his head grimly and handed Officer Franklin another file.

"Nicholas Tewksbury," Officer Franklin's eyes widened behind his thick spectacles as he read aloud. "This file is dated today, this morning!" He looked at the chief. "You think the leader grabbed a replacement for the guy on the cross who had the heart attack?"

"Seems that way."

Officer Franklin and Officer Tubbs were wide awake now.

"Holy shit," they said in unison. †

CHAPTER 35
Running

Running. Running. Running. Burning. Burning. Burning. Running. Running, Running. Stopping. Listening. Listening. Listening. Panting. Panting. Cooling. Looking. Sniffing. Sniffing. Sniffing. Smells. Turning. Listening. Listening. Listening. Panting. Cooling. Cooling. Looking. Sniffing. Sniffing. Sniffing. Smells. People! Turning. Running. Running. Running. Burning. Burning. Burning. Running. Running. Running.

Running. Running. Running. Burning. Burning. Burning. Running. Running, Running. Stopping. Listening. Listening. Listening. Panting. Panting. Cooling. Looking. Sniffing. Sniffing. Sniffing. Smells. Turning. Listening. Listening. Listening. Panting. Cooling. Cooling. Looking. Sniffing. Sniffing. Sniffing. Smells. People! Turning. Running. Running. Running. Burning. Burning. Burning. Running. Running. Running. Searching.

Running. Running. Running. Burning. Burning. Burning. Running. Running, Running. Stopping. Listening. Listening. Listening. Panting. Panting. Cooling. Looking. Sniffing. Sniffing. Sniffing. Smells. Turning. Listening. Listening. Listening. Panting. Cooling. Cooling. Looking. Sniffing. Sniffing. Sniffing. Smells. People! Turning. Running. Running. Running. Burning. Burning. Burning. Running. Running. Running.

Stopping. Heaving. Heaving. Heaving. Puking. Puking. Puking. Heaving. Heaving. Heaving. Retching. Retching. Retching. Gagging. Gagging. Gagging. Hacking. Hacking. Hacking. Shaking. Shaking. Shaking. Howling.

Running. Running. Running. Burning. Burning. Burning. Searching. Searching. Searching. Stopping. Listening. Listening. Listening. Hearing! Hearing! Hearing! Running. Running. Running. Burning. Burning. Burning. Stopping. Listening. Listening. Listening. Panting. Cooling.

Cooling. Looking. Sniffing. Sniffing. Sniffing. Smelling! Smelling! Smells! Running. Running. Running. Searching.

Running. Running. Running. Burning. Burning. Burning. Stopping. Heaving. Heaving. Heaving. Puking. Puking. Puking. Heaving. Heaving. Heaving. Retching. Retching. Retching. Hacking. Hacking. Hacking. Shaking. Shaking. Shaking. Looking. Turning. Listening. Listening. Listening. Turning. Running. Running. Running. Burning. Burning. Burning. Searching. Searching. Searching. Running. Running. Running.

Running. Running. Running. Burning. Burning. Burning. Running. Running, Running. Stopping. Listening. Listening. Listening. Panting. Panting. Cooling. Looking. Sniffing. Sniffing. Sniffing. Smells. Turning. Listening. Listening. Listening. Panting. Cooling. Cooling. Looking. Sniffing. Sniffing. Sniffing. Smells. People! Turning. Running. Running. Running. Burning. Burning. Burning. Running. Running. Running.

Stopping. Listening. Listening. Listening. Looking. Sniffing. Sniffing. Sniffing. Smells. Turning. Listening. Listening. Listening. Looking. Sniffing. Sniffing. Sniffing. Smells. Turning. Running. Running. Running. Burning. Burning. Burning. Running. Running. Running. Stopping. Heaving. Heaving. Heaving. Puking. Puking. Puking. Heaving. Heaving. Heaving. Retching. Retching. Retching. Hacking. Hacking. Hacking. Howling.

Running. Running. Running. Stopping. Listening. Listening. Listening. Looking. Sniffing. Sniffing. Sniffing. Smelling! Smelling! Smelling! Grasses! Eating. Eating. Eating. Chewing. Chewing. Chewing. Soothing. Soothing. Soothing. Listening. Listening. Listening. Looking. Sniffing. Sniffing. Sniffing. Turning. Listening. Listening. Listening. Looking. Sniffing. Sniffing. Sniffing. Searching.

Running. Running. Running. Burning. Burning. Burning. Stopping. Listening. Listening. Listening. Looking. Sniffing. Sniffing. Sniffing. Smells. Running. Running. Running. Burning. Burning. Burning. Searching. Searching. Searching. Running. Running. Running. Burning. Burning. Burning. Stopping. Heaving. Heaving. Heaving. Puking. Puking. Puking. Grasses. Heaving. Heaving. Heaving. Retching. Retching. Retching. Hacking. Hacking. Hacking.

Running. Running. Running. Burning. Burning. Burning. Running. Running. Running. Searching. Searching. Searching. Stopping. Listening. Listening. Listening. Looking. Sniffing. Sniffing. Sniffing. Smells! Smells! Smells! Running! Running! Running! Seeking! Seeking! Seeking! Stopping. Listening. Listening. Listening. Silent. Looking. Sniffing. Sniffing. Sniffing. Smells. Safe. Safe. Safe. Lying down. Lying down. Lying down. Sleeping. Sleeping. Dreaming... †

CHAPTER 36
The Reckoning

Julie looked at her Malamute, Rasputin. She smiled at him, which made him wag his tail gently. Her body tingled all over. The sex had rejuvenated her. She felt alive and powerful. She walked back to her full-length mirror in the main hall and looked at herself. It reflected someone else. Julie froze in place momentarily; the woman with the pink golf ball stared back at her. The aura of this woman reflected a bright, blinding white light from the mirror. It reflected pure power and perfect balance. Julie's knees became weak. She covered her mouth and felt breathless. She blinked her eyes. The vision faded as her own beautiful green eyes looked back at her from the mirror.

Rasputin had been sitting on the hallway floor looking up at Julie intently. His large, furry ears stood straight up at attention. Julie looked at him. She knelt down and he came to her. The two had a quiet moment together, with Julie gently scratching his head and behind his ears.

"You're right, Rass," Julie said aloud. Her voice sounded different to her. It was as if it had come from somewhere or someone else. Julie stood up and looked up the stairs leading to the second floor. There, on the windowsill by the first landing, was Don Juan. He stared at Julie with his intense green eyes. Julie smiled up at him. "Hi Don Juan," she said.

To her surprise, Don Juan did not move from the spot. He blinked his eyes once. Then he calmly got up and stretched himself. The little black cat then jumped down from the windowsill and began to hop up the remaining steps to the second floor. Julie could hear him softly ascend the stairs leading up to the attic. Rasputin started his way up those stairs. He stopped halfway and looked back at her.

Julie smiled and shook her head. "This is crazy," she said. The smile ran from her face. *No, it isn't.* Julie followed the dog up the stairs to the second floor. He then led her down the hallway to the stairs leading to the attic where Don Juan waited. Together, they ascended those stairs, and walked into the attic.

The shoebox in which some of her grandmother's things were was still opened where she had left it. Don Juan was purring audibly now. He rubbed up against the shoebox. Julie walked over to it and looked in. Rasputin began to sniff around the attic. He spent more time on each spot than normal, thought Julie. When he sniffed at the shoebox that contained her grandmother's special belongings, he wagged his tail. He seemed extremely interested in all of its contents. The dog began to drool. Julie laughed her throaty laugh.

"I guess someone likes that smell, huh, big boy?" The dog wagged his tail again. He then lowered his great head to sniff at Don Juan. To Julie's amazement, the little black cat gently bumped his head into Rasputin's nose. The dog wagged his tail and sat down. Don Juan climbed into the shoebox, still purring. Since the day Julie had rescued Don Juan, he had never let anyone touch him, ever, not even Julie. She wondered what had gotten into that little black cat? She was smiling.

Julie knelt down onto the old wooden floor and reached into the box and pulled out an old glass container. Inside were several roots from a plant. They looked quite familiar to her. The darkly rotted smell was even more familiar. There was no label on the glass container to suggest what the contents were. Julie put it back in the box.

She could see in the corner of the box an old, dog-eared picture. She carefully removed it and held it up to the light. It was an old black and white photograph. The picture had grayed with time and neglect. But Julie could plainly make out the two figures in the picture. She had only been six, maybe seven years old when the photo was taken. She stood next to her grandmother, who was in her mid-fifties at the time. They were standing in her grandmother's garden. Flowers bloomed everywhere around them. A tiny woman, her grandmother stood only a few inches taller than Julie in the picture.

Julie smiled as she took the whole picture in. She looked at her grandmother closely. She was dressed in a tight, dark dress that hugged her body. Her dark, raven black hair was long and fell freely, framing her beautiful, pale and delicate face. The sunlight seemed to nestle in her hair for warmth. It shone on her face. She was not looking at the camera. Her entire being seemed to be focused on her granddaughter. Her wide, beautiful and genuine smile radiated down onto Julie.

It had been warm, that day, Julie remembered. She was wearing shorts that came down to just over her knees and a light-colored T-shirt. She was filthy from working in the garden alongside her grandmother. She was not smiling in the picture. Julie laughed out loud at the expression on her own face in the picture. It was defiance. She was staring straight into the camera. Her mother was the one taking the picture. She had been trying, unsuccessfully, to get little Julianna to smile.

The little girl would have none of it. She stood next to her grandmother and positively glared at the camera. Her green eyes seemed to sparkle at the camera lens from behind all that dirt. Julie blinked her eyes as she looked at the picture. *How can I be seeing green in a black and white photo?* she thought. She held the picture up. The color was gone. Julie looked at Rasputin. He sat directly in front of her. He was staring directly into her eyes, unblinking. Next to him, in the shoebox, sat Don Juan. He, too, was staring silently up at Julie.

Julie looked back down at the photo she held in her hands. Those were very trying years for her. They were difficult for the whole family. Her mother suffered from a terrible depression. She was often hospitalized and when she was home was often heavily sedated. This took its toll on the Bernard family, particularly Julie. She was the oldest and therefore took care of the household and her younger brothers and sister until leaving home for college.

To make matters worse, her mother never seemed to get along with her grandmother. They argued, as mothers and daughters sometimes do, every day. Often times they would argue about Julie. On more than one occasion the point of contention was who, or what, Julie was. Julie felt a burning in the pit of her stomach. A cold rage engulfed her. She remembered now.

Julie drove her parents crazy when she was little. She was beyond adventurous. All one had to do was look away for a moment and Julie would be gone without a trace, as fast as her little legs could go. She loved nature and every one of nature's creatures. She would be found hours later, inevitably covered from head to toe in mud and muck, having rescued a frog or a butterfly from a certain death. That defiant expression would burn from her filthy, beautiful face as she was escorted back to the house.

As a little girl Julie also had the uncanny knack of knowing a person's thoughts and stating these thoughts out loud for all to hear. Though she did this with a childlike earnestness, there was also just the slightest hint of mischief in her eyes. This caused her parents no end of awkward embarrassments through those early years.

It was always Julie's mother who would overreact. Her grandmother would laugh and send the little girl up for a bath. She defended Julie in her gentle, soft-spoken way. But there were times when it would be too much for her mother. She would become hysterical. This was especially difficult because Julie and her parents and three younger siblings lived in a house owned by her grandparents.

To his credit, Julie's father would try to intervene and calm his wife down, sometimes with disastrous results. Her mother was given to histrionics. When Julie was older, she would call her mother "drama queen" more than once during their own heated arguments. The worst arguments always started whenever her mother found anything in the house that reminded her of witchcraft.

Her mother knew, Julie remembered. Not one other person in the entire family knew this, only Julie, her mother, and her grandmother. Her grandmother's name was Theresa. Theresa hid herself in plain sight. A devout Christian, she was a pillar of the local church. She was a powerful witch from a long line of witches that stretched back to time immemorial. Friends and neighbors who were in need of a cure or remedy for anything that doctors could not cure came to Theresa.

The bloodline of this particular family of witches skipped every other generation. Julie's mother, named Mary, was not a witch. She never forgave her mother, Theresa, for telling Julie the truth about the bloodline. The irony to Julie was that Theresa had never actually said a word to her. Julie just knew. In order to conceal all of this from the rest of the household and the rest of the family, Mary and Theresa would argue in a vague way. No one in the family ever could understand what the two women were arguing about—except Julie, of course.

But after Theresa's death, Julie had put it all away. Julie was only thirteen when her beloved grandmother passed away. She believed it would be best for herself, her mother, and the whole family if she simply pretended to not have any of these abilities. At first Julie had to go to significant lengths to quash any and all impressions, intuitions, or downright knowledge that came to her. She ignored her dreams and would dismiss anything odd that did occur as simply coincidence. As time went on, it became easier and easier. As she went deeper and deeper into the sciences as a student in high school and then college and beyond, she had all but forgotten that she had ever had any abilities at all. It was all a distant dream from a far-away time and a far-away place.

Julie stared at the cobwebs blanketing the attic ceiling, her eyes seeing nothing. *Who am I?* she wondered. Her body still tingled. She felt warm and light. She looked again at Rasputin, who waited patiently by her side. She looked at Don Juan. The little black cat stared straight into her eyes, unblinking. Julie felt as if he was somehow recognizing her for the first time. She scooped the little black cat up and held him while he purred. She remained there, kneeling in the center of the attic floor. She held the little black cat and the old photo against her chest. Julie closed her eyes. †

PART FIVE
The Witch
and
The Priest of Lies

"This is the end." —Jim Morrisson

CHAPTER 37
The Gathering

Julie opened her eyes. The night was pitch black. She looked around as her wide, green eyes adjusted to the darkness. She could smell the forest, the pine, the dew, the moss, the earth. Chills went down her spine and she wrapped her arms around herself, shuddering. Though she could not see, she knew where she was. She could sense, and actually feel the clearing. Electricity was in the air. She could feel her heartbeat sync with the rhythm and the heartbeat of the night and the wilderness. She swallowed hard.

Moonlight bathed the Great Woods and the clearing briefly. A large, dark shadow crossed over the clearing and over her head. Julie looked up at the night through the large opening in the canopy of the clearing. The moon was full behind the dark clouds as they raced across the sky, casting dark shadows that followed frantically along the treetops and the ground. This rendered everything in Creation to complete and utter darkness. The light of the moon would return just as quickly, bathing Creation in a naked, pale light. This made all the Great Woods and Wilderness of Littleborough flicker, like an old movie.

Julie sensed a powerful presence nearby. She looked across the clearing. A form appeared on the opposite side. Tall, dark, and thin, Julie knew it was the old woman, the witch. The moonlight danced in her wild, white hair and gleamed in the witch's green eyes. Or were they blue eyes? Julie observed that the witch's eyes seemed to change, as they did before, and went from green to blue, to a deep purple, then scarlet, and then jet black. The old woman held something in her arms, but it was too dark for Julie to see what it was. The witch began to advance. The flickering of the moonlight made her tall, thin motions seem erratic and grotesque. The wind carried her soft, singsong laughter to Julie.

Julie set her chin and began to advance slowly toward the old bat. As they neared the center of the clearing, it went dark and stayed dark. Julie looked up through the opening of the canopy above the clearing and saw that an enormous dark cloud had blocked out the moonlight. After a moment it passed, soaking the clearing in bright moonlight again. The witch was gone, vanished. A familiar looking shoebox sat on the forest floor in front of Julie. She stooped down and picked it up. She opened the lid carefully and, sure enough, Geraldine the rat blinked furiously up at Julie in the bright, flickering moonlight. Julie smiled, shaking her head. Her smile ran from her lips when out of the corner of her eye she detected movement. She gently stroked the rat and then closed the lid.

The dark form of a man, tall and muscular, loomed at the edge of the clearing. He carried something large in his arms. The undergrowth in the clearing crunched beneath his heavy steps as he strode toward the center of the clearing. He did not see Julie in the darkness as he went past her. The moon washed the clearing in light momentarily and she could see that this man was carrying a body. She gasped. This startled the immense man and he whirled around to face her. Julie looked up into his face.

"Oh, my goodness, is that you, Doctor Robinson?"

Doc Robinson had to peer hard at Julie for a moment. "Julie?"

"Yes, it's me."

The doc looked around nervously. "You've got to get out of here, now," he said.

"Don't you think we both should leave?"

"Julie, there's an animal in these woods. It's dangerous. It's killed at least twenty people, so far."

"But, then, why are you here?"

"There is something I have to do. Now, go."

"But, what in the world are you doing out here with…with that…oh my God?"

"Now, Julie, just stay calm…"

"Is that…is that…Father Torrez?" Julie looked up at Doc Robinson. He peered down at her through his glasses.

"Yes, it is." Julie's jaw dropped wide open.

"What are you doing with Father Torrez' body, Doctor Robinson?"

Before Doc Robinson could reply, the sound of footfalls could be heard coming toward the clearing. Voices were shouting. A thick, white mist started rising from the forest floor, permeating the darkness. Julie could see her breath. A tormented howl rose above the trees of the forest and lightly shook the ground. Julie cried out. The beast was nearby.

"Here he is," Doc Robinson said. "This way, my friend. I'm right here. That's a good boy." He looked down at Julie. "Get out of here now, Julie."

Julie and Doc Robinson stood in the center of the large clearing, right next to where the bonfire had been the night before. The voices were coming from the east. Doc Robinson carefully placed the body of Father Torrez on the ground at the edge of where the bonfire had burned. He straightened himself up and turned toward the sound of the approaching voices. Three men entered the clearing. Julie recognized Bishop Richter and Father Freeman. The other was a small, well-dressed little old man. One of the priests was speaking.

"This better be legitimate, you asshole. Miguel was a friend of ours, we knew him. He would never summon you."

"Oh, no. You're quite right about that. The summoning, I mean. With the help of a very dear, new, young friend and the advisement of a local witch, I have found the identities of those who summoned me. One particularly inept monkey and his fellow baboons attempted to summon me right here, in this very spot. However, there is one among them, I must say," Satan smiled a wide smile, "who is an old friend. He is a very old friend, and a faithful servant."

"Then, for Christ's sake, Lucifer, if he sold you his soul, take him! But what the hell does that have to do with Miguel?" They all slowly walked into the center of the clearing where Doc Robinson stood.

"As I said, I lay no claim to him."

"Then, why do you have Miguel's body here?" the bishop said.

"He doesn't," Doc Robinson answered.

"I don't?" Satan turned around to face Doc Robinson.

"No, you don't. I have the body here for a different reason, something much more important than any business you may have had, Satan." When Doc Robinson called this strange, little old man "Satan," Julie lost her breath. She looked wide-eyed at the little old man. The palms of her hands began to sweat, despite the cold autumn-night air.

"I think, good doctor, you may be forgetting about our little agreement, that small matter of your son's soul, which still belongs to me?" Though his manner seemed quite gentle to Julie, the menace in his light English accent sent chills down her spine. Her stomach turned in revulsion.

"What the hell are you bullshitting about, now, dink-weed?" Father Freeman said.

"No, no." Doc Robinson held his hand up. He regarded Satan through his large eyeglasses. The brilliant light from the moon still flickered intermittently amidst the rushing clouds. The small, dapper gentleman smiled up at Doc Robinson as the vet spoke. "This particularly meaningless individual is right. I did sell him my son's soul." Julie turned and looked up at Doc Robinson.

"Oh, my boy, my boy, no," the bishop said.

"Hey, fuck you, my boy," Doc Robinson said, glaring at the Bishop.

"Yes," Satan said, still smiling. Doc Robinson ignored him.

"If your sick, pathetic excuse of a god had an ounce of decency anywhere in his pitiful being, I never would have had to deal with this little piece of shit here. But no, that great almighty felt that my Belinda needed to suffer!"

"Everyone suffers, son. Jesus suffered," the bishop spoke gently.

"Oh my, mercy me, you shouldn't have said that, Pat," Satan said.

"Jesus did not suffer like anybody, ever!" Doctor Robinson's voice boomed in the clearing. "He was God, right? He knew he would live on. There is no human being alive that has such knowledge, by your own admission; it is based on faith, or belief and trust." Doc Robinson snorted at the idea. "The level of human, fuck it…all suffering, by all of 'His' creatures, is galling. Let me clue you in here; that great fraud in the sky has never suffered, ever. And no one, I mean no one, has ever suffered like my Belinda!"

"Take it easy, Doc, take it easy," Father Freeman said. Julie could only stare, wide eyed.

"I don't understand, son, what makes you think you've sold your son's soul?"

"I had to. You see, when my wife gave birth to our son, the doctors learned that she had contracted an incurable cancer. It slowly ate her alive, from the inside, out. It kept her in a perpetual agony, but she couldn't seem to die. God knows she wanted to. Late at night, when we were alone, she would beg me to kill her. She would cry out for me to end it, but I couldn't." Doc Robinson looked out into the darkness of the forest now, staring. His voice lowered to a whisper.

"I could never be sure. I couldn't be sure if it was really Belinda praying for death, or those fucking drugs they kept her on. There was a pill for this, and a pill for that, and then they would give her more pills to control the side effects caused by the other pills. It never ended. And she was never really herself. I could never be sure.

"One night I woke up to her screaming. She was screaming my name. She was screaming for me to please, make it stop, make it stop." Tears stung the corners of Julie's eyes as she listened to Doc Robinson. She looked up at him, but he was still just staring out into the black void, remembering. "I knew she was in terrible pain. She had flung the covers off and was wriggling and straining from the agony. I looked at her bedside table where we kept all her meds. They were gone. They were all gone. She had taken them all at once, but somehow, they had not killed her.

"When I realized this, I looked at my wife. She had stopped screaming and writhing around for a moment. She was looking right at me. Then, I knew. She looked up at me with love in her beautiful brown eyes, smiling, as I took a pillow and placed it over her face. I applied as much pressure as I physically could for as long as I could. But when I lifted the pillow off of her face, she was still alive. Her eyes were wide open, and she began screaming again.

"I tried one more time. I kept the pillow on her face until she grew still and quiet, and kept it on some more. When I took it off of her face, I thought that she might have finally died." Doc Robinson pointed a large finger at Satan. "That's when you showed up, at the foot of her bed. 'Doesn't look good, does it?' you said. Right then and there, Belinda drew in a deep breath, and screamed my name. 'Who are you?' I asked. 'Who, indeed,' you said." Chills went up Julie's spine when Doc Robinson said this. She covered her mouth with both hands and closed her eyes for a moment. "So, we made a deal, didn't we, Satan?"

"That is correct, Doctor Robinson."

"A deal that you proposed to me that night, right, Satan?"

"Yes, that's right, again."

"A deal that stated that you would end Belinda's suffering and let her die, if I signed over the soul of my first born to you?"

"Yes, it was all so very touching," Satan said. "She pleaded with me that I take her soul instead. As she quivered in agony, drenched in sweat, she begged me to take her. And then you, good doctor, pleaded with me that I take your soul, instead of hers. And round and round it went; however, I was resolute! It was the boy I wanted."

"Yes, it was the boy you wanted. But it is not what you will get," Doc Robinson said.

"I'm so sorry, dear friend, what was that?" Satan said.

"Which word was that muddled brain of yours not able to process, Satan?"

"I rather think, old boy, that you are the one who is muddled, as you put it. I already have the boy. Why else would you be here, delivering this mortal's remains to me?"

"I'm not. I need this body for something far more important than you."

"Now, wait a minute, Doc, what are you talking about?" Father Freeman said.

"So, you lied, then?" Satan said.

"Listen, seriously, Satan, do you really think you're the only one who does?" Doc Robinson said. He peered intently into the darkness of the woods outside the clearing, in the direction of the sounds of the beast. "I needed this body to lure that magnificent creature in here. I want to check its wounds and treat it if necessary. I want to study it, to learn about it."

"Now, just a minute, Doc," Father Freeman said, "you can't use Miguel's body for this. It's indecent and immoral."

"Oh my, yes, you tell him, John."

"Shut up, Satan. Doc, it's sacrilegious to desecrate a body like this!"

"I'm not desecrating anything. I'm just using it for bait. Don't worry, padre, Miguel won't feel a thing."

"Doctor Robinson, that's awful!" Julie said.

"Oh, is that you, Julie?" The bishop and Father Freeman had both jumped at the sound of her voice.

"Yes, it's me. What is going on here, Father?"

"Do excuse me, Pat, John," Satan said this softly, "but who might this charming young lady be?" He looked at Julie, smiling. Then he looked more closely. When Satan recognized Julie, his smile widened to what almost looked as if it went beyond the little old man's face. "Miss Bernard! What a wonderful surprise to see you here, my dear." The little old man's light, pale blue eyes seemed to get lighter in the darkness of the clearing. Chills crawled down Julie's spine, again. She shook her head defiantly.

"I don't know you."

"Oh, but you do, my dear, you do! You have seen me quite a bit more than the average mortal, I dare say." The little old man had taken off his hat respectfully. He held it against his chest, beaming at Julie. "Oh, allow me, then. My name is currently William Chester. Yes, yes, that's it." He stepped toward Julie and the two priests, dropping his London Fog fedora into the darkness of the forest floor. "However, I am very happy to report that my use for William Chester has temporarily come to an end. And it is as well as you shall see, Julie Bernard, as you shall see."

"I don't know you," Julie said this in a whisper, shaking her head. She knew she had never seen this person before. She also knew that she recognized those raging, tormented eyes. They burned white to blue, to violet to purple, to scarlet and then to black. His face still smiled as his body grew tall and shadowy. A sickly, crackling sound emerged from the little old man. It was the sound of bones, and sinews, cartilage and muscle, all cracking and breaking as the once dapper body of the little old man withered away and a great shadow was born from it.

"No! No, God no!" Julie screamed. Bishop Richter and Father Freeman had both moved over to stand by Julie's side. They watched in horror as the face and skin and fine suit of William Chester crumpled to the ground as ashes to dust. Towering above it all was a strange darkness that flickered in the full moon's light and the shadow of racing clouds.

"Do you not know me?" The voice was male. It was deep, clear, and beautiful. Julie wasn't sure if she had actually heard it or it was all in her head. The enormous shadow didn't appear to have a mouth. "My true name is unknown to you. Satan, Lucifer, Mephisticles, Belial, Beezlebub, and so many more; all are names mortals have tried in vain to put upon me." He took another step toward them. His foot crashed down onto the forest floor. The earth shook beneath their feet. Julie could see that his foot was cloven, large, and black. She slowly raised her eyes upward along his body as it gleamed in the fluttering moonlight and darkness of the clearing.

The devil took a second step toward them. He now towered over them. The boisterous and profane protests of the two priests were to no avail. What had been a tall, thin shadow now began to take a solid form. Lucifer, in his true, earthly form, was beautiful to look at. He appeared as an angel might, Julie thought.

He was winged. But he also had arms and legs. His head was high up on an elongated, slender neck. He had the head of a bull, or a large goat, with the face of a man. It sometimes appeared as if he had horns on his head, then, sometimes not. He had a large, long penis. Lucifer glowed like the ancient starlight bestowed upon him by God.

His eyes, however, did not. They appeared to Julie as black and lifeless...soulless. Satan lowered his huge head and face in order to peer into Julie's wide, green eyes. He was smiling again. She could feel it. He closed his eyes and began sniffing at her, holding his large head at odd angles around her face, her throat, and her head.

"I am no name. I am. Julie...you will need only call me...master." †

CHAPTER 38
A Rush to Judgment

"No! No way!" Julie lashed out at the devil, missing his face by mere inches. He straightened himself up as he laughed a deep belly laugh. Father Freeman and the bishop tried gently to restrain her. Julie had stopped struggling, however. She simply stared straight up at Satan defiantly as he grinned and leered down at her.

A deafening roar filled the clearing. The sheer force of it knocked Julie and the two men of God to the forest floor. Doctor Robinson calmly turned to face the direction from which it came. The roaring died down and silence reluctantly returned to the clearing. Julie rolled herself onto her belly and got herself up. She reached down and helped the bishop back up onto his feet.

"Thank you, my dear." They brushed the ash, sticks, and leaves off of themselves. As they did, they all looked around the clearing uneasily. The night and the forest flickered rhythmically under the moon and clouds. Satan had vanished.

"Where did he go, Bishop?" Julie asked.

"I don't know, Julie," the bishop said.

"He had to keep an appointment, I believe, but he'll be back." The voice came out of the darkness. It gave everyone but Doctor Robinson a start. "Oh, sorry, it's only me." The lady with the pink golf ball walked out of the shadows and into the flickering light of the clearing. She smiled warmly at Julie as she approached. "Are you feeling better, champ?"

"Yes, ma'am, thank you." Julie smiled up at her.

"Those mushrooms go better on a salad, know what I mean?"

"Yes, ma'am."

"Good." She turned and regarded the two priests. Her smile widened into a grin. "Well, well, well, what have we here? Why, men of the cloth are among us." The woman with the pink golf ball smiled sweetly and looked at Julie. She gracefully turned back toward Bishop Richter and Father Freeman. "Oh! Wait, don't tell me…ahhh, the eternal battle between good and evil, am I right?"

"Hello, your holiness? You're the Judge sent by the Teacher?" She nodded, still smiling. "I am Bishop Pat Richter. And this is Father John Freeman."

"Yes, I know who you are, gentlemen. I am Emily." She shook the Bishop's hand.

"You seem to know Julie. Over there is Doctor Robinson. And yes, you're right. We are in a struggle with Satan." The bishop was saying this as they shook hands. The Judge towered over the bishop and Father Freeman. She laughed out loud, shaking her head as she did.

"Men, you guys just don't quit, do you? Honestly," she looked at Julie, then back at the two priests, "consistently dumb as stumps. Seriously, men have the collective IQ of a lampshade. But do not despair, boys. Because yours is an amusing gender, sort of like watching nature programs on the television, I'd say." She smiled sweetly as she spoke.

"Oh my God, you're being so mean! They're trying to help! Don't be so mean!" Julie said.

"Oh, bullshit, these two aren't fighting anyone now. Are you, Bishop Pat Richter?"

"No, you're right, ma'am. We're not chosen to fight him. A young priest, Father Knight, was chosen."

"I'm familiar with James. Tell me, who chose him?"

"What? James is alone with that horrible angel?" Julie looked at the bishop and Father Freeman incredulously. "And you expect him to do what, exactly? Slay Lucifer with a pointy sword? Did you even give him a sword, or a gun, a really, really big gun? You saw him…the…devil, I guess, just now! He's huge! What is James supposed to do against that?" Julie thought about James' soft, kind, and gentle brown eyes. She shuddered at what she imagined he must be going through. She folded her arms across her chest, still holding the shoebox with Geraldine in her right hand. "Well? I'm waiting for you guys to tell me, how is he supposed to fight him?"

Bishop Richter smiled at Julie. He looked up at the Judge. "Perhaps you can give us a hint; you seemed to have no trouble making him leave this place. It's almost as if the devil could sense you were coming, and he was gone."

Emily shook her head sternly at the Bishop. "The reasons Lucifer flew from this place are two; one, he is quite afraid of that rather impressive creature here in these woods that we can all clearly hear is getting closer to us. And two, as I've told you, he has the decided appointment to keep with your poor lamb and sacrifice, Father Knight."

"Sacrifice?" Julie looked up at the Judge, wide eyed.

"Now, really, ma'am, we're not sacrificing Father Knight."

"Uh-huh."

"We believe in the boy! He can win this fight against evil."

"How could you sacrifice James to the devil? Oh my God!"

"Julie, we didn't sacrifice him. And he has God on his side!"

"Oh, yes. That should do the trick," the Judge said.

"Please, what do you mean by 'sacrificed'? Is the devil going to kill Father Knight?"

"He isn't here to marry him, babes."

"Isn't there something we can do to help him?" Julie touched the Judge on her shoulder.

"We can't help. He's on his own."

"But Bishop Richter and Father Freeman say that James will win."

"He will win, Julie," the bishop said.

"Yes. He will win. But he will not survive." The Judge looked straight at the two priests as she spoke. They both began to protest, and Julie started to cry, but their voices were summarily drowned out by another shriek from the beast. As it died down to a low, menacing growl, there could be heard rustling in the brush of the woods and what sounded like men's voices coming from the western side of the clearing. Within a moment, distinct footfalls could be heard approaching. Men were running and shouting.

"Oh, great," the Judge said to Julie, "just what we need now, more men and more testosterone. Fucking hooray." Julie laughed through her tears.

Officer Tubbs burst into the large clearing. He looked angry and alert. Officers Jones was right on his heels. Officers Marconi and Evers arrived within moments of that. Each man had his firearm in hand and at the ready. They were soon followed by Officer Ben Franklin. The chief and Inspector Dahms walked into the clearing calmly together several minutes later.

Officer Franklin and Officer Marconi were both quite winded from running so hard. Both were bent over, hands on their knees, several feet apart from each other, gasping in huge quantities of the cool, forest air. The moonlight still shuttered amidst the racing clouds. The thick, cold, and damp mist still covered the forest floor.

"Jones, Marconi, Tubbs, spread out and keep an eye along the perimeter." The men all nodded and fanned out. Inspector Dahms was still looking eastward. "That thing is getting closer."

"Who are these other people?" Officer Tubbs asked. The inspector looked around the clearing.

"What the hell are you all doing here?" Before anyone could answer, the beast screamed and then howled.

"We've got to get these folks out of here, Tom," the chief said.

"Sounds good, Chief. Any ideas?"

"Right now, it's circling us. When it gets to the southeast corner, Franklin, you take every civilian here back through the northeast opening. You and Lydon drive everyone back…" Another deafening roar filled the clearing. The chief trailed off, and he and Doc Robinson turned back toward the west. Everyone else covered their ears and crouched down. The beast was in the mouth of the clearing. The path to safety was blocked.

"Take it easy, Chief," Doctor Robinson said. "He won't enter this clearing with quite so much light. He prefers not to be seen."

"I see. And how would you know this, Doc?" Inspector Dahms said.

"I've been studying him. He's amazing."

"I seem to recall you telling me that you had no knowledge of this creature."

"I lied. I didn't want you and your men killing it. I want to know more about it."

"It's killed at least forty-two people, Doc."

The large vet looked at the inspector. "But, there were only twenty or so killed here."

"Closer to forty, and two more victims in town have turned up in just the last few hours, and that does not include possibly the hunting party and the search party."

"Well, well," Doctor Robinson said, "that is a remarkable animal."

"Doctor Robinson, it has attacked forty-two people. I think it's safe to say that it's dangerous," Julie said.

"Forgive me, Julie. But forty-two fewer humans on this earth is not such a bad thing."

"You are entitled to your opinion, Doc. And the first forty victims were all murderers. But innocent people are being torn to shreds."

"A remarkable creature, indeed."

"So, it doesn't like light?" Officer Tubbs asked.

"No, it doesn't. The full moon is what's saving you all from him at this very moment."

"And saving you, too," Officer Tubbs said.

"Have you seen this creature clearly?" Officer Franklin asked.

"Yes. I saw him very early this morning, a bit before you showed up, Julie, and you, too, Dahms. Well, you saw the fence. He crashed straight through it and then collapsed in my back yard. He's huge! Twenty-five or thirty feet from snout to the tip of the tail. I couldn't count the rows of teeth."

"But, what is it?" Officer Franklin asked. Doctor Robinson looked surprised.

"It's a wolf," he said "But there is an anomaly; he is winged."

"Yes!" Officer Franklin shouted this and thrust his fists straight up in the air. "I knew it! I was right, you guys! I told you it was a flying demon wolf. Didn't I?"

"Shut up, Franklin," Officer Tubbs said.

"Not flying, young man," Doctor Robinson said. "He is far too large to fly. But when he gets up enough speed, he can almost glide over the forest floor, or even just over the tree tops of the forest canopy. It's an entirely unknown species."

"That kills and eats people." Julie said.

"I believe that it has somehow been provoked, Julie. You see, I heard the fence crash down, so I went out to the backyard to see. He had terrible burns on his paws and belly. Both of his wings were badly burned underneath as well."

"See? Burns on his wings just like I..."

"Franklin!"

"I treated the creature for his burns then and there. He would not eat any of the food I brought out to him. But he drank water as if severely dehydrated. He smelled like smoke from a fire and probably inhaled quite a bit of the smoke. I couldn't fill the trough fast enough while he drank. The idiots he killed here have somehow disturbed this creature."

"I believe that's possible," the chief said. "Given what Miss Bernard has taught us about last night, that makes sense. My people still believe this clearing to be a powerful and magical place. And we believe in several beings that have lived in these woods for centuries, even longer. Maybe this thing is different."

"So, then, it can't be killed?" Doctor Robinson asked.

"I don't know, Doc," the chief said.

"I admit I didn't believe this thing was real. But it isn't immortal," Officer Tubbs said.

"He seems it to me," Officer Franklin said.

"No, the evidence suggests that the injuries to this creature this morning were sufficient to make him seek out the doc for help. If he can be hurt, he can probably be killed," the inspector said.

"Seek out...you believe, then, that this animal knew I could help?"

"It stands to reason. If the chief's right, and this area is his home, he would presumably know you and know what you do."

Doc Robinson nodded. "That makes sense. I think so, too," he said.

"Wait, someone's coming," Officer Evers said. "I hear people shouting!" Everyone turned his or her gaze away from the entrance of the clearing to look where he was pointing. There was movement along the far edge of the clearing. The clouds overhead moved across the sky faster than before. The moonlight flickered awkwardly, making it hard to see.

"Hey, over here!" someone shouted. His voice came from the woods just outside the clearing. "I see lights, follow me." People began pouring into the clearing led by Captain Little Joe and Danny, the fireman. As they entered, the beast's howling seemed to somehow come from all around and from above the large clearing. His every shriek made people cry out or scream. Patrolmen held their weapons at the ready, turning left, then right, sometimes straight up in the air to try to face the direction from which the sounds came from.

"What have we got, Tubbs?" Inspector Dahms said.

"It's the search party and Billy Pollard's group! We'll count again, but it looks like all forty of them are here, sir!"

"Okay, and the search party folks are still out here why, exactly?" the chief said.

"Don't know, sir."

"Chief! Oh my God, Chief!" Selectperson Barbara Wordsworth clutched his arm frantically with her perfectly polished nails as she searched his face. "You haven't the faintest idea of what I've been through! It was horrible! Horrible! There's an old woman! An old woman, Chief! She's evil! She's insane! And what exactly is that growling at us? What are you going to do about this? Inspector! Save me! You must! You must!"

"Calm down, Barbara!" Selectman Dick Pale said. "Well, what do you think we should do, Chief?"

"For starters let's get everyone, all of you, as close to the middle of this clearing and as far away as possible from the edges, please," the chief said. Everyone began to move.

"Oh, my God, Richard!" Julie said. He saw her and walked over and hugged her. "How did you all end up here?"

"That old bat showed up and we had to run out a different way. We were lucky to get out at all."

"Are you all right?"

"Yes, I'm fine dear. Stop fussing. How are you... Wait, what are you doing out here?"

"Oh, that's a long story for a bottle of wine, maybe even two."

Inspector Dahms looked at Julie. "What brings you out here, Julie?" he said. The howling momentarily stopped.

"I couldn't sleep. So, I just bundled up and resumed walking the woods looking for Sandra. So, why are you and your men here, Tom?" Before Inspector Dahms could answer Julie, another deafening roar filled the clearing. There was a moment of silence. Then the sound of light footfalls could be heard.

"Wait," the bishop said. "Someone else is coming." Everyone stopped talking and turned towards the mouth, or western entrance of the clearing where the beast had been only a moment ago. The footsteps of a man could clearly be heard approaching the clearing. A tall, dark, thin form appeared in the shadowy mouth of the clearing and came forward slowly.

"I do declare, do not fear my friends. It's only me." The tall, thin frame of Jeb was silhouetted in the shuddering moonlight. Holding his long, bony hand was little Sandra. She was still in her little pink and blue dress with the light pink bow in her blonde hair. Jeb smiled widely as he greeted the chief, the Bishop, and Father Freeman.

"You found her," the chief said.

"This is all so terribly embarrassing for me," Jeb said. "Please do forgive me, but I found my sweet, sweet Sandra playing in the Rectory with Father Knight's little shepherd dog. I believe he's called Ezekiel, after the fine prophet." Julie could not quite see Jeb's face clearly in the shadows of the clearing. "I am so terribly sorry to have caused such a fuss, and the moment I found her I felt I should let you all know right away. Yes, sir, right away."

Jeb stepped closer, smiling down at Sandra. He looked up from Sandra and down into Julie's eyes. Julie stared up at this tall, thin man's eyes in the flickering moonlight. She knew this face. She had seen it in a dream. †

CHAPTER 39
The Tall Man

Jeb, the clergy, Inspector Dahms, and the chief all gathered in a tight circle. They spoke in hushed tones. Officers Tubbs and Franklin stood close by and listened in. The townspeople from the search party and from the hunting party all whispered among themselves as everyone desperately tried to figure out what the hell was going on. Strange, muted snorts and growls emanated from just beyond the boundaries of the clearing as the beast ominously circled them all from just outside the clearing.

It all became quite distant to Julie. She could only stare at the face of this man who looked to her as if he was one hundred years younger than he looked only last night. It couldn't be, she thought. After all, it had all been a dream. She felt dizzy and nauseous. Her vision, and her thoughts, seemed somehow clouded. She struggled to make out the features of his face. Her mind raced as she tried to think, but it was as if her magnificent brain was running in quicksand. Julie walked over to where the inspector was standing and listened.

"You found her in the Rectory, you say?" the bishop said. "That's odd. I looked in the Rectory and the whole of the church grounds before joining the search. So did Father Freeman and Father Knight."

"Yeah, I took a look in the Rectory and found Father Knight there getting ready to go out and search. Sandra certainly wasn't there when we were there."

"You should've just called us," the chief said. "Coming out here at this hour and bringing Sandra with you was dangerous, Jeb. How'd you even know we were here?"

"I didn't, sir. Well, you see, I don't own a cell phone and when I called your station from the church phone, there was only a busy signal. I just knew y'all were still out here looking for my daughter and I couldn't bear the thought of you all out here in the cold and dark." Jeb looked down at his daughter with a toothy grin. "I brought Sandra along because I did not dare take my eyes off of her lest she steal away again."

"Okay" The chief looked at Inspector Dahms. The inspector nodded and drew out his cell. He pressed the call button for the station. He held out the cell as the universal busy signal rang out softly for all to hear.

"That's strange," Officer Tubbs said. He turned away and spoke softly into his radio.

Officer Lydon, stationed on Deerfoot Road, came back over the radio but there was a strange, squealing interference. Officer Tubbs asked Officer Lydon to repeat the transmission, but the same interference occurred. "Hard to be sure what he's saying, but it doesn't sound like he's getting through to the station either, Chief."

"Okay. Ask him to keep trying, please."

"Yes, sir." Inspector Dahms pulled out his pipe and slapped his open palm with it several times. Julie had now joined the small circle of men, still staring up at Jeb. For his part, Jeb looked down at Julie, smiling his wide, dimpled smile. She stepped toward him. She stared into his eyes, searching.

"It's you," Julie said.

"I beg your pardon, ma'am?" Jeb straightened up and put one of his large, bony hands to his chest.

"I said it's you." Julie was pointing at Jeb. Everyone in the clearing stopped talking, turned, and looked at Julie.

"Is there something wrong, Julie?" the inspector asked.

"Yes, there's a lot wrong, Tom. I saw this man before, here, in this clearing, last night." As she spoke, Julie reached down and took Sandra gently by the hand. Sandra squeezed Julie's hand.

"No, surely not, child," Jeb said.

"Yes, yes, you are…" Julie stared up at Jeb, then looked at the inspector.

"Who is he, Miss Bernard?" Inspector Dahms said. Julie could only shake her head.

"I don't know. I don't know who he is. But I know one thing: He is not Sandra's father."

"I am the child's father, ma'am. Just as sure as the word of the good Lord I am her…"

"You're a liar!" Julie stepped toward Jeb. Her voice had cut through the darkness that was the clearing.

"Easy now, Julie, take it easy." The bishop stepped between Julie and Jeb. "I've known Jeb for a couple years now." But Julie just shook her head.

"How do you know this?" the inspector asked. "When could you have seen him last night? You were here with us last night."

"It was before we all got here. He was here." Julie glared at Jeb. "He was the leader. He...he did all this." Inspector Dahms looked at Jeb. Jeb returned the inspector's gaze; he raised his eyebrows in surprise, shrugging his shoulders. He then looked down at Julie and spoke.

"The leader? The leader of what?" Jeb said. "My heavens to Betsy, I...I could never lead anybody out here for any reason." Jeb's cheeks dimpled as he seemed to smirk; he appeared to Julie to be stifling a laugh. "Now, suppose you tell me what it is I'm supposed to have done here, young lady?"

"I don't understand, Julie," the inspector spoke gently. "Were you here earlier, last night, before we all got here? Because we didn't see anybody when we all got down here; neither did you, or so I thought."

"No, no, I wasn't here earlier." Julie hesitated. She bit her lower lip. She looked up at the chief, and then at Inspector Dahms.

"Then, how could you know he was here?" Julie shook her head. She would not, or could not take her eyes off of Jeb.

"Julie, if you know something that we don't, we're going to need you to tell us what you know," the inspector said. "When did you see him? Where did you see him? And are you sure that it was this man?" Jeb stared back at Julie with his maniacal, toothy grin.

"Well, young lady?" Jeb said, his leering grin widening.

"Hey, you be quiet," the chief said. He looked at Julie. "Miss Bernard, a minute ago, you seemed very sure when you said that Jeb is the leader." Julie swallowed, shaking her dirty blonde head.

"I don't know," she said.

"I think that you do know," the chief said. "Take your time, breathe, and clear your head. Now, when did you see him, Miss Bernard?" the chief asked. But Julie just looked at him and shook her head.

"Well, that settles that, as far as I'm concerned," Jeb said. "I have notified you all that my daughter is safe with me. So, without further ado, Sandra and I will be bidding you all a good night." Jeb reached for Sandra's hand. But Julie gently pulled Sandra away from Jeb.

"No."

"I beg your pardon?" Jeb seemed genuinely surprised.

"I said no." Julie was standing between Jeb and Sandra now.

"Miss Bernard," Jeb stepped forward towards Julie, "please let me take my daughter out of this place now."

"Sandra is not your daughter. And you're not going anywhere with her."

"Julie," Inspector Dahms said, "unless you can clarify your statement, and explain to us how you know this man is connected with all this, you're going to have to let Jeb take Sandra."

"Julie?" the chief said. Julie looked at the chief, then at Inspector Dahms. She could feel Sandra squeezing both of her hands now, as the child stood right behind her, with Julie's hands pulled behind her back. Julie breathed out slowly through her mouth, puffing out her cheeks as she did so. She looked up at Jeb.

"I saw him in a dream," she said. "I saw all of this, the whole thing, in a dream. I saw you."

"In a...dream?"

"Oh, come on!"

"That's absurd!"

"This is ridiculous!" Voices rang out of the darkness around Julie, the chief, the inspector, the clergy and Jeb. Julie closed her eyes.

"I know, I know, it sounds crazy," she said. "But I did. I saw this man in a dream, doing everything that happened here last night."

"Why, that is utterly ludicrous!" Jeb said. "Now, see here, young lady, you unhand my daughter and we can forget about this whole dream nonsense."

"Not so fast," the chief said. He held up his massive hand, and everyone in the clearing went quiet. His wide, oval eyes glistened a jet black in the moonlight. He spoke slowly and softly. "Wasn't there something else you needed to ask Jeb, Tom?"

"Yes, sir. Jeb, you still haven't answered my last question. How did you know we were here?"

"Why, I simply followed the noise. Y'all make a terrible racket out here in these woods." Jeb smiled. A long and uncomfortable silence permeated the clearing.

"What sort of noises were you hearing?" Inspector Dahms said.

"Oh, I could hear y'all a screamin' and a hollerin'. Thought I heard a gunshot or two."

"I see. And so naturally you led your daughter toward the gunfire and the screaming you heard out here in the dark forest in the middle of the night." Inspector Dahms stared straight into Jeb's eyes. Jeb stared back, smiling. His long, gaunt cheeks dimpled as he regarded the inspector, who calmly filled his pipe with tobacco.

"Why, whatever are you suggesting, good Inspector?"

"I'm not suggesting anything, Jeb." Inspector Dahms lit his pipe with a wooden match. The smoke billowed out of his mouth and nostrils in a flickering hue of blue, gray, and moonlight. "It seems to me that your behavior is suggestive."

"Hey, what's going on here?" Father Freeman said. "What's with the Spanish Inquisition? Jeb's been a fine addition to our humble little church here. He hasn't done anything wrong."

Inspector Dahms nodded as he puffed his pipe thoughtfully. "On the other hand, Bishop, there is a reason we are here in the middle of the woods in the middle of the night."

"Okay, what?"

"We're expecting someone," the chief said.

"Indeed, we are expecting someone," the inspector said.

"Okay, who?"

"Apparently Jeb," Inspector Dahms said.

"Jeb?"

"What in blazes do you mean, sir?" Jeb said.

"He means we knew you were coming here tonight," Officer Franklin said.

"You mean to say that y'all knew I would be coming here?"

"That's right."

"Out here in the middle of these dark woods on a cold night like tonight?"

"Yes, sir." Jeb smiled at Officer Franklin. He turned and looked at the chief, then the inspector. He slowly turned to face Bishop Richter and Father Freeman. His maniacal, white-toothed grin widened. He regarded Julie.

"It was you," Julie said.

"Now, Miss Bernard, ma'am, you're not entirely correct. But you are not entirely wrong, either," Jeb said. His tone had changed. His voice was gentle, his smile menacing. He stooped down, his face inches from Julie's face. "It is me, Miss Bernard. Is, as in the present tense." He began to laugh. Julie stared into his face. An icy chill raced down her spine.

"Wait a minute, what's your name?" Julie said. Jeb did not answer her. He simply smiled smugly at her, occasionally suppressing a giggle. The chief turned to face Julie.

"Miss Bernard, his full name is Jeb Choate."

"Jeb...Choate?" Julie looked back up at Jeb. "Jeb Choate...Jeb...J...E... B." Chills raced back up Julie's spine. "Jedidiah, Ebenezer, B. Choate. You're him." Jeb was beaming. "You're him. But you can't be... You would have to be..." Jeb began laughing again. Officer Franklin stepped toward Jeb and looked into his eyes. The tall, thin man stared back at him, still chuckling.

"Miss Bernard, are you suggesting that this is the Jedidiah Ebenezer B. Choate? My God, he would have to be about a hundred and twenty years old. That's impossible."

Jeb nodded his head. "Right you are, young man. Right you are. Oh, I do declare, this is an exciting conundrum now, isn't it, Miss Bernard?"

"No conundrum here, you sick pig. I'll never give up Sandra now." Julie said.

Officer Franklin licked his lips, nervously peering into Jeb's face. "Mr. Choate, are you admitting to us that you are, in fact, Jedidiah Edmund B. Choate?"

"I am the very man." Jeb could not have had a wider grin on his face. He seemed to be absolutely delighted.

"Are you?" Inspector Dahms said.

"Yes, sir, I am!" The bishop and Father Freeman stared at Jeb with their mouths agape. Bishop Richter looked up at the chief.

"I don't understand. Who is he, really?"

"He is a devil worshipper. Some sort of priest, I guess," the chief said.

"You sonofabitch, you killed Miguel!" Father Freeman lunged at Jeb with his hands up around Jeb's throat. Jeb backed up a step, nodding his head, laughing at the two priests.

"Father Freeman! No. No!" The Bishop, the chief, and Inspector Dahms all had to restrain him and hold onto him as he screamed at Jeb. He clutched the man by the lapels of his coat with his thick, powerful hands. They all struggled and jostled awkwardly over the forest floor for a minute.

"He took you in when you had nowhere to go! You and your 'daughter'! Miguel opened his heart up to you, his home, our church!"

"Take it easy, padre, take it easy," Inspector Dahms said. "We've got him now."

"You killed him! You killed Miguel!"

The bishop stepped in front of his old friend. "John, stop. Just take it easy, friend. It won't bring Miguel back."

Both men of God had to choke back tears when the bishop said this. Father Freeman stopped struggling, nodded his head and let go of Jeb's coat. The inspector turned to face Jeb, who was still grinning.

"I take it you want us to believe that you have lived for over a hundred years?"

"I have lived many, many more years than that. Too many to be more precise, sir."

"That's interesting, Jeb. But not entirely true," Inspector Dahms said.
"Oh?"

"I think that you are a direct descendant of the old Baptist Minister. His great-grandson, I'd say. And he handed down this absurd belief in the devil and this nasty ritual to your grandfather, and he to your father, and then, from Daddy to you."

"I assure you, sir, I have not sired any children. Little Sandra there was adopted." Jeb paused, and he winked at Inspector Dahms. "It's part of the deal, you see. Eternal life, yes, but there can be no bloodline. It's just not possible. And I must say it is a small price to pay for such wonders!"

"A small price to pay? What about all this?" Officer Tubbs said.

"Yeah! You're the one responsible for the crucifixions!" Officer Franklin said. The word *crucifixions* rippled through the clearing like an electric shock. There was a pause of stunned silence that lasted a breath and a heartbeat.

"Crucifixions?"

"Oh my God!"

"What?"

"What is he talking about?"

"Oh my God!"

"What does he mean by crucifixions?"

"What crucifixions?"

"Oh my God!"

"You mean, right here?"

"Oh my God!"

"You did this? You son of a bitch!" Officer Marconi lunged at Jeb. For his part, Jeb nodded his head again and stepped back and leered at Officer Marconi. Officer Jones and Officer Evers stepped in front of him and tried to hold him back. Many of the townspeople started screaming and shouting at Jeb, the police, and each other. There was pushing and shoving as some of the townspeople tried to get at Jeb and some tried to get away from him. As all hell broke loose around them, Officer Franklin looked up at the chief. He started to speak but stopped and looked at Inspector Dahms, then back at the chief. His bosses were both looking right back at him, stoically.

"Shit," Officer Franklin said.

"Easy, Joe. Everybody, just take it easy," the chief said. "I want everybody to stay back. This is a police matter." The screaming and shouting within the clearing seemed to anger the creature as it stalked the perimeter of the clearing. It began to growl again. This made everyone quiet down and return his or her collective attention to the beast and the surrounding darkness.

"Harold, cuff Mr. Choate, please."

"With pleasure. Okay, asshole, turn around." Inspector Dahms gazed into Jeb's eyes.

"Jeb Choate, you are charged with the murders of—"

A deafening roar erupted into the clearing. The inspector ignored it and continued.

"How the hell are we all going to get out of here?" Selectperson Barbara Wordsworth said.

"We're not," Doctor Robinson said. She screamed. This started more screaming, pushing and shoving among the throng as everyone crowded into the center-most part of the clearing away from where they could all clearly hear the beast stalking. Selectperson Barbara Wordsworth became entangled with Binny Moran. They both tripped over the corpse of Father Torrez. When they each saw what they had tripped over, they resumed screaming.

Darkness enveloped the clearing. The screaming was muted by a thunderous rushing sound accompanied by a low, primal growl that sounded as if it was right on top of all of them. The dark shadow of the beast appeared and disappeared alternately in the manic flickering of the full moonlight as it raced into and through the clearing. The sound of flesh and bone being struck with tremendous force followed by a piercing, guttural scream cut through the night like a knife. The smell of a wild animal, feces, and fear wafted through the clearing. There were crunching, tearing, and gurgling sounds, punctuated by gunfire. The muzzle flashes appeared in a surreal pattern in the pitch darkness of the clearing.

"Hold your fire!" The chief and the inspector both spoke this at the same time. The moonlight returned to the clearing for a moment, revealing to everyone a dark crimson trail leading off to the east and into the forest. The acrid smell of gunpowder lightly spread over the smells of the forest night. The creature had returned to the darkness of the clearing edge and continued to thrash about in the underbrush.

"Oh my God!" Several people screamed. Several vomited. Many began to cry. The patrolmen were trying to get everybody back toward the center of the clearing. The bishop and Father Freeman began to give last rites.

"Who was taken? Does anybody know?" Father Freeman said. No one answered right away. He and the bishop moved to help several people back up and onto their feet.

"What are we going to do?"

"What is happening?"

"What the fuck? What the fuck?"

"Oh, please, God, what is going on here?"

"Listen, everyone, now," the chief spoke. "We need to focus on one thing. We have got to get everyone out of here."

"How?" Officer Tubbs asked. "Because I can tell you one thing: Bullets don't kill this thing."

"Are you sure, Tubbs?" the inspector said. The patrolman held up his firearm.

"I emptied the clip straight into his side. It hurt him, but that's it."

"Same here," Billy Pollard said. "I hit him twice at point blank and it didn't slow him down much, if at all!"

314

"Yes, it would seem that you can injure the creature, but killing it is another matter altogether," Doctor Robinson said.

"I didn't say anything about killing this animal," the chief said. "I said to get everyone out of here. I think if we light a large fire here, in the center of the clearing, we can prevent the animal from charging into the clearing the next time it goes dark."

"I don't think fire light will light this clearing enough to prevent that animal from another attack, Chief," Doc Robinson said.

"Probably not," the chief said. "But it was badly burned by fire only this morning." He looked out at the south end of the clearing where the creature currently stalked, snorting and grunting its displeasure with the light of the moon. "It fears fire."

"Right," Inspector Dahms said. "If the fire really works, we could make torches. Maybe use them to escort our people out?"

"No, it would never work," Doctor Robinson said. "Torches and flares don't produce enough light for that. The only light that seems to work is sun light and the full moon."

"True, but it may be all we can do." The Chief looked at Billy Pollard and his crew. "Could you cover us while we move out?"

"Yes, sir!"

"People, and I'm speaking only to police and rescue personnel, let's gather as much wood as we can find in this clearing! Bring it back here to the center of the bonfire area! Be careful and don't get to close to that thing. Let's go!" The rescue personnel immediately spread out around the clearing and began to gather up branches and sticks into their arms.

"Okay, I want everyone who is not a law officer to gather right in the center here to keep you all as safe as possible," the chief said.

"Come on now, everybody! You heard the chief!" the bishop said. "Come on, everybody." The bishop and Father Freeman herded the terrified people toward the center of the clearing while the patrolmen were busily piling up sticks and branches and brush for the bonfire. Julie, Bea, and Richard joined Captain Little Joe and the fire rescue crew and began to arrange the material into a more organized pile to help prepare the bonfire.

It was clumsy and awkward going in the flickering moonlight. There were people everywhere trying to stay out of each other's way while remaining as close to the center of the clearing as possible. Julie bumped into someone; it was too dark to see whom. Officer Franklin stumbled on something. His arms were full of sticks and branches. He fell forward with a light thud and the crunching of sticks and leaves beneath his chest.

"Damn it!" Officer Tubbs and Captain Little Joe helped him up. For its part, the beast continued to circle the clearing, growling and grunting. After a spell, an enormous pile of sticks and branches rose up in the center of the clearing.

"I think we're ready!" Officer Tubbs said.

"Good. Light it," the chief said. †

CHAPTER 40

"Allow me." Inspector Dahms struck a wooden match and stooped his tall frame down. He held the tiny flame to the dry leaves and twigs arranged at the base of the woodpile. The tiny flame danced amidst the leaves, and twigs and flame began to pop up here and there around the base. The inspector strode around the woodpile to the opposite side and struck one more wooden match, then he reached down and lit the kindling there. Captain Little Joe and Danny had joined the inspector. They stoked the flames and threw some of the burning branches up onto the woodpile. Fire quickly spread across the entire base of the woodpile.

The bonfire lit up with an audible whoosh and illuminated the gaunt, terrified faces of the townsfolk of Littleborough. They all stood perfectly still in a full circle around the bonfire. Their static shadows were cast against the remaining canopy above their heads amid the treetops. This created a dark, shadowy halo that mixed with the moonlight among the pine needles, leaves, and branches above. Though intense, the heat from the bonfire seemed cold.

Silence reigned inside the clearing. Only the snap and crackle of the bonfire could be heard. The beast was still stalking outside the clearing. The intermittent full moonlight, coupled with the flames of the bonfire, seemed to be enough to keep the creature at a distance.

Satisfied that the bonfire was burning sufficiently, the inspector walked over to where Julie and the chief were standing. Officers Tubbs and Franklin were also standing there, along with the handcuffed Jeb.

"I wonder," Julie said, "if we make this a large enough fire it could keep the creature away until sunrise."

"You know, it might," Inspector Dahms said. "It'll be light soon."

"Oh, I'm afraid not, good Inspector," Jeb said.

"Shut up," Officer Tubbs said. The clearing went silent again for a moment.

"Hold on a minute, Tubbs," the inspector said. "What are you talking about, Mr. Choate?"

Jeb smiled his best smile. "Why, I'm speaking of the light that is not to come, ever," he said.

"Skip the fanciful language and please come to the point," the inspector said.

"Very well, Inspector. I'll put it bluntly so that every single one of you ignorant fools will understand: There will be no dawn. For those of you too stupid to comprehend, I'm referring to sunrise, which, I am delighted to tell you, has been postponed…forever, it seems. Unless…"

"What the hell are you talking about, assface?" Officer Tubbs asked. Jeb ignored him, and simply stared at the inspector, smiling. Officer Tubbs stepped between Jeb and the inspector, grabbing Jeb by the lapel of his jacket and shaking him. "I asked you what the hell you're talking about, dirt bag."

"Hell is a good way of putting it, child," Jeb said. The chief and Inspector Dahms quickly moved to separate Officer Tubbs from Jeb, who never stopped grinning.

"Take it easy, Harold. Take it easy," the chief said. He turned toward Jeb. "What do you mean, Mr. Choate?" But Jeb only shrugged his slight shoulders.

"My watch has stopped," Officer Marconi said.

"Hey, mine too," Officer Franklin said. "Three o'clock in the morning on the dot."

"This is quite strange, quite strange, indeed." Inspector Dahms was looking at his wristwatch. He then looked at his cell phone. It was dead. "Does anyone have a cell phone with a signal?" Everyone there looked at his or her cell phone. Not one was working. They were all dead. No one spoke.

"As I have quite dutifully and kindly tried to tell you all, time and space have stopped, people. It is no more. Unless his glorious ceremony is completed, and the great master is properly honored, there will be no dawn," Jeb said.

"Shut up."

"If you insist, child," Jeb flashed his toothy grin at Officer Tubbs. "But I know the only way to truly rid us of that terrible creature, and to save our own lives, and to restore time to its proper passing, is if we complete the ritual."

"And, by that you are referring to the ritual you performed here last night?" Inspector Dahms said. Still grinning, Jeb nodded his head. "I see. So, you are proposing that we murder four more innocent people—no, excuse me, crucify four more innocent people so that you can finish some stupid, pointless 'ceremony,' as you call it? I don't think so."

"No, no, why, no, that's not what I'm suggesting at all, Inspector."

"Then, what is it you are suggesting?" Officer Tubbs said, glaring at Jeb.

"I'm merely suggesting the completion of the ceremony. It will require only the one sacrifice of a sweet, innocent soul who did not willingly come to this place." As he spoke, a light seemed to gleam in Jeb's eyes as he looked down at little Sandra.

"You're sick!" Julie backed herself and Sandra away from Jeb as she spoke, nearly tripping over a small tree stump. "You will never lay your hands on this child again. That much I know!"

"Oh, my graciousness, I believe I will be, and quite soon, too, my dear."

"Right, so, you want to kill your own daughter, sacrificing her to a devil, and this will somehow make that thing go away and restore time, is that it?" Jeb looked at Inspector Dahms.

"It pains me no end, Inspector. I wish there was another way. But it will require the life of my child to save all of us from that terrible creature out there. And, yes, it will, as it always has, restore the passage of time to its original state of Creation."

"So, you say," Inspector Dahms began to fill his pipe, "but, then, weren't you planning on 'sacrificing' your daughter regardless of the circumstances here? I think it's a safe bet that you were. And that's why you were so concerned when she disappeared."

"Why, of course that's why I was concerned, Inspector. Good people of Littleborough, I admit that I fully intended to sacrifice my precious daughter tonight, right here in these hallowed woods, in this most holy of places. But only to rid us of that terrible evil that is out there, right now. I did not kill all those people; the beast did, by God!"

The clearing erupted into a cacophony of noise as everyone there began to speak or shout at once. As their voices rose, tempers flared and several people had to be separated from each other when it appeared they might begin to fight among themselves.

"Everybody, calm down right now!" the chief said. His voice boomed in the large clearing. Every single person in that clearing stopped yelling. The chief never raised his voice. Even the beast in the woods ceased its snarling for a moment. "We will all surely die if we allow ourselves to become hysterical. We certainly can't allow ourselves to be divided at a time like this. There is a way to survive this, and in order to find it we must all remain calm and work together. I am specifically talking to those of you who volunteered for the search party. Let us do our jobs and just, please, do as we ask."

"You all shouldn't even be out here," Officer Tubbs said.

"Yeah, but here we are, Chief, totally screwed." Bea said.

"Yes, that's true," Inspector Dahms said. "However, we specifically told all of you to stop at sunset and resume in the morning. Why are you all still here? Where were you all?"

Each member of the search party looked around at each other. Some shuffled their feet along the forest floor. Some looked at the ground while others rolled their eyes. No one wanted to be the one to say it.

"Well," said the chief, "where are you all coming from now?"

"We were all grabbed by a witch," Richard stated this flatly. There was a long, pregnant pause.

"A witch," Inspector Dahms said. He regarded Richard, who nodded his head emphatically. "I see. Well, that's cleared that up, then."

"No, he's telling the truth," Danny the EMT said. "We were all picked off one at a time by this tall old woman. I mean, maybe she was a witch. I don't know. She used a drug to knock me out. Then, she dragged me into some cave somewhere underground. We were all there."

"That is absolutely ridiculous," Officer Tubbs said.

"But, Harold, given everything else going on around here, who can say that isn't possible?" Officer Franklin said.

"I'll say it," Officer Tubbs said.

"And I'll second that motion," Officer Marconi said.

"How, exactly, did this witch convince you all to take drugs?" Inspector Dahms said.

"She tricked me." Danny said. "She had a fistful of what looked like shit in her hands and she just blew it into my face. Next thing, I'm waking up in a bloody little cage in a bloody big cave somewhere."

"Same thing happened to me," Captain Little Joe said. "She just kind of appeared behind me, and then, bam!" He looked at the chief. "I think it's the old lady, Sam, in the legends. She totally fits the description." The chief looked straight into Captain Little Joe's eyes. Julie was looking at him, as well.

"Lila?" Captain Little Joe nodded his head. The chief turned and looked at Billy Pollard, his wife Nancy, and their son Peter. This was the hunting party. "Did this happen to you, too?" They each nodded their heads solemnly.

"Who is Lila, Chief?"

"Well, Julie, there's an ancient legend that goes back to our ancestors' creation stories. There was a princess called Lila; she was named after the storm spirit. Our ancestors called her 'Lilutu' and sometimes 'Lili.' 'She was a beautiful, strong, and independent girl, beloved by all her people. She was kind and gentle. Wild animals showed no fear of her or aggression toward her when she walked through the forest." As he softly spoke, the chief kept his wide brown eyes trained on the edge of the clearing. He had noticed that the subject of Lila seemed to have an effect upon the beast in the wilderness.

"She was betrothed to marry a prince from a rival tribe. She didn't love him. She ran away into the wilderness the night before her wedding. As she ran, an ancient, and some say evil, wilderness spirit saw her and was struck by her beauty and strength. Smitten, he followed her. He appeared to Lila in the guise of a giant wolf, and raped her.

She bore from this a child—a terrible creature, half-boy, half-wolf with wings. It drove her near to madness. It's believed that both Lila and this creature, who my people call Dam, still live here in these woods."

"Lila," Julie said.

"Well, that certainly fits the description of the animal given by the doc," the inspector said.

"And that's where you're all coming from just now?" the chief asked. "Where is this cave?" Again, silently, everyone looked around sheepishly.

"I don't think anyone can find it, Chief," Julie said. "But I can vouch for them; I saw the witch and the cave they were all in."

"It's true. Julie's the one that got us all out of there, Tom," Bea said. "If it weren't for Julie, we'd all be worm food."

"That's for sure," Danny agreed.

"I see," the inspector said. He looked at the chief, who shrugged his shoulders. "So, we're also looking for a witch, now, who we will charge with possession of a narcotic and kidnapping."

"I don't think she meant any harm to anyone," Julie said. This statement started another uproar of shouting voices among the townsfolk in the clearing.

"Oh, come on!"

"Not harm us? Not harm us?"

"Are you kidding me?"

"She drugged us!"

"You get into one of those little cages!"

"What the hell are you talking about, Jules?" Richard said. "That bitch almost killed you back there." Julie nodded her head.

"I know, Richard, I know. But she didn't. It just seems to me like she was simply getting all of us out of the woods and away from that animal out there; otherwise, why are we all still alive?" There was a silence. "She even took Sandra out of danger."

"Yeah, she took her out of the woods and stuffed her in a cage like the rest of us!" Selectperson Bert Snodgrass said. Julie held up her hand.

"I know, I know. But let me ask you this: Did she pee on any of you?" There followed a long silence.

"What?" Inspector Dahms looked at Julie incredulously.

"Did she pee on any of you? Answer me!"

After a long silence, Danny spoke up. "I guess I do remember her standing right over me after she hit my face with that shit and I went down. And I do smell like piss, now that you mention it."

"She peed on my chest," Bea said. "I remember it, now...kinky!"

"That old woman peed on you guys?" Richard said. "Actual...urine? My God, is that what I have been breathing in all this time?" He pulled at the fabric of his white dress shirt up to his nose and began to sniff. Almost instantly he jerked his head back from his own shirt while snorting for air. "Oh my God, she peed all over me!" Richard shook his head, shuddering. "So, it now turns out that that horrible smell has been me this whole time? And I wasn't even conscious while she did it, that bitch. Who knows, I might have even liked it!"

The creature stirred at the edge of the clearing and howled. It was a long, lonely and powerful howl. It literally filled the entirety of the Great Woods in Littleborough and echoed throughout the town.

"But don't you see?" Julie said. "This creature won't touch you if you smell like the old woman. She peed on us with a purpose, to protect us from him."

"But she didn't pee on me." It was Selectwoman Barbara Wordsworth. "She didn't pee on me! Oh my God, she didn't pee on me! Why didn't she pee on me? Why? Somebody help me, help me!"

"Damn it, Barbara, shut up," Bea said. "Just stand in between those of us who do smell and you should be fine."

"Yes, good idea, Bea, thank you." Inspector Dahms calmly refilled his pipe with tobacco as he spoke. "Anyone else not peed on by the witch?" As the inspector spoke, the chief and some of the patrolmen had to stifle their laughter. "Then, please, move to the very center of the clearing. Those of you who the witch favored by urinating all over you, could you form a ring around them? Yes, and then we'll form a ring of ourselves around you...okay? Jonesy, Tubbs, if you two could slide over toward the south opening, I'll cover the east with you, Chief?" The large man nodded his head as his large, brown eyes scanned the darkness.

"Franklin, you stay with us."

"Yes, sir."

"Billy, can you and yours watch the north opening?"

"Can do, Inspector."

"Very good. Evers and Marconi, you guys should cover the west opening, if you please...hey!" Someone had broken away from the group and was in a frenzied sprint for the mouth of the clearing and the path that led back to Flagg Road. His figure silhouetted and disappeared alternately in the flickering light of the clearing and grew dimmer and dimmer as he got further away from the protection of the bonfire.

"Dude, stop!" Officer Franklin said. A growl, low, primal, and barely audible, raised the hairs on the back of his neck. Everyone and everything in the clearing went quiet. Only the snap and crackle of the bonfire could be heard with the desperate footfalls of the running form and the growling of the beast. Then the growling stopped. Binny Moran's tiny voice could just barely be heard softly speaking. "Oh, my God."

A thunderous rush burst from the northeast edge of the clearing. It was too dark to see anything as clouds obscured the moonlight. The forest floor trembled beneath their feet as everyone stared, wide eyed, blindly into the darkness. The dark cloud passed and bright moonlight splashed over the whole of the clearing. And there it was.

The beast was, in fact, a huge wolf. His thick, dark coat could not mask the powerful muscles rippling as the creature raced across the clearing. Wild, piercing eyes burned fiercely out of his enormous, leonine head. His jaws snarled, revealing rows of large, jagged teeth in a surreal blur of rage. Forty voices screamed in unison at the sight of their deepest, darkest dreams.

"Fire!" the chief said. The patrolmen and Billy Pollard's group all had clear lines of sight to the beast so they fired their weapons at the animal. "Okay, hold, hold, hold your fire, now!" They all ceased fire as it got too close to the running man. As the beast overtook his prey, darkness mercifully returned to the clearing as another cloud raced across the full moon. There was a dull squishing noise followed by a piercing scream.

"No, no, no, no, no, no, no, no! God, no! God, no! God!" There was a terrible gurgling and retching. Silence followed.

"Oh my God."

"What was that?"

"You mean what is that?"

"Oh my God."

"What the hell was that?"

"Does anyone know who that person was?" the bishop said. This was followed by a murmuring among everyone for several moments. Selectperson Dick Pale whispered with Selectperson Tim White.

"Are you sure, Timothy?"

"Yes, he's not here now and he was paired with me for the search. He was here five minutes ago."

"Okay, thanks. It was Hank Hubbard, Bishop."

"Oh, dear," the bishop said. He and Father Freeman both began to pray.

"What the hell are we going to do?" Selectperson Wordsworth said. She looked over at the inspector and the chief.

"Die," Doc Robinson said.

"Shut up, Doc," Officer Tubbs said.

"No, young man, I fear the good doctor is surely right, my child, surely. We shall all die here—pointlessly, I might add—if we do not complete the ceremony."

"You shut up, too, whatever your fucking name is."

Silence permeated the cold, shuttering night. The clearing would light up with hues of yellow, green, and blood. Then it would return to the black of darkness. No one stirred. The beast was still for the moment. Julie was just able to hear his breathing and snarling in the shadows of the forest. The bishop and Father Freeman finished the last rites for Hank Hubbard. The flames from the bonfire licked upward at the night.

"You know what?" Julie spoke. "I hate it, but that really might be the only way we can survive this situation." A chorus of voices rose in the large clearing as many opposed what Julie had said.

"Miss Bernard, are you suggesting we kill Sandra? I can't allow anyone to do that," the chief said.

"No, of course not, Chief. I'm suggesting we kill Jeb." This time an even louder chorus of voices rose, most in complete agreement with what Julie had said.

"While I do like your thinking, Miss Bernard, it's still murder. Also, if we kill him, he can't help us complete this alleged ritual."

"I do declare, sir, you are right upon that point. I should also point out to you good people that it must be the blood of an innocent, and I certainly cannot in good conscience count myself among the lambs."

"That is the understatement of all time," Father Freeman said.

"My friends, it's better to die with a soul than to live without one, isn't it?" Bishop Richter said. "We must not worship anyone other than God! We mustn't, we can't put our faith in this man, this murderer! We cannot ever put our faith and our souls into the hands of the fallen angel!"

"You dare speak of faith, Bishop?" Jeb said. He grinned menacingly at the two priests. "And who should they put their faith in—you? How can they after you lied about Miguel's death?"

"We never lied about anything!" Father Freeman said.

"What about the way he died?" Jeb said.

"What about it?"

"You priests told the congregation that he had a heart attack."

"He did. The autopsy proved it."

"You butchers of truth, priests, police, and your elected selectpersons, failed to mention that the cause of the heart attack was pure fear from when he discovered me welcoming Satan into Father Torrez's own church, sirs. Into your church. You failed to mention a heart. The heart of an infant baby boy that I placed so carefully in your holy water as a gift for our master, Lucifer."

This statement seemed to suck the air out of the entire clearing itself and everyone in it. The clearing, the beast, the townsfolk, and the Great Woods of Littleborough fell silent in the flickering light. The only sound now was the bonfire's crackling, and Jeb's laughter as it filled the night. †

CHAPTER 41
The Town Meeting
or
the Liars' Den

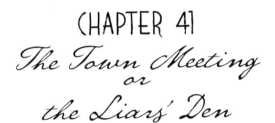

"Shut up," Officer Tubbs said. He looked at the inspector and then at the chief. "What is he talking about?"

"Yeah, what is he talking about?" Bea said. She was looking at selectperson Barbara Wordsworth, who was shaking her head and shrugging her shoulders.

"I have no idea what he's talking about!" she said. "Besides, who's going to believe a devil worshipper about anything?"

"Well, I don't know about you, Barbara, but so far, he's the only one to tell the truth.."

"Exactly," Richard said. "I mean, he's horrible, but at least he's being honest about who he is and what he's done"

"Right, not a damned fork-tongued liar face, like you suits are."

"That's right!" Jeb said. "Tell it on the mountain, Captain Little Joe!"

"Shut up."

"How dare you?" Selectperson Barbara Wordsworth's voice rose into a shrill screech. "I never lie! Never, do you hear me?"

"You're lying right now, Barbara."

"It's Selectperson Wordsworth!" Bea slapped her across her face. "Ow!"

"Shut up, for God's sake, Barbara, will you please?"

"So, what exactly is he talking about with Father Torrez's death?" Billy Pollard said.

"Nothing," Selectperson Dick Pale said, "there's absolutely nothing to it."

"Yeah, there is," the chief said. "The time for lies is over, people. I think it's high time for some truth telling."

"That's easy for you to say, Chief! But you were in on the lies, too!"

"No, he wasn't," Selectperson Tim White said. "The chief voted against not telling you all about the events in St. Mark's Church last night."

"Now Tim, we're never supposed to reveal any specifics about the way a person votes on something," Selectperson Dick Pale said. Selectperson Tim White shrugged.

"How the hell are we supposed to believe that, anyway?" Nancy Pollard said.

"At this point, what difference does it make?" Christo Papatheo said.

"I think it makes a big difference!" Gabby Mauro said.

"It doesn't make any difference," Dick Little said.

"We had a vote and we decided to keep it quiet until we had all the facts, that's all. It wasn't going to be kept a secret forever," Selectperson Dick Pale said.

"No, you were just going to wait until everybody died, that's all," Doctor Robinson said.

"That's just not true!" Selectperson Candy Dahlbright said.

"It sure seems to be the case."

"Who cares? It's done! Now, will you tell us what happened?" Billy Pollard said.

The chief looked down at Selectperson Wordsworth. She was staring out into the darkness and mumbling to herself quietly. "This isn't my fault. I never lie. I didn't lie. I was thinking about everyone else—their safety, the panic...the rumors..."

He shrugged his massive shoulders and then spoke. "The night before last we were called to St. Mark's Church. Someone had performed a ritual in the church that involved blood and candles and stuff," the chief said. He paused, regarding his friends and neighbors. The bonfire cracked loudly as the flames danced and sparkled in their eyes. He sighed. "There was a human heart placed in the holy water." An audible gasp came from all around the bonfire. "Father Torrez apparently woke up and walked into the church. When he discovered the heart, and what Jeb was up to, I guess, it was too much for him. He died of a heart attack right there on the spot."

"Oh my God," Binny Moran said.

"And you guys didn't think we should know about this?" Bea said.

"That's insane!" Dick Little said.

"You covered it up! You all covered it up!" Gabby Mauro said.

"We thought it would cause a panic!" Selectperson Dick Pale said.

"Well, you were right, Dick!" Dick Little said.

"Thank goodness you waited until now to tell me," Richard said. "Because if you told me earlier, I would have crapped my pants at work, instead of just now, here, in the middle of the woods."

"You assholes let us all wander into the woods looking for the daughter of an outsider, while knowing full well that there was a homicidal maniac running around Littleborough with an infant's heart? What the fuck is wrong with you people?" Peter Pollard said.

"Yeah, no shit, right?"

"Good plan, General Custer."

"Next thing you know, they're going to tell us they all knew about the giant, homicidal fucking wolf, too," Captain Little Joe said. The clearing fell silent.

"Oh, you've got to be kidding me!"

"You knew? You guys knew?" Bea said.

"Oh my God!" Binny Moran said.

"Dude, seriously?" Richard said.

"Who knew? I want to know who knew!"

The chief stepped forward and held up his hands as the din rose. "I knew," he said. The noise ceased. "I knew, and I decided it would be best to track and hunt the wolf quietly. We felt that it would be safe for you all to search for Sandra during the daylight hours. That's why we told you all to be out of the woods by sunset. We didn't like the idea of anyone being out here. But when we learned that a little girl from our town, even one who is an outsider, was lost out here, we had to act and act fast."

The group fell quiet. Dark clouds continued to stream across the full moon as if they were a cameo in a silent film. Jeb snickered. He stood, towering over Officers Tubbs and Franklin, with his hands cuffed behind his back. He could not contain himself. He started to laugh again.

"Shut up."

"Oh, right you are," Jeb said.

"What the hell are we going to do?" Selectperson Barbara Wordsworth said.

"Has time really stopped?"

"That's ridiculous, Christine!"

"Is it? Then what do you think is causing this, Pete?"

"I don't know, but…"

"Hey, butt munch, do you have a better theory?"

"Oh, what the fuck do you know about anything, George?"

"I know that my watch has stopped along with everyone else's, douche bag!"

329

"What does that prove?"

"It proves that time has stopped, Einstein!"

"Time has stopped? What the fuck does that even mean?"

"It means just that."

"Superstitious bullshit. Doc, you're a scientist. Tell them! Tell them time hasn't stopped."

Doc Robinson had largely been ignoring everyone and still stared intently at the edges of the clearing where he could hear the beast skulking. He did not take his eyes off of the forest.

"Time has stopped," he said. "Ask yourselves this: Has the moon moved in the sky at all since you idiots all arrived?" Everyone looked up.

"How would we know?"

"He's right," the chief said. "It's been in the same position for a while now." Bishop Richter and Father Freeman looked at each other. Neither spoke. Inspector Dahms reached into his coat pocket and pulled out his pipe and began to clean it. He looked at the chief, who was looking right at him.

"What are we going to do, Chief?" Julie asked. The chief did not answer.

"You're not thinking of…Chief, Inspector Dahms! This is not the way!" the bishop said.

"Bad plan! Bad, bad plan!" Father Freeman said.

"You can't be serious." Officer Evers said.

"Wait a minute here, how can we actually be contemplating this?" Officer Marconi said.

"Joe, do you have a better idea?" Captain Little Joe said.

"Yes, anything but this. We could pray, something!"

"Pray to whom, sir?" Jeb said. "Where is your God, people?"

"Shut up," Officer Evers said.

"Yeah, well, come to think of it, Jeb, where exactly is your devil?" Officer Tubbs said. "All I see is some weird, strange, nasty animal. I see no devil anywhere around here."

"Oh, he'll come. Rest assured, my sweet master always arrives when I come bearing special gifts."

"Hmmmm…not always, I think," Inspector Dahms said. "Unless I am mistaken, and the truth here is self-evident, you screwed up your ritual here last night, Mr. Choate. You didn't summon Satan; you awoke this creature instead. You say you didn't kill all the people we found in this clearing; I say you did."

"Surely not, sir."

"Surely so, Mr. Choate," the chief said.

"So, what are we going to do?" Selectperson Bert Snodgrass said.

"I think we should do the ceremony, like she said." Selectperson Barbara Wordsworth pointed at Julie. Many voiced agreement with her.

"As the police here, we can't allow any one of you to be killed, or sacrificed, or injured." the chief said.

"We should put it to a vote, like any town meeting," Selectperson Dick Pale said.

"My friends, my friends, this is a terrible, sincere mistake you are making. We must not worship any other!" the Bishop said. "We especially must not worship Satan! And the police are right! Thou shalt not murder, remember? Remember?"

"Calm down, Padre," Inspector Dahms said. "We will not allow a murder."

"Amen," Officer Tubbs said. "There shalt be no murder here tonight by any of you, ever." There followed a momentary silence.

"Wait a minute, what if we just do the ceremony without the sacrifice?" Selectperson Candy Dahlbright said.

"Without the sacrifice there is no ritual," Jeb said.

"Right, says the guy who conjured up a big-ass wolf instead of a little dude in a red suit with little bitty horns and a pointy tail," Officer Tubbs said. As he spoke, Captain Little Joe and his firemen fed the bonfire more sticks and branches and the flames grew higher. This was followed by a long, anguished howl from the beast.

"I tell you all that the ritual simply will not work without the sacrifice," Jeb said.

Officer Franklin walked over to Inspector Dahms. He turned his face up toward the much taller man, who stooped slightly and the two men's faces were inches apart. Officer Tubbs and the chief were also there. They spoke in hushed tones.

"I think Selectperson Pale is right," Selectperson Barbara Wordsworth said. "We should put this to a vote."

"But we need all the selectpersons to do that. Daphne isn't here," Selectperson Candy Dahlbright said.

"Of course she isn't here. This is actual work and beneath the great Daphne Phoeble," Dick Little said. "You can't walk around these woods with heels like those!" People were laughing.

"This is no joking matter, Dick," Selectperson Barbara Wordsworth said. "Daphne had to go down to the middle school to prepare for a campaign speech for tomorrow."

"I thought you said this wasn't a joking matter, Barbara," Bea said, "because that's pretty funny."

"Oh, stop it!"

"No."

"We can declare an emergency vote in a case like this," the chief said.

"Okay, let's do it," Selectperson Dick Pale said. "We'll do an open vote, by show of hands."

"She can't vote! She's new here. It's barely been a year!" Selectperson Barbara Wordsworth said. "And it's the same with him!" She pointed at Julie and the inspector.

"That's not fair," Selectperson Candy Dahlbright said. "This affects them, too. They're a part of this."

"Maybe we should have a vote to see if they can vote?" Selectperson Dick Pale said.

"Fuckin' politicians!" Billy Pollard said. "Will you just make up your fuckin' minds?"

"We're trying, Billy. We want this to be fair," Selectperson Dick Pale said. "All those in favor of allowing Julie and the inspector to vote, raise your hands! All those opposed?" There was a pause as the tall, distinguished gentleman counted the raised hands. "We have a deadlock."

"Oh, Jesus Christ! Now what do we do?"

"A tie means they do not get a vote," Selectperson Bert Snodgrass said. Julie and Inspector Dahms looked at each other. He shrugged. She shook her head and rolled her eyes upward, making him smile.

"Wait a minute, Chief," Officer Marconi said. "We're not seriously contemplating a murder, are we?" The chief smiled, shaking his head. He walked back over to where Jeb stood. The inspector and Officers Tubbs and Franklin followed.

"Mr. Choate, it would appear that it has been your goal to live forever, is that right?" Inspector Dahms said.

"Yes, sir, that is correct. I have lived a very long and happy life thus far."

"Uh-huh, well, even you can see it appears your time is at hand, at the present moment, Mr. Choate? Ironic, isn't it? The very beast you inadvertently raised is the very thing that will end your little run of good fortune, no?"

"It does appear to be so, sir." Officer Franklin had a small flashlight and a pen and pad of paper in his hands.

"Then tell us the exact ritual," he said.

"I will tell you, but I do not see what good it will do without the blood of innocents," Jeb said.

"You want the blood of innocents?" the chief said. "Look around you. You're soaking in it, Mr. Choate." The chief glared into Jeb's face as he spoke. "We're all standing knee deep in the blood of innocents."

"Very well, sir. But then I must tell ya'll before conducting your terribly important and democratic duties that if ya'll do indeed decide to follow me as I perform this rite, it will only work if every single one of you does exactly as I say and do. No exceptions, sir."

"No way!" Officer Marconi said. "Chief, you can't expect us to follow this bag of...bag of..."

"Shit," Officer Tubbs said. "Joe's right, Chief. We can't possibly put him in charge of all of us! We can't!"

"It would only be temporary if we did, Harold," the chief said. "We are voting on a temporary situation. Once the situation is concluded, we arrest Mr. Choate for murder." The chief looked at Jeb. "That's non-negotiable, Mr. Choate."

"This is unacceptable, my friends!" the bishop said. "Please, don't listen to Jeb! We can't do this! We can't!" He looked at Father Freeman. "Where's the Judge?"

"The who?" the chief asked.

"She disappeared some time ago, Pat," Father Freeman said. "I'm wondering if that animal got her?"

"But that was Hank Hubbard," Selectperson Barbara Wordsworth said.

"No, there was someone before him and we couldn't figure out who it was."

"Oh, no. No." Both priests crossed themselves. Julie looked around the flickering clearing in disbelief. *No, please no,* she thought.

"Who are you talking about?"

"The Judge, Chief. She was sent by our Teacher to help in this matter." The bishop paused, choking up. "She may be gone."

"Sorry, Father, I truly am," Selectperson Bert Snodgrass said. "This is a legal, voting matter, and you have no say in this as clergy according to our town charter."

"That may be true, Bert, but we can declare a spiritual state of emergency under that very same town charter!" Selectperson Dick Pale turned and looked at the Bishop.

"Spiritual?"

"Yes!"

"No! This is life and death, Pat!"

"You're talking about worshipping Satan, Dick! This is far more serious than life or death!"

"Nobody here is really worshipping Satan, Bishop. Except that asshole, of course," Officer Tubbs said. The chief nodded.

"Officer Franklin and the inspector have discovered that this clearing is subject to becoming an energy vortex at certain times. This fits in with what my people say about this clearing and several other spots in town. Somehow, it suspends time and space and general normalcy, I guess."

"That's right, Chief," Officer Franklin said.

Jeb was shaking his head. "If you truly wish to rid yourselves of that creature out there before it comes back in here, it will have to be my sweet master ya'll worship, or death. Your choice."

"We're wasting time!" Selectperson Barbara Wordsworth said.

"Actually Barbara, time is the one thing that isn't wasting around here."

"Good point, jerk." She looked at Selectperson Dick Pale. "I'm simply saying let's vote! Before Fido gets hungry again." Selectperson Dick Pale nodded.

"Is that what you wish to do?" the bishop said.

"Do you have a better idea, Bishop?"

"We want to try prayer, first. If everybody, all of us, pray together for the Lord to deliver us from this...this situation He will show us the way."

Selectperson Dick Pale turned and faced his friends and neighbors. He sighed. "Okay, that's fair."

Folks were nodding their heads. Everyone knelt and bowed their head except Doc Robinson and the inspector. The bishop and Father Freeman kissed their crucifix, and then began to lead everyone in the Lord's Prayer.

"Our Father, Who art in Heaven. Hallowed be thy Name. Thy Kingdom come; Thy Will be done..." Darkness blanketed the night sky, the forest, and the clearing. The entirety of the forest floor began to tremble and shake violently. People began screaming. Everyone tried to get up off of their knees, only to fall down onto the cold forest floor. Two loud, muffled shots rang out.

"Noooooooooooo! Noooooooooo!" Billy Pollard's screams were punctuated by more gunshots. "You son of a bitch! You son of a bitch! Noooooooooo!" Light returned to the clearing. Billy Pollard was running around the bonfire, covered from head to toe in blood. He was still screaming and firing his weapon randomly into the surrounding woods. There was no ammunition left in his firearm.

"Billy, Billy, calm down!" The chief and Captain Little Joe ran over to Billy Pollard and tried to lead him back to the relative safety of the bonfire. "Take it easy. Take it easy." They reached the bonfire and sat him down. He clutched at his rifle. Tears streaked down his blood-covered face.

"Are you okay, Billy?" Captain Little Joe said. Billy sat, staring into the fire. His son, Peter, stood and stared into the darkness of the forest, weeping softly. As the moonlight momentarily returned to the clearing, they could see that the entire right side of his body was covered in his mother's blood.

"Where's Nancy, Billy? Billy, where is Nancy?" The chief turned away. "Nancy? Nancy!"

"She's gone, sir. Gone with her God, I expect," Jeb said. "I am sorry. So very sorry." Jeb began to laugh. He turned and looked at the bishop and Father Freeman. "Your God is not here, sirs. No. But mine is. As sure as that full moon, the master is here, sirs. He is ready and waiting for us all. Satan is here."

Selectperson Dick Pale turned and, once again, faced his friends and neighbors. "People of Littleborough, the floor is now open for a vote by show of hands. Those in favor of performing the rite, please raise your hands." †

CHAPTER 42
Dawn, the Wolf, and the Lamb

"For to win one hundred victories
in one hundred battles is not the acme of skill.
To subdue the enemy without fighting is the acme of skill."
—Sun Tzu, *The Art of War*

And so, it had been voted on and agreed. Officer Tubbs reluctantly removed the handcuffs from Jeb's wrists. For his part Jeb could not stop beaming. He rubbed his wrists to get the circulation back into his hands and strutted around the clearing with an enormous grin on his face. He put Julie and Bea in charge of preparing the "brew," as he had called it. There was plenty for everyone in the large cast iron cauldron despite it having spilled over during the previous night's carnage.

Julie and Bea dragged the heavy cookware upright and over the several feet to where Jeb stood. He arranged small sticks and brush around the cauldron. He straightened himself up and looked at Inspector Dahms.

"May I have a light, please, Inspector?" Wordlessly, Inspector Dahms lit the kindling beneath the cauldron with a wooden match. "Thank you, sir." Jeb began to stir the thick, viscous fluid in the pot. Julie and Bea watched in disgusted fascination. The odor was a combination of feces and burning plastic.

"I'm not looking forward to that!" Bea said. Julie laughed her throaty laugh and shook her head. Jeb handed Julie the thick stick he was using to stir with. Julie began to stir the brew. Jeb joined the remainder of the group as they made preparations for the Ball. Most of them were gathering more sticks, branches, and brush with which to feed the bonfire.

Julie's arms tired from the labor. The brew was thick and nasty. She felt dizzy and nauseous from the fumes as they came into her face. Bea took the thick stick from her. Julie smiled at her gratefully. She had handed the shoebox containing Geraldine the rat off to Sandra so that she could tend to the brew. Sandra opened the shoebox and could not conceal her delight at the sight of Geraldine. The little girl sat on the cold forest floor and stroked the rat gently.

Julie now walked back over to where Sandra sat. She tried to think of the safest place she could find for her little friends. She knelt down by Sandra and peered into the shoebox. Geraldine was sleeping. The little rat awoke and looked up at Julie, sniffling. Julie smiled. She then became aware of a pair of golf shoes flickering in the moonlight in front of her. Someone was standing over her in the darkness of the clearing. Julie looked up. It was the Judge. Julie looked into the Judge's amazing eyes and breathed a sigh of relief. The Judge pointed to the center of the clearing, by the bonfire.

"Put her there. Lilith's baby will be all over us in a minute. Follow your instincts, and only your instincts." Julie turned to see where the Judge was pointing. As she turned her head back around and looked up, the clearing went dark. When the moonlight returned, she was not surprised to find that the Judge and Sandra were gone. She sighed.

"Yes, ma'am," Julie whispered.

The patrolmen gathered up the body and body parts of Hank Hubbard and the body of Father Miguel Torrez. There were no body parts, or a body, of Nancy Pollard anywhere to be found. Inspector Dahms walked over to Bishop Richter and Father Freeman as they furiously prayed for a blessing in the clearing and asked for forgiveness for everyone involved with what was to come.

"Excuse me, gentleman, I was just wondering how Father Torrez's body came to be out here. The last I heard, it had been returned to you both to prepare for final services in the morning."

The bishop and Father Freeman looked at each other. They both turned and looked at Doc Robinson.

"I took his body out of the chapel below us and brought it here to entice that incredible animal."

"I'm just curious, my boy. How did you know about the chapel, and how to find it?" the bishop said.

"What chapel are you talking about?" The inspector said this to the Bishop. "Is there something underneath this clearing?"

"Yes, there is an ancient chamber down almost ninety feet below our own feet. It is a most holy of holy shrines for several faiths, including our own humble form of Christianity."

"Can we use this to escape or hide from this thing?"

The bishop and Father Freeman shook their heads. "No, the entrances are well outside the walls of the hellish prison this clearing has become."

The inspector looked at Doc Robinson. For his part, Doc Robinson stared back.

"Well, Doc, how did you know about this chamber?"

"Satan told me how to find it, Inspector."

"Right." The Inspector shook his head and walked away. Doc Robinson and the chief stared eye to eye in silence. The beast howled frustrated rage as the moonlight dominated the clearing for several moments. The eerie, pale yellow light cast by the full moon flickered around the orange glow of the growing bonfire.

Jeb briefly instructed his new congregation on the basics of the ritual. He bid them to simply move as he moved and say what he said. The participants formed a line behind Selectperson Barbara Wordsworth. Jeb took the large, silver ladle from within the enormous metal pot and held it up to his mouth. He took a large drink from it. He then held it up for Selectperson Wordsworth. She sipped it and immediately gagged and covered her mouth, staggering away. Selectperson Dick Pale was next. He did exactly as Selectperson Barbara Wordsworth had done.

And so it went. One after another, each took their share of the elixir. The patrolmen of Littleborough had insisted that they would not partake of the drug. But the fumes from the heat of the little fire beneath the pot had filled the clearing and clearly had an effect on most of them. As Julie awaited her turn, she observed Officer Evers and Officer Jones struggling to walk in a simple, straight line. Almost everyone seemed intoxicated. Everyone also seemed to blissfully, momentarily forget that death was just outside of the clearing and trying to get into the clearing.

While the townsfolk prepared themselves for the ceremony on the western side of the clearing, the police gathered on the east side. There they stood in a small, tight circle around the chief. As the night flickered around them, he addressed his men.

"We all know there is a chance, a very good chance, that this thing isn't going to work," he said. "We have to approach it as if it won't. We will need to protect everybody from the wolf; we will also need to protect everybody from Jeb."

"Jeb? What can he do that he hasn't already done?" Officer Franklin said.

"He could try to get a hold of anyone here and sacrifice them to the devil, Ben. That's what he's admitted he's here to do."

"Why don't we just shoot the motherfucker?"

"If he makes any kind of move toward anyone at all that looks like he's trying to hurt them, you can shoot him, Harold."

"Just don't miss," Inspector Dahms said. "There will be people all over the place when this thing gets started. Be careful."

The chief nodded. "Any gunfire has to be executed with extreme caution, whether it's aimed at Jeb or the wolf. We also have to keep an eye on Billy and Peter Pollard." The group looked over at the raging bonfire where the two men quietly wept. "Everybody got it?" Everyone nodded. "Okay, fan out but keep close to each other, stay out of the way of the ceremony, and be careful. I'll see you all when it's over. Good luck."

The patrolmen all fanned out around the bonfire.

Julie raised the ladle to her lips. She stopped. She had quietly removed a mushroom cap from beneath Geraldine in the shoebox when she had placed the shoebox by the bonfire. Julie looked quickly around the clearing. No one was watching her. She ate the mushroom cap. Like before, it was foul tasting. The texture was coarse and mealy. She swallowed. It made her shiver and shudder to her core. Julie then took a deep breath and raised the ladle back up to her lips and sipped the dark ooze. Her entire body shuddered from the taste and the effects were immediate.

"It's not that bad," Bea said as she retched next to Richard, who was also retching. "If you don't mind shit, piss, and snot mixed with Diet Coke."

"Really, Diet Coke? That is so disgusting, Bea. What is the matter with you?" Richard said. They both began to laugh. Others around them began to laugh. Their laughter was contagious and uncontrollable. Richard tried to stand up. He swayed left and right as if blown by a strong wind. He felt light headed. Bea had also tried to get to her feet. She fell right onto her backside and laughed uncontrollably while pointing up at Richard.

Still laughing, Richard helped Bea onto her feet. Despite the horror they all had witnessed to that point, none could wipe the grin from their faces. The sound of drumming suddenly filled the night and the clearing. Jeb played a set of old conga drums. Badly scorched, they had nearly been lost in the fire. His large hands and long, bony fingers slapped the ancient, dry skins with an alluring, primal beat. Danny the EMT played drums in a band. He took over for Jeb. Selectperson Bert Snodgrass began to play on the bongo drums that were directly opposite from where Danny played.

Wordlessly and still beaming, Jeb led the rest of the group to a point just north of the bonfire. He began to move around the bonfire in a counter-clockwise direction. One by one, the townspeople of Littleborough followed him. Many joined hands.

They moved slowly and clumsily, at first. The drug was clearly taking its affect and the forest floor in the flickering light of the clearing was difficult to negotiate. Dick Little tripped on something and fell onto his side. He pulled Bea and Binny Moran down with him. They struggled back onto their feet. He tried to brush off the leaves and brambles off of the two ladies, but they both simply smiled and resumed dancing. Somewhere, church bells started ringing.

The beast continued to thrash around the clearing's very edge. After a number of times around the bonfire, Jeb changed the direction to clockwise. The townspeople followed. Jeb began to chant. It was a language no one had ever heard before. Everybody understood every word. They repeated after him, and the dance picked up pace.

The good people of Littleborough began to feel lighter. Their legs and feet no longer seemed to be bearing their weight. The forest floor felt like air. It was as if the dancing had created a breeze that carried them gracefully around the fire. They gathered themselves once more and sprang the other way with even more speed and aplomb.

Within the confines of the circle in which they danced, all was calm compared to the outside. Beyond the seven-sided clearing along the edge of the forest, Julie could see, hear, and feel trees, some of them enormous, bending and whipping in the wind. Large branches gave forth a deep cracking and snapped, hurtling into the black night of the forest. Dark clouds raced across the opening above the forest canopy and out of sight in seconds. The moonlight in the clearing flickered at a quicker pace, once again like that old, silent horror film.

The beast howled and roared menacingly as the light in the clearing dimmed. It appeared inside the mouth, his massive jaws agape. The rows of teeth glittered in the fluttering light. His eyes blazed white to light blue, scarlet to crimson, then purple to pitch black. Still, they glowed like the embers of a bonfire.

"Oh good, the puppy wants to play!" Officer Tubbs said.

"Everyone spread out a bit, but not too much!" the chief said. "Don't any of you go it alone, got it?"

"Right, you've got it!" Billy Pollard, still covered in his wife Nancy's blood, stepped forward and joined Officer Tubbs to face the demon. The winds that whipped around the clearing now howled at the clearing's edge. It was deafening. Jeb and his new found flock continued their strange dance. They moved and swayed, whirled and swirled around the bonfire facing inward. Their backs were turned on the forest and the beast, darkness and death. Their faces beamed like Jeb's. They smiled and laughed, light and gay, oblivious to the chaos around them.

"If anyone of you gets a clear shot, take it!" the chief said. "Be careful not to hit anyone with friendly fire!" The patrolmen all nodded their heads solemnly as they tried to take up various positions around the clearing while staying out of the path of the revelers' dancing.

"I'm not sure we should let anybody shoot their weapon, Chief," Inspector Dahms said. "I feel light headed just from the fumes of the narcotic." The chief nodded.

"I know. Me too, Tom. But I don't think we have any choice here."

"You're probably right."

"Come on! Come on, you devil!" Billy Pollard screamed at the beast.

"Billy!" the chief said.

"You want blood? Do you? Well, come and get it! Come and get it, you fuck!"

"Get back! Billy, get back! Don't get too far away from the fire!"

"Dad!" Peter Pollard said.

"Come on! You son of a bitch! Come on, what are you waiting for?"

The beast charged. Somewhere someone was heard saying, "Fire!" All the patrolmen opened up on the beast. Billy Pollard began to fire his weapon. Their volleys sounded like thunderclaps inside the clearing. Still, the dancers danced. They were smiling and positively beaming as they spun and swayed to the beat of the drums and the gunfire.

Suddenly, the clearing was completely bathed in moonlight. The wolf stopped short of reaching Billy Pollard. It howled straight up at the full moon and dashed for the darkness of the forest. But the powerful winds seemed to be preventing the creature from escaping the clearing. He shrieked in agony whenever the moonlight crossed his face. Julie felt like crying as she watched.

The clearing itself started spinning. Julie fell and found herself pinned down to the cold forest floor by the centrifugal force. She looked around the clearing from where she lay. Everyone had been pulled down to the ground. She closed her eyes. As the beast raged, voices seemed to echo in her head, calling her name. "Julie...Julie...Julie..." Though she tried with all of here being, Julie could not seem to block the voice out of her head. She curled herself into a tight fetal position, covering her head with her arms.

Julie tried to breathe. She concentrated on the voice that called to her in her head. *No*, she thought. *Go. Go back to your home. Go into the light.* Julie repeated this thought again and again as she continued to concentrate and breathe.

There were the voices of men shouting. Some shouted instructions; others shouted warnings. Their voices would carry all over the clearing on the wind and die in the center vortex. They would be punctuated by thunderous gunfire. The gunfire would die down and then one could hear echoes of the drumming and singing and chanting and still, the church bells ringing. Then there were the screams of men dying.

Julie watched as the chief and Inspector Dahms had both held their ground during the melee. They had remained calm, fixed, and focused. Each had produced his firearm and aimed exclusively for the eyes of the beast. Though killing it certainly did not appear to be possible, they were certainly causing the creature considerable difficulty by hitting its eyes.

Doc Robinson looked on. He stood by the bonfire. From time to time, he would call out for the creature to run and get away from here. He implored the beast to go, take flight, and come back later when it was safe.

For their part, the dancers all struggled, one by one, to get back up onto their feet. Jeb urged them to follow him back around the bonfire in the original direction. They all clumsily followed. Julie thought she noticed something different about Jeb. He seemed younger and taller now. Julie then noticed what he held in his hand: a knife. It was a long, thin blade that somehow wrapped itself up his arm. Her green eyes glittered. She tried to get onto her feet. As she got both her feet underneath her, Julie was smashed back down onto the ground by the backside of the beast as he whirled all the way around to face her.

"*Julie...Julie...Julie!*" She deeply felt the anguish in that voice. There was a desire, almost a lust. Was it love? Julie felt a terrible confusion at this. *Can this truly be evil?* she wondered. The torment in the voice, the tortured soul that yearned for Julie to go to him, to touch him, to heal him, was too much for her to stand. She began to give in. Julie felt as though she were willing to do anything to ease this creature's pain and burden. *It would also save everyone here,* she thought. She started to rise up to be devoured.

"No! No!" Father Freeman was shouting over the din. He crawled over to where Julie was and pulled her down onto the ground with his arms and legs. The bishop had belly crawled over and was helping Father Freeman. A blood-covered arm fell onto the ground next to them. The shirtsleeve was tattered and torn, but unmistakably blue. The hand at the end of the severed arm clutched a firearm that smoked from having been fired multiple times. Officer Marconi was dead. Julie, Father Freeman, and the bishop screamed.

Their screams got the attention of Officer Jones. The creature appeared to him as if it were standing over them. He ran to get to the people he thought were being mauled. As he ran, the flickering of the moonlight returned, making his gait appear quite odd and grotesque. As he neared it, the beast turned and faced him. It shot out an enormous paw with five huge, sharp claws protruding. It howled at the moment of impact as the beast sheared off the head of the police officer. The momentum of his headless body fell forward. His disembodied head carried forward through the air and the flickering light in a nightmarish flight, and near enough to the creature for it to snatch it out of the air with its terrible jaws. There were more screams.

Officer Tubbs heard screaming. He had finished reloading his firearm for the third time, and was preparing to fire yet another clip into the belly of the beast. He burst up from where he crouched and opened fire. Upon seeing this, the chief and Inspector Dahms resumed firing. Officer Franklin was also firing his weapon. He, along with Officer Evers, had stayed along the perimeter of the clearing. Each shot his weapon only occasionally so as to be sure not to hit anyone else.

"No!" Julie screamed when she saw that Officer Tubbs was running at the demon. But it was too late. The movement of the policeman caught the eye of the beast. It raced at Officer Tubbs, who now screamed and fired his weapon into the creature's face. There then followed a terrible splattering sound as the beast collided with Officer Tubbs. The collision made the man and the beast roll right to the edge of the clearing and right on top of Officer Franklin. The three crashed into the brush and out of view of the clearing and into the black forest.

There were several muffled gunshots and muffled screams amidst the roaring of the demon. The gun of Officer Tubbs fell silently to the forest floor. His blood and other bits of him seemed to rain down on everyone in the clearing. Only the guns and the shoes of Officer Franklin and Officer Tubbs remained.

The beast turned his great, leonine head back toward the center of the clearing. Father Freeman and the bishop had been kneeling and deep in prayer throughout the entire rite until they went to Julie's aid. They had returned to prayer. Each held his crucifix aloft, overhead. This clearly enraged the demon. It howled and charged across the clearing at the two men of God.

Julie knew that everyone here was going to die. She thought that she should, perhaps, pray. As she started to put her head down, she saw a flash of light cut through the twilight of the dawn. It seemed to startle the demon. Though it was blinding, it was brief. Julie was able to trace the source from where she lay in the center of the clearing. There, standing just outside of the clearing, was the Judge.

There was another flash of blinding light. It came from the opposite side of where the Judge stood. This flash also seemed to bother the terrible beast. Julie tried to see who was there, but she could not.

At one point she thought she saw Lila just outside of the clearing, her eyes twinkling green. The flashes of light continued, as did the gunfire of the few remaining patrolmen. The demon was having difficulty finding the two priests whom he so clearly wanted to kill. He could feel a tiny form struggling beneath him. The creature looked down to see that it was Julie. He began to sniff at her face. Time truly stopped and waited.

The demon smiled. Still a bit groggy from having been stepped on, Julie knelt on the forest floor. Her hands covered her face. She took them down slowly and looked up at the wolf, her wide green eyes looking directly into his tormented soul. The beast hesitated. It was as though he wasn't sure what he wanted to do with her.

The chief and Inspector Dahms moved in. They both emptied their clips into those tormented eyes as they charged. The demon reared up in pain. Officer Evers reached out his hand to try to pull Julie out from under the beast. But the creature's great jaws opened impossibly wide, and he shredded the brave man with one snap of his jaws. Two large, powerful hands grabbed Julie from behind. She looked up to see as the chief lifted her on the run, pulling Julie out from under the beast.

There was another flash of light. Julie could swear that it revealed multiple eyes, wide and staring, around the head of this creature. This time it made the demon turn toward the west. As he did so, his tail smashed into Inspector Dahms, sending him through the air and crashing to the forest floor. His firearm sailed through the twilight and into the underbrush. The beast turned back toward Julie and the chief. This time he would not hesitate. His great head and jaws shot downward. He smashed the chief to the forest floor. But Julie crawled away. The demon turned to see, or smell, where Julie might be hiding.

As he did, there were more flashes of brilliant, white light that illuminated the clearing, confusing and enraging the beast. He screamed and howled. At one point the creature turned, suddenly and violently. His leg whipped around and inadvertently kicked Richard while he danced. He fell back out of the clearing, hitting his head on the base of a large elm tree. His thick, black hair flung as he fell. He blinked his brown eyes once and passed out.

Julie thought she could see Sandra just beyond the edge of the clearing in the woods. She strained herself to see. Little blonde pigtails framed the dirty, defiant face. She was somehow creating flashes of blinding white light. As Julie looked around the clearing, she could see that Lila, the Judge, and Sandra were ringing the clearing with this light. They continued to flash it onto the demon.

But the demon would not be put off. Despite the best efforts of the witches, the many bullet wounds, the prayers of the priests, he found Julie. The two men of God threw themselves at the demon called Dam. He merely brushed them aside. *Julie…mmmmmmmmmmmm…Julie.* Again, the two men of God ran at the huge creature, cursing and swearing. Julie was punching and kicking the demon's face and head. He lunged forward slightly, knocking Julie back down onto the forest floor.

He sniffed at her, drooling all over her face and her hair. Julie could not breathe. She had the wind knocked out of her. She rolled over onto her hands and knees trying to get back up onto her feet when she saw the shoebox in the shuddering moonlight. She would not understand why she did what she did for many, many years to come. Julie tried to crawl the fifteen feet between her and the shoebox. The winds and the centrifugal force of the spinning clearing forced her back.

She dug into the cold, hard forest floor with her fingers and the toes of her sneakers as she tried not be lifted straight up and out of the clearing. Julie could feel her fingernails breaking and tearing from her fingers as she dragged herself along on her belly to get to the shoebox. She reached out for it. Leaves and ashes and heaven only knew what else blew into her face and eyes, blinding her. Julie closed her eyes.

A tremendous weight landed on her back, pinning her to the cold forest floor. Julie could not breathe. Somewhere above her a horn sounded. At least it sounded like an enormous horn, Julie thought. Deep and resonant, she could feel it more than hear it. Her entire body vibrated under the weight and pressure from the sound. It had completely drowned out the drumming, chanting, gunfire and screaming.

She thought about Geraldine. She pictured the tiny rat inside the shoebox. She could see her tiny face framed by the light blue markings from the disinfectant. She felt it. "Yes," the rat said. The time was now. Still pinned in place, Julie shut her eyes tight and reached out her hands without looking and gently felt around the ground. Finally her hands found the shoebox. Julie carefully pulled it closer and opened it. The tiny rat leapt out of the shoebox and onto the forest floor.

Julie opened her eyes. The little rat regarded her. Julie looked around. Everything now moved in a strange and sickly slow motion. The full moon light flickered on and off in the blood-soaked clearing. The drummers drummed. The dancers danced. Man and wolf waged war. Julie looked at the rat. When their eyes met, the tiny rat turned and began to run directly into the powerful winds. Suddenly Julie found that she was able to rise to her feet. She began to follow the little 'rat in the hat'.

As she ran after Geraldine, Julie realized that she was able to move freely, albeit slowly, without being blasted by the centrifugal forces of the spinning clearing. She looked around the clearing as she ran.

"Tom!" Julie called out to the inspector. He had managed to get back onto his feet and resume the fight. "Tom!" His firearm and hat were missing. His nose was bleeding. Blood ran from a gash on the side of his head as well. "Tom!" He looked over. Julie waved at him to follow her. He ran over to where the chief stood. He called over as he ran.

"Chief!" The chief saw him. Inspector Dahms pointed over toward Julie. The chief looked at her and she waved at him to follow. The two lawmen crouched down and carefully moved toward Julie and the little rat. As they did, they each grabbed the two men of God, who were still feverishly praying, pulled them up from their knees, and dragged them over to where Julie was.

"Follow the rat!" Julie said. Her voice sounded distant. It traveled strangely in the vortex as it could be heard in some places in the clearing and not in others.

"Where are we going?" the inspector said. The chief, the Bishop, and Father Freeman all looked at Julie. She shook her head and smiled.

"I don't know," she said. "We're going to follow that rat." The inspector looked at the chief. He shrugged his big shoulders.

"Good enough for me," he said. They all began to follow the rat in the hat. Julie noticed that Geraldine was running around the bonfire in the opposite direction of the winds from the vortex. She was leading them in a spiral, away from the fire. It was slow going. No matter how hard Julie ran, it seemed as though she was in slow motion, like in a bad dream. Sight and sound, smell and sensation traveled so strangely on this ethereal plane. It was as if they were deep under water or in outer space.

As they worked their way around the bonfire, the chief would reach out a massive hand and grab the nearest person, pulling them into the safety of the spiral. One by one, the dancers and drummers were pulled into the path of the rat, following Julie and Geraldine. Doc Robinson was the last to join. Despite the pure chaos around them, the ground beneath their feet was firm and the wind in the clearing seemed to howl all around them without affecting them. A strange voice carried over to them.

"Where's my daughter?" Jeb found himself alone beyond the safety of the spiral. He smiled his maniacal grin, brandishing his blade. "Where are you, my sweet, sweet Sandra? The master's coming and we don't want to disappoint him, now, do we? Come here, girl." His eyes locked with Julie's. A wide grin slowly spread across his face. His thin, gaunt cheeks dimpled.

"Keep moving!" Julie wasn't sure who had said this, but she knew they were right. She looked behind her. It looked as if the entire township was right behind her, working their way out of the vortex. She continued on.

"Sandra!" Jeb's voice carried over them. "Sandra! Where are you, lamb?" Julie looked up. A blinding white light burned directly ahead of her. She watched as the little rat in the hat disappeared into it. She turned back toward the townsfolk.

"Come on!" Julie turned to face the light and ran straight into it. Her body went from ice cold to red hot and back again. Time and space stopped. She couldn't see. She couldn't hear. She couldn't move. Julie could not breathe. She began to pass out. As darkness came, Julie's thoughts turned to her grandmother. Her beautiful, China-white face framed by her long, raven black hair glistened in Julie's mind. *What happened?* Julie wondered.

Before she could think of an answer, there was a cold slap to her face by the fresh, clean night air of the forest. She sucked the air into her lungs and then found herself sailing through the air. Julie landed on the cold, hard forest floor in a crumpled heap with an audible grunt. She lay there for a moment, panting.

"Watch out! Watch out!" It was Inspector Dahms. He landed right on top of Julie.

They both emitted a grunt. "Sorry about that." He could barely speak above a whisper as the fall had knocked the wind out of him.

"Look out!" It was the chief. He landed on top of the inspector.

"Oh, dear!" The bishop landed on the chief. "Sorry about that, Chief!" He was followed immediately by Father Freeman, who was followed by Bea, who was followed by Captain Little Joe, and then everybody. The entire town of Littleborough seemed to be piled on top of one another in the mouth of the western entrance to the clearing.

Julie had struggled up onto her feet. She was looking into the clearing for anyone they may have left behind. As everyone else slowly clambered to their feet, they were mostly silent. Some were coughing, some were still gasping for breath. But everyone seemed okay.

"You're not thinking of going back in there, are you, Julie?" Inspector Dahms said.

"I have to find Sandra before Jeb does, Tom."

He nodded. "Sit tight. We'll find her."

"You don't have to," Bea said, pointing. "She's right there." Julie looked to where Bea was pointing.

"Oh, my God." Sandra stood in the center of the clearing, by the bonfire's rage. The moonlight was still flickering; the night was still shuddering. Behind Sandra, clutching her by her head, was Jeb. He held the knife upward toward the sky. He was speaking in that strange tongue. Julies' green eyes sparkled. "Sandra! No!" She raced back into the clearing.

"Miss Bernard!" the chief said. "Don't!"

It was too late. Julie had burst back into the clearing and ran directly at Jeb and Sandra. The vortex had continued to rage. The witches continued to flash those brilliant lights into the clearing at Dam. Julie found herself slowing to a crawl as she tried desperately to reach Sandra. The winds from the vortex slammed her back down onto the ice-cold forest floor. Helpless, Julie looked up from where she lay.

"Sandra! Run! Run!" The little girl in the pink dress and blue ribbons did not seem to hear her. Jeb was beaming. "No, no you son of a…" Julie had managed to get back to her feet. She had not run very far when she was smashed to the ground by the beast. Dam stood over her. Julie struggled beneath him, kicking and screaming and punching. *Is he smiling?* she wondered. He licked her face. She became aware of others around her now. The chief, Inspector Dahms, and Doc Robinson were all trying to wrestle the wolf away from her. "Forget me! Save Sandra!" Julie screamed.

She was being crushed beneath the chief, Doc Robinson, and Dam, who were all locked in a struggle. Inspector Dahms had gotten down on the ground and was trying to reach beneath the beast and get a hold of Julie. Fire completely ringed the clearing in the woods. The white light flashed rhythmically, exposing the demon. It broke loose from the chief's powerful grip.

The creature suddenly turned and raced toward Jeb. Jeb could only stare in horror as the beast closed in on he and Sandra. He had not been able to complete the spell or incantations for his master. He tried, in vain, to kill Sandra with a strike from his blade. But the beast crashed into him before he could plunge the knife into her. Jeb flew backward through the air straight out of the clearing and out of sight.

Inspector Dahms had helped Julie back onto her feet. Julie knew this was her chance. She broke free from his grip and raced for the center of the clearing where Sandra sat, dazed. She scooped the little girl up into her arms and began to run for the mouth of the clearing on the western side. The giant wolf turned back toward Julie. He roared a deafening howl as he attacked. Doc Robinson and the chief managed to step in between Dam and Julie. The inspector took Sandra from her as they ran toward the mouth of the clearing.

The wolf chased after them. He caught up to them as they reached the clearing's very edge. He pounced and took them all down in a dull, squishy thud. They were all rolling around on the forest floor in a tangle of limbs and brush. Dam was on top of Julie. Despite their best efforts, the chief, Doc Robinson, and Inspector Dahms could not free her from Dam's grasp.

Then Julie watched from beneath the wolf as peculiar electricity filled the clearing. The early dawn lit up a bright, blinding white. Ash and leaves and debris filled the air as the wind from the vortex whipped and cracked through the clearing in every direction. It was as if a thousand tiny tornados burst up from the forest floor. Julie heard her name being whispered. She reluctantly closed her eyes. The wolf had been sniffing at her face again when he stopped short. The noise and flashing light subsided for a moment. The clearing was quiet. Everything went still.

The beast raised his great, leonine head up high and sniffed at the air. It was an all-too-familiar scent. He smelled it, but he could not believe it! Something was coming this way, to this clearing in these woods! He knew that he would have to strike it before it could strike him. He hated the thought of possibly losing this witch. She smelled special, truly special. But this other one, well, he smelled like sweet revenge! This was something his father had taught him.

The demon could not resist. The wolf turned to face the north opening in the clearing and Father James Knight. As the creature turned toward James, the clearing began to spin in the opposite direction. The noises and the flashing returned in an even more bizarre and chaotic fashion. Julie realized that she, Sandra, Lilith, and the Judge had somehow reversed whatever had been done here. Her intuition told her that this could send this creature and Satan back in the same way they had come.

James ran as fast as he could into the clearing. He could plainly see in the flickering moonlight an enormous creature attacking Julie. Julie saw James as he ran toward her.

"No, James don't!" she screamed. "No!" The vortex closed. It slammed shut with a tremendous force followed by a deafening thunderclap. But the creature was not in the clearing when the vortex closed. He was in the northern mouth of the clearing, face to face with James.

The wind from this thunderclap struck James with a terrible force. He was lifted and flung, unconscious, into the center of the clearing, along with the great demon. Though the thunderclap had knocked him off of his paws, the beast was unhurt. He rose up over Father Knight, laughing. His laughter filled the clearing. The bishop and Father Freeman screamed.

Julie screamed as she raced across the clearing as fast as she could. The demon seemed to be waiting for her. He grinned maliciously as she ran toward him. At the last moment before Julie reached where James lay, the beast lowered his head and snatched him up in his great jaws by the legs. Julie screamed and tried to grab at one of Father Knight's arms. Father Freeman tried to get his other arm.

They both managed to get a hold of one of Father Knight's arms, and a pathetic tug of war ensued. The demon was playfully shaking his great head from side to side, pulling Julie and Father Freeman along with him. He bit down and pulled only a little, so as to allow the fun to continue. Both Julie and Father Freeman were now covered in Father Knight's blood. The bishop joined in the struggle. When Julie saw that the demon was going to kill Father Knight, she let go of his arm and started punching and kicking at the beast. She was crying as she did so. The wolf nudged his enormous face forward, knocking Julie and then the two priests down onto their backsides. Julie hit her head when she fell. Everything flashed white, and then darkness came. That was when the beast belched. He stopped and stood quite still.

His eyes widened. The color of his eyes had stopped changing. They remained black and dilated. He belched again, and then again. His entire body rippled and quivered. A growling sound emitted from his belly. The wolf hacked, hacked, and hacked again, then vomited. James's upper torso came out in a hot, stench-ridden and watery mess. He vomited once more, and the rest of Father Knight emerged in a stew of human remains.

The demon screamed. The sound shook the ground, knocking everyone down onto the forest floor. He looked wildly in all directions with a look of stark terror in his eyes. He then burst out of the clearing, to the southwest, smashing trees and brush in his path. The wild creature half-ran and half-flew out of sight into the twilight of the forest, still screaming and howling.

There followed a tremendous thunderclap inside the clearing. It instantly extinguished the large bonfire and flattened the few remaining townsfolk who were upright. Silence returned and reigned the night and the Great Woods again. The night sky grew still. The full moon illuminated the carnage in the clearing. Nothing stirred in the forest. And time began to tick. †

CHAPTER 43

"Arise, shine; for thy light is come,
and the glory of the Lord is risen upon thee."
—Isaiah 60:1

Julie opened her eyes. She lay still for a moment on the cool of the forest floor. She felt the early morning sun splash lightly on her face. The smell of blood and gunpowder filled her nostrils. The sun was up and was warming the forest.

Carefully, Julie sat up and looked around. She could hear someone weeping softly, somewhere. She listened closely. Slowly and painfully, she got herself up onto her feet and began to limp back toward the clearing in the woods.

Inside the clearing she could see Bishop Richter and Father Freeman kneeling together and crying. All of the townsfolk who were there that night had gathered around the two priests. Some were kneeling. Some were sitting. Some were praying. They were all weeping.

The chief stood off to the side looking on. There was no sign of the creature. The inspector limped back into the clearing. He stood next to the chief. Doc Robinson was looking in the southwesterly direction that the wolf had run.

"I think Billy and Peter Pollard followed the wolf," the chief said to the inspector, who nodded.

"Where are Jeb and Sandra?" the inspector wondered to the chief.

"We have to keep looking," the chief said.

For the second time in a very short span, Julie Bernard found herself looking around this very clearing at blood-soaked body parts strewn all over creation. She stopped and looked down at something familiar. Though

353

slightly damaged, the shoebox was right in front of her. She picked up the shoebox and opened it. Geraldine was fast asleep inside. She looked up at Julie for a second, blinking her sleepy eyes. Julie gently closed the lid and continued limping over to where the remaining survivors were gathered.

There, in between the bishop and Father Freeman, lay Father James Knight. He was still alive and suffering terribly. Julie knelt by his side. She began crying and tried to comfort him. She stroked his face and head, whispering to him. "It will be okay," she said. "You saved us," she said. Julie was still bathed in his blood. He began to shake violently.

Bishop Richter knelt with James's head in his lap. He wept and prayed openly. He removed his frock and placed it over James's body to warm him. "I think he is cold," he said. Father Freeman placed his frock over the Bishop's frock. He burst up onto his feet and half-walked and half-ran in small circles. He alternately cried, swore, and muttered to himself.

There came a sniffling sound. Everyone looked. Officer Franklin had found his way back to the clearing in the woods, despite having lost his spectacles. Blood ran down his pudgy cheeks from a bad knock on the head. It mixed with his tears.

He slowly waddled around where James now lay, and over to where the inspector and the chief were standing. Inspector Dahms looked him over carefully for any other injuries. He patted Officer Franklin gently on the back. Officer Franklin began to weep again.

James still looked to be in pain and discomfort. He was in shock, no doubt, thought the Inspector. The bishop began to administer the last rites to James. "No, no, no," said Father Freeman as he knelt back down next to the young priest.

Julie closed her eyes, praying along with the Bishop. Her tears flowed freely. "It's okay, it's okay, it's okay," she whispered gently to James through those tears. Then she heard it. There was a splashing sound, like water. James opened his eyes.

Flower petals fluttered gently down onto and around James's head and face. Julie looked up along with Bishop Richter to see the Judge standing over all of them. She seemed to also be softly reciting a prayer. She held in her hand a burning smudge of sage. The mixture of the flowers and the sage was so beautiful. It seemed to instantly ease the pain James had been in. His soft, brown eyes seemed to focus for a moment.

The Judge whispered prayers in Latin, ancient Hebrew, and ancient Greek. The Bishop, Father Freeman, and Julie all silently joined her. There was that sound of water again! Julie looked up when she heard it.

James smiled. He could see the water, finally. It was so beautiful the way the sun was shining on the bluest water he'd ever seen. The water splashed again, this time playfully, and James could see his brother, John. He was sitting in a rowboat, waving, and smiling warmly at him. James climbed aboard, smiling broadly. As James closed his eyes for the final time, they went fishing together. Father James Knight was the last lamb to die that day. There was in that moment, the moment, a sweet and still silence in the forest.

The bishop pulled the frocks up and over James's face. He continued to pray, crossing himself and James numerous times. He prayed hard. Father Freeman had joined him, crying openly. The Judge had walked around the body of Father James Knight several times. She had continued to sprinkle the light mixture of flowers and sage around him.

When she had finished, the inspector thought that he could see just a hint of tears form in her striking eyes. But if there were, it was fleeting. The bishop had also completed his prayers. Still weeping, he slowly and stiffly raised himself up off of the warm forest floor. Upon seeing him struggle, Julie took him gently by his arm and helped him up.

"Why, thank you, dear child." The Bishop's voice was soft and hoarse. Father Freeman had also gotten up and was now standing next to the Bishop. The Judge looked at the two priests. Inspector Dahms and Julie looked at each other. They smiled wearily.

Slowly, one by one, the good people of Littleborough arose to their feet. The chief spoke to Captain Little Joe and Danny the EMT softly. They nodded their heads and then helped lead the bedraggled group of survivors out of the clearing, through the mouth on the western side and back up the path toward Deerfoot Road. No one said a word.

"James saved us, you know, Judge. It was his purity." The bishop stared into the Judge's beautiful eyes with his bright blue eyes.

"It's true, ma'am," Father Freeman added. "James carried the day. He must have somehow survived the challenge from Satan, and then got here in time to…well, you know."

"No, I don't know, John," the Judge said. "Please, do go on. Explain to us all what just happened."

Bishop Richter shrugged. "He defeated evil."

"Yes. But poor James isn't going to be at the big victory party tonight, now, is he, Pat?"

"Don't be mean," Julie said to the Judge.

"Well, is he?" The Judge began to circle the two priests as she spoke, 1 the clearing earlier. When she came back around to 1 at both men straight into their tear-filled eyes. She e. Her tone was calm and even.

for your loss. But this is everybody's loss. Was this e of possibly the best priest we've had in a century?

Think of the healing he could have done. Think of the teaching, the uniting he would have done. I know, I know." The Judge turned her back on them and regarded the chief and the inspector, then turned and looked back at the holy men.

"It was win at all costs, good versus evil. And that's true. But we lost a hell of a lot more than we won today. It was the slaughter of a lamb." The two men of God did not speak. These were exactly the words that each priest was thinking as she had spoken.

The Judge walked out of the clearing in the woods. Julie followed. She heard the voice of the Judge inside her head. *This isn't over, yet, dear.* She opened the shoebox and scooped Geraldine up into her arms. She clutched the tiny rat to her chest. Her wide, green eyes could only stare, unseeing. Doc Robinson followed well behind Julie.

Inspector Dahms and the chief had decided to look for more survivors in and around the clearing. The chief asked the bishop and Father Freeman if they would help Ben get back to Deerfoot Road and the two clergymen replied, "Of course." The inspector had managed to contact Officer Lydon back on Deerfoot Road, and he had called in multiple ambulances to tend to the injured. The chief and the inspector then split up to cover more ground in the search for survivors and for any clues as to where Jeb and Sandra may have gone.

The bishop and Father Freeman had waited for everyone else to leave. They each took one final look inside the clearing and prayed and blessed it. They stopped by Father Knight's body. They turned, each weeping, and walked away. Each took Officer Franklin gently by the arm and led him out of the clearing. All three men cried every step of that path.

When all were out of sight, Lila reemerged from the forest and into the clearing. She had been tending to Dam, who was in very bad shape from ingesting part of Father Knight. Lila peeled the blood-soaked frocks off of the body of Father James Knight and began to examine him. She then began to laugh and sing as she wrapped his body back up carefully and removed it from the clearing in the woods. The forest was back to normal now. It was alive with rhythm, vibration, and nature. The sun was shining. It was warm. It was no longer the realm of shadows. It was no longer the realm of the priest of lies. ✝

356